No More Mulberries

Mary Smith

For
Jon and David

With thanks to
Andrew Radford, Janice Galloway and Liz Small
for all their help

ONE

Sang-i-Sia July 1995

'Daddy's home!'

Hearing Ruckshana's delighted cry Miriam, hunkered in the shade of the mulberry tree, raised her head from the pile of rice she was picking over. She watched her daughter tear bare-footed across the compound, oblivious to obstacles. Chickens contentedly pecking at nothing scattered, squawking alarm, as the three-year old, flung herself at her father. He lifted her, throwing her high in the air, laughing at her squeals of mock terror when he pretended to drop her.

Iqbal lowered Ruckshana to the ground, smiling over her head at his wife. The late afternoon sun had lost some of its heat but the path to their home, crouched high on the mountainside, was steep and he was panting slightly when he straightened up. Farid emerged from the kitchen carrying, with the careful solemnity of his eight years, a glass of water. Balancing the glass on his outstretched right palm, left hand under his right elbow, he offered the water to Iqbal, who acknowledged him with a nod before drinking.

Miriam reached over and smilingly patted her husband's stomach. 'You've put weight on since we came here,' she commented.

'I'm blaming your Scottish Afghan cooking,' he replied. 'What are we eating tonight? And when? I'm starving.'

'Rice and chicken – totally Afghan. Ready in about an hour.'

Miriam put the rice to cook and began preparing a salad. Slicing tomatoes coaxed with determination and loving care from her vegetable plot's stony soil, she listened to the children and Iqbal talking in the background. Farid was telling with quiet pride how he'd done in his arithmetic test while Ruckshana chirruped non-stop, sounding like the mullah bird, as she tried to engage her father's undivided attention. When Miriam lifted the lid of a pot on the kerosene stove the rising steam carried an aroma of slow-cooked chicken, oil, tomato and garlic.

When the food was ready, she called Farid whose task was to unroll the *dustakhan* over the striped gillim on the living room floor then, while Miriam carried through the dishes of rice and chicken, he fetched the *nan* wrapped in a cotton cloth. Ruckshana squeezed in between her parents, sitting cross-legged on the *toshak* as they did. Miriam, knowing how easy it was to hurt her daughter's dignity, hid her smile at the sight of the dimples on the little girl's chubby knees.

Over dinner she and Iqbal swapped stories about work. As well as dealing with the usual skin infections and gastric problems, he'd been consulted by Murtaza, the determined hypochondriac from the next village. 'He swore he could hardly put one foot in front of the other. Insisted he really needed a course of injections. When I said I'd have to examine him,' Iqbal's eyes crinkled in amusement, at the memory, 'he leapt up onto the couch like a nine-year old.' Miriam laughed with him. Murtaza had been known to gatecrash the women's clinic in his attempt to acquire medicines.

'Oh, and I met Mother of Naeem on the road home,' Iqbal continued. 'She's pregnant again. I think she'll be up to see you soon for a check up.'

Miriam counted on her fingers, saying, 'It's barely a year since the last one and this'll be her fourth. Last time, she'd a problem with her blood pressure so it'll be good to keep an eye on her.' She paused. 'Did she mention why Naeem and Sultan didn't come for English class today? It's not like them to miss a lesson.'

'I told them there wouldn't be any more classes,' Iqbal said, mopping his plate with the last piece of *nan*.

'What?'

'They won't be coming back.' He popped the bread into his mouth, not looking at her.

'But why?' Miriam asked in astonishment. 'They're both so keen. And they've made such good progress in the few weeks they've been coming.'

Iqbal, continuing to chew, looked down at his empty plate and Miriam began to think he wasn't going to answer her. Finally, he said,

'I have my position to think about. My reputation. Not only in this village, but the whole district. It's not right for young boys to be here in the house alone with my wife. People will talk.'

'Come on Iqbal, Naeem is, what? Thirteen? Sultan is eleven, twelve at the most. How could that cause talk in the village?'

With a glance at Farid, Iqbal switched from Dari to English. 'Are young boys in Scotland not thinking about sex?'

'Oh, for goodness sake, yes, of course. Think about it, talk about it, fantasise about it – but not about doing it with a woman who's nearly forty, the mother of two children.'

Iqbal's eyes narrowed and his voice was cool. 'The subject is closed.'

About to protest, Miriam became aware the two children were still sitting in the room. For once Ruckshana had fallen silent, gazing round-eyed at her father. Farid's head was bowed and she couldn't see his expression, but knew his face would have the closed, tight look it assumed whenever there was the possibility of an argument. She'd wait until the children were in bed before continuing this discussion. Hoping to dispel the tension in the room she rose to her feet, saying, 'Come on, Farid, you clear the plates while I bring the *toot*.'

The children whooped as she placed a large basin heaped with a pyramid of mulberries – white, red, purple – on the cloth. Washed in icy cold well water the berries glistened like jewels in the light of the oil lamps. Everyone gathered round, busy fingers searching expertly for the choicest fruit, the children's faces and hands soon stained purple with juice. At last, Miriam sat back. 'My favourite, favourite fruit. I wish they were in season all year round. I'll put some up to dry tomorrow. They're not the same dried, though, with their chewy texture and…'she groped for the word she wanted, shrugged, 'dustiness. Right, you two,' she continued, pointing at Ruckshana and Farid in turn, 'hands and faces washed before you get a story.'

'I'll get them ready for bed and read to them,' Iqbal said. 'I don't need to go out tonight.' She gave him a fleeting smile in outward acceptance of what she understood was a peace offering, though inwardly she still seethed. It would take more than a bedtime story to make peace.

Miriam twisted the ends of her faded black chaddar behind her back to keep them out of the way then stacked the dishes from their meal into a large aluminium basin. She carried it into a little room adjoining the kitchen, before fetching the water heating on the kerosene stove. Darkness had fallen and, leaving the dishes to soak she went out, carrying a lamp, which she set on the ground. Its feeble light was barely sufficient for her to see the chickens as she rounded them up, shutting them safely in their house for the night. As usual, the little black one had to be coaxed down from the branch on which she liked to roost. 'Come on, you silly bird,' Miriam called, throwing a handful of grain at the bottom of the tree. 'The foxes will get you.' Greed overcoming her resolve to remain free the bird fluttered down, squawking when Miriam grabbed her firmly. Laughing at the hen's ruffled look of affront at her ambush, she returned to the washing up, squatting comfortably beside the basin. When she had finished she poured the wastewater down a hole in the bare, packed-earth floor.

Her thoughts kept circling around the cancelled classes until, feeling her simmering anger come to the boil she stepped outside into the cool night air. Iqbal was being ridiculous but if she was going to persuade him to change his mind, she must stay calm. She really didn't want it to turn into a major row. She took a deep breath, which ended on a yawn. Too tired for one thing.

Maybe she should agree to Iqbal's suggestion and employ a girl from the village to help with the housework? She'd always refused, telling him she'd feel uncomfortable having someone working in the house. She didn't admit to him she hated the idea of people thinking the foreign wife needed help to run her home, couldn't cope with hard work. Bad enough they knew she couldn't spin wool – or milk a goat. That bloody-minded animal, feeling her first tentative touch, had looked knowingly over its shoulder at her with its nasty, wrong-way-round eyes and walked away. Tightening her grip only made the goat go faster, forcing her into an idiotic crouching run, while her friend Usma, in between shouts of laughter yelled at her to let go. When she did, falling over in a heap on the stony ground, the pain of her scraped knees had been nothing compared to the hurt to her dignity and pride. For weeks after everyone asked her if she'd milked any more goats. The day she could join in the laughter at the episode had not yet arrived.

She sighed and looked upwards. Familiarity with Afghanistan's night skies never lessened her sense of awe. On moonless nights the

Milky Way was a magical white path through stars that didn't twinkle – they blazed. Constellations her father had taught her to recognise when she was a child – Orion, the Plough, the Seven Sisters – demonstrated proudly that here, they possessed far more jewel-bright stars than she had ever seen in Scotland. Tonight, though, the moon, almost full, had risen, dimming the stars' brightness, silvering the jagged peaks of the mountains that kept the valley safe. 'Our moon,' she whispered. 'Oh, Jawad, what have I done?'

'Miriam?' She jumped at the sound of Iqbal's voice close behind her. Had he heard her whisper?

She turned to face him relieved to see he was smiling. 'Children ready for bed?' she asked. 'I'll go say goodnight to them.'

He shook his head, coming to stand next to her, saying softly, 'Ruckshana's already asleep. Farid is learning his spelling words for tomorrow.' He reached for her hand. 'Miriam, look, I suppose I should have mentioned it to you – cancelling the boys' lessons.'

'Mentioned it?' She snatched her hand away, the need for calm forgotten. Tilting her head to look up at him, she asked, 'What about discussing it with me?'

He stepped back, stared down at the ground, 'I see no need for discussion. I told you – I won't have my wife talked about.'

'Shouldn't you have thought about that before you brought a foreign wife back home, then? Anyway, who's talking about me and those boys?'

'No one...'

'So why cancel the lessons?'

'Come on, you're making too much of this.' He spoke lightly, as though the matter were of little import. 'Someone mentioned it to me, asked me if you were still teaching English to Sultan and Naeem.'

Miriam gaped at him. 'Someone mentioned it? Maybe someone else wanted their son to join the class? I think it's you who's making too much of this. I don't understand...'

He interrupted her, 'Of course you don't. It takes a long time to learn the village mentality; to understand what kind of behaviour is acceptable, what's not...' his voice faltered, as though he'd thought better of what he was saying. He looked away from her.

'Don't patronise me, Iqbal. I didn't arrive here yesterday. Don't forget I spent ...' Now it was her turn to let her words trail away.

'Go on,' he said, his voice taking on a chilly edge. She sensed him tense, his expression hardening the way it always seemed to at any mention of her past life. This wasn't about her understanding the culture. It was about Iqbal and – she didn't know exactly – his concerns about his status – his fear, a fear that seemed to her quite illogical, of being made to look a fool. She shook her head and gave a sigh. No point in trying to reason with him He wouldn't change his mind and talking about how she used to teach classes, been encouraged by … She swallowed hard as memories threatened to overwhelm her. Stay in the present. This is your life now. Call a truce. She put a hand out, touched his cheek. 'I'm trying to learn, Iqbal, okay?' She felt him relax and added, 'Come on, let's go and see how our own student's getting on with his spelling for tomorrow.'

Farid, lying flat on his back, arms and legs spread like a starfish, was fast asleep. Miriam removed the open schoolbook from where it had fallen across his face. In sleep his face lost its habitual anxious expression. Kneeling, she pulled the blanket up to her son's chin, leant over and kissed him, wishing she could kiss away the sadness that seemed never to leave him.

Back in the living room Iqbal was sliding two *toshak* together, leaving a gap between them and the one on which Ruckshana slept, thumb plugged into her mouth. Miriam untied the bundle of bedding, stored during the day in a corner of the room, passing Iqbal the blue and green peacock-patterned blankets. Leaving him to make up their bed, she slipped into the adjoining bathroom to wash for the night prayer. The centre of the small room was taken up by a diesel-fuelled *bukhari*, which heated water in a round tank with a hinged lid for filling and a tap on its side. In the summer, when the sun could warm water left outside in buckets, it was only lit once or twice a week. In winter, when it was lit daily, taking a bath was a pleasure few people in the village enjoyed. She shuddered at the thought of stripping off in the bitter cold. No wonder people who didn't have such luxurious trappings were reluctant to bathe more than was strictly necessary in winter. Next to the *bukhari* stood an array of galvanised buckets, some containing cold water, and three plastic water jugs. Towels hung on nails driven into the mud-plastered walls alongside a small square mirror, in which she noticed her grey eyes still held a spark of anger.

Mentally preparing herself, Miriam washed her face, and then her hands, letting the water run from above each elbow to the tips of her fingers. When she finished *wadoo* she returned to the living room, where she placed the small tablet of baked mud from Karbala, representing Allah's earth, on the floor in front of her. Opening with the obligatory *Allahu Akbar*, Miriam began her prayer. As she murmured the words, followed the rituals of standing, bowing in *ruku*, prostrating herself until her forehead touched the *mohr*, the familiar repetition soothed her.

By the time she'd finished and returned the tablet to its embroidered pouch Iqbal was already in bed. Yawning, she turned out the lamp and slid down beside him. He pulled her close until she was snuggled against him, his hand sliding round her waist. He spoke softly, 'Miriam, I'm sorry about… well, about… the class.'

Knowing how difficult it was for him to apologise, she nodded her head against his shoulder. When she felt his lips seek hers in the dark, she turned more fully towards him, winding her arms round his neck.

Later, she gave a sleepy reply to his murmured *shubakhair*. Before long, his even breathing indicated he was asleep but Miriam found herself wide-awake, restless. Despite the continued intimacy of their lovemaking something had changed in their relationship – not suddenly, but gradually. Nothing she could pinpoint, but it felt as though Iqbal disconnected from her sometimes. Had his feelings for her altered in the five years since they married? He'd never been one for talking about emotions but back then she felt he loved her. Was it just that he showed it differently from…No, re-visiting the past won't help.

Her thoughts were interrupted as Ruckshana sleep-crawled across the room, burying herself, without apparently waking, like a heat-seeking missile between her parents. Moving to make room for her daughter, Miriam felt a stab of guilt – wishing for the past was to wish Ruckshana unborn.

Shortly before eight o'clock next morning Iqbal and Farid set off together down the path towards the village. Only one or two white puffs of cloud dotted the brilliant blue sky. It was already warm, would soon be hot. As one, the women waiting to consult Miriam in the female clinic averted their eyes, shielding their faces with their hands or the edge of their chaddars until Iqbal passed them. Miriam watched until Farid turned to wave where the path curved out of sight, smiling as his chanted spelling words floated back to her.

She turned to her patients, who'd resumed their chattering as soon as Iqbal disappeared from sight. Some of the older women wore baggy trousers, which fell in folds before tapering to a cuff at the ankle but the younger ones had adopted the more fashionable straight-legged *tunban* under knee-length, wide-skirted floral-patterned dresses. Most wore waistcoats richly embellished with silver and gold braid and some of the unmarried girls fastened broad, beaded chokers round their necks. Children were squatting on the ground together playing a game, which involved throwing small stones in the air and trying to catch them on the back of the hand before they fell.

Unlocking a door, Miriam wrinkled her nose as she breathed in the familiar crushed-aspirin smell of the room which doubled as both consulting room and office. An examining couch, two simple wooden chairs and a small table cluttered with Iqbal's paperwork took up most of the space. On the packed-earth floor, of what had originally been built as a storeroom, a covered mattress and a woven gillim with bright orange stripes added a splash of colour. Shelves on one wall held a selection of basic medicines, textbooks and teaching aids; on the wall opposite posters depicted the stages of a baby's growth in the womb. Two small windows, set high in the walls let in very little natural light, making it far from ideal as a consulting room.

Before Miriam had come to Sang-i-Sia, named after the black stone of the surrounding mountains, she had assumed when Iqbal had talked in Pakistan of them working together he had meant exactly that – together, under one roof. It had been a shock to learn he did not want her in his clinic. Oh, he had dressed it up with various reasons, some of which, like the fact the women preferred to consult Miriam away from the eyes and ears of male medical workers, were valid. It still came down to the fact he didn't want his wife seen working outside his home. Miriam shoved the papers aside, noting Iqbal's statistics were still not up to date. Deciding she'd better tackle them in the afternoon, she called in the first patient.

Bibi Gul, wisps of greying hair escaping her *chaddar*, hobbled in, carrying her small granddaughter in her skinny arms. Miriam invited her to sit, asking after her family. Only once it had been established that every member of both families, their livestock and their crops were all, thanks to Allah, in good health was it possible to learn what had brought Bibi Gul to the clinic.

'It's Chaman. She has diarrhoea.'

'Let's have a look, then. How long has she been sick?' Miriam asked, reaching out for the listless child who immediately let out a wail, clinging to her grandmother.

'Three or five days.'

'What's she been eating?'

'She's not eating. I told you she's got diarrhoea. She needs medicine.' Bibi Gul took a small plastic bag, pinned for safekeeping inside her waistcoat. Although they had no decent sized pockets, waistcoats took the place of handbags. Safety pins and sewing needles were embedded in the fabric, matches stowed away in a small side pocket while, pinned to the inside were the keys to unlock the tin trunks in which were stored sugar and sweets and other household valuables. Now she handed over a piece of paper from the bag. It was a scrawled prescription for streptomycin, a tuberculosis drug. Her son, she told Miriam, had been a *mujahid* with *Wadhat* in Kabul. A big doctor there had given him the prescription. She was sure it would be good for *Chaman*.

While Miriam tried to explain the prescription was not for diarrhoea, the child continued to cry until, with soil-begrimed fingers Bibi Gul scrabbled for the soother hung on a string around the child's neck. She plugged it firmly into her granddaughter's mouth. Miriam smothered a sigh.

'I'll be right back,' she said. She hurried to the kitchen where she tore off some *nan*. When she returned to the consulting room, she removed the soother at the same time offering the child the bread. The little girl lost her listless look and began to chew with evident relish. Ignoring Bibi Gul's disapproving clucking Miriam continued her examination of the child. 'Well, she doesn't have any fever,' she said a few minutes later shaking down the thermometer, adding, 'but she's very weak because she's so dehydrated. She needs to drink plenty to replace the fluid she's lost. And she needs to eat nourishing food to help build her strength.' She paused as Bibi Gul's silence told her she wasn't listening.

'She needs medicine,' the older woman repeated.

'No, Bibi Gul, she doesn't need medicine. The diarrhoea will stop by itself. In the meantime I'll show you what to do to help Chaman get better.'

Bibi Gul looked mutinous. It was going to be a long morning. Why did Bibi Gul have to be the first patient of the day? Now she would have to spend ages convincing her not only that Chaman didn't need medicine but she did need to eat, and especially, to drink. Many of the villagers attempted to cure illness by 'perhez', or fasting, cutting out foods they believed caused the problem. On the face of it, it was a logical treatment – eating and drinking often produced more frequent diarrhoea in the acute stage. Unfortunately they usually cut out the most nutritious foods. Miriam headed once more to the kitchen, returning with a jug of water, an enamel teapot and a spoon. Knowing she would at some point have to tackle the subject of the dirty soother – one of the most likely causes of Chaman's diarrhoea – but deciding to leave it for now she gave the child another piece of bread. For the next twenty minutes Miriam explained, with the help of her plastic baby, what happens to a child with diarrhoea and how the family should treat it. Several of the other women crowded into the room to watch.

Once, this lack of privacy had worried Miriam and she had shooed spectators away but now, unless she was examining a patient, or someone indicated they needed to speak to her alone, she let them stay. All the better if more than one woman got the message.

The women murmured amongst themselves as the doll plumped out when Miriam poured in more water than it was losing at the other end. At last Bibi Gul, seemingly convinced, or at least partly mollified by the packets of oral re-hydration salts she was given, rose to leave. Although not all her patients were so time-consuming Miriam found herself, as always, having to explain why she would not prescribe capsules or, most-sought after, injections. Even when it was something as simple as a child with worms for which she could legitimately hand over pills she felt compelled to explain to mothers how they could prevent a recurrence. 'I know, I know,' she said, almost laughing at the astonished expression on one mother's face. 'It's impossible to stop your kids playing in the dirt, or putting their fingers in their mouths – but at least please try to stop them playing near where people go to shit.'

By lunchtime the sweetish odour of unwashed bodies overlaid the room's medicinal smell. Miriam turned to invite the last of her patients into the consulting room. The older of the two women carried a tightly swaddled baby. Wordlessly she handed the bundle to Miriam who, unwrapping the layers of cloth, struggled to hide her emotions when she saw the wizened, old man face, the emaciated bundle of skin and bones that emerged. Addressing the younger woman she asked, 'What's his name?'

'Sadiq,' she replied in a voice little above a whisper.

'How old is he?'

'Two months.'

The other woman suddenly reached over and grabbed the young woman's breast, making her gasp in pain as she squeezed hard. 'She hasn't enough milk. Can't feed him. Useless daughter-in-law I have.' The younger woman's eyes filled with tears but she said nothing.

'You old cow,' Miriam murmured in English, before addressing her questions to the baby's mother, Bilquis, who explained she had three older children at home, the youngest only 18 months old. As well as the work in the house she sometimes had to spend whole days out on the mountain cutting *butta,* carrying the firewood home piled high on her back. The children were left at home until her return. Her mother-in-law, insisting she personally was too weak to work – besides, what else was a daughter-in-law for – kept up a running grumble of complaints until Miriam wanted to slap her. No wonder the poor woman's milk's dried up.

Sadiq whimpered as she weighed him. At barely six pounds, his chances of survival without intensive feeding were nil. She handed him back to his grandmother. She could think of only one solution. He'd have to stay here. She turned to the mother-in-law, the one who would make any decisions. 'You're right. Sadiq does need powdered milk. But because he is so weak I need to see him every day.' The old woman began to protest about the difficulty of making the journey to the clinic each day. Miriam nodded in agreement, 'Yes, I can see it would be a problem. Could you persuade your daughter-in-law to leave him here for some weeks? And,' she added, 'you would be most welcome to stay too – so you can keep an eye on me. Then when you go home you can show Bilquis how to mix Sadiq's feeds.' The woman's eyes flicked from Miriam to Bilquis, to the baby. 'Look, '

Miriam said, 'I'll leave you for a few minutes to talk about what you want to do.'

Miriam stepped outside, blinking in the sunshine. She must be mad. He'd probably die and she'd be blamed. No one would trust her again. She should just send them home with a supply of milk powder – but then he would die, for sure. Closing her eyes she saw again the tiny scrap of skin and bones, the eyes huge in the skeletal face and marched back into the consulting room ready for battle. Bilquis was holding Sadiq, tears streaming down her face and Miriam knew she was going to leave her baby. The distraught woman held the re-wrapped bundle out to her. Oh shit! What had she let herself in for?

TWO

Sang-i-Sia July 1995

Ruckshana had spent the morning playing with two of their neighbour's little girls, occasionally wandering into the consulting room to check on her mother's activities. Now, well past her usual lunchtime, her daughter was grumbling and hungry, but Miriam first mixed a bottle for the baby. His grandmother, Uma, watched her suspiciously, although what she suspected her of Miriam had no idea.

It didn't take Sadiq long to work out that the teat in his mouth was a source of nourishment and he sucked hungrily for a few moments. When, almost immediately, he threw up most of the feed Miriam caught a smug, 'knew it would happen' look on Uma's face. With a tight-lipped smile she handed the baby to his grandmother, murmuring, 'There you go, you old harpy. You can clean him up.' She headed for the kitchen to prepare lunch. They could make do with eggs. She was too tired and uptight about Sadiq to cook anything more ambitious.

Ruckshana was bursting with important news. 'Zainab's cat's got four kittens. They're yellow. Eyes like this,' she screwed her eyes tightly shut to demonstrate. 'Jemila says I can have them. Can I, mummy, can I have the kittens?'

'I think you might have one kitten – certainly not four. We'll talk about it tonight when daddy's home.'

Ruckshana, dipping bread into her fried egg, was silent for a moment. 'Two kittens?' she bargained hopefully.

'One kitten – maybe. Now, eat up.' Later, with Ruckshana settled for an afternoon nap, Miriam prepared another bottle for Sadiq. She thought he brought back less of it this time and left him with Uma, who had settled on the mattress in the consulting room. Miriam lifted the heavy basin of mulberries. Using the rickety ladder with its uneven rungs Iqbal had cobbled together, she climbed onto the flat roof, whose main beams, formed by huge, straight-trunked poplars, were concealed beneath the layers of mud creating a weatherproof coating. Their house was the highest in the village, built almost half way up the steep mountainside and as always, Miriam caught her breath at the stunning views.

Immediately below her the village's handful of adobe houses looked as though they had grown out of the hillside. Further down, the bazaar's half dozen or so shops straggled alongside a narrow, unpaved road, which led towards the valley's cultivated strips and orchards showing as vivid splashes of green, before climbing towards a narrow coomb. The river threading its way through the valley, sometimes parallel to the road, sometimes meandering off on another route of its choosing, glinted blue and silver in the sunshine. Towering all around, the jagged-peaked mountains always drew Miriam's eyes. Over thousands of years natural forces had formed their rocky outcrops and pinnacles into fantastic shapes. Opposite, it was as if a fort, complete with battlements and towers had been carved from the perpendicular walls while behind her, gigantic black rocks thrust against the blue sky.

Miriam allowed the utter silence to seep into her, soothing her before turning reluctantly from the view to put sheets down on the roof on which to spread the mulberries. Her neighbours' rooftops were already covered with fruit and the white, black, red, purple berries produced patchwork quilts of colour around the village. In a few weeks the rooftops would be covered with golden apricots drying in the sun.

'Oh! Mother of Farid!' Miriam could see two women beginning the steep ascent to her house. She waved to them before hastily laying out the last of the mulberries. By the time she had climbed down the ladder to put water on to boil for tea, she could see her neighbours, Fatima and Shahnaz, emerging to join the others. Two or three afternoons a week Miriam's women friends came to visit. Usually she welcomed their company, and the chance to keep up to date with village events, but today she'd have preferred some peace. There was so much to do. Oh, well, Iqbal's statistics would have to wait. Why couldn't he deal with them himself, anyway?

When the women appeared at the gate of the *auli* Miriam moved forward to welcome them into the compound. The two older women kissed her forehead, a greeting she returned by taking and kissing the backs of their hands. The other two, nearer her own age, kissed her on both cheeks before she led them into the house. As they settled themselves on the mattresses around the walls Miriam watched how Fatima and Shahnaz, her nearest neighbours who lived in the house below hers, hovered until the two older women seated themselves, then each chose a place as far from the other as possible.

This was not, she knew, out of respect for age but because the two younger women were not on speaking terms. Both were married to the same man, a state of affairs neither enjoyed. Miriam had heard the story – Fatima's account of it – not long after she and Iqbal had arrived in Sang-i-Sia. When Daud had announced his intention to take a second wife Fatima had protested. 'I was angry,' she told Miriam. 'Very angry. I'd always been a good wife. Never refused him when he wanted to sleep near me.' Miriam had smiled at the local euphemism for sex, for the usually forthright Fatima was rarely coy. 'I'd given him three children, two boys and a girl. Kept them healthy, cooked for him, cleaned his house. He had no reason to take another wife.'

Fatima's anger, arguments, tears and pleas had had no effect. Daud went ahead with his marriage plans, but before the wedding took place Fatima had won some concessions. 'He agreed he would spend equal time with us – this is as Islam says, so he couldn't argue,' she explained to Miriam. 'Also I said I would never share a kitchen with her, nor cook for her.' Daud had worked out a timetable so each woman had access to the kitchen area at different times. Each family had its own room. Fatima also made it clear she would never speak to her husband's new wife. Ten years later, she still kept to her word.

Miriam had been astonished the two women had lived under one roof for so long without talking. They looked after each other's children, making no difference between them. She had herself seen that if a child fell, whichever mother was nearer would pick it up, dust it down, kiss it and stop the tears. Fatima had had three more and Shahnaz, with four, was catching up so the house was overflowing. They attended weddings in the village or went to offer condolences to bereaved neighbours without speaking to each other, and when they visited Miriam they sat, drinking tea in each other's presence, joining in the general conversation without ever once acknowledging the other's existence. However closely she watched them, she never saw one of them as much as look in the other's direction.

By the time Miriam brought the tea, Ruckshana had awoken. 'Where's Zainab?' she asked Fatima.

'Why, she's right there, in front of you,' replied Fatima, indicating one of the older women.

Ruckshana giggled, 'No, your Zainab, where's she?'

'Down below minding her baby sister.'

Ruckshana looked at her mother who, with a nod, gave her permission to find her friend. 'Behave,' she called after her, 'and come back when Farid comes home.' Miriam poured the tea, placing the enamel teapot and dishes of sweets within easy reach of her guests. The almost toothless Zainab reached out a calloused hand, dirt-encrusted fingers adorned with three silver and aquamarine rings, for a sweet, which she sucked noisily while slurping her tea. Miriam tried not to wince. The women settled down to the serious business of catching up on news of the village and surrounding area. Zainab and her sister-in-law Aquila, whose weathered features reminded Miriam of a pickled walnut, had reached a stage in their lives in which they could hand over the burden of work at home to daughters-in-law. With time on their hands for the first time since childhood they visited neighbours, complaining about how lazy their sons' wives were, gathering and disseminating gossip. They were probably still a few years younger than her mother and occasionally Miriam tried, but failed, to imagine them in Scotland, attending one of her mother's bridge parties or committee meetings.

The women had already heard about Miriam's unexpected guests. When she brought the baby through for a feed they shook their heads and clucked their tongues, not holding out much hope for the infant's survival. The biggest talking point of the day was the forthcoming marriage of one of the village girls to the son of a local landowner. 'Father-of-Zohra's done well for himself there,' remarked Zainab authoritatively, popping another sweet into her mouth.

'How much was the bride-price? I heard it was …?'

'Wait a minute,' Miriam interrupted, 'which Zohra are we talking about?'

'Oh, you know her,' Fatima replied. 'Her mother and my sister-in-law are cousins.' From Shinia way – half an hour from here.' Miriam, once she'd placed the girl, voiced a regret that the young girl was to be married so soon.

'Soon?' exclaimed Fatima, *chaddar* slipping as she shook her head. 'That one should have been married a long time ago. You should see her at the well, laughing when the boys tease her. Too free, by far.' She refilled her glass before continuing, 'Last year at harvest time I saw her hanging around the threshing ground. She brought apples from her father's orchard for Daud's young brother.'

Aquila spoke up, 'And I suppose you never hung around the well when you were young? No giggling to encourage the boys?'

Fatima winked. 'Maybe – but I didn't go offering them apples. My father would've killed me.'

The women discussed how Zohra's marriage would give her father access to some of the land her future father-in-law owned, moving on to talk about the growing animosity between two villages over the re-routing of a small burn. Miriam left to make fresh tea. When she returned to the room the conversation had moved onto dreams. Zainab was telling the women about her dream of the previous night in which she had seen her son, who had been working in Iran for the past two years.

As she described in great detail the clothes he wore – the suit she'd sewed herself with thread blessed at the shrine – what he was doing – cooking his meal – and what he said to his mother – that he could not cook *surwa* as well as she could – Miriam smiled ruefully. Women were always telling her about their dreams of loved ones; dreams reassuring them of the well being of family members living far from home, dreams of forthcoming marriages or pregnancies. Even Miriam, apparently, frequently featured in the women's dreams.

Miriam wasn't sure if they were really dreams, experienced when the women were asleep, or waking reveries occurring as wakefulness slips towards oblivion. Whatever, she was still surprised, not only by the frequency of these dreams but, by their normality. Though, occasionally, the dreams were warnings of impending tragedy. She gave a shiver. Sometimes in her dreams she'd see Jawad, his arms reaching towards her, his mouth open in a silent scream. Other times, she would be running after him but no matter how fast she ran or how loudly she called his name he never stopped or turned. She'd awake, afraid that she'd been calling his name in her sleep.

The door opened and Farid entered, panting after running home from school. He nodded to the women. '*Asalam 'alaikum. Chator asteed* – how are you?' he asked politely, though Miriam could see from his constant hopping from foot to foot, he was impatient to share something with her. Of course, the spelling test. His eyes danced in his solemn face when she asked about it, 'First position – none wrong.'

'*Mubarak* – Congratulations,' Miriam smiled at him and the other women all added their congratulations until Farid dipped his head, embarrassed to be the focus of so much attention.

'Is Ruckshana not with you?' Miriam asked, coming to his rescue. 'Will you fetch her please, Farid?'

'Don't bother,' said Fatima, rising to her feet. 'I have to go anyway. I'll send her home.'

The other women also rose to leave, murmuring about tasks still undone, meals to cook. Fatima paused, 'I forgot I had a joke to tell you,' she said. 'Have you heard about Mullah Nasuridin's wife and the BBC?' Everyone shook their heads, smiling in anticipation.

'Well, every day Mullah Nasuridin went home and told his wife he had heard such and such from BBC. He told her about things happening in Kabul and in America and all over the world – all these things he heard from BBC. Nasuridin's wife became jealous and angry and finally shouted at Nasuridin, 'Who is this Bibi See? She seems to know an awful lot and does a lot of talking to my husband. Who is she?' Everyone laughed and Miriam made a mental note to try to remember the story for Iqbal. Despite the fluency of her Dari she still found humour one of the most difficult things to tune into and sometimes the women would be crying with laughter over a joke that had gone right over her head. By the time they had explained it to her, it no longer seemed funny. Fatima's BBC joke was simple enough for her to grasp and, delighted she had 'got the point' of it she hoped to re-tell it without messing up the punch line.

Miriam walked her visitors to the gate, where she said goodbye, asking Farid to watch for Ruckshana coming up the path from Fatima's house. She smiled at her son, ruffling his short-cropped dark hair. "Well done with the spelling test. Your father would be so proud you're doing well in school. He was a clever boy, too. Always took first position in his class.' Farid gave a half-smile and, dodging from under his mother's fingers on his head, suddenly bolted down the path calling his sister's name although, Miriam noticed, she was nowhere in sight. She headed towards the kitchen.

Iqbal arrived home later than usual. Miriam heard Ruckshana run to greet him, demanding to know what was in the plastic carrier bag he held. 'Don't be nosy,' he said, placing the bag out of reach on a high shelf. He came to where Miriam sat feeding Sadiq, a watchful Uma by her side. 'I heard we had visitors.'

'Oh, Iqbal, I couldn't think what else to do. I just acted on the spur of the moment because…' not wanting to express her fears in front of the grandmother her voice tailed off. Switching to English she added, 'He wouldn't have survived if he went home… but… well, now I think it was pretty stupid of me. Look at him – what chance is there?'

'I don't know.' He reached out and stroked the baby's cheek with a fingertip. 'But I do know he has more chance with you than with anyone else.' The warmth in his voice – his faith in her ability – touched her.

Over dinner, when Ruckshana, tripping over her words in her excitement, started to tell her father about the kittens, his eyes twinkled in amusement. Suddenly realising he was about to sanction the immediate transfer of all four kittens to their house, Miriam cut in, 'Iqbal, one kitten's enough, please. And they can't come tonight – it'll be a few weeks yet. Their eyes aren't even open.'

As her daughter, hands on hips, glared at her mother for interfering, Iqbal roared with laughter until Ruckshana's eyes filled with tears. He scooped her up in his arms, 'It's okay, it's okay – I promise you'll have a kitten. But mummy's right – four is too many – and we need to wait until your kitten's big enough to leave its mummy.' Mollified, Ruckshana slipped back to her place and began to attack her *shurwa* as though she had not eaten for days. Harmony restored, Iqbal winked at Miriam who smiled back. Was this a good time to tackle him about the paperwork piling up? Maybe not. Why spoil things? Another day wouldn't make much difference. She asked instead if he'd heard the news of Zohra's engagement.

Iqbal said, 'We've been invited to the wedding.'

'All of us?'

He nodded. A huge grin spread across Miriam's face. It had been months since she'd been anywhere – and then it had been to pay her condolences to a friend whose husband had died. A sudden thought struck her. 'What'll I wear?' Iqbal reached down the package he had brought home, handing it to her with a slight bow. Miriam pulled out a length of cloth. 'Oh, this must be the design Fatima was talking about,' she cried. The pattern of vibrant orange roses swirling over a green background was hideously loud and, she suspected, not at all what smart women were wearing in the city. Still, it was what the other wedding guests from the village would be wearing. Giddy with excitement at the prospect of going out, she shook out the fabric. 'There's enough here for a dress for Ruckshana as well.'

Miriam pirouetted up to Iqbal the length of cloth draped around her and kissed him on the lips. He started to return the kiss but broke off at the sound of Ruckshana's giggles and Farid's throat clearing. 'It's time you were asleep,' he said to Ruckshana, grabbing her and tickling her until she shrieked with laughter. 'And you'd better be by the time I come home.' At the door, he added to Miriam, 'I won't be late.'

'Iqbal…' She stopped. Wanted to say don't go out – stay, play with the children, talk to me. He was opening the door. 'Thanks for the material.'

'I'm pleased you like it and – well, I'm…' She looked at him, unable to read his expression. He stood for a moment then, 'Seeing you so excited about the wedding … well, it made me realise…I know there aren't many chances for you to get out of the house.' He sounded almost wistful, looked embarrassed. He cleared his throat as though to say more, shook his head and left. She stared at the door for a few moments, wondering what he'd been trying to say, until Ruckshana tugging at her chaddar reminded her she'd to get her daughter ready for bed.

When Ruckshana was asleep Farid said goodnight and went to his own room to finish his homework before bed. Miriam kissed him goodnight, promising to look in on him later. She'd persuaded Iqbal to create a room for Farid by partitioning off a section of the guest room because she felt it was wrong for him still to sleep in the same room as she and Iqbal. Fatima, whose children, ranging in ages from two to twelve, still slept in the same room she shared every other night with Daud, had been amazed at her explanation. 'Oof, it can't be anything to make a noise over by now, surely?' she'd laughed. 'With Daud, it's over and done with before any of mine have time to wake up.' Not feeling up to sharing such frank declarations about her sex life, Miriam had changed the subject. She was relieved when Fatima, amused at her embarrassment, finally became bored of making teasing remarks about noisy lovemaking.

Thinking about how in Scotland both Farid and Ruckshana would have been expected to sleep alone since they were babies, and wondering how and where she could create another room for her daughter, Miriam went to the consulting room to check on Sadiq. Uma was asleep. She stood for a moment, listening for the baby's breathing and, reassured, turned to leave when she caught sight of the untouched paperwork on the table. Dr Jeanine, co-ordinator of Hansease, the organisation, which employed the couple, was due to visit them anytime now. She would need the clinic's statistics and accounts for her reports to overseas donors, without whom none of the ten clinics throughout Hazara Jat would exist. She'd have a fit if she were to see this mess.

Miriam sat down with a heavy sigh. It was almost as if Iqbal was deliberately setting himself up for a confrontation with Dr Jeanine. He wasn't looking forward to her arrival, had been grumbling for weeks about 'being inspected' by some foreigner who'd not been in the country five minutes. Who would want to know, down to the last afghani, how the budget had been spent. Why should the person at the top of the organisation be a foreigner? Did the donors think Afghans weren't clever enough – or did they not trust them to work honestly? She lifted the top paper from the pile and stared, unseeingly at it. Anxiety about Jeanine's visit wasn't enough to explain how much he'd changed. What was happening between her and Iqbal? He'd started going out most evenings, soon after the family had eaten, returning when the children were already in bed. She knew he met with Moosa, the local *mujahideen* commander, and the headmaster, Malim Ashraf, some of the teachers.

When they first came here – how long ago? Eighteen months now. He used to refer to Moosa and Ashraf as the *bozurg* – Afghanistan's VIPs – laughing a little at how self-important they were with their meetings. She sighed again. Now he was one of them, a *bozurg*, a big person, involved in plans for the local schools, a member of the local council, the *shura*. When she asked him what they talked about his answers were vague and unsatisfactory, as if such important matters were of no concern to a wife. But they used to discuss everything – the political situation, what was happening in Kabul. It was ages since they had talked to each other like before. They used to plan their future, the new clinic he hoped to build, hoped one day to run without relying on foreign donors for support. One day – when there was peace.

He'd changed since they came to Sang-i-Sia but she couldn't pin down exactly when or why. He was more – not possessive, exactly – it was more this obsession with what people might be saying about him, about her. The cancelled classes. He hadn't always been like this, and it wasn't as if she gave him any cause. Apart from members of his own family – which was a rare enough occurrence – she went for days, weeks even, without ever seeing or talking to a man.

Had she done the right thing? She'd been sure of her decision five years ago when they married in Pakistan. But now? She felt the only things she and Iqbal did together now was eat and sleep. Sadiq stirred, whimpered and Miriam realised with a start she'd been sitting for almost an hour in front of the untouched statistics. She hurried out to mix a feed for the baby.

THREE

Sang-i-Sia August 1995

By the time Zohra's wedding took place there were no more
mulberries, and apricots were already giving way to peaches. As she
set off with her husband and the children Miriam, self-conscious in her
new clothes, felt ridiculously excited about the outing. Were it not for
the fact Iqbal would be mortified, she would have skipped and sang
her way down the path like Ruckshana was doing.

The clinic's Toyota was parked at the foot of the mountain. As she
clambered in Miriam realised she had not been in a vehicle for almost
nineteen months since, her arrival coinciding with spring's fresh
greening on the trees, she came to live in the village. Settling herself
beside Iqbal, she brushed dust from the hems of her white, wide-
legged *tunban*. They wouldn't stay white for long. She admired the
hand-stitched embroidery. Years ago she'd tried the patience of her
friend Usma who attempted to teach her the delicate stitches. However
hard she'd tried she could never manage more than three stitches
before Usma was taking them out again, complaining they were too
big, too ugly. The white cloth was a dirty shade of grey before Usma
admitted defeat, asking how it was possible someone supposedly so
clever could be so useless at such a simple task. It had been a less
public humiliation than the goat, though no doubt Usma had not kept
the story of the *kharijee's* ineptitude to herself. Years ago, now, but
since then she'd never even managed to master the simple task of
operating a hand sewing machine. Now, Miriam smoothed down the
wide skirt of the dress Fatima had made for her. She couldn't
remember when she had last felt so dressed up. Not that she ever gave
much thought to clothes here, or her appearance – wearing and

washing the same couple of suits over and again. Whenever she felt her light brown hair, nearly always hidden under a chaddar, became too long she asked Iqbal to give it a trim. How she'd hated putting herself in the hands of a stylist in Edinburgh – torture – and no matter what he tried she knew it was a fruitless exercise – she'd never looked stylish.

As they passed through a neighbouring village, a mere six houses huddled low on the mountain, Iqbal pointed out Sadiq's house. Miriam looked out hoping for a glimpse of Uma but there was no one about. Sadiq had returned home only the week before. Although by no means plump, at least he was a stronger baby with much the same chance of survival as any other infant. 'Don't ever let me do such a thing again,' she said with feeling to Iqbal.

'I don't remember having much say in it. Anyway, you know you would if another Sadiq was brought to the clinic.'

Would she? It had been such a struggle, especially in the beginning, when Uma appeared completely disinterested in anything Miriam tried to do, taking a perverse pleasure whenever Sadiq vomited or lost a few ounces in weight. Over the first few days Miriam experimented with different strengths of formula until finally finding the amount and frequency of feeds that worked best.

Uma was unhappy when Miriam suggested leaving off the baby's swaddling, unconvinced by her explanation that Sadiq, free to wave his arms about and kick his legs, would build up his muscles. Although at first the tiny mite had not had the strength to do much kicking he could squirm, alarming his grandmother who, unused to holding a wriggling baby, struggled to keep her grip on him unless he was tightly wrapped up. Miriam would have loved to bath the baby but, knowing no one would immerse a baby in water until it was much older, she contented herself with wiping the important bits with cotton wool and warm water. She insisted, however, on cutting his long, dirty fingernails, despite Uma's protests that it would bring bad luck.

'Uma, see how he scratches himself, and the dirt from his nails will infect the scratches. He's too weak to fight off an infection.'

'If you let me wrap him up properly he wouldn't scratch himself,' Uma pointed out. 'Cutting his nails – you want the evil eye to fall on my grandson?' The old woman's eyes filled with tears and Miriam, with a sudden flash of insight, realised how deeply distressing the situation was for her. She felt ashamed. The older woman's apparent disinterest in the baby's welfare was a mask to hide her hopes for his survival, a way of not tempting fate. Not only was she afraid that her grandchild might die, she was having to cope with a never-ending series of assaults on her long-held beliefs about childcare handed down through generations.

'I'm scared too but believe me, Uma, everything I do is to help Sadiq become strong. Try to trust me.' Miriam reached out and hugged her, feeling the older woman's body tremble with suppressed tears. The nail-cutting incident marked a turning point in their relationship. The day Sadiq weighed in at nine pounds on the clinic scales was also the day he first smiled. Both women had wept together. Turning now to Iqbal, Miriam said, 'Yes, I'd do it again. Definitely.'

Half an hour later they reached the village where the wedding was being held and she and Iqbal parted company. As the bride's father ushered Iqbal towards the room for male guests, Miriam looked questioningly at Farid who was considering his options. Young enough to be still allowed to sit with the women, he was old enough to be embarrassed by this. Finally, though, he followed his mother and sister into a smaller room where the bride sat. It was crowded with women and children, who had to shout above the Indian film music playing at full volume on a ghetto blaster. Hoping the batteries would soon run out, Miriam fought her way through the crowd to reach Zohra's side. '*Mubarak*' she mouthed, handing over the envelope containing a wedding gift of money, realising as she did so she had no idea how much Iqbal had put in it.

An unsmiling statue, Zohra sat almost completely hidden by the scarlet and gold wedding *chaddar* draped over her head. When she glanced up in a brief acknowledgment of the gift Miriam saw tears brimming in her eyes. The layers of heavy make up could not disguise how pale and drawn her face was. The girl's mother and sisters surrounded her, fussing and clucking, tweaking at the folds of her perfectly arranged sequin smothered satin suit, dabbing at the sheen of sweat on her forehead, applying a fresh coat of lipstick. As other guests arrived to greet the bride Miriam relinquished her place, squeezing back through the throng. Two women moved over to make room for her to sit beside them on the *toshak*.

'*Asalam 'alaikum*, Dr Miriam, *chator asteed*?' they greeted her. As far as they were concerned all foreigners were doctors – unless they were engineers. Miriam used to be uncomfortable about her elevated status, imagining what would happen at home if she went around impersonating a doctor. Once, when she'd explained quite forcibly to three women who hailed her on the road that she was not, not, definitely not a doctor they gazed at her in astonished silence. Finally one said, 'If you are not a doctor, why are you here? What use are you?' After that, Miriam, who most certainly did want to be of use, gave up trying to explain she was only a midwife.

She could smell the newness of the deep red needle cord cloth covering the mattresses around the rooms. A curtain, embroidered with stylised flowers, hiding the bundle of bedding stored in an alcove, was also new. On a shelf above the alcove sat the Qur'an, wrapped in a silk cloth. A few framed photographs on the walls showed various family members who had worked in Iran and Pakistan. In each, in front of studio backdrops of Alpine meadows or tumbling waterfalls, the subject sat or stood ramrod straight, gazing directly at the camera with no hint of a smile. The room had been decorated with shiny tinsel garlands for the wedding and the air was heavy with the mixed odour of perfume and perspiration. Tea and a tray of cakes and sweets appeared. Instead of the usual boiled sweets these, in honour of the occasion, were wrapped toffees. '*Choclet*,' whispered Ruckshana in delight to Farid. Their mother now completely absorbed in conversation with her neighbours, the children stuffed their mouths and pockets before rushing outside to find other children at play in the *auli*.

Hearing someone call her name, Miriam craned her neck until she spotted Iqbal's brother Hussain's wife Masooma, struggling through the crowded room. In her arms she carried a screaming baby, two more small children clutched at her skirt. People obligingly squashed further up to create a space. She sat down, fumbling at the front of her dress until she exposed a milk-filled breast. The wailing ceased. Watching her sister-in-law fan her flushed face with the sleeve of her dress, Miriam realised they were wearing similar outfits, only Masooma's roses had a blue background.

While the women chatted, an army of small boys served food. *Kabuli*, topped with plump sultanas, almonds and carrots, chicken, *subzi* and saucers of sweet *firni* were laid out on a long white *dustakhan* around the edges of which were colourful embroidered birds, horses and teapots with the words *khushamdeed* – welcome – at either end. More tea was being served when a small boy threaded his way through the women to whisper in Masooma's ear. She nodded. 'Hussain is ready to leave, ' she explained, beginning to get to her feet. 'It's been good to see you Miriam-*jan*.'

'Yes, I wish we saw each other more often.' Miriam stood up to embrace her sister-in-law.

'Well, whose fault is that? You're invited often enough.' Her words stopped Miriam in her tracks.

'What do you mean?'

Masooma shrugged. 'Oh, I know it's not you. It's Iqbal. He's always got some excuse about work whenever we ask him to come to a *mehmani*, or,' she added, 'just to come and see us.' She put her arms out to hug Miriam who stepped back, looking bewildered.

'But why?'

'I suppose he…' Masooma looked suddenly embarrassed. 'Oh, don't ask me, I've no idea what goes on inside men's heads.' She stepped forward again and this time, distractedly, Miriam returned her embrace. She sat down, turning over what Masooma had said until her thoughts were interrupted by the arrival of more guests.

Two hours later Miriam was still sitting in the same spot. The only time she had moved was when, desperate to pee, she had ventured outside, grateful to find the village boasted a latrine. She squatted over the hole, attempting to hold the torn sacking across the entrance with one hand. Would she ever stop worrying about someone walking in on her? One of the first things she had done when she arrived in Sang-i-Sia was to insist Iqbal fitted a door complete with a bolt to their own latrine.

In her excitement about getting out of the house Miriam had forgotten how mind-numbingly tedious a wedding could be unless you had a role to play other than guest. Were the men next door talking about more interesting topics? Once, in that other life with Jawad, she'd been treated as an honorary man, invited to join the men at an engagement. The future bride's family brought gifts – a gold watch, a turban, shoes. She'd watched the young man strap the watch around his wrist, slip on the smart black leather shoes. His father had wound the yards of silk round his head. She'd panicked slightly when he handed over a pair of western style trousers. Had he forgotten her presence? Was he about to strip off in front of her before trying on his new suit? However, he'd pulled the trousers on over his *shalwar*, creating a peculiarly lumpy appearance. For the rest of the time she'd been bored; her grasp of the language in those days not enough to let her take part in the conversation.

She was sleepy and dizzy from the constant noise, the heat and the continuous questioning about life in Scotland, which the women insisted on calling London. They always wanted to know how much money she earned as a doctor in London, gasping at such unimaginable wealth, but ignoring her explanations about how much rent and food cost. She preferred to keep the conversation centred on the women's own lives where there was some common ground. She smothered a yawn. What had Masooma been on about? She didn't know about invitations. Must ask Iqbal later. Some women in the centre of the room moved and Miriam caught a glimpse of Zohra now dry-eyed but still pale and silent.

Not the happiest day of her life, poor love. What memories of her wedding day will she choose to look back on? She smiled at a sudden memory of her own wedding. Unlike Zohra, Miriam had spent her wedding day grinning all over her face. Her new mother-in-law had tried to explain why she should look sad. 'This is the day a girl leaves her father's house forever. She says goodbye to her mother, sisters and brothers, not knowing when she will see them again. That will be for her husband to decide. Her life changes completely from this day and although it's hoped her husband and his family will be good to her she doesn't know what her *kismet* will be.'

'Well, I left my father's house years ago,' Miriam had replied. 'In my country it's part of growing up and being independent. And I'm so happy today, I just can't look sad and miserable – besides,' she added beaming, 'I know my husband's family will be good to me.'

'You are an exasperating girl,' Zakia had said, shaking her head, though she could not entirely hide her own smile. 'But you will be good for my son I think.'

Did Zakia still believe that? Or, did she also play the 'what if' game? What if Miriam had never met Jawad? They wouldn't have, if Janet hadn't been so insistent. God, it had been a dreadful party. Janet, a nurse working on the maternity ward had urged Miriam – or Margaret as she still was then – to go with her to the party. She closed her eyes, hearing her friend's voice in her ear.

***

'Come on, don't be so boring – you'll enjoy it once you get a couple of glasses of wine down you. There'll be loads of talent.'

'I'm not looking for talent, thanks.' Janet was always trying to fix her up with men. 'I'm still seeing Dave, remember?'

Her friend rolled her eyes. 'And where is Mr Cool Lab Technician this weekend? Fishing?' Margaret nodded. Dave was a friend of a friend of Janet's – blind date material – who'd been part of a group of hospital staff who went bowling one night. To Margaret's surprise, for never having mastered the art of flirting, she'd given him no encouragement, he asked to see her again. He was good-natured, generous and amusing when not talking fish and they'd drifted along ever since – like a placid river with no unexpected eddies or exciting whirlpools to ever disturb the surface. Sex with him, though infrequent because of her work shifts and his fishing trips, was satisfying – in a comfortable sort of way. Dave was a thoroughly nice man. She didn't want to settle for nice but it was easier than being forced into the horrors of Janet's talent scouting forays and, usually, he provided a good enough excuse to wriggle out of invitations. Not this time. It was clear, although initially delighted with her matchmaking success, Janet was now determined Margaret should widen her horizons. Without quite knowing how it happened Margaret was dragged along to the party.

They'd no sooner got drinks than Janet disappeared into the crowd, mumbling, 'Back in a tick.' Miriam left alone at a table near the entrance, plastered a smile on her face in an attempt to look as though she were enjoying herself. She spotted several colleagues, but they were all part of laughing, chatting groups. She had no idea how to go over and join them, convinced the moment she approached everyone would stop talking and stare at her – or worse, ignore her. Occasionally, people arriving paused to say hello before wandering off in search of drinks, to be swallowed up by the crowd and never seen again. Her frozen smile slipped. She was angry with Janet for abandoning her, even more angry with herself. Why was she so bloody spineless? She knew some people thought she was aloof, stuck up. If only they understood the agonies of the socially inept. Gauche, her mother had described her to a friend – 'Margaret is terribly gauche. No social skills.' Right, go find another drink and someone to talk to – or leave. The sight of Alan Johnston advancing towards her propelled her into action. Grabbing her coat she moved towards the door determined to escape being trapped by the nursing lecturer. It worried her that she was a magnet for a man who appeared to believe she was fascinated by tales of how he had to call the plumber on a Sunday morning to attend to his mother's blocked overflow pipe. 'Not leaving already, are you, Margaret?'

'Yes, 'fraid so, Alan. I've, em, just remembered I should be somewhere else. I'm late. See you around.' Thrusting her arms into her coat she accidentally delivered a right hook to a man standing in the open doorway. 'Sorry,' she gasped. 'Are you all right?'

'No problem,' he murmured, rubbing gingerly at his nose and following her outside. 'Can I call a taxi for you?'

'What? No, no, I only live round the corner. Thanks anyway.'

'Oh,' he paused for a moment, looking confused. 'I thought you had to be somewhere else. Perhaps I misunderstood? My English is sometimes not so good.'

Intrigued by his accent she paused, turning to face him. She had to look up he was so much taller than she. In the light of the street lamps his features were indistinct. She sensed his deprecating comment about his English hid some amusement. 'Um, yes, well I said that because I wanted to escape.' Wondering why she felt any need to explain to this stranger who had caught her out in an untruth, she added earnestly, 'I don't usually tell lies.'

'I also would like to escape. I do not feel comfortable amongst so many people. Maybe we could escape together?'

Janet would have taken the question as a chat up line and come back with a smart answer; within seconds they would both be laughing together, planning an escape to Mars or something equally outlandish. She felt though this man was not chatting her up, sensed something wistful, lonely about him. She suddenly smiled, 'Okay, why not? There's a coffee shop in the next street, should still be open. I'll buy you a coffee as an apology for breaking your nose.' She must be mad wandering off into the night with a complete stranger.

In the café, cappuccinos in front of them, she looked properly at him for the first time, taking in the high cheekbones, dark, almond shaped eyes with long, sooty lashes. Instinct told her she was safe with this man. 'My name is Jawad.' He offered her his hand, which she shook, smiling.

'Margaret.'

'It is a pleasure to meet you, Margaret.' She found herself watching the shape of his lips as he sounded each syllable of her name carefully.

'You too, Jawad. Where are you from?'

'I am from Afghanistan.' He said it with pride, mixed with a painful sadness. Remembering how many Afghans had fled after the Soviet invasion she wondered if he was a refugee but, no, he explained he was studying engineering at Edinburgh University. He would return to his country equipped with skills and knowledge to help his people rebuild their country. He talked of the devastation his country had suffered in the war, now in its fifth year, between the *mujahideen* and the Soviets. He told her of the lack of roads and bridges, of towns and villages without electricity and water, of the absence of an infrastructure, and he talked of the beauty of his country, of the blue-domed shrine to Ali in the city where he grew up. He conjured up the high snow-capped mountains and remote valleys of Hazara Jat, his ancestral homeland. She listened captivated, not only by his words but by the way he spoke them; his accent, the slightly old-fashioned sounding English, the way his eyes came alive with love for his country, his sweeping arm gestures, his passion.

'I think it is enough about me and my country – what about you, Margaret, what work do you do?'

'Oh, I'm a midwife.' Delivering babies suddenly seemed a bit dull compared to the prospect of re-building a destroyed country brick by brick.

'My country needs more midwives – nurses and doctors, too, but especially midwives – to work in the rural areas. In the cities the situation is better but in Hazara Jat...' And he was off again, occasionally pausing, searching for a word to express himself more clearly, telling her about the lack of health services, of people having to walk for hours to reach the nearest clinic, of women dying in childbirth. 'Almost half of Afghanistan's babies die before they are five years old,' he said, quietly, 'almost half.' He shrugged. 'Forgive me, Margaret, I am taking too much of your time. Usually I do not speak of all these things. Not everyone wants to know, they have their own problems. You are very sympathetic to talk to.'

The waiters were stacking chairs, glaring at the couple, who for far too long, had managed to ignore the signs of closing. Miriam glared back at them. She wanted to stay here forever; afraid once they moved a spell would break. Outside, Jawad fell into step beside her as they walked towards her flat. Please let him ask to see me again, please let him ask for my number, please, please. When she told him they had reached her home, however, he only said, 'It has been a pleasure talking with you, Margaret. Good night.'

'Oh, yes, well, goodnight.' Damn it, was she just going to let this man walk away? 'Wait, Jawad…' she swallowed. 'Look, I've enjoyed your company tonight, hearing you talk about Afghanistan and, well, look, would you like to meet up again, sometime, em, for another coffee?' He smiled, patting his pockets until he found a crumpled envelope. They exchanged telephone numbers and she contented herself with that, though she fretted about him throwing away the envelope by mistake. She'd give him a week – no, four days – would three be too forward? – then she'd call him. She didn't need to summon up her courage. He phoned the next day.

Although she feigned indifference to the gossip about her in the maternity unit and the staff canteen, secretly she revelled in it. Her colleagues were amazed dreary Margaret Anderson had captured such an amazing man. They drooled over him when he came to meet her at the end of a shift. She dumped a rather surprised Dave, although Jawad gave no indication he regarded her as anything more than a friend. It didn't matter. Nothing mattered as long Jawad wanted to spend time with her. Each time they said goodbye she counted the hours until she would see him again.

Over the winter they spent more and more time together. Hating the cold Margaret would never have suggested visiting the Castle in January. However, Jawad's enthusiasm for exploring Edinburgh's every nook and cranny was infectious and she found herself muffled in layers of her warmest clothes, eyes watering in the bitter wind actually enjoying herself as she stood next to him on the battlement or ventured down yet another hidden close to study the Old Town's architecture. What she enjoyed most was when they finally headed for a café where they could sit in the warmth and she could listen to him talk. Very occasionally, a little voice in her head asked what possible future could they share? She silenced it.

In the spring, Jawad told her he was going home to visit his family, asked if she would like to join him. She didn't need to think for a second before saying yes. 'Won't you have to wear a veil over there?' asked Janet. 'And what's his family going to say when their son comes home with a white girlfriend?'

'Jawad's family are educated. Their women don't cover their faces. And I'm not ...' She broke off, confused. Janet stared at her.

'Haven't you slept with him yet?' Margaret flushed and Janet hooted, 'You've been seeing him for months! What's wrong with you? Or is he gay?' As her colleague hurried off, presumably to pass on this tasty bit of gossip, Margaret sighed. Was she his girlfriend? How did Jawad view their relationship? That he liked her was clear but was it only as a good friend, a platonic relationship? She sensed there was more to it than that. Sometimes she caught him looking at her when he thought she wouldn't notice. What she saw then made her tingle and melt inside. Yet, whenever they met and parted Jawad would take her hand in both of his, squeeze it gently and immediately release it. He had never even tried to kiss her.

***

'Mummy! Time for the procession.' Ruckshana's voice shrilled in Miriam's ear. Limbs protesting at moving after so long, she rose stiffly to her feet, blinking herself back to the present. The babble of voices around her rose as the women fussed over the bride, kissing her goodbye, praying for her as she began the journey to her husband's home. There was a clatter of hooves outside and Miriam, disorientated, stuck somewhere between past and present, hurried out with Ruckshana.

Someone led a pretty grey mare up to the door and her father helped Zohra to mount. She sat side-saddle, eyes downcast. The groom, in his fine new turban, was already astride a black stallion. He didn't look at his new wife as the horses were turned around and led out the compound. Outside the gate a string of donkeys, each laden with tin trunks, still mirror-shiny in their newness, was urged into line behind the bride and groom. Guests gathered round, counting the boxes, shrewdly calculating the value of what lay within – quilts and blankets, clothes for both Zohra and her new in-laws, teapots, glasses and dishes from Iran, striped *gillims* for the floor of the couple's room – agreeing that her father had given his daughter a respectable send off. A group of horsemen came galloping up firing kalashnikovs in the air and guests formed a procession, which followed the bridal couple towards the next village.

A few yards from the groom's home half a dozen grinning children blocked the way with a length of rope pulled taut to form a barrier. 'What will you pay to pass here?' demanded a young lad sternly of the groom. The crowd laughed as Zohra's husband fumbled in his pockets for the customary 'toll' before he would be allowed to take his new wife any further. The laughter grew louder when the boy, glancing disdainfully at the proffered money asked, 'Is that all you think she is worth to bring home?' More money was flung on the ground and at a signal the rope was dropped and the wedding party continued on the last stage of the journey.

Miriam, carrying Ruckshana, was thankful when Iqbal appeared at her side and took the child into his own arms. She snuggled into him, her eyes closing in sleep almost immediately. 'I've asked someone to bring the Toyota,' Iqbal said. 'I think it's time to go home.'

FOUR

Sang-i-Sia

Iqbal looked across at Miriam, sitting rigid in the front seat of the Toyota, Ruckshana asleep on her lap.

'Stop fretting,' he murmured, 'he'll be fine. Daud'll watch out for him.' Farid had looked so crestfallen when he realised they were leaving before the *buzkashi* started Iqbal said he could stay to watch the game with their neighbour. Now, however, Miriam's doubtful expression made him feel he was in the wrong. He added, 'You would've embarrassed him if you'd insisted he came home with us.'

Eyes straight ahead, she replied, 'Rather he was embarrassed than injured. You know how dangerous it can be for spectators.'

Iqbal grunted. So few people kept horses around here now, he doubted there would be as many as twenty riders taking part. It was only in places like Mazar-i-Sharif the big *buzkashi* games were still held with upwards of eighty horses, their riders fighting for possession of a headless calf. Miriam was probably imagining Farid being trampled under flying hooves as he tried to scramble to safety when, as sometimes happened, riders were unable to prevent their over-excited horses charging towards the audience on the sidelines. He fell silent, knowing nothing he could say would reassure her.

Back in Sang-i-Sia, carrying the still-sleeping Ruckshana up to the house, Iqbal could have sworn the path had become steeper. Breathing heavily, he was relieved to lay his daughter down, sinking beside her on the *toshak*. He shook his head at Miriam's offer of tea, suggesting instead they spend some time on the paperwork. During the last couple of weeks, at Miriam's insistence, he'd put in an hour most days bringing things up to date. She'd worked alongside him, their joint efforts bringing a satisfying order to the chaos, and the task was nearly done.

'Let's leave it until tomorrow – I'm too tired to think straight now,' Miriam said.

'Come on, it'll take your mind off worrying about Farid. I want to finish it tonight.'

'Why the urgency all of a sudden? Oh, I know. You've heard Dr Jeanine is coming?'

He nodded. 'She could be here any day.'

'Oh, Iqbal, why didn't you tell me? How long's she going to stay?'

'The letter's here somewhere.' He patted his pockets, finally pulling out a folded sheet of paper. At the same time an envelope fell on the floor. Miriam stooped to pick it up. Iqbal froze. 'Leave it, I'll get it.' Although he knew she couldn't read the Arabic script, she'd recognise whose hand had written it. His voice was sharper than intended and he felt her glance searchingly at him before she looked at the envelope in her hand.

'This is for me. Why didn't you give me it?' She turned the envelope over, 'You've opened it.' The anger in her voice took him by surprise. 'You've no right to open my mail.'

'But you would need me to read it to you.' Even to his ears it sounded a pitiful defence. Swallowing, he added, 'I didn't want you to be upset. I wasn't keeping it from you, but I wanted to find the right time.'

'My God, Iqbal, surely I'm entitled to have my letters given to me unopened. Anyway, how could you know it would upset me before you opened it?' He watched her remove the single sheet of paper from the flimsy envelope, stare at the closely written script. As though suddenly struck by what he'd said her face paled. She looked at him, anxiety in her eyes. 'Why will it upset me? Tell me. Read it to me.'

Iqbal took the sheet from her shaking hand and began to read aloud, though he knew the contents by heart.

Dearest daughter,
We send many greetings from Mazar-i-Sharif. We hope you and
Farid are well and pray for your continued good health. We miss
you.

Miriam-jan our hearts are still aching – as yours must be also - at the loss of our son. It is great sadness for us that we do not see you and our beloved grandson in our lives. With your permission we would like to welcome Farid to our home for a short visit before the winter. It would bring such joy to Jawad's mother. Please let me know if you are agreeable and we will make the necessary arrangements.

Miriam sank to her knees, burying her head in her arms. 'Oh, God, what should I do? I can't lose Farid, too. I can't.'

'You won't lose Farid.' Iqbal slid down beside her, pulling her into his arms. 'They only want to see him. A few weeks and he'll be home again.'

'What if they decide to keep him? How could I stop them?'

Iqbal wiped away the tears spilling down her cheeks. 'Miriam, they won't keep him. Anwar is an honourable man. I promise I'll go and fetch him myself if they try. Come on, this is what you always said you wanted.'

'I know, I know. It's the shock of realising it'll happen so soon.' She wiped her eyes. 'It's so good Farid will get to know his father's family.' She gave Iqbal a watery smile. At that moment Ruckshana appeared in the doorway, grumpy from her too-long sleep and Miriam took her off to wash her face and find her something to eat. Later, Farid arrived bursting with excitement, and the importance of having been out without his family.

'Jan Ali won the *buzkashi*. He has such a strong horse.'

Miriam, patting a place beside her, said, 'Come and tell us all about it and how well Jan Ali rode this strong horse of his.' She looked over at Iqbal, 'Tomorrow – we'll write to them tomorrow.' He heard the tremor in her voice but, knowing she wouldn't want him to do or say anything to alert Farid to her distress, he gave only a brief nod. He would send word to Anwar, suggesting a halfway meeting place.

Once he heard about his visit to Mazar, Farid, animated by this great adventure, hovered at the gate every afternoon, waiting for Iqbal to come home from work. His stepson's disappointment, each day no letter arrived from his grandfather, contrasted with the look of relief on Miriam's face at the delay in losing her son. When at last the reply came, it was to say Farid's uncle Daud would travel to Bamiyan to escort him to Mazar-i-Sharif.

They left before it was light. Farid, who'd been in a state of high excitement the night before, fell asleep almost before Iqbal drove clear of the village. Iqbal slid a cassette into the player, keeping the volume low. He usually travelled with his driver, wasn't used to silent journeys. After an hour or so he wished Farid would wake up. Talking would help pass the time – father and son. He gave a rueful smile. Farid behaved towards him as though he were a distant uncle – polite, respectful. When he had his own son, he'd have to ensure he didn't make any difference him and Farid. Well, Miriam would ensure he didn't but when would Miriam be ready for another child? Last time he broached the subject she'd asked him to wait a bit longer, be patient. Allah knew he had been – but Ruckshana was three already. People would start to wonder. He'd talk to her when he came back from Bamiyan. Farid stirred, mumbled once in his sleep then sat bolt upright as though pretending he had been awake all the time.

Iqbal put a hand out, ruffled the boy's hair, asking if he was hungry. Miriam had packed a lunch for them and he pulled up so they could stretch their legs before eating. 'So, how's school,' he asked to break the silence.

'It's fine, thank you.'

'Still want to be an engineer?'

Farid, biting into a hardboiled egg, nodded. Iqbal struggled on for a few more minutes before rising to his feet to resume the journey. As though realising how far away he was going, and for how long, from his mother, Farid became more than usually subdued. When, in the late afternoon, they approached the edge of the bazaar, however, he suddenly came to life, exclaiming, 'Oh, look, look, the Buddha.' Iqbal smiled at his excitement, promising as they drove slowly past the towering figure carved into the rock, he'd soon see an even bigger one. At the hotel on the main road Farid hung out of the window, directly opposite the larger of the two figures.

The main Hazara mujahideen group, Hisb-i-Wadhat used the area as its command post and tanks and armoured personnel carriers were parked in front of the cliff. The caves, once occupied by pilgrims, were now used as ammunition stories and provided accommodation for fighters. Almost at the feet of the giant Buddha soldiers were playing volleyball. 'Please, can we go and look?' Iqbal was about to agree when a voice spoke up from the doorway.

'How about I take you tomorrow, Farid-*jan*, and introduce you to some of the Commanders?' Farid's uncle, Daud entered the room, continuing, 'Maybe they'll let you climb up inside the Buddha.' It was a suggestion designed to win the boy over and Iqbal saw, with a sudden pang of envy, how Farid's eyes lit up even while he hung his head shyly. Why hadn't he thought up the idea first? Now he'd been relegated to the position of delivery boy, of no further consequence. He moved forward to make the somewhat unnecessary introductions between uncle and nephew.

'Well, look how tall you have grown, *Mash 'Allah*,' Daud smiled at Farid. 'You won't remember me, Farid-*jan*, but we did meet once before, a long time ago. You were a very little boy.' His smile slipped. 'A sad little boy.' An awkward silence fell as both men thought about the circumstances of Daud and Farid's first – and until now – only meeting. Iqbal was relieved when the serving boy brought in a tray of tea.

Later in the evening, over kebabs and rice, Daud suggested after a day exploring the Buddha and the ancient citadel of Bamiyan, he and Farid make a detour to visit Band-i-Amir and its famous lakes before setting out for Mazar-i-Sharif.

'Has your *padder-adari* – stepfather – told you the legends of Band-i-Amir?' Daud asked. Farid shook his head, eyes gleaming at the prospect of a story.

Iqbal sat back against the wall, staring into his glass of tea as Daud held Farid spellbound with the tale of how Hazrat-i-Ali, son-in-law of the Prophet, created the dams. 'It was way back in the days of the cruel tyrant, King Barbar. He sent a thousand of his slaves to build a dam but, despite working day and night for many months, they could not contain the river. Barbar was furious and became even crueller towards his people, making them pay high taxes, punishing them for the smallest thing.

'There was a young man, a poor farmer, who couldn't pay his tax. Barbar threw his wife and children into prison. The young man was terrified he'd never see them again. He heard Hazrat-i-Ali was visiting the king's territory and he asked him for help. Ali devised a cunning plan. He disguised himself as a slave and told the young man to offer to sell him to the king for enough money to pay his debts. So the young man bound Hazrat-i-Ali with strong ropes and went to Barbar who agreed to buy the 'slave. But, unfortunately…' Daud paused to pour more tea and Iqbal could see Farid squirm with impatience waiting for his uncle to continue. He wished Farid hung so eagerly on his words. Why had he never told him stories? Would it bring them any closer? Sometimes he felt Farid… judged him? No, that wasn't quite it. With Ruckshana it was so different – and it wasn't only because of the blood connection.

Daud was continuing his tale, 'Unfortunately the king was not prepared to pay the money until his new 'slave' carried out some challenges. He was to build the dam, he was to slay the dragon of Bamiyan, which was only kept from devouring everything in the king's territory by the sacrifice of a young girl every day – and he was to bring Hazrat-i-Ali to him in chains. He had to complete all those tasks within one day. Well, everyone knew it was impossible and the king's courtiers laughed at the young man and the 'slave.'

'Hazrat-i-Ali was angry at the injustice of the cruel king and strode immediately to the mountaintop where, his temper making him impossibly strong, he kicked down masses of rocks to form the Band-i- Haibat, the Dam of Awe. Next, he took up his sword and sliced another chunk off the mountain to create the Band-i-Zulfiqar.

'You will never see such brilliant blue water anywhere in the world,' Daud was telling an open-mouthed Farid. 'The first time I saw Band-i-Amir, I wondered what names to give so many different shades of blue – deep dark sapphire in the centre to clear turquoise. The Band-i-Haibat, is supposed to have miraculous curative powers. I'm sure you'll know the place, Dr Iqbal?'

Iqbal nodded though at the mention of Band-i-Haibat he had given an involuntary shudder, disguising it by raising his arm to signal for the boy in the kitchen to bring more tea.

***

He was a small boy again – Farid's age – about the time some of the children refused to sit beside him and taunts of 'leper' followed him from school. He could scarcely believe his ears when his father announced that he was taking the whole family on a special outing – a picnic at Band-i-Amir. After hearing the fabulous stories so often, the thought of being able to see Hazrat-i-Ali's handiwork for himself kept Iqbal awake with excitement the night before the trip.

When they arrived Iqbal, his brother and sisters helped their mother carry the rugs, cushions, bundles of nan, the big black pot in which she'd cooked the *shurwa*, the kettle and all the other essentials to the chosen spot. It was a long walk from where they parked the jeep his father had borrowed, along rocky paths at the base of towering cliffs, between two lakes. Tripping over the ends of the rug he carried, Iqbal stared, mesmerised, at the water; its blueness even more than he'd imagined. When soon after the family settled themselves, his father suggested they go for a walk, Iqbal's happiness was complete. Taking his father's hand he strolled importantly beside him along the edge of the lake. Even his brother, who he often suspected was their father's favourite, was left behind. 'You know it's said Hazrat-i-Ali blessed this water to give it the power to cure diseases?' his father asked. Iqbal nodded, wondering if they should collect some of the water to take home – perhaps it would smooth away the patches on his forehead. His father said, 'Yes, we'll fill some bottles later, but there is another way to cure this sickness you have. Come.'

As they walked on together Iqbal puzzled over this sickness he seemed to have. He didn't understand it – he didn't feel sick, not like his friend Ali had been. He'd had a cough, which never went away and gradually he became thinner and weaker, and then no one saw him any more. No, he was strong and healthy, apart from these lumpy reddish patches appearing on his body. He fingered his earlobes with his free hand – they'd become thicker recently. Together he and his father walked round a small promontory. Here the water's darker blue reflected its greater depth, a high cliff blocked the sun and air was chilly. There were fewer people about, standing in tight little groups. Instead of the noisy laughter of the families they had left behind there was the sound of praying. A cry, a splash and giant ripples suddenly roughed the calm water. 'Oh, someone's fallen in,' Iqbal cried out in alarm. 'Be quick, father. Help him!'

His father motioned him to wait. From under the choppy surface of the water a man emerged and, arms milling wildly, began swimming towards the rocky shore. The sound of praying grew louder as hands reached out to help pull the shivering man out of the water. Iqbal shivered in sympathy, knowing, despite the hot sun, how bitterly cold the water, its rivers fed by snowmelt, would be. He felt his father's hand on his shoulder, urging him forward, towards the water. A sudden spasm of fear gripped Iqbal as he understood what his father intended. 'No! No, father, please no,' he screamed, trying to move back, away from the edge, away from that dark water. 'I'll drown. I can't swim. Please don't, father, please don't.'

His father, although struggling to remove something from his bag, still managed to prevent his escape by gripping his arm, hard. 'Ssh, you won't drown,' he tried to reassure the terrified boy. 'I'll tie this rope around you – see. It'll go round your middle and I'll pull you in again.' Iqbal continued to fight, striking out at his father, pleading with him not to throw him in the water. He might have succeeded in breaking free had not another man come to help his father. Together they pushed and dragged him to the very edge of the rocks and he heard himself scream, once, then there was a loud roaring and rushing in his ears, a feeling of being dragged down through darkness, of a giant's icy grip squeezing the life from him.

Then he was pulled, choking and heaving out of the freezing water. His father, tears pouring down his face, struggled to loosen the rope while trying, at the same time, to wrap a blanket around him. 'I hate you! I hate you!' Iqbal screamed at him. Freed from the rope, he turned and ran, his clothes slapping cold and wet against his goose-fleshed skin. He thought he heard his father call out, telling him he was going the wrong way but he didn't stop, his only impulse to get as far away as possible. Finally, exhausted, he stopped, his chest heaving from the exertion. He rested on a smooth flat, sun-warmed rock. The sun's rays felt good, taking away the outer chill and when his breathing gradually slowed he allowed his eyes to close.

He didn't remember dozing off but when he opened his eyes again, the sun was slipping down the sky. He looked around him, disorientated. The rocky, dusty landscape made him think of the time he'd looked at the moon through a telescope a *mujahid* said he'd taken it from a Russian soldier. The *muj* also said men had landed on the moon, walked on it. Iqbal hadn't liked to argue with him but he was sure it couldn't be true. A soft breeze, blowing the scent of wild mint towards him, was creating gentle ripples in the water, which sparkled in the slanting rays of the sun. He shivered as the memory of its coldness came back to him. When he heard voices, he thought his father was coming to find him. Not yet ready to face him he slipped from his perch and hid behind the rock and then…

A man and a young girl were walking his way. The girl's hair was damp. He heard the man tell her to stop, to wait for their father. When both hunkered down on the other side of the rock behind which Iqbal was crouching he could no longer see them nor hear what they were saying, though he was sure the girl was crying. He felt uncomfortable hidden there, as if he were spying, and was about to cough to make his presence known when he heard more footsteps approach. There was a sudden muffled cry, a crunch and a thud, as though something heavy had fallen on the ground.

A voice cried out, 'Father! Why?'

'Because it didn't work. Help me. Quickly. Take her feet – move!'

'But maybe it takes time. How…?'

'It's better this way. Leprosy doesn't only affect the victim. We'd all be outcasts. Now, move. Over there, where it's deep.'

There were scuffling sounds, and laboured breathing. Iqbal, now terrified he'd be discovered, pressed his body against the rock as though trying to get right inside it. How long he remained with his eyes screwed shut, expecting any second to hear a shout as one or other of the men saw him, he didn't know. He heard a splash. Footsteps hurrying in the direction from which they had come. He hugged the rock, listening, long after the footsteps faded. After what seemed like hours, he dared to move his cramped limbs, paused, still listening, then stood up and slid cautiously round the side of the rock. It was deserted. Then he saw in the low rays of the sinking sun, bloodstains on a stone, on the sandy soil – and he was running again.

Instinct directed him towards an area where people were packing their picnics away, others already strolling in groups towards the road. He began to cry. A woman stopped him. 'Are you Iqbal?' she asked. He nodded dumbly. 'Your family has been searching everywhere for you. Your poor mother is frantic. Come on, I'll take you back to them.' He allowed himself to be led, still hiccupping sobs, to where his mother was sitting, her head in her hands. She sprang to her feet and rushed towards him, enfolding him in her arms, hugging and scolding him at the same time. She sent his brother off to find his father who was still searching among the thinning picnic crowds. Iqbal let them think he was upset because he'd been lost. When his mother finally let him go his father moved towards him but Iqbal, terrified, shrank from him.

***

'Dr Iqbal? I was asking if you know Band-i-Amir?'

'Oh, yes, yes, though it's a long time since I visited,' Iqbal replied. 'I'm sure you will enjoy seeing it, Farid, but now, I think we should sleep – you have a long day ahead of you again tomorrow.'

Next morning, when it was time to leave, Iqbal could see Farid was fighting back tears. He wanted to reach out and hug him, but was unwilling to risk the hurt of rejection if the boy shrugged off his offer of comfort. Instead he said goodbye with a handshake and the traditional blessing. 'Go quickly, Farid and come back safely.'

He turned to Farid's uncle, now standing with a hand on the boy's shoulder, 'Daud, Sahib, have a safe journey.' He put out his hand, which the other man, after a brief, almost imperceptible, hesitation shook firmly. Iqbal, however, had noticed. Politeness, perhaps even a degree of shame at his attitude, may have overcome Daud's revulsion, but Iqbal knew he had not wanted to shake hands with a leper. He turned away swiftly, one hand rising automatically to shield the tell tale absent eyebrows.

As fast as the potholed road allowed, he headed out of Bamiyan but, however much distance he put between himself and Daud, he couldn't forget the slight pause before the man shook his hand. Although the disease had been curable for years, people still feared it, or rather, they feared those who had it. Long-held beliefs based on ignorance: some said it was a sign a man had had sex with his wife while she was menstruating, others maintained the disease was Allah's punishment for some wrongdoing, the mark of a sinner. How to convince people it was caused by nothing more sinister than a simple bacterium, cousin to the one that causes tuberculosis?

Only a year ago he'd heard of a man turned away from his village mosque because people were afraid he would spread leprosy amongst them. And the girl, Zakia, from Jaghoray. Her family, recognising the signs of the disease and, terrified their neighbours would drive her out of the village, hid her in an outbuilding for years. By the time she was discovered no amount of reconstructive surgery could repair the damage – a hole where her nose had been, mouth distorted, eyes… But her family had loved her. He shuddered again at the memory of Band-i-Amir. He still woke some nights, sweating and shaking from nightmares about the girl's murder. Miriam would hold him, stroking his head, soothing him until he grew calm again.

He'd never told her what he saw in his dreams, what he'd witnessed all those years ago. It was difficult to find the words to explain some things. He gave a wry smile. Had his immunity been higher he might have got the tuberculoid type of the disease and, given how long he went without treatment, would probably have ended up with deformities like Zakia. Instead, his was the kind of leprosy involving loss of body hair, in particular the eyebrows. The only sign he had ever had leprosy was the missing *abru* – the word meant both eyebrow and reputation. The loss of the first leading, inevitably, to the loss of the other. Would he ever be free of the stigma?

FIVE

Sang-i-Sia, September 1995

Dr Jeanine's arrival, a few days after Iqbal's return from Bamiyan, was preceded by the appearance of a large, dishevelled sheep. Driven into the *auli* by the combined efforts of her driver Zahir, and Iqbal's field assistant, Hassan, the confused animal charged around scattering chickens, upending the bowl of rice Miriam was about to clean and trampling over her vegetable patch before being cornered by the latrine. Miriam, clutching her empty rice bowl, was still dazed when Iqbal led a short, dumpy woman through the gateway. Coated in layers of dust from the road, her dark hair mostly concealed under a *chaddar-i-namaz*, sturdy hiking boots on her feet, she was panting heavily.

'My God,' she was gasping, 'oxygen – you should provide oxygen tanks before making people walk up such a mountain.'

Miriam moved forward to shake hands. She knew little about her boss other than she had worked for a couple of years in Pakistan before taking on the co-ordinator's post with Hansease. They'd met only once before, shortly after Jeanine had been appointed and was about to fly to Mazar-i-Sharif to open the office there, while Miriam had been in the middle of organising her own departure with Iqbal, by road, for Sang-i-Sia. They'd expected to meet again before now, but Jeanine's first proposed tour of the clinics under her charge had been postponed when fighting between two *mujahideen* groups had closed the roads. By the time the security situation had improved, the roads were still closed, this time by snow.

Miriam pointed at the sheep, now standing docile, Ruckshana's arms around its neck, 'Did you think we wouldn't be able to feed you?'

'A present for you from Ismail from Zard- somewhere or other. Zardgul? When he asked if I'd deliver something to you I thought he meant a letter. You've no idea the problems your sheep caused us on the way.'

'From Ismail? Where did you meet him? How is he? The family? Oh, did he not send a letter?' As Miriam's questions tumbled over each other, she sensed Iqbal tensing beside her.

He interrupted, 'Come on let's go inside. Let Dr Jeanine sit down and breathe more easily.'

Jeanine rummaged in the capacious bag on her shoulder then handed a small package to Miriam. 'From me for you – and for me,' she grinned. 'I'm not insulting your national beverage,' she said to Iqbal, 'but sometimes you know, only coffee will do.'

When Miriam, mouth watering in anticipation, brought through the coffee, Jeanine and Iqbal were deep in conversation about the political situation. She didn't think if she lived in Afghanistan for another twenty years she would ever fully grasp the complicated manoeuvrings of the various political parties. The way they gave or withdrew their support from each other was like a giant kaleidoscope of ever-changing patterns of allegiances. Only instead of the brightly coloured chips of glass in a child's toy, the shifting shapes were in drab military shades of grey, green and brown. Regardless of how often factions switched sides the balance of power never really changed one way or the other. No one was ever a winner – and thousands of Kabul's civilians lost their lives in rocket attacks and bombing raids, which had reduced vast areas of the city to ruins. Over a million citizens fled the prolonged bombardment. A few had returned to Sang-i-Sia, some had left the country for Pakistan or Iran but many others sought refuge in Mazar-i-Sharif. Miriam was relieved to hear Jeanine say that under General Dostum's control the northern city continued to remain relatively stable.

In reply to Jeanine's question about the local security situation, Iqbal said, 'Here is peaceful for now. Who knows what will happen next week, next month? Hisb-i-Wadhat is in control in Hazara Jat for the moment but...' He shrugged.

'What about Taliban? Do you think they can really take over the country like they say they will?'

Iqbal shook his head. 'I do not believe they can do so. I am talking often with local commanders. They tell me Taliban do not have so much power to take Kabul. They are not so organised. In Pushtoon areas only they are strong.'

'I heard they are gaining more supporters,' Jeanine argued. 'People are fed up of the current situation – the roadblocks and robberies, the rule of the warlords. People want peace. Taliban say they will bring peace and stability to the country.'

'Of course, you must know better than I do,' Iqbal spoke quietly, inclining his head as though to a higher authority. Miriam winced, wondering if Jeanine would realise he was being sarcastic but Iqbal continued smoothly, 'When Taliban killed our leader, Mazari, I think the people saw how these religious students really are. Torturing an old man then murdering him.'

Jeanine nodded, 'My driver had a set of photographs – they were circulating in the city – showing Mazari with his hands and feet bound. They say over 60,000 mourners came on foot from Hazara Jat for his funeral.'

Miriam, pouring coffee, said, 'Many went from here. He was much loved by Hazaras. They knew he wanted to see them gain political equality. And he spoke out against those who put politics before Hazara national interest – and against those who put religion before politics.' She handed round the coffee, offering sugar and milk while Iqbal attempted to explain the circumstances which led to Mazari's death. Taliban had supposedly offered Mazari some kind of deal, offering to negotiate between Wadhat and the Kabul government.

'Taliban's Mullah Borjan asked for a face-to-face meeting with Mazari,' Iqbal said, 'but as soon as he entered Taliban territory he, along with his, companions was taken hostage. Within a few days they were dead.'

'Why did they kill him?' Jeanine asked.

'They hate us, we Hazaras, because we are Shia.' Iqbal said. 'They thought Mazari's death would finish Wadhat. They were mistaken. Khalili – he is a good leader. He has succeeded in making this area free again. Now no government troops are here and he is trying to rebuild the administration. Even, they've established a university in Bamiyan. And,' he winked at Miriam, 'they have shown they do not discriminate against women. A number of women have seats on Wadhat's central council.'

Miriam nodded. Khalili had done much to bring unity to Wadhat after Mazari's murder, and appointing women like Dr Sima and the others to the council was a great step forward. But, so much still had to be done. Although eight separate Shia parties came together to form Wadhat as long ago as 1988 even now peoples' loyalties often remained with the individual party they had originally joined: Nasr, Mustazifin or, her throat suddenly constricted, Sepah, rather than the umbrella body. Disputes between families belonging to different parties could escalate into periods of fighting between the groups. They were lucky here in Sang-i-Sia. Despite the outward signs of military activity – men carrying kalashnikovs, strutting about with rocket launchers strapped to their backs, bandoliers of bullets around their chests – the action was usually in far off Kabul. Not much consolation for mothers there who lost their sons. Aware of a change of mood she tuned back in to the conversation. What had Jeanine said to cause Iqbal's tense expression?

'You think the Lion of Panshir is the hero of Afghanistan? What do you know of this man?'

Jeanine seemed unaware of having put her foot in it. 'Well, everything you read is about how well he fought against the Soviets. He does seem to be a brilliant tactician, no?'

'Dr Jeanine, with respect, I cannot say you are wrong, of course, but perhaps there are some things about the situation in Afghanistan you have not yet understood. Perhaps, you should ask questions before believing everything you read.'

'What do you mean?'

'This 'hero' as you call him, killed – no, what is the word I want – more than killed?' He looked to Miriam.

'Massacred?'

He nodded. 'This man massacred 700 Hazaras in Kabul. Not 700 soldiers. Civilians.' He looked as though he was going to say more but stood up and, hand on his heart, bowed slightly to Jeanine. 'Please excuse me, Dr Jeanine. I must see Zahir is comfortable in the guest room.'

Jeanine looked slightly astonished at his abrupt departure. 'Goodness, did I say a wrong thing? How can I understand everything going on in this country?' She was churning the contents of her bag, eventually producing cigarettes and a slightly crumpled envelope she passed to Miriam. 'From the sheep man.'

Miriam tore it open eagerly. 'Damn!'

'What?'

'It's in Dari. I'll have to get Iqbal to read it to me.' Asking Iqbal to read a letter out to her was the last thing she wanted to do right now. 'How did you come to meet Ismail?'

'He came to the clinic at Yakolang. He'd heard I was coming to Sang-i-Sia – said he knew you and could I take a letter. The sheep was an afterthought. He produced it the morning we were leaving. Up until then I rather liked him. I take it from Iqbal's cool acceptance of the gift he's connected with your first husband's family?'

'He worked with Jawad and me in Zardgul,' Miriam began but was interrupted by Ruckshana begging for food for 'her' sheep. 'There are some potato peelings outside the kitchen. I'm sure she'll enjoy them – then come in and wash your hands.'

'Don't you have two children? An older boy?' Jeanine asked.

Miriam nodded, 'Yes, Farid. He's gone to stay with his grandparents in Mazar-i-Sharif. He'll be back before winter.'

'I expect you miss him.'

'You wouldn't believe how much. I know he'll have a wonderful time and his grandparents will spoil him but I can't help worrying. Mazar is such a big city. I imagine all sorts of things happening – Farid getting lost, or being run over, or caught up in fighting.'

Jeanine shrugged, stubbing out her cigarette in an empty sweet dish Miriam provided as an ashtray. 'As I said, the situation in Mazar is pretty good. He'll be fine.'

Sensing the doctor's boredom with her maternal anxieties Miriam, giving a shaky laugh, said 'Let's change the subject. How long are you going to stay with us? Which clinics have you been to already? How are the other clinic workers? Have you seen…?' Miriam paused, shook her head, 'Listen to me! A million questions and you must be exhausted and desperate to clean up. Sorry, Jeanine. I'm just so pleased you're here – we don't often get visitors from outside. Come on, I'll show you where you'll sleep – it's my consulting room but it's quite comfortable – then you can take a bath and have a rest until dinner is ready.'

Over the evening meal a refreshed Jeanine entertained the family with tales of her travels with the sheep. 'And so when we made a pee stop I thought we should check on her condition. All the boxes in the back of the Toyota had slipped and the big bundle of blankets had fallen on top of her. Poor thing. She was squashed – legs stuck out so – like you see in cartoon pictures.

'We took her out while Zahir re-arranged all the boxes – then we had to catch her again because she thought she would just return herself to Zardgul. I never knew before how fast a sheep can move. When we stayed one night in a chaikhanna Zahir was worried our sheep would be cold in the back of the Toyota so he gave her a blanket – my best blanket. Was she grateful, this horrible sheep? No, she peed on it. Phew! The stink was unimaginable. At least, thank God, Zahir did not request that she sleep in the hotel with us.'

Jeanine swallowed the last piece of chicken on her plate and leaned back on the cushion behind her. 'Where is he, by the way? It's not like Zahir to miss out on food – especially when it's as delicious as this.'

'He's eating in the other room with Hassan,' said Iqbal. 'In fact, if you'll excuse me, I should go to them now.'

'I'll come with you.' She started to rise to her feet.

'No, no, stay. Take tea with Miriam. I know you have too much to talk about.'

'Yes, but I need also to talk to Zahir about getting the leaf spring mended and the spare tyre. And I'd like for us to make a rough plan of what's to be done while I'm here.'

'No problem,' Iqbal said from the doorway. 'I will tell Zahir where he should get this work done.'

'Well,' Jeanine asked Miriam, as the door closed behind Iqbal, 'do I assume I'm now in purdah? Is this the *zenana*?'

'It's our family room, that's all. Zahir will be more comfortable eating in the other room. You'll see him tomorrow. Will you go down to the clinic with Iqbal in the morning?'

Jeanine groaned, 'Oh, God, going down to the clinic means having to climb **up** your bloody mountain again. Oh, well, a few days here should cure me of this filthy habit.' She waved a cigarette in the air before lighting it. She accepted a glass of tea, refusing a sweet with a shake of her head.

When Iqbal returned, Jeanine outlined her plans for the next few days. As Miriam had expected she wanted to collect the clinic accounts and statistics – thank goodness they were up to date – and, as well as dealing with medicine requisitions for the following year, intended spending time observing the work in both clinics. Although Iqbal nodded in quiet agreement with Jeanine's suggested timetable, the deepening furrow on his forehead told Miriam he was becoming edgy and defensive at the thought of someone looking over his shoulder.

'Right then,' said Jeanine, 'sounds like we're organised – there's just the teaching camp arrangements to settle. Will you be free for the whole month, Miriam?'

Miriam, trying to smother a yawn, looked startled. 'Sorry Jeanine? What teaching camp?'

'In Charkoh, next month. You know, to provide practical clinical training for the most recently qualified paramedics. I've three doctors coming, two French, one German. She's in obs/gynae, which I thought you would find useful.' As Miriam continued to look blank, she continued, 'I wrote asking if you could come along to work as a translator for us.' She turned questioning eyes from Miriam to Iqbal. Miriam too, turned her gaze on her husband.

'Ah,' he said, 'I meant to talk to you about it Miriam but it, em, well, you know how busy we've been working on the statistics – and with Farid going away well, it slipped my mind.'

'Odd how much correspondence seems to slip your mind these days,' she replied.

'I'm sorry, Dr. Jeanine, it's my fault entirely,' Iqbal confessed. 'I think your teaching camp is an excellent idea. The boys will learn a great deal I'm sure and while I would like very much to attend, I really didn't think I could take a whole month away. I have to make a field tour next month….'

'Hold on a second, Iqbal,' Jeanine interrupted, raising a forefinger in the air. 'I think there is some misunderstanding here. I'm not expecting you to come with us to the camp – it is only Miriam I need as a translator.'

Miriam could have sworn she heard her husband's mouth snap shut with shock. She watched his colour deepen to an unpleasant shade of puce while he grappled to find a way to give his boss an answer she wanted to hear, while leaving the way open for him to ensure the matter would later be quietly dropped. He swallowed hard, 'Of course you are quite right, Dr Jeanine. Miriam's Dari is excellent. She will be very useful at a teaching camp, but,' he raised his arms in a gesture of helplessness, 'it would be difficult for her to go to Charkoh without me. Besides there are the children to think of.'

Jeanine turned to Miriam. 'What's the difficulty? Ruckshana can go with you – your son is away. In fact coming to the camp will help take your mind off worrying about him. Or is there some other problem?'

Miriam opened her mouth but Iqbal cut in, 'Next month is very soon. Perhaps if there is another camp next year? You could hold it here in Sang-i-Sia, even. Really, Dr Jeanine so much would need to be organised before Miriam could go.'

'*Naturellement*. Which is why,' Jeanine replied, 'I sent the letter weeks ago – to give you time to make arrangements before I arrived.' She ground her cigarette out and scrambled to her feet. 'I think now I will say goodnight. It's been an exhausting day.' She closed the door firmly behind her. In the ensuing silence Miriam waited for Iqbal to say something but he seemed to have lost the power of speech. Not knowing what to say herself, she moved about the room arranging the bedding, checking on her sleeping daughter, trying not to think about how wonderful it would have been to go to Charkoh.

Eventually, without looking directly at her, Iqbal said, 'Of course, you realise it would put me in an intolerable situation. That woman has no understanding of Afghan culture – expecting a wife to travel alone, leaving her husband and home, to be a *tarjuman*. This is what happens when foreigners are in charge of projects – we should have an Afghan doctor as *rais*, not a foreigner. We wouldn't need translators then either.' Finally he met her eyes. 'I hope tomorrow you will make her understand it is impossible.'

Miriam took a deep breath. 'No,' she said. Though her insides were churning, she spoke calmly. 'You'll have to make her understand, because I don't understand either why it's impossible. The teaching camp's a great idea and I'd learn a lot from working with those doctors. You forget I'm not a qualified doctor. I'm a midwife and sometimes the gaps in my knowledge scare me witless – turning down the chance to learn more seems crazy.'

'So you will defy me and go to Charkoh?' Iqbal's voice was icy.

'No, Iqbal,' Miriam sighed, 'I won't defy you – just as I didn't defy you about teaching the boys English, just as I didn't defy you when you said I shouldn't work in the village clinic. No, if you really don't want me to go to Charkoh then I won't – but **you'll** have to explain to Jeanine. You explain to her how your reputation as the big respected doctor depends on making sure everyone knows his foreign wife understands her place is hidden away in her home.' Feeling tears of frustration and anger threaten to spill, Miriam stopped, determined not to let Iqbal see her cry.

He headed for the door, 'I'm going to check Zahir has everything he needs. Don't wait up for me.'

When the door closed behind him, Miriam, hands balled into fists, sat down heavily. Well, hadn't she handled that really well?

Over breakfast next morning Iqbal, seemingly relaxed, discussed the working day ahead with Jeanine, but noticing the tic pulsing under his left eye, Miriam knew he was still furious. Avoiding eye contact with her he gulped down his tea, drumming his fingers on the empty glass while Jeanine went to collect her stethoscope and blood pressure set.

When Miriam accompanied them to the door only three women were waiting outside. Most of her patients had defected to Iqbal's clinic, their inherent shyness at consulting a male doctor overcome by the prospect of being treated by the new *feranghi* doctor. The influx of female patients wouldn't do much to improve Iqbal's temper. Jeanine, returning alone in the late afternoon, confirmed her suspicions. 'Iqbal says to tell you he'll be late. He's just starting on the men now. He's not in a good mood,' she said. 'I left as soon as I'd seen the last of the women.' She tugged off her boots at the door, giving a heartfelt sigh as she removed her socks. 'That feels good,' she said wiggling her bare toes. 'There's been a big rush of female patients in all the clinics but I thought it would be different here, when you're available.'

'They hope you've brought some new, powerful injection to cure everything,' said Miriam. 'There'll be even more tomorrow as the word spreads. Anyway, come and meet some of my friends – they've been hanging on, hoping you'd be back before they had to leave.' Jeanine followed her round the room, greeting each of the women with her few words of Dari before lowering herself onto a mattress, attempting to tuck her short legs beneath her. Miriam translated the questions the women fired at Jeanine – why did she not speak Dari, which country was she from, was she married, would it not be a problem to find a husband after being so free – and so old?

'Do they always ask such personal questions?' Jeanine asked when they'd gone.

'Believe me, you got off lightly today because they hadn't time to stay for a thorough interrogation. I've been asked if Iqbal doesn't mind my small breasts, if it's true that foreign women let their husbands put their tongues in their mouths. Kissing on the mouth is considered a bit of a no-no, here. Although,' she added with a smile, catching Jeanine's questioning look, 'from my, admittedly, limited experience the men don't appear to have such hang ups.' At her daughter's appearance, clutching a kitten firmly round its neck, Miriam changed the subject, turning her attention to showing her the kindest way to carry her pet.

When Ruckshana left, holding a slightly less uncomfortable kitten Jeanine said, 'I wish I had your command of the language. It's rather shaming that I still know so little Dari. Miriam, I really want you to come to the teaching camp. Your skills as a translator will be an enormous help. I think you know Chaman? She is also coming because she wants to gain experience with the gynae doctor.'

Miriam had met Chaman in Pakistan where the girl grew up as a refugee until, after marrying Ali, she returned with him to Afghanistan. Now she worked as a field assistant alongside her paramedic husband in the area neighbouring Charkoh. Would Iqbal feel differently knowing an Afghan man was allowing his wife to go? She shook her head, 'You'd better find someone else.'

'I thought I'd wait for a couple of days to let Iqbal think it over before I say any more to him.'

'He won't change his mind.'

'It can happen if you want it to,' Jeanine said, a conspiratorial smile curving the corner of her mouth. Miriam looked at her curiously. 'Well, do you?'

'Of course I want to go, but...'

Jeanine held up her hand, saying, 'All right, let's leave it for now.'

Iqbal looked tired when he came home in the evening and Miriam, dreading a continuation of the previous night's argument, was glad Jeanine wasn't going to raise the subject of the teaching camp again. Even so, the atmosphere was strained, although he did at least look pleased when Jeanine announced she'd work in Miriam's clinic the following day. When he finished his meal, Iqbal excused himself saying he'd take tea with Zahir in the guest room, Miriam gave a sigh of relief.

Next day it didn't take long for the female patients, and a couple of men, who'd gone to Iqbal's centre to consult Jeanine to make their way up the path and it was late in the afternoon before the clinic ended. Miriam made coffee and joined Jeanine in the sitting room where she was already puffing at a cigarette. Despite being aware of the doctor's disinterest in Farid and Ruckshana – she'd seemed genuinely surprised the latter required nourishment at lunchtime, complaining about having to interrupt the work – Miriam couldn't stop herself talking about Farid. She missed him terribly; his absence a constant shadowy presence. 'I'm afraid next time,' she confided, 'they'll want him to stay for longer. They may even suggest he lives with them, goes to school in Mazar. I couldn't bear it.'

'Well, this problem you will solve when you return to UK. The boy would be out of reach of his grandparents and have the advantage of a proper education.' Miriam stared at Jeanine, who continued, 'I do not want Hansease to lose you, of course, but I assume it is something we must be aware will happen one day. I'm only surprised you did not do it when your first husband died, when there was nothing to keep you here.'

'Nothing to keep…? There was everything to keep me. It never occurred to me to go back. I'd made my life in Afghanistan with the man I loved. This is where our child was born. This is Farid's country and his father's….'

Jeanine, reaching for her cigarettes, glanced up at Miriam and cut in, 'But it is not yours.'

Miriam sighed. Pointless trying to explain – she'd tried with others more sympathetic than Jeanine and couldn't make them understand. When she received the news of Jawad's death her only thought was to find a way to be as near to him as possible. Apart from taking care of Farid, her determination to return to Afghanistan was all that kept her sane at times but Jeanine would think her mad if she tried to tell her this. She shook her head as though in agreement with Jeanine. No, it wasn't her country.

'Surely,' the doctor continued, 'you must long to go home, to family, friends, to be part of your own culture again? What about your children's education. Why do you want to remain here, always the outsider?'

'Farid is doing well at school. He will go to university in Kabul or Mazar – possibly abroad. By the time Ruckshana is old enough there will be a school in the village, then university for her, too.' Miriam stopped. Why was she justifying herself to this woman? She shrugged. 'I was more of an outsider in Scotland than here. This is where I belong.'

Jeanine gave a faint, disbelieving smile. 'You think it is possible to cross such a wide cultural gulf?'

'Not easily but, yes, it can be done. After living here for years I've still much to learn but I believe I'm bridging the gap.'

Again the disbelieving smile flickered over Jeanine's face. Miriam could feel herself bridling. Jeanine asked, 'So you do not miss your Scottish friends?'

Miriam considered before replying, with a shake of her head, adding, 'Besides, I have good friends here.'

'Oh come on, Miriam,' Jeanine replied. 'You don't truly think of the women I've met here as real friends? What do you have in common? You can't discuss the books you're reading. How can you talk to them about your life in Scotland – what can they understand about it? Can you even confide in them when you've had a row with your husband, as you would a friend at home?'

'Books I'm reading?' Miriam laughed, side-stepping the reference to possible marital discord. 'I don't remember when I last had time to read a book – other than a medical text. And, yes, I do think of Fatima and Zainab as proper friends.' Before she could say any more Iqbal flung open the door.

'*Mudder-i-Farid*, Dr Jeanine, please come. We have an emergency.'

SIX

Sang-i-Sia September 1995

Iqbal was guiding two women, the younger, heavily pregnant, into Miriam's consulting room.

'She's been in labour for over two days,' he said. 'Mother thinks the baby's stuck.'

Jeanine, scooping up books, notebooks and items of clothing to make space on the mattress exclaimed, 'My God, Miriam, she's a child.' Miriam, intent on settling the girl nodded without comment. The girl was maybe about fourteen, exhaustion obvious in the purplish circles under her eyes, which Miriam saw, were dark pools of fear. Murmuring soothingly, as though to a frightened puppy, she began, with practised hands to palpate the distended abdomen.

'Right way round, head's well down.' She looked questioningly at Jeanine. 'Do you want to do an internal?' When the doctor nodded, Iqbal, about to leave the room, handed Miriam the case notes he'd already made. 'Don't worry,' she murmured to the mother, '*Insh 'Allah*, everything will be fine. Sit closer to your daughter, help her feel less afraid. Maybe massage her back?' The woman made no move towards her daughter but remained where she squatted on the floor beside a cloth bundle she'd brought.

To help calm the frightened girl Miriam, while Jeanine went to wash her hands, began to go over the routine questions Iqbal had already asked. From his scribbled notes she saw the girl's name was Kulsoom. The mother cut in to give the name of the village. 'Oh,' said Miriam, surprised, 'but you could have gone to the German clinic – it's surely nearer than here?' The woman stared at her for a moment then shrugged. Miriam, addressing Kulsoom, asked for her husband's name. A contraction gripped the girl making her grit her teeth and again it was her mother who replied. Miriam looked at Iqbal's notes. Even allowing for his untidy scrawl there could be no mistaking Naeem, the name the woman gave her, for Jan Ali, the name written on the form. When Jeanine returned she excused herself to have a word with Iqbal.

'I also thought it strange they didn't go to the German clinic,' he said when she told him about the different names. 'The mother told me they were offered a lift in a truck for part of the way but even so they still had to walk for half a day up the valley to get here. It's as if they don't want anyone in their village to know.' He looked at Miriam, 'I suspect the girl's not married.'

Miriam returned to the consulting room where Jeanine had completed her examination. 'Fully dilated. Everything's fine. Child's far too young for pregnancy. Sheer terror's made it such a long labour.' Miriam had seen it before. Occasionally Iqbal had sent a woman whose labour had stopped out in the jeep – her family attendants accompanying her. Usually half an hour on the rough roads was enough to re-start a labour. There would be no need for such treatment today. Despite her fears the girl's time was near and within a couple of hours the baby, a boy, was born, small but strong. Jeanine handed him to his grandmother who began to swaddle him. Although she didn't speak, her features softened and on impulse Miriam reached out a hand to her. The woman looked up and Miriam saw a glimmer of tears.

Kulsoom's mother was adamant they should return home the next day. 'Can't you make her stay longer?' Miriam asked Iqbal, 'Tell her Ismail is too busy tomorrow.'

'What difference will it make? She is quite capable of walking out of here if we try to delay things. At least the girl will be spared walking all the way home carrying her baby.'

'If she's not married I'm worried about how the family will treat her. Do you think the mother will pass the baby off as hers?'

He shrugged. 'Probably. Even if people suspect, they won't say anything directly – though it's unlikely they'll ever find a husband for the girl now.'

At five o'clock next morning Ismail arrived to take the family home. Miriam had prepared food for the journey, which she handed to

Kulsoom's mother. At the gate Kulsoom turned to Miriam, her eyes full of tears, but whatever she had been going to say was drowned by a sudden sob. She kissed the back of Miriam's hand then turned, head bowed, to follow her mother.

In the evening, while Miriam was bringing the food from the kitchen, Iqbal went to answer an urgent knocking at the gate. Recognising Ismail's voice, she strained to hear but couldn't make out what was being said. After a few minutes, Iqbal stuck his head round the door. 'Ismail's coming in.' Miriam nodded, easing her chaddar up to cover her hair before the driver entered the room. He paused in the doorway to slip off his shoes and Miriam gasped when she saw him. Sweat runnels tracked across his dust-covered face giving him a bizarre appearance, which might have caused laughter had it not been obvious from his expression something terrible had happened. His hands and forearms were covered in scratches, some still showing red beads of blood, and his clothes were ripped in several places.

'An accident?' Miriam asked looking from Ismail to Iqbal.

Ismail shook his head, 'No, not accident.' He sat down, rubbing his palms over his face. 'I don't know how it happened – how I didn't notice anything.'

Miriam suddenly shivered. 'It's the baby isn't it?' Ismail nodded.

'What's going on?' Jeanine interrupted.

'Sorry. It's the baby. Look, I'll explain after Ismail's told us the story.'

It took a while to hear the whole tale. Although Ismail's words came tumbling out in a rush he paused often, correcting himself, going back to repeat parts. He told them he saw the girl was crying when they set out and her mother had spoken sharply to her. His attempts to make conversation were ignored so he'd listened to a Daud Sarkhush cassette. At some point in the journey the mother requested he stop. Understanding one or other of the women needed to pee he'd been careful not to look in the direction they took.

When, later, the woman again told him to stop – they would walk from this point – he reckoned they were still half an hour by foot from their village. It was only when they moved away he realised neither woman was holding the baby. He at first thought they'd deliberately left it in the Toyota but a quick check told him no. He'd run after them, but when he asked what they'd done with the baby, Kulsoom's mother had simply asked, 'What baby?'

Ismail stopped speaking, his head bowed. He looked up at Iqbal and Miriam. 'I didn't know what to do. I thought about trying to force them back into the Toyota. I thought about driving on to the village and finding the girl's father, telling him what had happened. But,' he scrubbed at his face with his hands, 'I knew it would take too much time so decided to try and find the baby.' Already mid-afternoon and knowing the light would soon be fading he had driven as fast as he dared, praying that he would recognise the place where they had stopped earlier.

'But everywhere around that area looks the same,' Iqbal interrupted. 'It's all desert and scrub – no landmarks.' Ismail nodded. He'd lost count of the times he pulled up at what he thought was a likely spot to search amongst thorny shrubs and occasional rocky outcrops. Even when it became dark he took a torch and continued his fruitless search.

'I kept listening hoping to hear a baby crying. Finally the torch batteries ran out. I had to give up.'

'You did all you could,' assured Iqbal, while Miriam translated for Jeanine, whose eyes widened in horror as she listened. Iqbal readily agreed to her suggestion that they resume the search next morning although he pointed out there was little chance of finding where the baby had been abandoned. 'And,' he added, 'there's no chance it would have survived the night.'

'It was well bundled up,' Jeanine argued. Miriam knew Iqbal was not only thinking about the bitterly cold night but of the packs of jackals roaming the area beyond the valley. Jeanine was now demanding that the *Shura* – the local government – be informed, that the family be brought to book.

Iqbal cut in, 'Dr Jeanine, with respect, I understand your concern – we are all shocked – but reporting this matter to the *Shura* will not help. Sometimes we have to leave things to Allah for judgement and punishment.' Jeanine looked set to continue the argument but Iqbal continued, 'Tomorrow you can continue the search but I must ask you not to take any other action. You do not understand the consequences that may result from talking to the authorities about this.'

Miriam slipped quietly out the room. In the kitchen she tidied up, putting away the uneaten food for which no one now had any appetite and stepped outside. There was no moon to dim the stars but tonight Miriam saw their brilliance as ice cold and dangerous. Thinking of the tiny bundle lying somewhere in the desert she shivered, pulling her chaddar more tightly around her. From inside, the sound of Jeanine and Iqbal's voices reached her as a low murmur. She thought about Ismail. He must be exhausted. She should tell him to go home. But she remained where she was, staring up at the blaze of light in the sky thinking about Kulsoom, probably lying sleepless at home, her breasts achingly full of milk, feeling as though someone had ripped out her heart. Jeanine was right, the family, or at least the girl's mother, had committed an appalling crime for which there could be no justification.

How would she feel at home reading a newspaper report about a mother abandoning her newborn baby? Compassion, concern for both mother and child rather than a desire for the woman to be punished. But in Britain a baby was usually left somewhere it would be found, not left to die. And what would the punishment be at home? Prison? Maybe sometimes, but also counselling, help.

Here, regardless of whether her mother had been the one who abandoned the baby it would be the fourteen-year old Kulsoom who would be punished. In some parts of Afghanistan she might even be sentenced to stoning, her pregnancy evidence of illicit sex. As for the boy responsible for sweet-talking the girl into taking the step, the consequences of which would bring such shame on her father's head – shame only a baby's death could…It was if Kulsoom had managed to become pregnant all by herself. A wave of pure rage swept over Miriam. She wanted to go after Kulsoom's mother, drag her from her bed, force her into the wasteland to feel the cold, feel what the baby would go through. What had she said to Jeanine about bridging the cultural divide? Still, she agreed with Iqbal about not reporting it to the *Shura*. She made no attempt to brush away the tears of anger and pity, which ran down her cheeks.

Lost in her thoughts she was scarcely aware of how cold it was until she heard Iqbal exclaim, 'Miriam, you're frozen. How long have you been out here?' He held out his arms and suddenly shivering violently Miriam went to him, glad to feel the warmth of his body as he pulled her close. 'Let's get you inside.'

'Where's Jeanine?' she asked.

'Bed. She's determined to be off tomorrow morning by six o'clock.'
'I don't want to see her again tonight. She'll want to talk about the baby. I can't face talking about it anymore.'

Late the following afternoon Jeanine returned empty handed, her face drawn and pale. Even before she sat down, she burst out, 'How often does this happen, Miriam? Surely not always this way?'

'Not always. Sometimes the girl's family arranges for her to marry the boy. It's not a major problem when the baby arrives a little early. Occasionally, the girl's mother might pass the baby off as her own. But,' she sighed, 'usually when the girl goes into labour the girl's mother will send her father and brothers out of the house. Kulsoom was only brought here because the labour had gone on so long. The baby might be drowned if they live near a river, or left outside in winter snow.'

'It's barbaric.'

Miriam agreed adding, 'As long as a father's honour depends on his daughters being virgins – or at least not having been caught out by pregnancy – until they are married it will continue. It'll be many years, generations, before the Pill brings about a sexual revolution here, particularly in the rural areas.'

Jeanine returned to work with Iqbal in his clinic for the next few days. Each afternoon he came home with a throbbing pain behind his eyes due to her constant quizzing. Wasn't it a waste of time checking everyone's blood pressure, regardless of whether they came reporting chest pains or a sore toe? Why did every patient leave with some form of medication, even if only a handful of analgesic? Why this, why not that? As if her main aim in life was to pinpoint flaws rather than note good practice. He imagined being handed a 'could do better' report at the end of her stay.

'It's what patients expect,' he explained, in reference to blood pressure checks. 'Many of them have their sleeves rolled up ready – they'd feel cheated if I didn't check their BP.'

He agreed some patients didn't really need the medicines he prescribed, adding, 'But, again it's expected. Doctors are supposed to give medicines – that's our job. In the beginning I used to try explaining they didn't need anything for a cold or a bout of diarrhoea but people became angry and abusive.' He spread his arms wide in a gesture of helplessness, 'I can't afford to have people say I'm a bad doctor.'

Jeanine shook her head, 'You must educate them better. It's a waste of our resources.'

He smothered a sigh. 'You are right, of course. But it will take time. You know people have lived for years with no medical services, seen measles or chest infections strike down their children. Newborn babies die for no apparent reason or from fear...'

'Fear?'

'Neo-natal tetanus. When the baby goes into the final spasm people believe it is dying of fear.' Iqbal kept his voice as free of expression as he could. 'They've still little access to medicine other than those carried by unqualified pharmacists in the bazaar. People are desperate to consult a doctor about even the slightest ailment, convinced a handful of pills or a course of injections can cure everything.

'This is not helpful,' he said, sliding open a desk drawer from which he pulled out a handful of glossy advertising flyers and posters from pharmaceutical companies. Fanning them out in front of Jeanine, he stabbed at a picture of a chubby baby with golden curls. 'People want their children to look like this. They come crying for whatever this child's being given – in this case some useless and expensive vitamin tonic.' He shook his head, flicking through the advertisements, 'No aspirin or penicillin. Only the latest, expensive drugs get this kind of advertising. People round here know the names of the latest antibiotic even before I do.'

Jeanine, either not understanding what he said or choosing to ignore it, impressed on him again the need to reduce unnecessary prescribing. Iqbal replaced the adverts. What brought people like Dr Jeanine to his country? Oh, he'd heard her talk about how much she wanted to help his people by providing proper health services, but she clearly believed her way was the only way of doing things. She talked about the need to educate his patients – like you could just dump a heap of 'education' onto someone's head and problems would be solved – but it was so one-sided. She hadn't even learned enough of the language to hold a conversation. He couldn't help but notice the little Dari she did know was all imperatives – come here, sit, cough, go. But then why would she need to learn more, she would move on before long. Did she believe she'd sorted out the health problems in Pakistan in two years? Which struggling, impoverished country would benefit from Dr Jeanine's knowledge when she tired of Afghanistan?

By the time he arrived home he wanted only to sit quietly and have Miriam massage away the pain in his head, but couldn't with Jeanine in the room. He was prevented by the rules of hospitality from asking her outright to leave him alone with his wife for an hour. As she had not grasped the subtlety of Afghan requests, his attempts to suggest that she might like to rest in her room before dinner were shrugged off. After the evening meal he was glad to escape. He just hoped her silence on the subject meant she had given up the ridiculous idea of Miriam going to the teaching camp.

Only Miriam heard his grumbles, late at night when the doctor finally went to bed. 'I know,' she agreed when he sounded off one night about the intensive grilling he'd been given regarding the accounts. 'She's not the most relaxing person to have around.'

'I thought you liked her, you both seem to have plenty to talk about?'

'I don't dislike her – though I think I might, if she was here for much longer. She's been very condescending about my friends and was rude to Fatima yesterday. Her ankle's still sore from when she twisted it so when she was here having tea I took a look at it. Jeanine came in and started on about how Fatima should consult me during working hours the same as everyone else and not expect private consultations. Although Fatima didn't understand what she was saying she knew Jeanine's anger related to her. It was embarrassing.'

Iqbal, unfolding blankets, shook his head, 'I'm sure she thinks I am eating Hansease's money. If she asks me one more time to account for…' He shrugged, flipped the blanket onto the *toshak*, and sat down. 'It's like people in Europe and America are saying they want to help Afghanistan but they don't trust Afghans not to steal the money so they must send a foreigner to be in charge.'

Miriam moved behind him and began to knead his shoulders and neck until he could feel the tense knots loosen. 'Trouble is,' she murmured, 'we need their money.'

He turned to glare at her. 'It should be freely given – after using my country as a venue for their wars.'

Fingers still working on his neck, she replied soothingly, 'Forget Jeanine for now. She's leaving the day after tomorrow and you won't have to see her again for months.'

Jeanine was to travel on to the Behsud clinic, the last on her tour. For once, buoyed by the prospect of her departure, Iqbal came home without a headache. He'd arranged to give a *mehmani* on her last evening. Daud would kill the sheep and help turn it into korma and kebabs. Personally, feeling as he did about Dr Jeanine, he would've preferred to ignore the custom of honouring a guest with a dinner but people like Malim Ashraf, his own father and brother, were expecting invitations, would wonder at his failure of duty. Let her have her honour. Soon he would have his life back. No more why this, why that, why not? He kicked off his sandals and strolled into the living room where Jeanine was sitting talking to Miriam.

'Iqbal, I've been thinking about the camp.' He froze. 'It would make sense for me to stop off here on the way back from Behsud to pick Miriam up – say in about five days?'

In the name of Allah, would she never give up? He swallowed hard, somehow managing to plaster a regretful smile onto his face. 'I really don't think it is possible. I am sure by now you understand enough of our culture to realise it is completely unacceptable for an Afghan wife to go away alone without her husband.'

'Firstly,' Jeanine snapped back, 'Miriam would not be alone; there'll be a whole team of people. Secondly, Miriam is not an Afghan wife – she just happens to have an Afghan husband. Thirdly, she is an employee of Hansease and as such is subject to the same terms and conditions as any other worker, which,' she paused as though to give added weight to her next words, 'in theory means she could be transferred to work at any of our clinics.' Iqbal opened his mouth in protest, but she continued, 'I said 'in theory'. Of course, I'm not going to send Miriam anywhere else, however, I do want her at Charkoh next month.'

Furious, but realising he was defeated, he shrugged. 'You are the *rais* – the boss – Dr Jeanine. Of course, Miriam must go to the teaching camp.' He rose to his feet. 'Excuse me, please, I must go and help Daud prepare the kebabs.' He thought he caught Jeanine throw a triumphant glance in Miriam's direction as he left the room. And now he was going to cook kebabs for the daughter of a…

Each afternoon following Jeanine's departure, he came home to be met by further evidence of Miriam's imminent departure. Piles of freshly washed clothes and half-packed boxes stood around the room.

'Iqbal, we have to talk,' Miriam said one evening. 'I'm fed up living with two bad-tempered babies. The way you're behaving is not only upsetting me, Ruckshana's becoming clingy. She doesn't understand what's going on but knows things aren't right between us.'

Iqbal felt a stab of guilt. Over the last couple of days he'd noticed how when he went out after dinner Ruckshana cried in a way she'd never done before. He had taken some pleasure in seeing how much it hurt Miriam, hoping she would realise it was wrong to take Ruckshana away from him, but now he realised with shame it was his daughter who was hurting more. 'Look, you've got what you wanted – but don't expect me to be happy about it. I'm the one who has to explain my wife's absence to everyone.'

'You talk as if I'm leaving forever. It's only four weeks. What's so difficult about telling people why I'm going to the teaching camp? I don't understand your attitude – Jawad would have been delighted if this opportunity had come up when we were in Zardgul.'

'Oh, yes, throw Mr Perfect Jawad's name in my face.'

'He would never have stopped me from doing something like this. Jawad trusted me. He wasn't always worrying about his reputation.'

'It might've been better for him if he had listened to what people were saying.' As soon as they were out, Iqbal regretted his words. Miriam looked as though he had slapped her.

'What are you saying?' she asked in a voice barely above a whisper. 'That Jawad was killed because he was married to me?'

'No, of course not. I said it without thinking. I'm...' He moved to put his arms round her, but the words of apology died as she shrugged him away.

'Just go away Iqbal. Leave me alone.'

He stared at her for a few moments, not knowing what to say or do. Finally, with a sigh he rose and left the room. He strode down the path towards the village, turning left at the bottom, in the opposite direction from the clinic.

The village consisted of a handful of one-storey buildings of sun-dried brick. The shop selling bolts of cloth provided the only vivid splash of colour along the dusty street. Next door to that the tailor sat all day cross-legged at his sewing machine. Although most people only ordered new clothes once a year to celebrate Eid at the end of Ramadan, always someone was getting married and Ali made a passable living, even engaging a boy to learn the trade. A general shop – the village's equivalent of a city department store – stocked everything else the residents required from sugar, rice and dried fruits to oil lamps, plates and dishes, batteries, boiled sweets and Russian shoes. Passing the *chaikhanna* Iqbal responded mechanically to greetings called out by the few men sitting cross-legged on a low wooden platform outside. Refusing their invitation to join them for tea he continued to the end of the village.

Crossing the river by the single poplar tree trunk serving as a bridge he reached the site of his proposed new clinic. The river ran shallow here, lazing its way around boulders gleaming in the sun. Two boys sat on the bank, cooling their feet in the water while a mixed flock of goats and sheep nibbled at the sparse grazing. The scent of lavender, growing in wild clumps, drifted on the breeze. Iqbal smiled with satisfaction as he paced out the boundary, imagining how it would look – purpose built with bright, light rooms, including a laboratory and a separate pharmacy. Dr Jeanine would present the plans and estimates to European donors this winter and seemed confident they would find the funding. She'd also insisted he add an extra room to his plans, a consulting room in which Miriam would work.

The walk had calmed him but now this reminder of Miriam renewed his anger at the way she'd thrown Jawad's name at him. Although he had to admit she rarely mentioned her former husband he could never shake off the feeling Jawad's shadowy presence was constantly between them. He often thought Miriam kept a mental tick list of comparisons, sensing her former husband always came out as the better person in every way. So, Jawad would have been delighted to let her go off for a month, wouldn't have worried what people might say? His anger now, though, was less about his ghostly rival, more about Miriam's failure to understand how her actions reflected on him. She seemed not to care about his loss of face.

Her women friends wouldn't say anything to her but they would whisper amongst themselves about the doctor's wife being so free. They would talk about it to their husbands who, though saying nothing directly to him, would have a pitying look in their eyes. He'd catch glimpses of meaningful glances and sly smiles behind his back. The doctor's foreign wife behaves as though she were in London, going off alone, working alongside other men. They'd say he had, by becoming a doctor, reached heights no one with that horrible disease – surely a curse from Allah – should ever have dreamed of reaching. Miriam had no idea what it was like for him to live with the knowledge people still talked about him and his past. People, especially the old ones, remembered the child with leprosy, the child even Hazrat-i-Ali could not cure at Band-i-Amir. They probably still talked about the time the leper had done the right thing at last and left the area – only by running away on his brother's wedding day he had broken his mother's heart.

Deep down he knew he was being unfair to Miriam. There was much he had not told her but somehow the words in his head became lost whenever he tried he explain his feelings. In her eyes he could never see the understanding he hoped for, only her resentment over the loss of freedom she had enjoyed in Zardgul. Without having reached any resolution he began to retrace his steps towards home.

SEVEN

Journey to Charkoh

When Iqbal left the house Miriam sat for a long time staring blankly at the closed door. Why, oh, why had she brought up Jawad's name? She'd learned not to mention him, knowing how it irritated Iqbal. Reminded him, perhaps, despite the status of marrying a foreigner, he had won a slightly tarnished trophy, rather than a virgin bride.

She heard the words he'd thrown at her playing over and over in her head. He knew she always harboured the fear if she had not married Jawad he would still be alive. What he didn't know was her fear stemmed from guilt about the fact Jawad never would have married her had she not forced his hand. She had proposed to him. All those years later she could still recapture perfectly the expression on his face – a mixture of amusement, disbelief, and sadness.

***

They were visiting the beautiful blue-domed *mazar* from which the city of Mazar-i-Sharif took its name. For once, they were alone – if being surrounded by hundreds of other visitors to the shrine could be regarded as alone. Usually, at least one, often more, member of Jawad's family was glued to her side. It was not something she'd expected. But then, lots of things were unexpected here.

The mountains Jawad had so often talked of were miles away on the horizon. The city itself was in a flat plain, a desert. Everything was dry and dusty – dust everywhere. She felt it coating her teeth no matter how often she brushed them in the bathroom, which in itself was a puzzle. How to dry herself properly, for one thing. The shower cascaded onto the floor and took so long to run through the drain in the floor she was paddling in water, balancing on one foot as she tried to dry the other. Finally asked Jawad who'd shown her the two inch-high wooden stool on which to stand.

She wished he'd explained table etiquette to her. Well, not table, exactly – she'd known the family ate sitting on the floor round a cloth called a *dustakhan* but not how someone would bring a coffee-shaped jug and basin so she could wash her hands before eating. Although the cook – she hadn't realised the family was so well off either to have servants – a cook and a girl who cleaned – walked down the length of the cloth distributing *nan* she hadn't realised it was not done to allow any part of her own foot to rest on the cloth. No matter that Jawad mentioned her *faux pas* in private, she still felt like a naughty child – feet off the table, if you please.

Worse, one evening a bowl containing chicken in a sauce was passed to her. Only after she'd helped herself and passed the bowl on did she notice everyone else took only sauce, which they spooned over their rice. To her horror, she saw Jawad's father, Anwar, divide the rest of the meat. She felt herself turn scarlet when he passed her share to her. Mortified, she refused it, indicating the chicken – which by now seemed to have grown into a giant-sized portion – already on her plate. He insisted. She refused, looking across to Jawad, who appeared to be the only one not watching the drama, for help. 'Don't ever let anyone offer me food first,' she begged him later.

She'd intended to keep a diary during her stay but gave up after the first couple of days; impossible to find the words required to record her impressions, sort out and make sense of her emotional response to everything she was experiencing. Jawad had brought it so much to life when talking to her in Edinburgh, but the reality was much more, and in some ways much less, than she could have dreamed. The war seemed not to affect people in ways she imagined. It was discussed, yes, and people listened eagerly to the BBC news – somehow she'd thought news broadcasts would be banned – but in the crowded streets and bazaars overflowing with consumer goods there was little indication the country was embroiled in a war. She'd been half expecting to remain indoors a lot of the time, hiding in cellars during bombing raids, not be taken sightseeing or to wedding parties with music and dancing.

The blue tiling of the magnificent twin domes gleamed in the sunlight as they strolled along a path, the air heavy with the scent of roses. She listened to Jawad, in tour guide mode, telling her the history of the shrine, built to honour Hazrat Ali. Son-in-law of the Prophet Muhammad, he was assassinated in 658AD.

'Wasn't he buried in Najaf?' she interrupted, always eager to show she did know some things about his country.

'You are right,' Jawad agreed. 'Well, partly right. You see, Ali's followers were afraid his enemies would take revenge on his body. So they placed Ali on the back of a white she-camel. It was turned loose to roam wherever she wanted. At the very spot where, eventually, she fell dead, Ali's body was buried.'

She loved hearing Jawad tell stories, captivating her with the legends of dreams and mystics surrounding the shrine; even the thousands of white pigeons living in the shrine complex had their story. 'People believe feeding the pigeons,' he indicated with a sweep of his arm the birds fluttering around pecking at the grains of wheat people were scattering, 'will give them merit in Allah's eyes.' He bought a tin plate of grain from a vendor.

'People say every seventh pigeon is a soul,' he continued, 'and some believe this place is so holy, if a grey pigeon joins the flock, it too will turn white within seven days. Others say,' he gave her a grin, handing her the plate, 'if it does not turn white within a week the mullahs eat it to be sure the legend is kept alive.'

She laughed and he took a photograph of her as she threw the last handful of seeds to the birds clustered round her feet. She felt her smile freeze when she saw his expression change to one of sadness. 'Why so serious all of a sudden? What's wrong?'

'Nothing's wrong, but I do have something to tell you.' She nodded, waiting for him to continue, suddenly dreading what he might say. 'Margaret,' as always he lengthened each syllable of her name, making it sound so much more exotic. 'I've decided I am not going back to Edinburgh.' At her sharp intake of breath he raked his hands through his hair, making it stand on end. She resisted the urge to smooth it back into place, stood silently, the empty tin plate still clutched in her hand, waiting for his explanation. 'You know I always say one day I will go to Zardgul to work with my people? I cannot wait any longer. I am going this year.'

'But your degree,' she said, 'you can't give up now. Only two more years – it's nothing.' She could hear a pleading note in her voice, felt the threat of tears. Knowing neither would have any effect on his decision, she took a deep breath, continued, 'When you qualify, you'll have so much more to offer.'

Jawad shook his head. 'It's now they need help – not when I've wasted another two years. So, I will learn to draw plans for fine bridges. This is no help to the children of Zardgul today. Malnourished children don't need bridges. They need food, health care, education. No, Margaret, I will not wait. I know this is what I must do.'

Jawad often talked to her about the remote village area, from where his family came, enthusing her with his plans for building a clinic, a school where girls, as well as boys, would receive an education. Zardgul. Its name meant yellow flower. Imagined Jawad filling her arms with the golden blooms she pictured carpeting the mountainsides in spring. Not now – sometime far in the future. Suddenly Zardgul turned from a distant fantasy into an immediate threat.

'What about us?' She blurted out the words, wondering as she did so what exactly she meant to this man she knew she would love until her dying day.

During the day they never seemed to have a moment to themselves and had taken to sitting up late in the evenings to talk, long after the household had gone to bed. One night he'd turned to her, 'I'm talking too much as usual. I think you are falling asleep?' She shook her head, blushing as she realised she had been watching his lips instead of listening to his words, wondering what they would feel like on hers. Suddenly deciding she had nothing to lose but her pride, she leaned forward and kissed him full on the mouth. He returned the kiss then pulled back, his hands on her shoulders looking anxiously into her eyes. 'Margaret, are you sure?' When she nodded he groaned, pulling her to him. It had been so simple. It was so exactly right between them. Why hadn't she done it months ago?

'Us?' She thought he sounded puzzled, as though their relationship was irrelevant.

'Yes, Jawad, us – you and me! Do I just say goodbye to you on Saturday? Go back to Edinburgh not knowing – not knowing,' she swallowed hard, 'if I'll ever see you again?'

He sighed. 'Why do you think it has taken me so long to tell you this? I hate the thought of us being apart but...' He sighed again, shook his head.

'Then I'll stay – go with you to Zardgul.'

'Why not?' she asked, bursting into tears, when he continued to shake his head.

He caught her hand. 'Margaret, don't cry. The idea of you coming to Zardgul is wonderful but,' he shook his head, adding, 'it is impossible. It's not like living in the city – there's no electricity, no sanitation. Water is carried from the river. Zardgul – it is ten, twenty times more basic than here.'

Stung, she retorted, 'I would manage.'

As if he hadn't heard her, he continued, 'What could you do? You can't dig wells or build latrines or the clinic. You don't speak the language.'

'I'm a midwife – you're always on about the need for medical professionals. Well, I am one. In fact I'm a damned sight more qualified than you.'

He nodded thoughtfully, 'We do need midwives and if you spoke Dari you could...But there are other problems. Bringing a foreign woman with me to Zardgul – well, I don't know how the people would react. It would cause talk, may lead to trouble if people thought...'

'Then go as a married man.' Jawad stared at her. Embarrassed by her forwardness Margaret felt herself turn scarlet. She stared at the pigeons still flocking around her feet, swallowed hard and carried on. 'I love you Jawad, I want to spend my life with you. Let's get married.' His silence lengthened until she shook his arm. 'Jawad?' Her sudden movement startled the pigeons into a flurry of flapping wings as they rose into the air.

'Margaret, I want to say yes. I do love you. I would like nothing better than to spend my life with you beside me. But I can't. My family – already they are searching for a suitable girl. They would never agree.'

'An educated, city-born-and-bred girl? No more suited to life in Zardgul than I?' He nodded. 'You would marry someone they choose for you? But if you love me....? Surely they wouldn't stop you marrying the person you love? Doesn't sound like the actions of people so proud of their progressive ways.'

'They would never force me to marry someone I did not care for. But I could not marry against their wishes, marry someone without their blessing. It would cause them too much pain and make so many problems for my sisters....'

'But if they agreed to give us their blessing? Or would you have another excuse?'

'Margaret, if my family agreed to our marrying then I would be the happiest man on the earth. But it's not ...'

Placing her hand over his mouth she stopped him. 'Right, then,' she said, 'I'd better go and see your father - ask him for his son's hand in marriage.'

Since her arrival in Mazar-i-Sharif, Anwar, a professor at Balkh university, had shown her nothing but kindness and respect. He'd arranged family outings, regretting a trip to Bamiyan was not possible for security reasons but taking her instead to Balkh, reputedly once the capital city of Bactria. Here Margaret marvelled at the beautiful turquoise blue dome of Khwaja Parsa's shrine and heard the romantic, heartbreaking story of the tragic poet, Rabi'a Balkhi. The first woman of the Islamic period to write poems in Persian, her wealthy, powerful family were furious when they learned she had fallen in love with a Turkish slave. After slashing her wrists they threw her into a dungeon, where in her own blood she composed her final verses.

Anwar organised dinner parties to honour his son's guest, advising her on a carpet buying trip and seemed to enjoy her eagerness to learn about his country and its culture. Miriam understood, though, this was no more than the hospitality he would show any guest, that as foreigner and a non-Muslim, she was certainly not being entertained as a potential bride for his son. It took all her courage to tell him she wanted to marry Jawad. He didn't, as she had feared, laugh at her, nor react with anger. Instead, with gentle courtesy he told her it was impossible.

'But Jawad and I love each other. We want to be together.'

'For a marriage to start in the strongest way possible, there should be compatibility, similarity in backgrounds, in beliefs, in culture. Love, the kind of love you talk about Margaret, is a transient thing – at the very bottom of the list of reasons to marry, if it has any place at all.

'I know now you feel as though your heart will break if you cannot marry Jawad. I am not denying the pain you feel is real but believe me

Margaret, your heart is a tough muscle, not so easily broken. You and Jawad will always remember each other – and the memories will, in time, be pain free.' He rose, to show the conversation was at an end, subject closed.

Miriam rose too. 'How do you know Jawad and I are not compatible? Oh, I'm sure plenty of girls from your social background are queuing up to marry Jawad. But how many will be so eager when they know they'll have to leave the city to live in Zardgul? What kind of marriage will your son have, married to a girl who can't cope with the way of life he's chosen?'

Finally, Anwar agreed to discuss the matter further with the family including, of course, Jawad. On her last day in Afghanistan he gave his answer. 'I accept you believe you love my son. I am still not convinced this love you both say you have for each other will last.' As Margaret opened her mouth to argue, he raised his hand. 'Wait. Let me finish. His mother and I, and,' he added with a hint of a smile, 'I think at least two dozen members of our family, have thought and talked much about this matter. Here is what we propose. You return to Scotland. Carry on with your life there. If, after a year apart, you both still feel the same, I am prepared to change my mind.'

'I'll never feel any differently about Jawad,' she replied.

***

The room had become dark. Rousing herself, Miriam set about lighting lamps, forcing herself to think about what to cook for dinner. Iqbal's appearance in the kitchen made her jump. 'A truck's just come in from Behsud. The driver says Dr Jeanine is on the road. She'll be here tomorrow.' They looked at each other in silence. Although she couldn't read his expression, for a moment she considered telling him she would not, after all, go to Charkoh. Instead, she nodded, turning away to stir the sauce bubbling in the pot behind her.

'*Zilla shudeed?*' Jeanine's driver, Zahir, glanced over his shoulder at his passengers. Miriam, whose head had slammed against the window when Zahir swerved the Russian jeep to avoid a boulder, grabbed the strap above the door, bracing herself as the jeep juddered over a pothole. She'd forgotten the agony of travelling in this country until the journey began.

'What did he say?' Jeanine asked.

'He's asking if we're tired,' Miriam translated, adding, 'to which the expected reply is 'no, not at all' otherwise he'll take offence at the implication his driving makes us tired. She smiled at a memory. 'The first time I was asked I thought the driver said *zillzilla*, the word for earthquake. It seemed,' grabbing the strap again, 'a particularly apt expression.' She looked down at Ruckshana sitting between herself and Jeanine on the back seat, wedged in with some of their blankets to protect her from being thrown about like a rag doll. Sound asleep. Miriam tried to ease herself into a more comfortable position but the back of the jeep, including the floor space behind the front seats, was so packed with bags and bedding, thermoses, a water cooler, space was limited, comfort impossible. She stared out at the scenery. On her right a sheer wall of mountain, while on Jeanine's side, a vertigo inducing drop to a valley far below, its orchards beginning to turn from green to the first gold and orange of autumn. If she screwed her neck round to look out the back window she saw the road corkscrew down the mountainside.

Her thoughts turned to Iqbal. He'd stayed at home on their last evening, played with Ruckshana and her kitten and read her a bedtime story. Despite Miriam's efforts to act as if things were fine between them, however, Iqbal rebuffed all her attempts at conversation, replying to her questions in monosyllables. He sat listening to a cassette, a hurt puppy expression on his face while she finished her packing.

'Iqbal, can we please talk about this?'

'What is there to talk about? You know how I feel about your going to Charkoh. Still you choose to go.'

'Jeanine….'

'Oh, yes, of course, the *reis* – her wishes are more important that your husband's.' He turned the sound up on the cassette recorder. Miriam gave up, finished her packing and went to bed. In the morning, when she was packing a box with food supplies for the journey, he sought her out in the kitchen, pulling her into his arms. She hugged him back, holding him tightly but feeling a gulf had opened between them. How could she continue with this kind of life of sulks and silences, of restrictions? What was the alternative? Giving herself a mental shake she pushed Iqbal from her thoughts, determined to make the most of the weeks ahead at Charkoh. Perhaps separation would give her a more positive perspective on things.

She heard Zahir swear under his breath. He brought the jeep to a halt: a puncture. Miriam climbed out. Grateful of a chance to stretch her legs, she ignored Jeanine's exasperated sigh. You'd think the woman would have got used to such unscheduled stops by now.

'Are we there, yet?' Rucksana asked, rubbing her eyes as Miriam lifted her out of the jeep.

'Not yet,' Miriam replied, hauling bags out, 'but it's picnic time.' Apart from the sounds of mechanical tinkering there was total silence. Under the huge, vivid blue bowl of the sky the mountains with their jagged peaks marched ahead, seemingly to infinity. Nothing grew – not a patch of grass, not a tree, not even the low scrubby bushes that were such a ubiquitous part of the Afghan landscape. Enormous boulders lay around, as though hurled from the mountaintops by quarrelsome giants and everything the eye could see was in shades of brown and grey. It was a lonely, desolate place but awesomely beautiful.

'What are those?' Jeanine's voice broke Miriam's reverie.

'*Busrauq*,' she replied, explaining, 'dough fried in oil. They're given to travellers on long journeys. Before they're fried you press a ball of the dough over a sieve to make the pattern, then roll them up loosely. Although they're quite soft when first cooked, they harden up and last forever – the equivalent, I suppose, of ship's biscuits.' Jeanine crunched cautiously before nodding in approval. Zahir joined them on the rug, wiping his oily hands on a rag before gulping down the tea Miriam handed him.

It was after dark by the time they approached Bamiyan, the first few lights of the bazaar flickering on in the distance. A primal scream, blood chilling, cut the air. Jeanine clutching at Miriam said, 'My God, what the hell…?'

Zahir, braking hard, flipped on the interior light, 'Checkpoint,' he muttered. Miriam, gathering Ruckshana onto her lap, caught sight of two figures, pointing guns at the windscreen just before Zahir switched off the headlights. The figures, heads and faces swathed in checked head-cloths so only dark eyes glittered, approached, one on either side of the jeep, kalashnikovs pointing, one at Zahir the other at the passengers in the back. Checkpoint. Keep calm. It's only a checkpoint. She listened to the guard questioning Zahir: who were they, where they were going, why they were driving at night? The driver gave his replies in an even tone. The guard's voice was hectoring – after dark was dangerous, thieves were about. A sudden giggle from Ruckshana caused Miriam to turn her head slowly to see the second figure, cradling his weapon, had removed his bandanna and was engaged in making faces and wiggling his ears at the little girl. He groped in his pocket, producing a handful of *kishmish*. A swift enquiring look at her mother and Ruckshana crammed the raisins into her mouth. Both guards laughed and with a final warning about night driving, waved them on. The release of tension in the jeep was palpable.

'That scream,' Jeanine shuddered. 'never in my life did I hear anything so terrifying.'

'It's how the *mujahideen* say 'Stop',' Zahir explained. 'Everyone understands it.'

'Indeed,' muttered Jeanine.

Ten minutes later they pulled up outside the hotel. Miriam, realising this must have been where Farid met his uncle on the way to Mazar, felt a stab of longing for her son, aching to hold him in her arms. Blinking back tears, she lifted Ruckshana down from the jeep hugging her so fiercely the little girl protested she was being squashed.

Climbing the uneven wooden steps to the first floor the aroma of kebabs made Miriam realise how hungry she was although her first wish was for tea to wash away the dust from the road clogging her throat. The hotel owner, Sufi, greeted Zahir as though he was a long lost brother before, hand on heart, he bobbed his head in a semi-bow towards the women. Addressing the two customers finishing their meal, he requested they move to another room, allowing the women privacy. He shouted to a young boy, scarcely more than eight years old, hovering in the shadows cast by two hurricane lamps suspended from the ceiling, to bring tea. He turned his attention to the rows of kebabs sizzling on a barbecue, constructed from half an oil drum. It was situated outside on the wooden balcony.

Miriam sank down onto the mattress the two men had vacated. 'I really do feel as though I've been earth-quaked,' she groaned, rolling her shoulders to ease the muscles. The boy brought the tea in battered enamel teapots before laying a filthy cloth on the floor on which he placed a large *nan* for each person. A tray of rice followed while Sufi carried over another tray, heaped with kebabs.

Before settling for the night the women, each with a torch in her hand, made their way back down the rickety stairs with Ruckshana. Their destination was the '*shayiste tashnab*' or 'proper toilet' Sufi proudly told them they would find in the courtyard. On the flat-roofed, mud building facing them, were three wooden doors. 'This **is** an *hôtel de luxe*,' said Jeanine, opening the first door.

'What's wrong?' Miriam asked as Jeanine leapt backwards, almost trampling Ruckshana.

'See for yourself. It's disgusting.'

'I'll take your word for it.' Miriam tugged at the second door. In the beam of her torch she saw previous visitors had somehow managed to miss the hole in the floor; turds of an interesting variety of size and colour decorated the perimeter. She closed the door hurriedly, though not before her nostrils had been hit by the stink. The third latrine was not much better but by then Ruckshana was dancing with impatience. 'Can you hold the light steady, while I hold Ruckshana over the hole?' she asked Jeanine, who had one hand clamped over her nose, the beam of light from her torch pointing uselessly upwards towards the star-studded sky.

Jeanine went in after Ruckshana, closing the door behind her. '*Merde*, how am I going to manage this?' she called out.

'You'll have to hold the torch in your mouth,' Miriam instructed, 'and roll up the legs of your *tunban*, and make sure the ends of your *chaddar* don't dangle on the ground.' At the sounds of Jeanine's grumbles, now muffled by the torch in her mouth, she suddenly started to giggle. The whole performance took so long an anxious Zahir appeared in the courtyard, as the women, washing their hands, were pouring water from a plastic jug for each other. Between bursts of laughter Miriam tried to explain the delay but it wasn't until Zahir opened the door of one of the latrines he understood.

Shaking his head, he said, 'I think it's better to go outside. Behind a rock is nice and clean.' The women followed him upstairs, struggling to control their giggles. Ruckshana was soon snuggled under a blanket and, despite the amount of time she had spent napping on the journey, was asleep before Miriam was half way through her story. The thin *toshak* on which she spread her own sleeping bag offered little protection from the hard floor but she was too tired to care.

Wriggling into a comfortable position, enjoying the luxury of stretching her cramped limbs she murmured, 'I could sleep on broken glass.' The only response was a gentle snore from Zahir, and a less gentle one from Jeanine.

EIGHT

Charkoh

Sleep, however, did not come swiftly and Miriam found herself thinking about Farid. Was life in the bustling city – with its electricity, television, cinemas – so exciting that he didn't want to return to Sang-i-Sia? What if his grandparents were trying to convince him to stay in Mazar?

   She scratched at her ankle. A fleabite, damn it. Slithering out of her sleeping bag she found antihistamine cream in her bag. Between the maddening itch, Jeanine's increasingly loud snoring and her concerns for Farid she felt sleep slipping further away. What if Farid was miserable? No, his grandfather was a kindly man who would do all he could to ensure Farid's happiness. Thinking about Anwar, reminded her of his reaction when she told him she wanted to marry his son. She hadn't thought he would give in so quickly. Of course she smiled to herself, anointing a fresh crop of bites around her ankle, he believed the marriage would never happen, convinced that once she returned to Scotland she would be re-absorbed in her western lifestyle and what he imagined was her full social life. Anwar knew nothing of the emptiness in her before she met his son. She felt as if she had been in hibernation until Jawad had come along. Returning alone to Edinburgh, she'd wanted nothing more than to go back into hibernation for the next year.

***

'Did you have to wear a yashmak? And walk ten paces behind Jawad when you were out together?'

She and Janet were in the canteen at lunchtime on her first day back at work. She was desperate to talk about her engagement to Jawad, about their plans for their future together, if only Janet would stop asking her stupid questions.

'No one wears a yashmak in Afghanistan. Some women wear a burqa, but no, I didn't. Except for small headscarves when they go out, none of the women in Jawad's family cover themselves.' Her answer came out more sharply than intended and Janet flushed. 'Sorry, didn't mean to snap. It's just that, well…Oh, hell.' She felt tears threatening and scrubbed at her eyes.

'Margaret, what's wrong? Have you and Jawad had a bust-up?' Janet sounded contrite.

Searching for a tissue in her bag, she shook her head. 'No, we didn't have a bust-up. Quite the opposite, in fact. We're getting married.'

'Married? My God, Margaret – married! When? Wow! I don't know what to say.'

'How about "congratulations, Margaret, I'm delighted for you"?'

'You're not pregnant are you? Even so, you don't have to…Oh, no you couldn't be – you haven't slept with him, have you?'

Margaret slammed her coffee cup down on its saucer, making Janet jump and others in the canteen turn to look at her. 'For God's sake, Janet, I'm telling you I'm going to marry the most exciting, wonderful man I've ever met in my life and all you can do is stutter and stammer and wonder if I'm pregnant. Can't you just be pleased for me?'

'I am pleased. If this is what you really want. It's just… well… Look, how well do you really know him and what he wants from you?'

'I've got a feeling that any minute now, Janet, you're going to tell me you're not a racist but…'

'Well, I certainly don't think I am,' Janet shrugged, 'but if being aware of the problems you might face marrying an Afghani and being in a mixed marriage in Britain makes me racist, maybe I am. Not to mention the religious aspect.'

'Afghani is a unit of currency. Jawad is an Afghan. If you're going to bring his ethnic origin into this at least get it right. And being in a mixed marriage here won't be an issue – we're going to live in Afghanistan.' She paused. She'd wanted to confide in Janet about the year's wait. She'd need to have a friend to whom she could grumble when the months of waiting seemed to go on forever, as she was sure they would. Now, afraid of how Janet would pounce on the fact that Jawad's family were less than ecstatic about the prospect of having a Scottish daughter-in-law she decided to keep quiet about it. 'It'll be a year before we marry – by which time I'll be a Muslim, too, so another of your concerns won't be an issue.' She stood up to leave, adding, as she slung her bag over her shoulder, 'And by the way, he's fantastic in bed.'

At the door she turned back. The dumbstruck expression on her friend's face would have made her laugh if she hadn't been so angry. 'Did your mother never tell you not to sit with your mouth hanging open, Janet, or flies might get in?' She let the canteen door swing shut behind her and marched off towards the ward to resume her shift.

***

Her persistent scratching at the fleabites had drawn blood, bringing Miriam painfully back to the present. Adding a final dab of cream to her ankles, she slid back into her sleeping bag, telling herself to remember to hang it out in the sunshine once they reached Charkoh, to rid it of unwanted visitors.

In the morning, when Miriam woke, Ruckshana was chattering to Sufi who was hunkered on the veranda cracking eggs into a frying pan. Jeanine was sitting up against the wall, her legs still encased in her sleeping bag.

Retrieving her chaddar, which had slipped inside the sleeping bag, Miriam covered her head before sitting up, sniffing the air. '*Subakhair* – Good morning. Mmh, something smells good.'

'Special breakfast,' Sufi said in English, addressing Jeanine. 'Very good breakfast for big journey.' Miriam saw Jeanine eye with suspicion the contents of the bowl he put in front of her. The house speciality was a cholesterol addict's delight: the fried egg sat on top of fried tomatoes on top of a meat stew and everything swam in several inches of oil. Miriam sighed happily as she reached for the fresh, warm *nan*, tearing off a chunk to use as a spoon. Ruckshana scooted across the room, eager to tuck in but Jeanine pushed her own plate away.

'Tell him I want an egg, cooked in water – no oil.' When Miriam translated Jeanine's order into a request for a boiled egg Sufi's expression changed from incredulity that someone was rejecting his signature dish to concern that the foreign woman was ill. At her insistence that she was fine, just couldn't face so much oil so early in the day, an expression of hurt pride crossed his features. Not one, but two eggs were boiled and presented to Jeanine, by which time Miriam and Ruckshana had wiped clean their dish and were rewarded with a smile of approval from Sufi.

As soon as Zahir returned from the bazaar where he'd been buying spare parts for the jeep they headed out of Bamiyan along the one dusty unpaved road lined with little shops that made up the bazaar. It was already crowded with both *mujahideen* and civilians and Miriam, after so long confined to Sang-i-Sia, where she saw only Hazaras, stared at the mix of tribal features – Uzbeks and Tajiks, even some Pathans. From her corner of the back seat Jeanine said, 'I was so disappointed the first time I came to Bamiyan. Everyone had told me how wonderful it was – that you could find almost anything in its bazaar. I expected it would be a smaller version of Mazar but it's like every other one street bazaar.'

Miriam felt a pang of disloyalty when she remembered her own initial disappointment the first time she saw Bamiyan, the provincial capital of Ghazni. She'd been upset too at how little care the soldiers took of the Buddha complex. The caves, encircling the feet of the Buddha, perhaps once used by priests or visiting pilgrims, had become ammunition stores, bomb shelters and living accommodation. It had saddened her to see a soldier empty kitchen slops that splashed and ran down what once would have been the painted robes of the Buddha. She had tried, and failed, to visualise how it might have been when the monasteries were filled with robed monks and pilgrims from India, China and other far away lands, mingled to pray and seek enlightenment and peace at the Buddha's feet. However, not liking Jeanine's dismissive tone, she felt defensive and made no reply. Jeanine didn't seem to notice her silence.

'Have any of your friends or family been out here?' she asked.

'My father came out when Jawad and I married.'

'What did people think about you marrying an Afghan? Had your family met Jawad?'

'It's strange, I was thinking about that last night when I couldn't sleep,' Miriam said. She recounted Janet's reaction. 'I'd expected her to be pleased for me because I was so happy. We became quite distant for a while – silly I suppose, but I was hurt she was convinced our relationship couldn't work. As for my family,' Miriam smiled, 'my father would have welcomed an alien from outer space as long as I was happy. On the other hand no one could've ever reached the standards my mother set so her hysterics were to be expected really. She met Jawad once. Was quite charmed by him, though she never forgave him for not being an exotic tribal chieftain.'

'Did Jawad's family insist on you becoming a Muslim?'

Miriam shook her head. 'That was my choice. Even Jawad didn't know about it until after our year apart.'

'So why did you?'

How to explain something she barely understood herself? Thinking back to those days in Edinburgh without Jawad, every day had seemed like a week and every week a month. She'd written to him every single day. They were long letters filled with the details of her life, her work, what she was reading – every book on Afghanistan she could find – about how much she loved him and looked forward to them being together again. She never posted the letters. What had she done with them? Perhaps they were amongst her few possessions stored in her mother's loft. One day Farid might want to read them. Feeling Jeanine's curious gaze, she realised she hadn't answered her question about her conversion. She shrugged. 'I wanted to immerse myself completely – marriage, religion, the whole works. It seemed the right thing to do. I'd probably have changed my nationality if I could.' She smiled, shrugging slightly at Jeanine's disbelieving look. Now it was the doctor's turn to fall silent.

With no punctures and only the briefest of tea stops they arrived at Charkoh, shortly before dark. The scenery had been changing gradually throughout the day and here the mountains had lost the jagged peaks with which Miriam was familiar, and their slopes and summits, though still high, were more rounded, smoother. The clinic was situated about a half hour's walk from the Charkoh bazaar. Surrounded by four mountains it sat on a flat plain, edged on one side by a river along which straight-trunk poplars grew, their leaves turning now to red and gold. Two large, weather-beaten tents, the sort used in refugee camps were pitched close to the clinic, United Nations lettering still faintly visible on their tops. As the jeep approached, Miriam could see dozens of people emerge from the tents to watch their arrival. 'My God,' said Jeanine, 'Patients. I didn't expect so many already. Hope you're ready for what's ahead.'

Miriam recognised Dr Anwar, who was in charge of the Charkoh clinic, and several of the paramedics from Hansease's other clinics as they hurried forward. By the time she had lifted Ruckshana out of the jeep, the welcoming party had descended on Jeanine. There was a hubbub of voices, each calling greetings, enquiring about her health, the journey, each person eager to be seen to show due deference to the boss. Hands reached out to grab pieces of luggage, determined that the *rais* should not have to carry anything herself. Miriam watched the performance with amusement. Would Jeanine be irritated or pleased by this over-the-top greeting? She grinned to herself as the doctor walked towards the clinic, unencumbered by even her handbag, smiling graciously at everyone – a benevolent despot.

Dr Anwar suddenly bobbed up beside Miriam. '*Zen-i-Dr Iqbal*, excuse me for not greeting you properly. The *rais*…' He spread his arms, dipping his head in self-deprecation. 'You know how it is. How is your good health? And how is Dr. Iqbal? It was a sadness for me to hear he could not come to Charkoh. Come, tea is ready in the staff room. Other foreign doctors all arriving yesterday. ' As they walked towards the clinic building Anwar rattled on like a steam train. His title of doctor was, like her own, an honorary one, bestowed on everyone who worked in the health profession. Ancillary staff in some of the clinics – cooks, watchmen, cleaners, put up no objections to being called doctor. Anwar had studied tuberculosis in Pakistan before returning to take charge of the Hansease clinic in Charkoh. His caseload was higher than any of the other clinics in Hazara Jat, one of the reasons Jeanine had decided to hold the second teaching camp here.

Ruckshana, squirming in her arms, wanted down. As Miriam straightened she heard a voice. '*Asalam' alaikum, Miriam-jan. Chator asteed?*' She grinned in delight as Chaman came forward to hug her. Despite the three little girls Miriam could see hanging shyly behind their mother, the young woman still didn't look a day older than when they last met, although, mentally calculating the years, her friend must be in her mid-twenties. Anwar excused himself and hurried off towards the staff room leaving Miriam and Chaman together. As she stood back to study her, Miriam saw Chaman was still as slim as a whippet. Dark wavy hair escaped her chaddar to frame a round face with rosy cheeks. Her dark, almond-shaped eyes sparkled with a hint of mischief.

'It's so good to see you again, Chaman. It's been too long.'

'You know you're welcome to visit any time.' She glanced around, 'Where's Farid? And Dr Iqbal?'

'Farid's visiting his grandparents in Mazar,' Miriam felt the familiar pang of longing for her son as she spoke. 'Iqbal's not coming. Jeanine said she only required my services as translator.'

Chaman raised her eyebrows, 'Must have gone down well with Dr Iqbal. It's good she didn't try to make Ali stay behind. I wouldn't leave him on his own again after what happened last time.' She gave a throaty chuckle, 'Let me introduce my girls. Feroza's eight now, and this is Leila. You saw them in Pakistan and this is Raihana, who wasn't even on the way then. Feroza is going to watch out for the little ones while we're working. Come on, let's have some tea.' Miriam said hello to the girls who answered with shy smiles. She linked arms with Chaman as they crossed the compound. When her friend had gone to Pakistan to visit her parents she'd returned to Afghanistan to find her husband had, in her absence, become engaged to another woman.

'How are things now between you?' she asked. 'Did the marriage take place?'

'Oh, it happened all right,' Chaman replied, 'but it didn't last long. As for Ali and I – yes, we're all right again now. For a while, though, it wasn't easy. Tell you about it later.'

The flat-roofed clinic buildings took up three sides of a square while on the fourth an enormous wooden gate was set into a high wall. 'The main consulting room is spacious,' Chaman said, 'but the windows are too small. Not enough light. The lab's good, though. Latrines are over there,' she pointed, 'and it's been agreed they're for staff only. They're digging some temporary ones outside for the patients.'

Miriam asked about the tents outside the compound. 'Dr Anwar borrowed them from the UN office in Bamiyan,' Chaman explained. 'As soon as he began telling people about the teaching camp patients started arriving. By yesterday about sixty were already waiting to see the doctors and I think about another fifty arrived today. They've been coming from miles away. Some by horse or donkey and at least one family travelled for two days on foot. Right, staff room's up there.'

She pointed to a wooden staircase leading to the first floor. Half way up, the uneven steps, almost ladder-like in their steepness, dog-legged round a corner in darkness.

The room was crowded. Miriam and Chaman squeezed together on the end of a *toshak*, accepting the tea someone poured from an enormous enamel kettle. Apart from the three foreign doctors, and Jeanine, paramedics from other clinics had arrived, most of whom Miriam had met either in Pakistan where they'd trained or on her journey with Iqbal to Sang-i-Sia. She returned their greetings with smiles and nods, feeling suddenly self-conscious at being in a room with so many men. She noticed Chaman pull her *chaddar* further forward, concealing her hair and most of her face but resisted the temptation to tug her own head covering more firmly into place.

When Jeanine rose everyone quietened. She welcomed everyone, thanking Anwar for his hospitality, promising the paramedics they would learn a great deal in the coming weeks. She introduced the doctors beside her. Dr. Helene, a tall, slim woman with mousy hair who, Miriam guessed was in her early sixties, was French and would run the internal medicine clinic. Dr. Adele, also from France, was a tiny woman, not much over five feet, with an impish grin, specialised in joints and bones and Dr Eva, from Germany was the obstetrician/gynaecologist. 'Where's Miriam?' Jeanine asked, looking round the room. 'Oh, there you are, couldn't see you hiding away there.' Miriam reddened as everyone turned to look at her. 'Miriam will be Eva's interpreter. Chaman, you should also work with Dr Eva and will be excused morning lectures.'

Miriam was pleased to see Eva looked friendly. In her twenties, she was tall with blonde hair pinned untidily on top of her head. Unlike the others, who, Miriam thought, wore a strange assortment of garments – long skirts, cheesecloth tops over tee shirts – they probably thought looked suitably ethnic, Eva was wearing a Punjabi suit. In a geometric pattern in shades of red the *shalwar kameez* had a matching chaddar with which she'd attempted to cover her head, though the chaddar had slipped to rest on her shoulders. As if she knew she was being studied the doctor looked up and winked at Miriam before turning back to Jeanine who was outlining the training programme. Following lectures each morning the paramedics would work alongside the doctors putting theory into practice. 'Lectures and clinic consultations,' she concluded, 'will start promptly at 7.00 each morning. Any questions?'

'What time do we finish in the afternoon?' Miriam recognised Hussain from the clinic in Jaghoray, one of the youngest, and brightest, of the paramedics.

'When we've seen the last patient of the day,' Jeanine replied with a smile that made Hussain sit down smartly, giving an emphatic shake of his head when she asked if he had further questions. 'Right then,' she turned to Anwar, 'I suggest we eat now and have an early night.'

Chaman was telling Miriam how much her girls were looking forward to having Ruckshana stay in their room when Jeanine made her way towards them. Without waiting for Chaman to pause, she cut in, addressing Miriam, 'I asked for somewhere quiet to stay. I know what this lot will be like, up talking 'til all hours – so they've found me a house between here and the village. There's plenty of room, so you can join me.'

'That's very…' Not wanting to be rude, her voice trailed away. She glanced at Chaman, saw the look of intense disappointment on her face and continued in a rush, 'Oh, Jeanine, I've just agreed to share with Chaman. Her girls want to be with Ruckshana.'

'But you'll be very crowded. And Ali is there. I don't …'

'Ali is sharing with the other men.'

Jeanine looked as though she would argue further but gave a shrug. 'Fine, if that's what you want. If you decide you want some peace and quiet, Miriam, let me know.' She went back to sit beside Dr Helene as the cook, Asif, and his assistant appeared with the food.

Breaking her bread into her soup, Chaman said, 'It is a small room, but we can fit us in.' She looked anxiously at Miriam, 'Only if it's your wish, Miriam-*jan*. I mean, you might want to share with Dr Jeanine – she'll have a much bigger room – but I hoped…'

'No, no, I'd rather be with you,' she lowered her voice to a conspiratorial whisper, 'besides, Jeanine snores.' When the remains of the meal had been cleared away Asif, appeared with another kettle of tea but Jeanine indicated to her driver she wished to leave. Zahir hastily put down his own glass of tea and jumped to his feet. The three foreign doctors at her heels, Jeanine left the room amid a chorus of *Shubakher* and *khau khush*. There was a second's silence after the door closed behind her then a babble of voices broke out – some calling for more tea, some bemoaning the early lecture times, others wondering who would work with which foreign doctor, all of them hoping to assist the blonde Dr Eva. Hussain was heard asking if they would be allowed to have Friday off or if Dr Jeanine thought they were machines.

Miriam indicated to Chaman she was ready to go. The two women rose to their feet. 'No, no, stay and talk to us,' a voice, which Miriam thought might be Hussain's, called out while another suggested a game of cards. 'I'm sorry, I'm really tired after the journey,' Miriam excused herself, adding with a slight smile, 'but just wait until tomorrow night – then I'll be ready for anyone who wants to challenge me at *fis-coat*. *Shubakher* – goodnight.' After negotiating the tricky descent to the ground floor she said to Chaman, 'I mean it, too. I learned to play in Zardgul and had quite a reputation as a demon card player.'

The children were fast asleep, sprawled together on one mattress. Miriam and Chaman prepared for bed, even said goodnight to each other, but soon they were chatting, eager to catch up on news. Chaman brought her up to date with what happened when her husband decided to take a second wife.

'I was devastated,' she said. 'I arrived late in the afternoon and the staff at the clinic came to welcome me back. No one said anything and Ali behaved just as you'd expect a man to behave when his wife comes home after a long time.' She grinned at Miriam. 'Everything was fine, very loving, and the girls were pleased to be with their daddy again. Next morning as he was getting ready to go to the clinic – almost like it was something he'd just remembered, you know, like "by the way the cat had kittens while you were away" – he said he should tell me he became engaged the week before.'

Chaman thought at first it was a stupid joke until she asked a friend in the village who, with huge embarrassment, confirmed it was true. 'Although I asked why a thousand times, Ali couldn't give me one good reason for doing it. It was as if he'd had some kind of brainstorm. He said he loved me, was happy with me, loved our children. He'd no complaints about me. He kept saying he was sorry he'd hurt me, but when I asked him to break off the engagement he refused. He said he couldn't.'

'But why couldn't he? It's an outrageous way to behave, totally against what Islam teaches.'

Chaman shrugged. 'Oh, he knew all that, Miriam, but he wouldn't do it. He would lose face, he said. You know, some nights he actually cried about the mess he had got himself into but he would not end the engagement. He thought everyone would say the girl's family changed their mind because he had leprosy. No one would believe he wanted to break it off.'

'Loss of face!' Miriam shook her head. 'If someone gave me 500 afghanis every time I heard that expression on Iqbal's lips I'd be rich. The family must have known he had leprosy when they agreed to the engagement, surely?'

'Ali would feel he had lost face,' Chaman said. 'If someone believes it – then it becomes the truth. Life was horrible. In the evenings after work he'd go to see her, instead of spending time with his daughters. It's strange,' she mused, 'I wasn't really jealous of her – she's called Fatima – I think I was too angry to feel any jealousy. He'd paid two *lakh* – two hundred thousand Afghanis – money I had earned working for Hansease. I was furious.' She shifted into a more comfortable position on her mattress, pulling the blanket round her knees. 'Talking's thirsty work. I could do with some tea.'

Miriam stood up, pulling her chaddar over her head, 'Let's raid the kitchen.' She glanced at Ruckshana and Chaman's girls sound asleep. 'They won't wake up – come on, let's go.' The two women crept out of their room, heading across the compound towards the kitchen. The cook had left out thermoses of boiling water so he could quickly re-boil it for the morning tea and Chaman added a pinch of tea leaves to the smallest one while Miriam found the glasses and sweets. Back in the room, glass of tea in hand, she settled back against a pillow to hear the rest of her friend's story. 'Did you know the girl – this Fatima?'

'Of course, everyone knows everyone – must be the same in Sang-i-Sia.' As Miriam nodded in agreement, Chaman continued, 'It was worse than that, she was my friend. Well, I'd always thought she was. We spent a lot of time together and she used to look after Feroza when I was busy in the clinic. I went to her house, to talk her into breaking off the engagement but she refused to see me. Although Ali wouldn't admit it, I suspect part of it was because he desperately wants a son, and I'd produced two girls by then. I know,' she continued as Miriam opened her mouth to protest, 'and Ali knows very well, it's the father who determines the sex of a child. Goodness knows we've had to explain to people in the clinic often enough. As the date of the wedding came closer he became more depressed. I thought about leaving him, going back to Pakistan with the children but there was no way I could make the journey alone. I didn't have anyone to help me make travel arrangements.

'A few days before the wedding I told him I would never accept his new wife in our home, he must go to his in-laws' house and not come near me or his daughters. Of course,' Chaman raised her arms, palms upward and shrugged, 'I couldn't have physically prevented him from seeing his children.' She paused to cover the sleeping children with the blanket one of them had kicked off, then poured more tea for herself and Miriam. 'He said he couldn't live without me. Why was I killing him in this way – I had thrust a dagger in his heart. You know the sort of thing.' Miriam nodded. Although she'd never experienced this sort of thing personally, she'd heard enough stories from her friends to be able to visualise Ali's dramatic performance. 'I told him he'd killed me when he refused to break off the engagement.'

Ali had gone ahead with the wedding, moved in with his new wife. Two weeks later he pleaded with Chaman to allow him to come home. 'My heart was breaking but I was determined to be strong,' she said. 'I stopped working in the main clinic, holding consultations in my own room so I wouldn't have to see him every day. He used to slip little notes under my door, begging me to talk to him.'

'Did you really want him back after what he'd done?' Miriam was amazed.

'I love him,' Chaman replied simply, adding, 'and despite what he did I knew he never stopped loving me. Ours was a love marriage, remember, and before all this we were strong together – oh, we had fights and difficult times of course – but I didn't want to live without him. Eventually I agreed to meet him and we talked. He was a mess. He knew he'd made a huge mistake. In going ahead with the marriage he had actually lost face more than if he had ended the engagement. The people in the villages from round about were all on my side. Not only the women, but their husbands too, thought he had behaved badly.

'He couldn't bear to be with Fatima and she, poor girl, knew very well he didn't want to stay. Finally it was she who brought things to an end. She told Ali she wanted a divorce – wanted it so much she, or at least her family, were willing to pay back most of the bride price. So, I got my husband back, although it took a long time for us to get back to where we were before he became engaged to Fatima.'

Although pleased her friend's marriage had survived such a traumatic event Miriam felt the story may not have ended happily for everyone. She shifted uncomfortably on her mattress, not sure how to say what was on her mind. Chaman, yawning, was gathering their empty glasses and thermos. Finally Miriam spoke up, 'But although things worked out for you and Ali, it still left Fatima with her life in ruins. How could she find another husband with everyone knowing what had happened?'

Chaman shrugged. 'She should've thought of that before trying to steal my husband,' she said coolly. 'Actually, she has married since – has a little girl now. Her father owns a lot of land and she has no brothers so it wasn't difficult for her family to find someone willing to ignore what had happened. But you're right, what Ali did would have destroyed the marriage prospects of a girl in different circumstances. Knowing my husband was so careless of the happiness of so many people is not easy to live with.' She began to rearrange her bedding adding, 'It's been tough but I know he's truly sorry for what he did. We have to build on that.

'Now,' she said, shaking out a blanket, 'unless we're going to get a severe telling off from Dr Jeanine for being late on our first morning, I think we should sleep.'

NINE

Charkoh September 1995

Miriam felt she'd scarcely closed her eyes when Chaman shook her awake. 'Miriam-jan, it's time for *fajr*. It'll soon be sunrise. Come on, stir yourself.' Miriam groaned, pulling the blanket over her face but Chaman insisted. 'We didn't pray last night. Up you get. There's water in the bathroom next door.' Miriam shivered in the chilly morning air as she emerged from her cosy nest.

'I have to get to bed a lot earlier tonight,' she said, heading for the bathroom to wash and prepare for prayer. 'I'm too old to sit up half the night talking if I'm to function properly next day.' As the cold water on her face chased away her sleepiness, Miriam was glad to share a room with Chaman rather than Jeanine. At the thought of the boss she hurriedly left the bathroom to pray before waking the children.

By the time the women reached the staff room the paramedics, most of whom looked as though they'd barely slept, were already seated around the *dustakhan* in front of bowls of hardboiled eggs and piles of yesterday's leftover *nan*, cold and leathery in texture. Miriam peeled an egg for Ruckshana. 'No Jeanine?' she asked Anwar who was pouring tea over several, heaped teaspoons of sugar in his glass. 'Didn't think she'd be late.'

'She's taking breakfast before she comes over,' he replied. Almost immediately everyone heard the sound of an approaching jeep. As if someone had pulled a switch, shocking the men into sudden action, they swallowed their last mouthfuls of breakfast. Gulping tea, grabbing notebooks, checking pens were in their pockets they rushed off to the room set aside for lectures.

'She has quite an electrifying effect, no?' Eva gave Miriam an amused look. 'Shall we get started?' Crossing the compound, the doctor said how glad she was to have an interpreter work alongside her. Her English was excellent and Miriam thought her German accent contained a hint of an American twang. 'Yes,' Eva agreed, 'I studied there for one year.'

Dr Anwar led them to a room furnished with a small table, a couple of folding metal chairs and an examining table. Outside, a crowd of women had already congregated. As Anwar bowed his way out of the room, half a dozen of the women shoved their way in. Chaman pushed them back out, explaining they would be seen in turn according to the number on the cardboard squares the *chowkidar* had distributed when they entered the compound. With none of the women able to read and each insisting she'd arrived before the others, it took Chaman some time to sort them into order. Finally, the first patient, an old woman triumphantly waving her card in a hand black with ingrained dirt, marched in, toothless gums open in a wide grin. She sat gazing expectantly at Eva. Miriam and Eva looked at each other. 'How do you want to do this?' Miriam asked.

'I'll ask my questions in English if you can translate for the patient. Then tell me what she says. Does that sound okay?' Miriam nodded and the work began.

A steady flow of women began to pass through Eva's consulting room: women with back pain, stomach pains, headaches, eye infections, women who desperately wanted children, women who didn't want more. They brought malnourished babies, children with earache, coughs, diarrhoea, others with worms, some with scabies. Day after day they came, often with anxious husbands waiting outside the clinic, and every evening, when Eva, Miriam and Chaman emerged, exhausted, from the consulting room, women were still waiting. The tents outside the clinic compound were never empty. Anwar organised a third tent to serve as a male admissions ward. Somehow they managed to find accommodation in rooms inside the clinic buildings for women and children who required treatment as inpatients.

Over snatched lunches and more leisurely evening meals, staff room conversations centred on patients and their problems. Family planning was a major issue with many women requesting *goli* to prevent pregnancy. Carrying an infant in her arms and currently in the middle of her ninth pregnancy, one woman was desperate for a rest. The local headmaster's wife, her superior social standing was evident in her slightly haughty manner and clean hands, though she was no more educated than the women she looked down on, women who had to work in the fields. 'I've been using a pill,' she explained. 'It said it would prevent pregnancy for twelve months but,' she gave a heavy sigh, 'my last two pregnancies happened after I took it.'

Neither Miriam nor Chaman had heard of this contraceptive pill and Eva sent for a sample from the bazaar. Manufactured in China, it turned out to be a herbal preparation and, as the headmaster's wife had discovered, totally useless. Through Miriam, Eva suggested the woman persuade her husband to use condoms.

'He won't. He says they would spoil his pleasure. I need the *goli* – the pills.' The clinic did stock genuine contraceptive pills but with roads often closed because of fighting there was always a danger supplies might not arrive, resulting in a rash of unplanned pregnancies. Miriam had brought her own personal supply with her – enough for the next couple of years. Iqbal would like her to stop taking them but…Maybe next year?

She and Chaman had encountered other obstacles to oral contraception being effective. Miriam told Eva, 'I couldn't understand why a woman who was taking the pill became pregnant twice. It turned out her husband often travelled to Pakistan to buy stock for his shop. He would be away for weeks at a time and whenever he left home he took her pills with him.'

Chaman nodded in agreement, adding to the conversation from her own experiences. 'Once a man asked me if he should give his wife pill before or after they are having sex. Afghan men are not trusting their wives.' She glanced over at the paramedics who had abandoned their own conversation about TB patients to listen in. 'Also,' she continued, 'they are not understanding a woman must take pill for some weeks before it works. How does she persuade her husband to postpone sex? I am thinking some women are becoming pregnant when pills are still in their pockets.'

'So, there are many reasons to encourage people to use condoms,' said Eva. Sniggers from the men made Chaman turn her back to them, pulling her chaddar onto her head. Miriam, ignoring the laughter, agreed with Eva but despite all her efforts she'd only persuaded two couples in Sang-i-Sia to use condoms.

'But why are they in the bazaar if no one will use them?' Eva asked.

'Oh, yes, children do use. They use them for,' Chaman groped for the English word, shrugged, ending, '*pakana*.'

'Balloons,' Miriam provided the translation.

Eva laughed, 'No wonder it's not easy to make people take them seriously.' Her face clouded. 'I wish I could do more for those ones desperate to have babies. That young woman, today, Aquila was it? So afraid her husband will divorce her. Why is it always the woman's fault if there are no children?' Miriam didn't reply though gave a wry smile when she noticed the men suddenly lost interest in the conversation, returning to their earlier topic.

In such basic field clinic conditions Eva was limited in what she could do to determine if any medical reasons prevented a woman from conceiving. Apart from taking a case history with questions about menstrual regularity, history of miscarriages and the frequency of sexual intercourse – a question provoking much blushing and giggling – she could, if the woman was willing, carry out an internal examination. Often the moment they were invited to remove their *tunban* and lie down on the examining table the women's desperate desire to conceive took second place to their terror that a man might walk into the room. Even when assured, with either Chaman or Miriam on sentry duty, this would not happen, a sense of shame made some women fight Eva every inch of the way. Tensing their muscles made it difficult for her to introduce a speculum. 'Bit of a problem, here,' she muttered on one occasion. 'Hand's stuck.' The woman had clenched her muscles so tightly they had gone into spasm, trapping Eva's fingers.

When the woman had no apparent problems the only advice Eva could give was to make sure the couple had sex during her fertile time. Husbands were called in to hear this method explained. Chaman, adopting a cool professional tone, her face straight, using a *tesbe* as a teaching aid, counted out the prayer beads to represent the days of the woman's menstrual cycle. By the time she reached the part where she recommended the couple abstain during the days the wife was unlikely to conceive her lips would be twitching. 'I can't help it,' she said to Miriam. 'The men can barely look at me they are so embarrassed. I don't think they've ever in their lives talked about sex except when telling dirty stories and they've certainly never had a woman tell them when and how often to have sex with their wives.'

One other option was to ask if the husband would agree to a sperm count check. Referred to the laboratory with a note from Eva he was handed a container by the lab technicians. 'This is too disgusting,' Eva exclaimed when Chaman told her why a husband had returned to the clinic to collect his wife. 'Can't they just get on with it on their own? Should I have brought a collection of sexy magazines?' Chaman shook her head.

'Islam forbids masturbation but...coitus interruptus?' she stumbled over the Latin mouthful, 'is acceptable. So, wives must participate.'

Finding a suitable place offering the necessary degree of privacy was a problem. One afternoon Miriam noticed two couples, both of whom Eva had sent to the laboratory an hour earlier, hovering around the clinic entrance. She called Ibrahim, the chief laboratory technician to explain again what was required but half an hour later they hadn't moved. 'Did Ibrahim not explain? Did you not understand?' she asked.

One of the men nodded sheepishly. 'So what's the problem?' she demanded impatiently.

'He didn't tell us where to go.'

Exasperated, Miriam opened the door to a small storeroom. Catching hold of the man's sleeve and the arm of the woman next to him she pushed them towards the room. 'You two,' she pointed at the other couple, 'you see the pharmacy? Where the medicines are? There's another storeroom beside it. You can go there.' No one moved. 'If you don't go now it'll be too late and you'll have to come back tomorrow.' She caught the sound of a smothered snort of laughter and saw one of the women hiding her face in her chaddar. 'What is it?'

The woman indicated the man Miriam had been trying to push into the storeroom with her. Blushing furiously she whispered, 'He's not my husband.'

'Oh, God, I'm sorry. Oh, God... well, sort yourselves out. Sorry.' Hiding her own blushes Miriam hurried away. 'Actually, they'd probably have been a lot quicker had they swapped partners,' she added when telling Chaman and Eva the story.

Whenever lab results showed a low or negative sperm count Miriam and Chaman allowed themselves a little smirk. Although Miriam was sure she was breaking some ethical rule, she always managed to let the wives know the result. As she pointed out to Eva, 'We don't know the husband will tell his wife the truth. At least she can have the satisfaction of knowing it's not her fault she's never become pregnant.'

That still left the difficulty of telling the husband; something Chaman refused to do because she would find the situation too embarrassing. Some of the paramedics were reluctant to tell a man he would never make his wife pregnant. On one occasion Miriam overheard Hussain telling someone he didn't have to believe the result as 'sometimes in laboratory they are making mistakes.' When she tackled him he was unrepentant. 'You don't understand. It is very big shame for a man to be told he cannot father children.'

'The wives don't feel too good about being blamed for not getting pregnant. Why should they go on being made to feel they are useless, when it's the husband's fault?' She glared at him, continuing, 'Anyway, we shouldn't be talking about blame and shame. We should be educating people, helping them understand these issues.'

'Why you are saying there should be no shame for Afghan people to not have children? In your country, there are test-tube babies. Fertility treatment. Why you are not educating people in your own country to accept it is okay to not have children?' Miriam stared at Hussain, not sure how to respond.

'I'm sorry,' she said at last. 'I didn't mean to make it sound it's not a problem for Afghan people. I have a lot of sympathy, especially for the women. All the pressure, is on them. I...'

'No. Not only on women. Men are under big pressure if they have no sons.'

'But they aren't afraid of being divorced, sent back to their father's house like a piece of rubbish. A woman isn't going to take a second husband because the first can't give her children.' She stopped. Getting into an argument with Hussain wasn't going to change anything. She drew a breath, continued, 'Yes, you are right about how different it is in the west. We have money and scientists trying to find new ways to help couples have children. And I can't see when these things will be available here. In the meantime can't we at least try to remove this sense of shame attached to childlessness?' When Hussain didn't respond, Miriam continued, 'It was wrong of you to try to bolster that man's ego by not telling the truth about the lab tests. We must be honest. If he thinks the tests are wrong he might decide to take another wife, who also won't become pregnant – more misery for everyone.'

'All right, I'll talk to him again,' Hussain sounded sulky. 'But I say is not so easy as you think,' he added as he walked away.

Dr Anwar was the best person to explain laboratory results to husbands, speaking sympathetically and honestly, usually to the couple together. Often the husbands accepted the situation. One man returned to Eva's clinic to thank her, saying, 'Now I know it's not possible to have children, I can stop worrying about it. It is Allah's will and we must accept it.'

Miriam threw herself one dinner time, on a *toshak* in the staff room, where most of the staff had already gathered for their meal. 'I know I say this every evening but tonight I am definitely going to sleep early.' After eating, two huge kettles of tea beside them, some of the men played cards and Miriam usually joined in. Now Hussain looked at her appealingly.

'But, Dr Miriam, you said you'd be my partner at *fis-kut* – we're going to thrash the rest of them.'

'Oh, okay, I'll play tonight, but it's the last time.' A chorus of dissent made Miriam laugh. Despite her exhaustion at the end of the working day, the teaching camp was exhilarating. As well as learning much that would benefit her patients back in Sang-i-Sia the stimulus of being surrounded by so many people made her almost light-headed. After the first evening's qualms about being in the company of so many men she'd relaxed and now enjoyed the good-natured banter, joining in the telling of stories and jokes herself. When the food arrived she groaned. 'Not *dal brinj* again! Does Moh'd Amir not know how to cook anything other than lentils and rice?'

Chaman's husband Ali jumped in, 'He can do red kidney beans, too. Two days lentil, two days lubia then two days lentil.'

'I'll have to show him how to make a good Scotch broth,' Miriam declared. Cheers of approval from around the room met her words, loudest of all from Moh'd Amir. Jeanine came in and people quietened as they moved around to allow her the place of honour. Helene and Adele sat, one on either side of her like mismatched bookends, but Eva squeezed in between Ali and Hussain. She was popular with the staff,

not only for her striking looks but because she was genuinely
interested in the people with whom she was working, and keen to
practise the few words of Dari she'd picked up. Miriam smiled as she
heard her declare '*dal brinj khub ast*.'

When Moh'd Amir brought in the tea, Chaman, declaring she was
unable to understand the fascination for cards, took her own children
and Ruckshana off to their room. 'What about you, Dr Eva? Will you
play?' Hussain asked. She shook her head but agreed to stay and
watch. Dr Jeanine and the other two doctors left as the card players
formed a group in the centre of the room. Miriam felt Jeanine's eyes
on her as she walked past. She was still wondering what the look
signified when Hussain pulled her back to the game. 'Why did you
play that club? Weren't you watching?'

Chaman was still awake when she returned to the room. 'Did you
win?'

'No we lost. Hussain's furious.' She shook her head, 'It was very
clever of the Prophet, (Peace Be Upon Him) to forbid gambling. If
Hussain can become so angry at losing a friendly game of cards I hate
to think how he'd react if he had his wages riding on the outcome.'

Chaman nodded. 'Hussain has a lot of growing up still to do. Ali
says he's like a little boy who has to be told all the time he's the best –
best doctor, best boss, best card player. Most men are the same,
though, aren't they? Even when they're grown up with
responsibilities, they behave like small boys if they don't get their own
way.'

Miriam grunted in agreement. 'Iqbal's probably still stamping his
feet and sulking about my coming here without him.' She slid under
her blanket. She'd thought this time apart would give her a chance to
think about her marriage, her life in Sang-i-Sia, maybe understand why
things seemed so wrong between her and Iqbal. In fact she'd hardly
given Iqbal a thought in days. By the time she and Chaman said
goodnight she was too tired to think. At least being kept so busy meant
she missed Farid less than she would have at home. Snuggling close to
Ruckshana she felt a pang of guilt about spending so little time with
her daughter. What a terrible mother she was. Tomorrow she'd read to
her instead of playing cards. And the day after was Friday. Thinking of
the bliss of a day's holiday she drifted off to sleep.

Next day the first patient to enter the consulting room was a woman called Amina. Her much-patched *chaddar* covered a dress so faded it was impossible to tell its original colour. She carried a child, her son, wrapped in a dirty blanket. She was weeping by the time she uncovered the tiny scrap. Moh'd Sarwar's eyes, huge in his gaunt face, glittered feverishly and his skin was stretched taut over too-prominent cheekbones. When Chaman weighed him, he barely registered six kilos. Bit by bit, Amina explained he'd been a healthy little boy until he had whooping cough. He had survived, although his older brother and baby sister did not. Shortly afterwards, he contracted measles. 'He was so weak. He never became any healthier,' she said. 'His father went all the time to the bazaar for medicines. He bought injections and syrups, pills – nothing worked.'

'Did you see a doctor?' Eva asked.

When Miriam translated the question Amina shook her head, 'There is no doctor. We went to the mullah. He told us *perhez* was the only way for Moh'd Sarwar to recover. He made us a *tawiz*. It took the rest of our money. We had to borrow from our neighbours to come here.' She looked at Eva, 'You're our last hope.' Overcome by sobs, she hid her face in her chaddar before adding on a whisper, 'He's our only child now.'

'*Perhez* is fasting, yes?' Miriam nodded at Eva's question. 'And what is this *tawiz*?'

'Some verses from the Qur'an fastened inside a piece of cloth. You must've seen them – most people wear them.'

'How long has he been fasting?' Miriam translated Amina's reply. For the last month the child had been given nothing more than weak tea. Moh'd Sarwar was starving to death.

Chaman brought a bowl of rice from the kitchen. Moh'd Sarwar dug both hands in and began cramming the food into his mouth. His mother fussed about his dirty hands but Eva shrugged. 'Better he eats than we worry about a few germs.'

'You know,' Chaman said, 'I see many malnourished babies in the clinic but never one looking so strange. Now I understand. Mostly I see them not so old as this, only babies. He has already teeth. They are looking enormous.'

'In fact,' Eva commented, her face expressionless, 'he looks like a particularly ugly, bad-tempered monkey.' Despite the tragedy of the situation, Miriam's lips twitched and Chaman hurried out, shoulders shaking. She returned with Amina's husband to explain the child would have to stay for some days for an intensive feeding programme. Eva curtained off a part of the consulting room to provide accommodation for the family.

'Good start to the day,' Eva said as they finally called in the second patient of the morning. 'It will be lunchtime soon and we have not yet had our tea break.' By lunchtime, however, Moh'd Sarwar had presented them with a new problem. After the first handfuls of rice he seemed determined to continue his fast to the death, refusing to eat anything else.

Chaman said, 'He shuts his teeth tight and turns away when I offer him food. I think when he sees a spoon he is thinking about all the medicines his parents were making him eat.' Reluctantly, Eva decided to insert a feeding tube.

When Jeanine said she wanted Chaman to spend the afternoon working with Dr Helena, Eva mildly protested that her clinic was particularly busy that day. 'For goodness sake,' Jeanine snapped, 'It's only one afternoon and you've got Miriam. Besides, you take far longer with your patients than the other doctors – you need to speed things up.'

'Cow,' Eva muttered under her breath to Jeanine's retreating back. 'Does she think we can just hand over a prescription and call the next patient? If she wants European style clinics, then I think she should have stayed in France.'

In the staff room over dinner that evening Miriam gave Chaman a résumé of the afternoon's workload, and an update on Moh'd Sarwar. 'His mother hates the feeding tube as much as her son hates spoons. Whenever our backs are turned, she pulls it out, then says he did it himself. We'd to keep interrupting the clinic to reinsert the tube. Oh, and Eva got an eyeful from one of the 'no milkers,' Miriam grinned at the memory.

The women had created generic nicknames for various kinds of patients. Miriam was impressed by Eva's ability to guess the reason for a woman presenting at the clinic. The 'pain and weakness all overs' were women exhausted from a combination of too many children, backbreaking work and never enough rest or good food. There were the 'infertiles' and the 'I've had enoughs.' The 'no milkers' were mothers who insisted they had insufficient breast milk and wanted powdered milk. Miriam and Chaman both knew from their own work how the network of mothers-in-law, aunts, grandmothers, even neighbours nagged mothers about not producing enough milk. The more the mother worried, the less milk she produced.

Several times a day either Chaman or Miriam explained the process of milk production to a woman who, more often than not, sat staring blankly until they had finished speaking then, without having listened to a word, renewed her demand for milk powder. When diluted cow's milk was suggested as a supplement the woman declared cow's milk would give her baby diarrhoea, causing Eva to burst out on one occasion, 'For God's sake what do they think milk powder is?' However, to the women, the powder in tins had no connection to the milk cows gave – it was medicine, the preparation of which would turn it, magically, into liquid milk.

Dr Jeanine could complain all she liked about their slowness; it took time to provide convincing explanations for the women. 'We need to get the men to sit in while we explain,' Chaman said to Miriam. 'If we can convince them, they'll help their wives stand up to the relatives at home.' It was Chaman, too, who hit on the idea of using a farming analogy to explain how mothers could ensure a plentiful supply of breast milk.

'What do you do if your cow starts giving less milk than it should?' she asked one nervous looking husband.

Shrugging, he replied, 'First, I'd give her more fodder. More to drink helps – and I'd milk her more often.' He looked enquiringly from Chaman to Eva to Miriam as though wondering what other aspects of animal husbandry they needed to know about. As they nodded encouragingly at him a light seemed to go on in his head. His thumb indicated his wife. 'It works with same with humans?'

Several times a day Dr Eva would ask, 'What do you do when the cow gives less milk?' Usually, the reply would be – 'give it more food' and they knew at least part of the breast milk producing process had been understood. One day, Miriam asked the question of the young woman in the consulting room. Before she had a chance to reply, a male voice from behind the waiting room curtain provoked laughter from everyone by calling out, 'Take it from the goat.'

Today, though, Eva, perhaps worried about Moh'd Sarwar and niggled by Jeanine's criticism, was less patient with the 'no milkers.' Miriam turned to Chaman, 'The patient was a young woman with a nice healthy baby. Insisted she'd no milk. Eva asked her to open her dress. They were like enormous melons – bursting with milk. You know the way Eva's eyes glitter when she's exasperated?' Chaman nodded. 'Well, she looked at these huge breasts for a moment then she leant forward, grabbed one and squeezed. She only meant to express a few drops to show the woman there really was milk.' She stopped as giggles overtook her. Chaman nudged her to get on with the story. 'Well, the first few drops appeared and then …' she spluttered, 'it was like a tap had been turned on. The milk gushed out. I don't know whether Eva or the patient looked the more surprised.'

Laughing, the two women collapsed against each other, everyone in the room joined in the laughter.

'After Dr Eva had mopped up the patient,' Miriam continued at last, she put a rubber glove over the tit and expressed the rest of the milk into it. I'll never forget the woman's face as she watched each of the fingers fill up.'

The conversation moved on to plans for the next day's holiday. Miriam rose to her feet saying, 'My holiday starts now. I'm going to say goodnight, have an early night and please,' she turned to Chaman, 'don't even think about waking me in the morning for prayer. I'm going to sleep until at least mid-morning. Come on, Ruckshana, let's go and read a story.'

TEN

Charkoh September 1995

As Miriam led Ruckshana out of the room she heard Jeanine say goodnight and follow her out. Once they'd negotiated the staircase the doctor turned to her. 'We've not had a chance to talk recently,' she said. 'How is it going? Enjoying the work with Eva?'

Miriam nodded. 'Oh yes. It's hard work but I'm learning so much.'

'It seems to be bringing you out of your shell, too. Is this the real Miriam beginning to show herself?' she asked.

'How do you mean?'

'Well I never saw the woman I met in Sang-i-Sia rolling about the floor laughing the way she does here.' Miriam's expression must have shown she didn't know how to respond for Jeanine hurried on, 'I didn't mean I thought you dull in Sang-i-Sia but you seem to be having a lot more fun here – as well as working hard, of course. When you go back Iqbal will agree I was right to insist you came.'

Miriam smiled faintly, 'I'm sure he will. Well, I've promised this young lady a story before bed so, if you don't mind, I'll say good night.' As she headed for their room she felt her spirits sink. Damn Jeanine. Why did she have to remind her about Iqbal? She was already feeling guilty about how easy it was not to think about him. Determined not to spoil this precious time with her daughter, she'd worry about it later. 'Come on Ruckshana, what about a game of Ludo after your bath?'

'And a story?' Ruckshana asked, ever ready to strike a bargain.

'Okay, Ludo first, then a story. What'll it be tonight?'

'Winnie the Pooh.'

After their game, while her mother bathed her, Ruckshana kept up a running commentary about what she and Chaman's girls had been doing. When her daughter said she'd been teaching Feroza, Raihana and Leila how to hunt for heffalump traps Miriam laughed, wondering what the Afghan girls made of the game. 'Did you find any?'

'No, Feroza says they don't have heffalumps in Charkoh. But I think they do – just we're not good at finding them. Need Farid to help us.'

Miriam hugged her. 'Do you miss him?'

She felt Ruckshana's head nodding against her shoulder. 'And daddy. When will they come?' At the hint of tears in her daughter's voice, Miriam hugged her close.

'They won't come here to Charkoh but when we go home to Sang-i-Sia, daddy'll be there, with your kitty, waiting for us. Farid'll come home soon afterwards. Into bed now for your story.' Miriam scarcely read a page before Ruckshana was fast asleep. She sat watching her daughter for a few minutes, wishing Farid here too. And Iqbal? Tossing the book to one side she lay on her back staring at the ceiling, thinking about her husband. If he were here would she play cards in the evening, join in the jokes, laugh as often? Or would she be the woman – the dull woman – Jeanine met in Sang-i-Sia? When they'd travelled from Pakistan they'd stayed at various Hansease clinics along the way. He'd not seemed then to mind her mixing with men. Odd it was in his home area, where he should've been relaxed, sure of himself, he'd become so obsessed about what other people might think and say.

She started as the door opened and Chaman, carrying a sleeping Raihana in her arms, came in with the two older girls straggling behind her. 'Would Ali mind if you played cards with the other doctors?' Miriam asked.

Chaman looked startled by the question. 'Well, he would – but only because I'm so useless, he'd be embarrassed. Why?'

'Oh, nothing.' She watched Chaman's shadow flickering on the wall as she prepared her daughters for bed. 'Goodnight', she murmured in the darkness after her friend put out the lamp.

She was only vaguely aware of Chaman creeping out of the room, shushing the girls as she took them off for breakfast and sunlight was streaming in the window before she woke again fully. It was almost 10 o'clock. She stretched luxuriously and lay for a few more minutes enjoying the thought of the leisurely day ahead. She was folding the bedding when an urgent knock sounded on the door.

'Dr Miriam! Dr Eva wants you. An emergency.' Recognising Anwar's voice, she opened the door. 'I'm sorry to disturb you but Dr Eva sent me. Please can you come now?' Miriam hurried to Eva's consulting room, concerned Moh'd Sarwar had taken a turn for the worse. He was sleeping peacefully in his mother's arms. She pulled the curtain back. A young woman, her face as white as paper, lay on the examining table. Eva and Chaman turned as she came in.

'Sorry to spoil your holiday,' Eva said, 'but I could do with some help.'

'What's happened?'

'This is Zohra. She has a retained placenta. She had the baby,' she pointed to the tiny swaddled bundle lying next to the woman, 'two days ago and they say only part of the placenta came away.'

'Two days ago? But...'

Eva rolled her eyes heavenwards. 'They thought they'd wait until the bleeding stopped before moving her. It's too late to remove the placenta, or what's left of it, manually – the cervix has closed. I'll have to do a D & C under anaesthetic.'

The barely conscious woman was stretchered to Dr Helena's consulting room, which had a slightly larger window. Chaman explained to Zohra's husband, Qurban and his mother what the problem was. When he heard the word 'operation', Qurban turned pale and tried to escape but Eva made Chaman call him back saying she needed him. Zohra's mother-in-law began calling loudly on Allah for help. Despite the larger window the light was poor, even when Eva dragged the examining couch close to the window. 'Still not enough,' she grumbled. 'Miriam, can you stand at the foot of the table – here – and shine this torch where I direct you.' Miriam took up her position, torch at the ready.

With no stirrups on the table, Eva slid Zohra as far down as possible, her buttocks right to the edge. The mother-in-law starting speaking excitedly, pointing at the window. 'What's she saying?' Eva asked. Miriam explained the woman was worried someone might look in the window and was asking if she could put a curtain up. 'My God,' Eva muttered, 'it gives a whole new meaning to death before dishonour.' She positioned Zohra's legs, heels resting on the edge of the table, knees bent upwards. 'I need the husband and his mother to hold her legs open,' she explained. 'Look,' Eva told Qurban through Miriam, 'all you have to do is keep a firm hold of her leg – see, like this?' Qurban gingerly took hold of his wife's knee as instructed, resolutely turning his back to the business end of proceedings. 'And you,' pointing to the mother-in-law, 'take the other leg. Come on, hurry up, I need to work fast. Chaman, once I've inserted the half speculum I want you to kneel down and hold it in place. Take this kidney tray in your other hand. Sorry it won't be very comfortable but it's the best I can do.'

Miriam, terrified she would start shaking, stood behind a crouching Chaman, directing the torch beam where Eva indicated. As Eva began, she explained how she was scraping round the inside of the uterus to ensure all the pieces of the placenta came away. 'Shouldn't I be wearing gloves?' Chaman asked.

'Technically yes, but there's no time now. You're not touching the patient so there's little risk of infecting her.' A flood of blood and blobs of disintegrating placenta shot out – all over Chaman's hand. She stared at the gory mess in shocked silence for a moment.

Turning her face up to Eva she hissed, 'I just **asked** you if I needed gloves.' Miriam admired the way she managed to hold her position, without letting go of the speculum or the kidney tray. She knew how furious Chaman was. Blood was dirty and a now polluted Chaman would have to take a bath, which would entail begging someone to heat water for her – or, as it was a holiday and the staff would be away, doing it herself – and carry the buckets upstairs to strip off in the cold bathroom. Eva, she realised, would not be aware of this, thinking only that Chaman had been concerned with the risk of infecting the patient. She flashed a sympathetic smile in Chaman's direction, which caused the torch to wobble and Eva to tut at her.

Every so often the mother-in-law sobbed loudly, declaring her daughter-in-law was dead, or of she wasn't, she soon would be. Sobs were immediately followed by loud prayers. Unable to do two things at once, she invariably slackened her grip on the leg she was holding. This allowed it to begin slowly to drift to its natural position until the foot rested inches from Eva's nose. '*Scheisse*. Get that damned foot out of my way,' she yelled and Miriam, trying to keep the torch steady in one hand, used the other to push the offending leg outwards again – like opening a gate.

Finally it was over. 'Clean as a whistle in there now,' Eva said, a hint of quiet satisfaction in her voice. 'Let's get her into bed somewhere – we can probably make some space beside Amina and Moh'd Sarwar. Don't know about you two, but I'm ready for a cup of tea.' Chaman, glaring at Eva, said she had to take a bath before drinking tea.

Anwar had arranged a fishing trip and picnic to which most of the staff were going, despite Jeanine suggesting if anyone was bored with nothing to do there were statistics to record. She, to everyone's relief, was going to stay behind to write up reports. In the early afternoon those going on the picnic headed out of the compound. As they walked towards the river their feet kicked up puffs of dust on the path. The flat, dry earth here was barren although in the distance a thin line of green showed where trees grew beside the river. 'How are they going to catch fish?' Eva asked when they reached their destination. 'No one has fishing poles.'

'Rods,' Miriam corrected her absentmindedly. 'Don't need them. You'll see,' she smiled, sitting down on a blanket Anwar spread under a willow tree. The men were undoing various bundles: wood for fires, frying pans and kettles, cooking oil, bread and a collection of plastic medicine containers. Miriam nodded towards the latter. 'They say the ones for Rifampicin are the best.'

'What does TB medicine have to do with fishing?' Eva asked. 'God, what was that?' She leapt up in alarm as a dull explosion sounded only feet away. Cheers and whoops came from the men. A whole series of explosions was followed by a mini tidal wave. 'They bomb the fish?'

Miriam nodded. 'They put explosives into the empty tubs, light a fuse and chuck it in. First time I saw it I was shocked. Lobbing bombs into a river seemed so unsporting. In Scotland people would be jailed. Now,' she shrugged, 'I can see it's much easier than spending hours hoping a fish will be fooled into biting a pretend fly. Let's face it the fish is dead whichever way it's caught. If they did it the 'sporting' way they'd never catch enough for lunch. '

The men were jumping about in the river grabbing fish, which rose, stunned, to the surface. Several fires were lit and the small fresh water trout were cooked whole, fried until crisply edible on the outside with tender, melting flesh inside. Afterwards Chaman and Ali took the children further upstream to a shallow pool where they could splash about. Miriam and Eva leaned back against the tree, sipping tea.

'How did you meet Iqbal?' Eva asked.

'In Pakistan. I was working on a health project for Afghan refugees in Quetta and he'd come to do some work at the provincial tuberculosis centre. Jeanine's predecessor introduced us. She thought Iqbal was the man I was looking for.' She fell silent, remembering.

Standing beside Dr Anna Kramer, she'd been watching the rugby scrum at the huge buffet table where the male delegates jostled and pushed as if the great platters of mutton biryani would vanish before they'd filled their plates. She could never understand what prompted the behaviour – it was the same at weddings. Surely they knew there would always be enough food to go round?

She heard Anna murmur in her ear, 'Look, Iqbal's coming over.' Miriam watched a taller than average Hazara detach himself from the crowd, a plate of biryani held high in each hand. He came towards them and handed a plate of food to Anna with a smile, and an apology for the men's behaviour. He had a round, open face and Miriam took in a flash of gleaming white teeth. She liked the way his eyes crinkled when he smiled. He turned to give her the second plate.

Anna made the introductions. 'I've heard a lot about you, Dr Iqbal,' Miriam said, putting out her hand.

He shook the proffered hand firmly. 'And I've heard much about you,' he replied. They both turned to look accusingly at Anna, forking biryani into her mouth.

'I've said only good things about you both,' she declared. 'I admit I've been hoping to get the two of you together.' Iqbal flushed, looking down at his feet. Miriam could only ask a banal question about how he found the morning's discussion. Iqbal chatted for a few minutes, mostly to Anna. When a bell sounded they moved to take their seats and Miriam realised Iqbal's gallantry in looking after them meant he hadn't eaten. 'Well, what d'you think?' Anna whispered. 'I said he was nice, no? Perfect for you – just like your Jawad.'

'Shh. They're starting,' Miriam said, ignoring Anna's question.

'Well, was he?' Eva's voice dragged her back to the present.

'Sorry? What?'

'Was he the man you were looking for?'

Miriam gazed unseeingly at the river for a long moment before giving a slight shrug of her shoulders. 'I really don't know the answer to that, Eva,' she replied.

'Sorry, I didn't mean to pry,' Eva said.

Miriam shook her head. 'No, no, you weren't – it's just me. Anyway, as I said, I met Iqbal in Quetta. It was a very quick courtship.'

'That is so romantic. Was it love at first sight? Is he very handsome?'

'No and yes,' said Miriam, laughing. 'No it wasn't love at first sight and yes, he is handsome.'

'You married without being in love?'

'I liked him. He was – is – a kind man. I thought he would be good to Farid, my son.' She paused, 'You know I was married before?' When Eva nodded she continued, 'I wanted to come back to Afghanistan – for a variety of reasons. Iqbal was supposed to open a clinic in Sang-i-Sia. He was a bit reluctant to return to his village unless he had a wife – I needed a husband – it was a good arrangement.'

Eva's face creased in a frown. 'You make it sound so businesslike and detached. Didn't you feel anything for him?'

Miriam said, 'You know, thousands of Muslim girls enter into arranged marriages every day, often without ever having met their future partner. While I'm not an advocate for arranged marriages, nor am I trying to say they work better than our western 'love matches', many do work out. And it wasn't as if Iqbal and I hadn't got to know each other.'

'But you just said you weren't sure if he was the right man.'

Miriam sensed, if not disapproval, a coolness in the other woman's voice. She sighed. For most westerners brought up to believe romantic love was a requirement of marriage her situation seemed too alien to understand and she never could seem to explain herself properly. She didn't want to give the impression her relationship with Iqbal was nothing more than a marriage of convenience. She touched Eva's arm. 'I was doing what I thought was right for all of us. Of course I had feelings for Iqbal – though not the Hollywood 'head over in heels in love' kind. I knew…' A shout from Anwar made both women look up. The men had rigged up a net for volleyball and were now calling the two women to join them. Eva got to her feet.

'Coming?'

Miriam shook her head. 'You go ahead. I'm feeling too lazy. Besides, I'd better go and find Ruckshana before she starts thinking I've abandoned her.'

Watching Eva stride towards the makeshift volleyball court scratched in the dust, Miriam felt prickly and defensive. Instead of going to find her daughter, she remained sitting under the tree. She thought fondly of Anna, remembering how they'd met.

***

Finding a way to return to Afghanistan became almost Miriam's reason for living – that goal, and Farid. She found work co-ordinating a basic health care project for Afghan refugees and had spent the day observing how classes were conducted in one of the camps. Not wanting to leave Farid with strangers she took him with her. The visit to the Serena Hotel – the poshest in Quetta, where she and Jawad had planned to enjoy two nights of romantic luxury before returning to Afghanistan – for ice cream was a reward for his good behaviour on what must have been a boring day for the little boy. Her own ice cream was melting, untouched, into a puddle in the dish when a voice said, 'You should've had strawberry – much nicer than the pistachio. They grow the strawberries in the gardens here.'

'Sorry?' she looked up at the woman who'd addressed her then down at her ice cream. Pushing the dish away, she said, 'I forgot it was there. Miles away.'

'May I join you?' The woman was already sitting down beside Farid who glanced briefly at her, his dark eyes large and solemn. Miriam had no inclination to make polite conversation with a stranger and gave her assent with a barely polite shrug. 'So where were you? Oh, I'm Anna, by the way, Dr Anna Kramer – from Germany,' she added unnecessarily in her strongly accented voice. 'I work with a medical programme that has clinics here in Quetta, and in Afghanistan.'

Miriam introduced herself and soon found herself telling Anna about her job and her frustration at the way the teaching was done. 'I mean,' she exclaimed, 'the health trainers treat the women they're supposed to be teaching like they're third-rate human beings. How do they think anyone will want to listen to them when they know they're being looked down on?' She described the session she'd witnessed in which the trainers perched on chairs set on a low platform, while their students sat below them on the bare ground. Although Miriam couldn't fault the content of the lesson, she was appalled at the delivery of it. At the end of the lesson, tea was brought with a dish of hardboiled eggs. Miriam had almost finished her egg when one of the trainers, Jemila, suddenly said, 'Oh, she's eating the egg! We never eat anything when we're here.'

Miriam felt instant guilt – had the refugee women offered the eggs as a token of hospitality, which the guests, knowing they couldn't afford to give away food, were expected to ignore politely? 'Oh, no,' Jemila scoffed, 'These women are so dirty – we don't want to risk getting sick by eating food they've prepared. Tea's all right – they boil the water.'

'They've been teaching health care in that camp for months, but they still think the women are dirty.' Miriam's voice rose. 'And it doesn't occur to them if that's true they should be questioning their teaching methods. I don't know how I'm going to change their attitude and if I can't the project will continue to fail these refugee women and their children.'

'But that's not what's really worrying you, is it?' Anna asked quietly. 'There's something else.' When Miriam remained silent Anna turned to Farid, who'd long since finished his ice cream and was sorting sugar packets into piles beside his plate. 'You come with me, young man. There's someone you should meet who can tell you exciting stories about brigands and stuff.' Farid, to Miriam's surprise, went off with Anna who returned a few minutes later saying, 'I introduced him to the doorman – you know the one with the moustache and a waistcoat covered in badges? He'll keep him entertained while you tell me the real reason you've been shredding your napkin under the table. They're not throwaway paper ones here you know – takes a pretty traumatic event to shred one of these.'

Miriam found herself talking, for the first time, to someone about Jawad – and once she'd started she couldn't stop. Words poured out – not about his death, which she explained in a few short sentences, almost dismissively in a voice devoid of emotion – but about how wonderful a man he was, as if by painting him larger than life she could, literally, bring him back to life.

Miriam allowed Anna to take her under her wing, though since her
first outpouring in the Serena, she no longer mentioned Jawad. She
was afraid talking about him, sharing him with others diminished him
in some way. He belonged to her alone. She'd keep him safe, locked in
her heart. Only to Farid did she talk about Jawad. Lying beside him
when she put him to bed she reminded him of how his father would
sing to them in the evenings, of how strong and handsome he was, of
the time they built a snowman together. Never mind if Farid had been
too young to remember, she would give him memories of his father to
keep with him always. Her son would fall asleep, his cheeks
sometimes wet with tears. For the rest of the time, at work, visiting
Anna, shopping for food, Miriam lived her life as though in a bubble –
like those children, she thought, who have to be protected from germs
– a defence against whatever else fate may throw at her.

Anna began to introduce Iqbal's name into their conversations,
telling Miriam of his enthusiastic support for women's rights,
education for girls, providing health care in rural areas. After
engineering their first meeting Anna continued to bring them into each
other's orbit although she must have been disappointed by Miriam's
disinterest in the man. Iqbal barely impinged on Miriam's
consciousness until one day the doctor mentioned she was trying to
persuade him to return to Afghanistan to open a clinic in his village.
'His medical training was paid for on the understanding he would go
back but now he's not so keen on the idea. Seems to think he needs to
find a wife first.'

Miriam said nothing at the time but something clicked in her brain.
The next time she was in Iqbal's company she led the conversation
round to his future plans.

***

'Sorry!' Hussain's exclamation broke into Miriam's thoughts. The
volley ball landed next to her, showering her feet with dust. She
jumped up, threw the ball back with a flourish and headed off to find
Ruckshana.

The week following the Friday holiday was even busier, with more
patients arriving every day. Eva's consulting room had further shrunk
to provide floor space for more admissions. Moh'd Sarwar had worked

out a spoon was preferable to a feeding tube and was now eating soups and mashed foods. Zohra was discharged. The day after her operation, she'd been sitting up chatting to Amina while her mother-in-law sat beside her feeding the baby on milky tea from a filthy bottle. Chaman had wasted no time in wresting the bottle away from her and setting to work to start the baby feeding at the breast. Now, Fatima and her malnourished daughter Leila had taken Zohra's place. Miriam, fed up with the unchanging diet of hardboiled eggs for breakfast gave hers to either Leila or Moh'd Sarwar. One morning she found Eva handing over her egg as well. 'Scrambled would make a nice change,' they agreed.

Miriam, with Chaman and Eva, was crossing the compound towards the consulting room after a ten-minute tea break when Jeanine stopped her. 'There's someone I want you to meet, Miriam,' she said from the door of the room serving as her office.

Miriam stepped into what was usually Anwar's store for laboratory materials, wrinkling her nose at the chemical smell that still hung in the air. Something was familiar about the tall, broad-shouldered man who stood, his back to the door, looking out the small window. As he turned, she let out a cry, 'Ismail!'

For one split second, she thought he'd come to tell her it had all been a mistake; Jawad was alive after all. The wild hope fled as instantly as it had come but left her shaken, as if seeing Ismail now, for the first time since she left Zardgul, was the final confirmation of Jawad's death. 'Ismail! Oh, I....' She swallowed hard, trying to control the tremble in her voice. Rooted to the spot she watched him move towards her. Although his hair was receding slightly it was still thick and black, the moustache, of which he had always been so proud, still luxuriant above the full lips. Ismail took her hand in both of his, a huge smile lighting up his face. 'Miriam-*jan*, I'm happy to see you after too much time.' When she made no reply he continued, 'I am bringing patients. In Zardgul, we are hearing news of the foreign doctors at Charkoh.' Switching to Dari, he continued, 'Mostly I came to see you – to take you home.' With a glance at Dr Jeanine he reverted to English, 'I hope this doctor will agree there is need to open a clinic in Zardgul.' Miriam opened her mouth but no sound came out. Thoughts whirled in her head: this man had probably spoken to Jawad the day he died. Perhaps he'd seen, could tell her what happened. What did he mean 'take her home'? She felt his hands grip hers more tightly. She extricated her hand gently, tried a smile, still didn't know what to say.

'You might thank him for the sheep.' Jeanine's voice, sounding exasperated, reached her, as though from far away.

'Yes, thank you for the sheep. It was delicious.' She shook her head, as though to re-start her brain. 'What a ridiculous thing to say. Ignore me. It's such a shock to see you here.'

Jeanine cut in briskly, 'Right, now you've found your voice, can you sort out accommodation for his patients? Later, I'll hear what he has to say about the need for a clinic in his village. I'd like your input, Miriam, as you know the area.' She grabbed a couple of folders from the desk and headed for the door, muttering about being late for a lecture.

'Miriam-*jan*, it's good to see you. Usma sends many salaams. She wanted to come but...'

Interrupting him she said, 'I'll send someone to sort out space for the patients in the tent. I'm sorry the accommodation isn't up to much. They didn't expect so many patients. They had to find an extra tent. Still, it won't be for long. I'm sure your group will get appointments tomorrow and then you can...' She broke off when Ismail caught her hands in his, turning her round to face him. She sighed.

'Let's start again, Miriam-*jan*. I ask how you are and you ask how I am, then I ask about your house and you ask about mine. We'll hope that neither of us will ever be tired and by then it'll be easier to talk about other things.' He released her hands saying, 'In fact I believe I can see the edges of a smile at last. Now, tell me where is Farid? And don't you have a daughter now?'

Miriam explained about Farid's visit to his grandparents and by the time she was telling Ismail about Ruckshana she felt herself begin to relax. Now she could ask him about his family, trying to imagine his sons being old enough to work on the land, how grown up his daughter must be. 'Oh, it would be wonderful to see everyone again,' she cried.

'You can. I meant what I said. I've come to take you home.' Miriam shook her head, but Ismail continued, 'I'll find a good horse for you – it's only one day's ride to Zardgul.'

'Ismail, we're so busy here. You've seen the patients, we see hundreds every a day. I can't...'

'If Jeanine was willing to let you go for a few days?'

She shook her head. 'Look, Ismail going to Zardgul is impossible. Let's drop the subject.'

'No, Miriam, I can't. Look,' he produced from a scruffy envelope a sheet of paper so flimsy from the many times it had been unfolded it was falling apart. 'The letter you wrote from Pakistan. You promised to come back to Zardgul – if not to live and work, at least to visit us, to hear what happened to Jawad, where…'

'Things are different now, Ismail.'

'You mean Dr Iqbal will not bring you to Zardgul.' It was a statement, not a question. Miriam didn't reply. 'Please don't say no without taking time to think about this chance. It may never come again.' He looked pleadingly at her. 'Miriam-*jan*, there is such sadness in your eyes. You need to come back – not just to keep a promise made to us but one I am sure you made to yourself – and Jawad.'

Miriam looked away, staring unseeingly through the window. Finally, she turned to Ismail standing silently beside her. 'I have to go now. Eva needs me in the clinic.' Seeing him about to say something more she whispered, as much to herself as to him, 'I will think about it.'

ELEVEN

Sang-i-Sia September 1995

'Why didn't Ismail Khan stop them?'

'He's gone.'

'Stop who? Who's gone?' Iqbal asked, removing his shoes at the open doorway of the headmaster's door. He straightened up and stepped into the room, embracing the two men who'd risen to their feet, their arms outstretched. 'What's happened?'

Malim Ashraf, a small, wiry man whose metal-rimmed spectacles gave him a bookish appearance that fitted his role as headmaster, sat down saying, 'You've not listened to the radio today then?'

Iqbal shook his head, not admitting he seldom bothered to tune in to the news since Miriam and Ruckshana went away. He missed them, more than he could've imagined. At first, anger had sustained him. After work each day he climbed the steep path to the house, calling at Fatima's to collect the bread, lingering for a few minutes to chat before walking the final few yards home. Self-pity replaced anger when he sat in the silent house that was so cheerless without his family. Ruckshana's kitten, also lonely, would pounce on his bare toes, encouraging him to play with her. Later, she'd sneak onto his lap, curling into a tight ball as though hoping he'd not notice and send her out. He let her stay, the purrs vibrating the tiny warm body reminding him of Ruckshana.

He spent less time with his friends. At first he avoided their company, fearing they'd think him weak for allowing Miriam to go to Charkoh. When, however, he met Ashraf for the first time after Miriam's departure the headmaster took him by surprise by commending him for allowing his wife to go to the teaching camp to further her medical knowledge. He'd searched the man's face for any hint that he was secretly mocking him but only admiration showed in his expression. Even so, other than a mumbled acknowledgement, Iqbal kept quiet about Miriam's disappearance from the family home – not everyone would be as progressive in their thinking as Malim Ashraf. Now, though sure, almost sure, his friends were not laughing at him he still visited less often to avoid that lonely homecoming for a second time in the day.

He looked questioningly from Ashraf to his companion, Commander Moosa whose face wore a worried frown in place of its usual good-natured smile. Stroking the wispy moustache scarcely visible on his upper lip, Moosa said, 'Taliban have taken Herat. Ismail Khan, with some of his men fled across the border to Iran. Many others were captured.'

'How could it happen?' Iqbal exclaimed. What's Rabbani doing about it?'

Malim Ashraf, his voice laden with contempt for the President in Kabul, said, 'He makes noises, that's all. He told Taliban they must leave Herat immediately or he'll bomb them.' He shrugged, adding, 'Taliban replied by saying if Rabbani doesn't leave Kabul at once they'll bomb **him**.'

'They think they can capture Kabul?' Iqbal's voice was incredulous. 'Don't they remember how they failed last time they tried?'

When Moosa remained silent, Ashraf replied, 'They've had time to re-group, re-arm and become better organised, but even so,' he added, 'I don't think there's a chance they can take Kabul. Surely now, Rabbani, Gulbedin, Dostum and Wadhat will get together to re-take Herat and stop any further advance.' He checked his watch and turned on the radio. 'We might hear something more now.' The three men fell silent as the World Service came on but other than a short item reporting the city appeared peaceful there was no information on the situation.

Over the next few days it became apparent the 'peace' in Herat was achieved through Taliban's brutal enforcement of new edicts. The men in the city were summoned to the sports stadium to witness the execution of a young man accused of shooting two Taliban soldiers. While Islamic slogans were played at full volume through speakers around the stadium he was hanged from a crane. Women were summarily sacked from their jobs. Girls' schools were closed. Televisions and video recorders, considered a corrupting influence and therefore un-Islamic, were hanged in mock executions, while music cassettes were broken open, their miles of tape festooning the city like strange garlands.

Iqbal listened to the talk around him. Malim Ashraf, who was on the point of securing funding from an overseas agency to open a school for girls in Sang-i-Sia, kept telling people it was Taliban who acted in an un-Islamic way by denying girls an education. Someone else pointed out that if women were not allowed to work there was no point of educating them anyway. Drivers who passed through Sang-i-Sia told of how much easier and safer travelling had become on Taliban controlled roads. Iqbal felt increasingly uneasy as more stories came out of Herat – of a man accused of murder being shot in the back by a member of his victim's family, of thieves having their hands amputated. As a Muslim he wanted to see his country become a true Islamic state but if these stories were true then they were the actions of extremists who'd gone far beyond anything Islam taught.

His thoughts turned again and again to Miriam, wondering what her reaction to the fall of Herat had been. She would surely have heard it on the radio; everyone at the camp would be discussing it. Would she be afraid Taliban's fist would grab more of the country? She wouldn't be fearful for herself, but for her children. How would Ruckshana receive an education if there were no girls' schools? Would Miriam think of leaving Afghanistan? Always at that point his thoughts would stop, circle back and begin again.

What worried him most about the current situation was how, as the days went by with no action from Rabbani's forces, it seemed already an accepted fact that Herat would remain in Taliban's grip. Gradually, discussions about what was happening in the city became less frequent as people turned their attention to more pressing aspects of their own lives. The miller was working full time, his donkey engine providing a constant background throb to village life. People waited for travellers returning from Kabul with winter supplies of sugar, rice, tea. Others spread fresh mud on their flat rooftops to make them weatherproof before the first snows came.

At the clinic one day Iqbal received a message that his father urgently wished to see him. Fearing he was ill, he asked his field assistant Hassan, to take over and, excusing himself to the remaining patients hurried out to the Toyota. His sister Zakia met him at the door of his father's house, bursting into noisy sobs the moment she saw him. Alarmed, he rushed by her without bothering to remove his shoes. His father was sitting in his usual place by the window. He looked well enough, though clearly distraught. 'What's wrong? What's happened?' Iqbal knelt beside his father, taking his hand. His father's eyes filled with tears but although he opened his mouth to speak, no sound came out.

Zakia appeared beside him, wiping her eyes. 'It's Hassan,' she whispered. For a moment Iqbal, thinking of his assistant, was confused then he understood she meant his brother Hassan. 'A letter came...' she gulped back her tears, 'he had a fever – we don't know what it was but... Oh, Iqbal,' she wailed, 'he's dead.'

'Who sent the letter?'

'His son. He says the family is coming home.'

'When? When are they coming?' Iqbal realised he was asking the wrong questions but ignored the disapproving look his sister gave him.

'They'll be here any day now, may even have arrived already. They'll go first to her family.' She stared hard at him. 'Do you have no tears for your brother? Nothing to say to your father in his grief?'

He looked at his father. He seemed to have suddenly shrunk. 'I'm sorry for your loss, father.' He reached out for his father's hand, placing his fingers on the pulse, counting silently. 'I'll send something over with Ha... with my field assistant, in case you can't sleep.' He rose and left the room. Zakia followed him, catching hold of his sleeve as he reached the front door.

'Iqbal! He needs you – not as his doctor, as his son. Please stay. Talk to him.'

'I'm sorry Zakia, I can't stay.'

She tugged again on his sleeve as he made to leave, pulling him round to face her. 'He loves you, Iqbal.'

He shook himself free and scrubbed at his face with both hands before answering. 'I used to think that, too. Even after the horrors of Band-i-Amir I thought he loved me as much as he loved all his family. Then, after what happened over Zohra... ' He shook his head, clearing a painful image. 'I'll come back in a day or two – but if you're worried about his health send for me immediately.' He looked at his sister's tear-streaked face for a moment before leaning forward to drop a kiss on her brow. 'Sorry, Zakia, I can't be a hypocrite.'

He drove to the site of the new clinic, bumping the jeep off the road. He sat for a while, engine idling, feeling a sense of shame – it was no way for an Afghan son to act towards his father – but unable to return to the house, to sit wearing a shabby veneer of filial respect and love, beside his heart-broken father. His father would ask for, expect, his forgiveness, needing it to absolve himself of any blame for Hassan's death. He switched off the engine, climbed out and began to pace. How much would Zohra have changed? Had she been happy? Had she thought of him during those years in Iran?

**

Zohra was chattering with a cluster of girls at the well, waiting her turn to draw water. Some boys hiding behind a boulder on the mountainside were trying to attract the girls' attention by throwing small stones to land with a gentle thud and a puff of dust at their feet. More stones fell close to Zohra's feet than those of anyone else but, unlike the other girls, she didn't giggle or cast quick, furtive glances towards the boulder from behind which the boys' grinning faces sometimes peeped. That was what attracted Iqbal to her; even more than her lovely face with its creamy complexion. He longed to reach out and touch it, see if it was really as soft as it looked. Zohra would never look at him, not with his disease.

He was sitting under a tree in the empty schoolyard one day, putting the finishing touches to a toy donkey cart he was carving. Absorbed, he didn't hear footsteps approach and started when a soft voice spoke close to him.

'That's lovely. You're so clever.'

Looking up, he caught a gleam of dark eyes, full lips curved in a smile before, embarrassed, he looked down again at his hands holding the wooden cart.

'You can have it.' He held out the toy. Stupid, stupid, what will a girl want with a donkey cart?

'Oh, I couldn't take it.'

His shoulders slumped and a soft sigh escaped him.

She spoke again, 'My brother would love a toy like this.'

'Take it – give it to your brother.' He felt her take the toy from his hands. Most people preferred not to touch anything he had touched but he saw Zohra was now running her fingers over the carving.

'You're Iqbal, aren't you?' He nodded. 'Why are you always alone? I never see you with the other boys.'

He hung his head, mumbling, 'They don't want me.'

'Why do you think that?'

Her voice was gentle, but was she taunting him? Surely she must know of his illness, that he was *jizami*? He sneaked a look at her expression and saw only interested concern.

'I have leprosy,' he said, pointing to the nodules on his face.

She nodded, 'Mhm. My father said he knew a man once with the same disease. He went to Pakistan because they have medicines there to cure it.'

Iqbal was speechless with astonishment. Firstly that Zohra hadn't recoiled in horror from him and secondly that she had been talking to her father about him. Over-riding all of that, she spoke as though leprosy could be cured.

'Me…medicine?'

She nodded. 'But I don't know anything about it. Only that in Pakistan people can be treated. I have to go now. Thanks for the cart.'

Iqbal stared after her as she hurried off, then jumped to his feet and ran for home to tell his father the amazing news that his disease could be cured – if only he could get to Pakistan. His footsteps slowed – could his father afford to send him there? By the time he was kicking his sandals off at the door his excitement had cooled. Being taken to Pakistan was an impossible dream. His father made it clear to him often enough he thought Iqbal should leave school and, like his older brother, Hassan, start earning his keep by working on the land. Only his mother's gentle, but persistent, intervention, persuaded his father to let him stay until the twelfth class.

He repeated Zohra's conversation to his father but the question of whether or not the family could find the money to send him to Pakistan didn't arise – his father simply refused to believe that any such medicine existed. 'I don't know why Allah has put this curse on you, my son. If Hazrat-i-Ali's power in the waters of Band-i-Amir could not cure you then there is nothing men in Pakistan can do. It's a hardship to bear, and I am truly sorry for you, but bear it you must for

whatever reason.' Iqbal didn't argue with his father but privately
resolved to ask Zohra – if he ever had the chance to speak to her again
– more about this medicine.

He saw Zohra on several occasions over the next couple of weeks. It
took him some time to understand these meetings were not the
fortuitous accidents he at first thought. Gradually it dawned on him
Zohra sought him out, most often in his favourite place under the tree
in the playground but sometimes on the path leading to his father's
fields, and she did so because for some reason she enjoyed his
company. This realisation went a long way to compensate for her
knowing nothing more about the medicine she'd mentioned. She only
knew her father had met the man when he lived in Kabul. The only
other thing she said on the subject, which Iqbal stored away in his
memory to be taken out and re-examined whenever he felt the
hopelessness of having leprosy, was that her father had told her that
for every illness in the world, Allah provided a cure, or at least gave
people the means of discovering it.

Zohra often brought her small brother along, telling Iqbal he wanted
to see how he carved the wooden toys he made. He would have
preferred to talk to Zohra alone but he knew the real reason for
bringing her brother along was that she was already aware of the need
to protect herself from pointing fingers and village gossip. He
willingly tried to teach a somewhat resentful Ali – who would have
much preferred to play with his own friends – how to do simple
carvings. Having a friend – someone who took away a loneliness of
which he hadn't been aware – brought a joy into Iqbal's life that made
the world brighter. Still shunned by his class fellows, called names,
made fun of, he spent most of his time out of school alone, but the
time he spent in Zohra's company, made life, not only bearable, but
happy. He loved her.

Over the winter months, when snow reached the rooftops, it was
impossible to meet. School was closed. The animals were kept inside,
their body heat rising, sweetish, steamy, to add to the overpowering
stuffiness of the living rooms above. Iqbal carved more wooden toys
than Zohra's brother could ever play with. When at last the thaw
began, the livestock were let out, dancing and prancing around stiff-
legged and astonished at the snow, recovering their forgotten freedom,
Iqbal looked forward to meeting Zohra.

He went to the tree in the playground, its branches still bare, and waited. She didn't come the first day, nor the second, nor the third. He took to wandering around in the weak sunshine, re-visiting other old haunts. His longing to see her gnawed at him. School started and he sought out her brother, Ali. He was with a group of friends who stared with hostile eyes at Iqbal. Ali looked uncomfortable.

'I've been making more toys for you,' Iqbal said after greeting the younger boy. 'Do you want to…?'

'Oh, I'm too old to play with such baby things,' Ali replied, cutting him off. Stung, Iqbal turned and walked away, the boys' jeers in his ears.

It was weeks – miserable weeks – before he saw Zohra waiting her turn at the well. She was wearing a chaddar and when she saw him approach she pulled an edge of it across the lower part of her face, turning her head away. She was turning a knife in his heart and he about-turned, walking swiftly in the opposite direction, blinking back hot tears. She'd liked him all summer – how could her feelings have changed? Anger rose. Surely he deserved some explanation? He paused, glancing back to where she was drawing up the bucket and filling her water jugs. Almost without thinking, he changed direction again, moving, unseen, behind the well until he came out on the path to Zohra's home. In a small copse of poplar trees he waited, hoping she would be alone.

He watched her approach. Her chaddar had slipped and he could see her black hair, pinned back on either side with silver clips in the shape of birds, framing her face. Her cheeks still had that same creamy complexion he remembered, the same full lips, though now they were not smiling. He saw with a pang that she looked unhappy and his anger dissolved to be replaced with a longing to comfort her, to make her happy, see her smile. She walked past his hiding place without glancing in his direction but after a few steps, her pace slowed and he realised she'd spotted him. He was by her side in seconds.

'Zohra,' he said her name softly then stopped, not knowing what to say next. He suddenly knew everything was different although he couldn't have articulated what or why. She was different. She was still Zohra, but there were something about her that made his heart beat in a way it never had before. His mouth went dry and when she looked up at him, her lips now forming a shy smile he felt a stirring of arousal and, thoroughly embarrassed, afraid she would notice, he suddenly lurched towards her, his hands reaching for the water containers. 'Let me take those for you.' She pulled away, slopping water on the ground. He stared at where it splashed her feet shod in the black rubber Russian shoes all the women wore.

'No, it's all right. I can manage.' She tightened her grip on the handles. 'Iqbal, I'm sorry but…well…it's difficult now. I…I can't talk to you like before.'

Putting the water jugs on the ground, she pulled her chaddar back onto her head, tossing one end over her shoulder to keep it in place. She blushed under his gaze, turning her head away. He realised what she was trying to tell him – she was no longer a girl child, but a young woman. He, standing here talking to her without a chaperone, was putting her honour, her father's honour, at risk. He should say goodbye, walk away, not cause her any trouble but he stood, irresolute. For the first time in his life he gave conscious thought to the rules governing his life. He suddenly wanted to challenge these unwritten laws dictating how he must now behave. He didn't feel that continuing last summer's friendship was wrong. And yet, and yet, his physical response a moment ago had shown his feelings towards Zohra had changed. It was his turn to blush and Zohra picked up the water jugs and began to walk away.

'Goodbye Iqbal,' she murmured over her shoulder.

'No, wait.' He caught up with her, moved in front of her. 'Please don't think badly of me, but I don't want to stop seeing you …' He gulped, 'I need you…you're my…' He was going to say friend but realised in that instant Zohra meant more to him than any friend ever would. She was his life. 'Zohra, last year – though you maybe didn't know it – I gave you my heart. It's still yours. Please don't break it.' When her eyes met his this time, she didn't look away and he felt hope rise, leaping like a crackerjack in his chest.

'I know, Iqbal, and you have mine.' She fell silent for a moment then continued, 'Maybe I can meet you tomorrow, in the afternoon. I can't say what time – or even if I can manage to get away. Where will I find you?'

'I'll wait for you in the *assia*.' The flourmill stood idle at this time of year. Zohra nodded, frowning slightly and Iqbal could have kicked himself. What made him choose a place that so often featured in jokes about illicit relationships? Then she gave him an impish grin and walked away leaving him wanting to shout the news of his good fortune to the whole world. Instead he went home to lie on a *toshak*, daydreaming until his father shouted at him to go and chop fuel wood.

They met as often as they dared in the following months; sometimes in the *assia*, once or twice they crept into a field when the wheat was tall and golden, hiding them from prying eyes, or at the far side of the copse of poplar trees. Those meetings, whether they were for a snatched ten minutes or a more leisurely hour or two, were never long enough. He told her, one day about the nightmarish 'treatment' to which his father had subjected him at Band-i-Amir. He ended saying, 'I've always believed my father would rather I was dead than have this disease.' She reached forward to brush away the tears glistening on his cheeks. He caught her wrist and kissed her fingertips before turning her hand over to plant a soft kiss on her palm. When she didn't pull away Iqbal wished an earthquake would open the ground and swallow them up before real life intruded and this moment of perfect happiness would vanish.

Iqbal was desperate for his final year in school to end. He was seventeen. He was a man now and though he'd little desire to join his brother on the land he wanted the world to see he was an adult. Sometimes he told Zohra he was sick of school but she always persuaded him it was important to continue his studies, that his learning would be useful when he went to Pakistan. She never doubted his leprosy would be cured. He used to look in a mirror at home, wondering how she could bear to touch him – his eyebrows had almost disappeared, his earlobes were, to his eyes, repulsively thick and hideous red nodules spotted his face. She shook her head, telling him he exaggerated, but did not play down his need to seek treatment. He had no idea how long he would have to be away and the thought of leaving Zohra behind was torture.

'How can I live without you?'

She gazed calmly back at him. 'You wouldn't need to.'

***

Iqbal gave a sudden shiver. That was the moment when a thunderbolt should have struck them both – when Zohra said she would marry him.

He shook his head to dislodge the memories trying to crowd in, tormenting memories of his helplessness when his dreams had turned to dust and Zohra was lost to him. She would be back to the village soon, but would she be back in his life? He could marry her now – if she would still have him. People would think it only proper that he took on the role of provider for his dead brother's widow. The woman he should have married long ago, if only his father had not been so afraid that his grandchildren would be born bearing the marks of leprosy.

'I can't, I can't forgive you.' Realising he'd spoken the words aloud he turned back to the jeep, slamming the door behind him. His thoughts turned to Miriam. She would understand his turmoil. If only he could talk to her about all of this – about Zohra, about his father's actions, about the loss of his dream. He gave a wry smile as he started the engine – no, perhaps not.

TWELVE

Charkoh September 1995

Miriam, along with everyone in Charkoh, heard the news of Taliban's capture of Herat with shock, which turned to horror as details of the atrocities filtered through. The staff room buzzed with animated talk, which even Jeanine's arrival in the room didn't quieten for a moment, about whether or not Rabbani would carry out his threat to bomb the fundamentalists, about whether they would once again advance on Kabul.

Listening to the discussions, Miriam desperately hoped Anwar and the others were right to believe Taliban would be stopped. If they weren't, if they took Kabul, then what would be the country's future – her children's? Ruckshana wouldn't be attending Malim Ashraf's new school. There would be no school for girls. Most of Hazara Jat had been too remote for the Soviets to bother with but even if the same held true for Taliban Ruckshana and Farid couldn't remain there forever – university meant Kabul or Mazar. What sort of education would the universities provide under Taliban? It was so impossible to imagine Taliban could enforce its draconian laws throughout the country she took comfort in the others' assessment of the situation. But then no one had thought a bunch of students could take Herat. And all the time a part of her brain continued to whirl with thoughts of Ismail and Zardgul.

Eventually, people began to speak less about Taliban, turn their attention from the larger political stage to matters of importance in their daily lives: Jeanine held her daily lectures, patients queued up to consult the doctors. Miriam had avoided meeting Ismail alone and still had no answer for him. When he came to tell her he was returning with the patients to Zardgul he didn't, to her surprise, try again to persuade her. Without thinking she repeated the travellers' blessing, 'Go safely and come back quickly'.

'I'll do that,' he said with a smile, 'bringing a horse for you.' She opened her mouth to protest but he shook his head. 'Don't say anything now. Give me your answer when I return.' He turned and walked away. She watched but he didn't look back. What should she do? She headed for the clinic. Work would stop her having to think for a few hours, but she must make a decision soon.

She stopped to speak to Amina and Fatima. Now both Moh'd Sarwar and little Leila were gaining weight and no longer so much at risk, the atmosphere in the tiny space, curtained off from the consulting room, was cheerful. The two mothers spent most of the day listening in on consultations behind the curtain. Sometimes Miriam would hear them giggling quietly when she or Chaman were teaching a woman how to calculate her fertile days, both able to recite the formula word perfectly. In fact they had picked up so much medical knowledge Eva told them they must surely be halfway to becoming doctors themselves. Sometimes she referred mothers with sickly children to 'Dr' Amina and 'Dr' Fatima to reinforce messages about good nutrition and suitable weaning foods. Today, Moh'd Sarwar was going home and Amina was packing their meagre belongings.

Chaman arrived, the first patient of the morning at her heels. The woman, holding a plump toddler on her lap, sat down. When Eva asked what the trouble was she complained of not having had any children. Pointing to the infant, Eva asked whose it was. 'It's my daughter's baby.' The woman looked crossly at Chaman who had been unable to stifle a sudden giggle when Eva pointed out to have a grandchild, she must have had children. 'But that was twenty years ago,' she declared. 'I never had any more – and I would like a son. Can you not give me medicine?' Eva shook her head but the woman went on, 'I heard there's a medicine women take in your country and afterwards they have three or four babies.' She looked expectantly at Eva, adding, on a pleading note, 'I only need one.'

Eva raised her eyes heavenwards, muttering something in German. Seeing Miriam and Chaman's blank faces she apologised, saying, 'I was asking myself why I didn't specialise in orthopaedics.'

The women were finishing their tea break when they heard a truck pull up outside the compound. Even as they were beginning the steep descent from the staff room the sound of running feet and shouted directions alerted them to an emergency. Dr Helene, running past, carrying two saline drips, called out, 'Your room, Eva, quickly.'

There was hardly space in the room for all the people crowding in. Miriam glimpsed Fatima, cradling Leila, huddled in a corner watching in bewilderment as Dr Helene knelt on the floor inserting a drip, instructing Eva to take the second one. Two children, pale and listless, lay on mattresses on the floor. Their parents, along with an older boy stood watching in silence. Hussain appeared at the doorway carrying glasses and two enamel teapots. 'ORS,' he announced, his usual cheerful expression solemn, adding, 'though they'll need a lot more than this. They're completely dehydrated – had diarrhoea for days.'

'Where have they come from?' Miriam asked, taking the drinks from him.

'Iran. You know the Iranian government's been evicting refugees. By force they are making them to go back to Afghanistan.' At Miriam's nod, he continued, 'In last weeks, thousands are crossing border. This family is with big convoy. Too many people are sick. One already has died. In Lal sar Jangal they are hearing about teaching camp and doctors here.'

By the time Dr Helene left to return to her own clinic the children, a boy and a girl, were lying side by side each with a drip inserted, nails banged in the wall providing makeshift drip stands. Their mother, Zubeida, her face expressionless and her eldest son, Ghulam Ali, a youth, Miriam guessed of about fifteen, sat beside them. The father had disappeared to the bazaar. The cheerful atmosphere present in the room that morning had vanished. Fatima, still holding Leila in her arms, was crouched in a corner as far from the family as possible. Eva rose after making a final adjustment to one of the drips and moved towards her consulting room, asking Miriam if 'Dr' Fatima would encourage the mother to keep offering the children ORS and, if possible, get them to eat.

Miriam translated but before Fatima could reply, Ghulam Ali snapped, 'We don't need her help. You should move her out of here, we need more space.' When Miriam began to explain there was no other space he turned his back on her. Taken aback by his bad manners, an angry retort rose to her lips then she glanced at the children. Probably worry over their condition was the cause of his rudeness. She smiled apologetically at Fatima and called the first patient. Throughout the day one or other of the women checked on the children, urging their mother to get them to drink.

'They don't like it,' she replied. Seeing the little girl eyeing the glass she held in her hand Miriam offered it to her. The girl nodded. Miriam helped her to sit up and she took a few sips after which her brother took a drink before sinking back, exhausted from even such slight exertion. Their mother shrugged. Later, she shook her head at the apples Eva brought and only when the children indicated they wanted to eat did Ghulam Ali, with ill grace, peel, slice and share out the fruit.

The father returned and for the remainder of the day he and the older brother helped one or other of the children to the latrine, one supporting the child, the other carrying the drip. The only time Zubeida voluntarily spoke to anyone was when she pointed out her son was fouling the mattress because he could no longer tell them on time when he had to use the latrine. After Miriam found some plastic sheeting she sat with the mother for a while, hoping she might become more responsive but to all her questions about Iran the woman answered in monosyllables, never volunteering information nor asking any questions in return. Later, admitting her failure to Chaman she added it was sometimes difficult to understand what the mother said when she did speak.

'It's her accent,' Chaman agreed. 'They lived in Iran for more than twelve years. Only the oldest boy was born in Afghanistan. They come from Naoor originally but are thinking for many years Iran is their home.'

Next morning the two children seemed a little brighter, the girl even managing a smile when Eva handed her a hardboiled egg. Fatima, called Miriam over and whispered urgently in her ear, 'I don't care if you send us home,' she said, 'but I'm not staying here another minute. I've tried my best. I've offered to make the ORS for them. Said I'll sit with the children if she wants to go out but I just get abused. They've brought bad luck in here. I don't want it affecting my Leila.' Although she knew she should ignore Fatima's superstitious fears Miriam couldn't help feeling the family from Iran had brought something dark into the room. She managed to find space in the waiting room tent in which to squeeze Fatima and Leila.

It was at the end of the day, shortly after Eva had seen the last patient, the boy died. After a few moments Eva reached up to stop the drip. Ghulam Ali refused to believe it was over. Feeling for a heartbeat on the lifeless body he screamed at Eva to say his little brother would be all right, while his mother wept, tearing at her clothes, crying out for her son to live. 'He was my heart, my liver, my light. Why not take the other one? Why did it have to be him?' Chaman moved to the mother's side, putting her arms round her. Miriam stood rooted to the spot, her eyes on the little girl, lying as still as death herself, listening to her mother try to barter her life with Allah in exchange for her favourite. Her eyes shifted to the mother who was tearing at her hair, having pushed Chaman's restraining arms away. No longer able to bear being in the room, she rushed out, breathing in gulps of cool, evening air.

She hurried, almost running, to the staff room, where she knew Ruckshana would be waiting for her to come and eat. She was suddenly desperate to hold her daughter in her arms, wishing with all her being Farid was here with her. The thought of losing either of her children was equally devastating. She had witnessed, too many times, the near-madness of a mother whose child had died, had heard their attempts to plea bargain with Allah, but it had always been their own lives they were willing to exchange for the life of their child. She reflected on all the woman had been through over the last few weeks: the trauma of the family's forced eviction, travelling for days crammed in an overcrowded truck, not knowing whether their family land in Naoor would still belong to them, witnessing the deaths of several fellow travellers followed by the illness of her own children. The death of her youngest son, she thought, may well have tipped the woman over the edge into some kind of, hopefully temporary, insanity – establishing a whole new set of problems for which none of the medical workers at the camp had expertise to solve. The most they could offer was a few Diazepam.

Although on admission she had been the stronger of the children, Latifa's condition deteriorated over the next couple of days. Zubeida sat all day, speaking to no one, her dull eyes staring into nothing. Usually Ghulam Ali ignored his little sister so when they heard him talking to her Miriam and Chaman shamelessly eavesdropped. Seeing them flush with anger, Eva asked what was being said. Chaman translated, 'He's asking her when she's going to die. He's saying,' her voice trembling with rage, Chaman continued, 'will you die today or tomorrow? He is saying her if she's going to die she should do quickly so they can leave here.' Eva wanted to intervene but Chaman shook her head saying it wouldn't do any good and intervention might even turn him more against her.

'Okay, but we're going to monitor them closely from now on. I want to know the child's not being denied the fluids and food she needs. She's going to get better.' Whatever the truth of the matter no one ever really knew but within two days of the women's increased watchfulness, Latifa was showing marked signs of improvement. Miriam watched her tucking into a plate of rice and *lubia* with evident relish. Her cheeks were already looking fuller and her eyes were bright and clear. She would be able to leave soon. Miriam saw the child hand her empty plate to her mother with a satisfied smile before leaning forward to hook her thin arms around the woman's neck and plant a kiss on her cheek. She turned away, a catch in her throat, marvelling at a child's unconditional love for a parent.

It was a relief to everyone when the family left to resume their journey, bringing a lightening of the atmosphere throughout the whole clinic compound. Their departure, however, reminded Miriam Ismail would soon return. What was she to tell him? When she broached the subject of taking three or four days to visit Zardgul with Jeanine, the doctor was in favour of her going. 'Yes, good idea. I'm sure we should open a clinic there but I need more information to prepare the funding application. Explore a little, find out if there is a suitable location, what accommodation is available and information on the distance to the nearest health services.'

'But what about my work here? We're still so busy – we never finish before 6 or 7 in the evening. How will Eva manage without a translator?'

'Oof, Eva tells me Chaman's English is quite good. She'll have more opportunity to practise if you're not around for a few days. For heaven's sake, Miriam, why ask me if it's all right to go then put forward arguments when I say yes? Really don't have time for this.'

Trying to understand her inability to make the decision kept Miriam awake. She had talked to Chaman who after listening to her going round and round in circles, had encouraged her to go. 'It is good chance for you. I think so good chance does not come again. But, Miriam-*jan* only you can make decide what to do.'

Now, with Chaman and the children fast asleep she lay awake. It had been her dream to return to Zardgul to visit Jawad's grave, to say goodbye properly. To hear exactly how he'd lost his life. She grimaced in the dark at the thought of Iqbal finding out she'd done this behind his back. He'd be beyond anger. She'd be doing something – not just going to Zardgul without him, but going off alone with a man who was not family – that would be talked about the length and breadth of Sang-i-Sia valley. Wouldn't it confirm he was right to try and prevent her from coming to Charkoh?

Need he ever know? It would be impossible to hide her trip from people here at Charkoh but the chances of Iqbal meeting anyone from the teaching camp in the near future were slim. Winter was coming and the snow would make travel between clinics impossible. It would be months before he met anyone who knew she'd gone to Zardgul. By then it would have been forgotten, not worth mentioning. She sat up, turned her pillow to the cool side, lay down again. She didn't like being sneaky. Would she be able to look him in the eye knowing what she'd done? She thumped her pillow with her fist. He'd promised her in Quetta, hand on his heart, that he would take her to Zardgul. They'd taken Farid for a picnic. Iqbal had borrowed a car and they'd driven into the wildness of the rugged countryside outside the city. Wasn't so concerned about what people would say then, driving around the countryside without a chaperone.

***

Instead of heading for Hanna Lake, a favourite picnic spot with both local people and the many foreign aid workers living in the city, Iqbal turned the borrowed car in another direction. Soon they were driving on a deeply rutted, stony track between barren mountains whose precipitous slopes were cut by deep ravines and gorges. 'We'll stop at a place I know a little further on,' Iqbal said. 'There's a small stream. Perhaps Farid will see some fish in it, or go for a paddle. I hope you won't find it boring?' This last remark was addressed to Farid who replied with a slight, non-committal smile.

Miriam saw Iqbal's face cloud over at the boy's lack of enthusiasm. She knew he was trying hard to win her son over but Farid remained distant and uncommunicative with Iqbal. He was always well mannered, thanking him politely for gifts he brought, but he never played with any of the toys Iqbal gave him. She longed to be able to hug and kiss away Farid's pain as she had when he was a toddler and kisses could soothe everything from scraped knees to lost teddies. A lost daddy was something else and her heart ached for her son. For the year they were in Scotland she'd done everything she could to make sure Farid would remember his father while they were apart. Photos of him were all around the house. Every night she'd asked Farid what he wanted to tell his daddy about his day, and she would write in the big scrapbook they were keeping to show him when they went back home. She looked, now, at Iqbal's set jaw and murmured, 'Give him more time – it's too soon for him.'

He opened his mouth to reply but at that moment as they rounded a spur of mountain a volley of shots rang out. A band of *dacoits*, turbaned, bearded, wearing loose baggy trousers, bandoliers slung across their chests with rifles held aloft, galloped towards them. 'Oh, my God,' she screamed, 'get us out of here.' The track was too narrow to turn the vehicle and, his face white, Iqbal slammed on the brakes. As the car skidded to a halt, Miriam, reaching for Farid, was astounded to hear Iqbal give a huge shout of laughter.

'It's all right. It's a movie. Look! Look over there.' He was pointing towards a cleft in the mountains into which the riders, before reaching their car, had veered off. Now they were milling about listening to a man with a film camera on his shoulder. Another, carrying a furry microphone, seemed to be adjusting the controls on a recording device. 'I'd heard this area was sometimes used for filming.' He opened the door saying, 'I'll go and check we're not going to be in the way.'

'Can I come with you?' Miriam hadn't heard such excitement in Farid's voice for a long time. Iqbal looked pleased but nodded as though nothing was unusual in the boy voluntarily addressing him, much less ask to accompany him. They headed towards the gorge, where now Miriam could see other people had joined the horsemen and cameraman, including a glamorous creature, with pouty lips, whom she took to be the leading lady. Dressed in a gorgeous, crimson *ghagra choli* encrusted with stones that dazzled in the sunlight, the woman was smiling at Farid who hung back shyly.

Iqbal returned alone. The leading brigand had invited Farid to help 'direct' the movie. He was now sitting beside the real director, taking occasional furtive peeps at the sultry actress. 'The picnic spot is only a couple of hundred yards over there,' Iqbal indicated a place where a few stunted shrubs grew. 'We can leave the car here.' He lifted out a rug and the basket Anna's cook had packed with their lunch, handed Miriam the thermos of tea and moved away. Miriam lingered for a few moments watching Farid, noting with pleasure how animated his thin face had become, before turning to follow him. She gazed at the rocky landscape. It looked like some parts of Afghanistan. As though he'd read her mind Iqbal said, 'It reminds me of home – though Sang-i-Sia is not as bleak as this place. In the springtime the orchards in the valley are beautiful with blossom – almond, cherry, apple.'

'There's no fruit in Zardgul,' Miriam said. 'It made things difficult when advising mothers on what to give their kids to eat. I always worried about Farid's diet although we grew our own vegetables and had plenty of dried fruit.'

'Despite your worries, he's a fine healthy boy, *Mash'Allah*.' Iqbal nodded in the direction of where they'd left Farid with the film crew, 'Have you told him about us?'

Miriam had not been surprised when Iqbal had asked her to marry him. She had not even pretended to need time to consider his proposal. The look of sheer delight and gladness on his face when she said yes, took her aback. She experienced a pang of guilt. Would he realise he could never make her feel such happiness? How was she to tell Farid?

'Not yet,' she said in reply. Before he could say anything she hurried on, 'Right now he's a very confused little boy. I took him away from his father then, just when he thought he was going back home to be with him again I'd to tell him he'd died and that we couldn't go back to Zardgul. He's too young to express his feelings – probably doesn't even understand what he's feeling. I can't tell him just yet his mother's going to marry someone else, giving him a new daddy.' She looked at Iqbal, pleadingly, 'I will tell him – soon, I promise.'

Pulling the picnic basket towards her she began unpacking. There was a whole, cooked chicken, salad, hardboiled eggs, yoghurt, *nan*, fruit and a plastic box of brownies. 'Wow!' she exclaimed, 'Hassan must've thought we were going camping for a week.' Indicating the film people she added, 'Should we invite them to join us?'

Iqbal, dismembering the chicken, shook his head vehemently. 'The first time I have the chance to be completely alone with my future wife she wants to invite a film crew along?' Piling some choice chicken pieces on a *nan* he added a bunch of red grapes and handed it to Miriam. Their fingers brushed as she took it from him and for a moment or two they held each other's gaze. Miriam thought he was going to kiss her but the sound of voices carrying from the film set reminded them they were not entirely alone. They smiled shyly at one another before turning their attention to the food. Miriam put some chicken on one side for Farid.

'What does he remember about Zardgul?' Iqbal asked.

'Very little. He wasn't quite three when we left.'

'That will make it easier,' Iqbal said. 'He'll soon forget.'

Miriam stared at him, resisting the temptation to throw her tea over him. He seemed not to notice the change in her expression but continued, 'I mean if you stop telling him stories about Zardgul he'll...' He left the sentence unfinished. 'What's wrong?'

'Get this straight, Iqbal,' Miriam remained calm though she was raging. 'I will never, repeat, never, stop telling Farid about Zardgul. It's his place of birth, and I will continue to remind him of that and of the time we lived there as a family. It was the place his father loved most in the world, and it was the place to which he dedicated,' she gulped, faltered, continued, 'gave his life.' Iqbal put a hand out towards her but she jerked away, continuing, 'You should understand, too, that **I** will never forget Zardgul.' Her hands twisting and pulling at the end of her chaddar, had found a loose thread and she was now, unconsciously, unravelling it.

'Oh Miriam, I don't expect you to forget. I was only thinking Farid would be less upset if ...I didn't mean what I said to sound so... so, well, maybe I was being insensitive.'

As though she hadn't heard him, Miriam went on, 'I wanted to go back as soon as I heard about Jawad. They said it wasn't possible then but I swore that one day I would take Farid back to Zardgul.' Choking sobs cut off her words and she buried her head in her lap. When she looked up, her face streaked with tears, she spoke, without looking directly at him, with a quiet intensity, 'My only wish, other than to see my son grow up healthy and happy, is to see where Jawad is buried, to say goodbye properly.'

'Miriam-*jan*, I'll take you there. Look at me, please.' She turned towards him as, kneeling before her, he placed his hand on his heart, saying, 'I promise I'll take you – and Farid. When we go to Afghanistan, I'll take you to Zardgul myself. I promise.'

This time she did not pull away when he reached out, but let him take and hold her hand. She lifted her eyes to his, 'Do you really mean that?' she whispered. When he repeated his promise she nodded. 'Thank you,' she said softly.

***

When they first moved to Sang-i-Sia she had asked from time to time when they would go to Zardgul. At first, it was because it was too soon, they hadn't yet settled but later there was always an excuse – fighting in the area, the jeep needed spare parts from Pakistan or he was expecting a consignment of medicines and couldn't leave in case it arrived when he was away. Once she'd asked outright if he didn't want her to go to Zardgul. He'd acted so hurt and angry – barely speaking to her for two days – that she doubted his word she'd felt guilty about asking. Eventually she stopped asking. Like she'd stopped asking to go out somewhere – anywhere – on a Friday for a picnic, for a walk. She'd tried so hard to fit in with the way Iqbal expected his wife to behave, staying at home, hidden away, not socialising with men, not even talking to them unless strictly necessary. And he had reneged on the only thing he had promised to do.

She sat up in bed, suddenly furious, not with Iqbal, but with herself. No one at home in Scotland would believe she was actually lying awake having this internal debate on whether or not to visit the grave of her late husband. What had happened to the woman who had married Jawad – the woman who knew her own mind, who went after what she wanted in life? With her right hand she held her left index finger. First question – did she want to go to Zardgul? Yes. She caught up the middle finger of her left hand. What's the worst, the very worst, that can happen if Iqbal finds out? He could divorce her, make her pack her bags and leave. But that would be a public acknowledgement of her unacceptable behaviour. Would Iqbal risk losing face by divorcing her? Was she prepared to take the risk?

The children stirred in their sleep. Chaman sat up, rubbing her eyes. '*Chi shood*?' – What happened?' she asked groggily.

'I'm going to Zardgul,' Miriam replied. 'Go back to sleep.' As Chaman threw herself back down, pulling the blanket over her head, muttering something inaudible but clearly in reference to her friend's mental stability Miriam laughed softly. She lay down and was asleep in seconds.

THIRTEEN

Charkoh September 1995

The decision taken, Miriam woke next morning refreshed and light-headed with relief. Chaman, who remembered nothing of being woken in the night, broke off combing Feroza's hair to hug Miriam when she heard her decision.

'I'm glad,' she said, 'you should've gone years ago.'

'I wish I was taking Farid.'

Starting to comb out the tangles in a squirming Leila's hair, Chaman said, 'When Farid's older he won't need someone to take him. He'll be able to go when he wants.'

Now Miriam was impatient for Ismail to return. Each morning, making her way towards the consulting room through the crowds of patients milling about, she was glad to know work would keep her mind occupied until he arrived. Pity there wasn't more time in the day to spend on changing mothers' beliefs about nutrition. It was frustrating to hear the same responses when asking women what their infants ate.

'You and Edwina Currie should get together sometime,' she muttered, to the bewilderment of the woman explaining the dangers of giving her eighteen-month old daughter an egg to eat – whether hard-boiled, poached or fried.

'These women believe you should starve a child, no?' demanded Eva. 'What is the problem with eggs?'

'Oh, they cause speech defects at the very least.'

'And mashed potatoes make them cough?'

'As well as swelling the stomach and giving the child wind. Dry nan, tea or water – all the nutrition a child needs. And where do you start,' she exclaimed in exasperation, 'when a woman tells you her arm injury was caused by a star falling out of the sky and hitting her?'

Eva shook her head. 'I think I cannot cope with more than one or two months of this. And I have always the knowledge I will return to Germany soon but you – you go back to your village to see these women every day. How do you stand it?' She ran her hands through her hair, dragging it back from her forehead. Her shoulders sagged.

'But I don't have so many patients every day in Sang-i-Sia,' Miriam protested. 'I'd be on my knees. And when I see a child such as Moh'd Sarwar, or little Leila, going home healthy …'

'But so few we can help,' Eva interrupted. 'I keep seeing the woman with mouth cancer.'

Miriam winced. Cancer, most probably from *naswar*, the powdered tobacco many people used, had eaten a hole completely through the woman's cheek. Her husband, when Eva said she could do nothing other than provide painkillers, said he would take her to Kabul. Miriam had struggled to translate when Eva said it was already too late.

'And that poor girl with the fistula,' Eva continued. 'Three days labour and a stillborn child is more than enough. To be left incontinent is too terrible. Her husband, I think should be shot for what he did.' Miriam agreed, remembering the pretty young woman, whose husband, believing force would hurry along his wife's protracted labour had jumped on her abdomen. He had later sent her back to her family because of her offensive smell. Repair might be possible in a city hospital but the family could not afford to take her. The smell of urine lingered long after the woman left the room.

'You have to remember the successes,' Miriam said. 'You can't afford to think about the overall health picture. It's too overwhelming.'

When Ismail arrived his face broke into a delighted smile the moment he saw Miriam. 'You don't have to tell me your answer,' he said, 'I can see it in your eyes. Oh, Miriama-*jan*, I am so happy you are coming back to Zardgul. Can you be ready to leave tomorrow?' She nodded, pushing away doubts creeping into her head.

The first fingers of light were barely showing when Miriam and Ruckshana left their room, moving quietly so as not to disturb Chaman and the girls. Just as Miriam's hand reached for the door handle, Chaman said, 'Don't you dare go without saying goodbye.'

The two women hugged and with Chaman's, 'Go quickly, come back safely,' sounding in her ears Miriam set off, Ruckshana's hand in hers, towards the gate. The cold air caught at her throat and the world gleamed white, sparkling with hoarfrost. Standing beside his own big chestnut, Ismail waited outside the compound, holding the reins of a grey mare for Miriam. She stroked the horse's nose, speaking softly to her, before swinging herself lightly up into the saddle. Ismail grinned at her as he settled Ruckshana, bundled in layers of warm clothing, in front of her. 'So, you still think horses can understand human talk, Miriam-*jan*?'

'Of course,' she replied, returning his grin, remembering his disbelief all those years ago when he'd first heard her talking to the horse Jawad had bought her in Zardgul. She'd called her Zeba, meaning beautiful. Ismail had laughed when he heard her talking to her, asking if her horse understood English or Dari and what the horse said in reply. No one, she discovered, talked to their horses, nor gave them names. They were a mode of transport.

'What shall we call our horse, Ruckshana?'

Her daughter thought for a few moments before saying in a decided way, 'Her name's Miveri.'

'Oh,' said Miriam, urging the horse to walk on. 'That's an unusual name. What does it mean?'

Ruckshana tutted, 'Nothing – it's her name.'

'Hear that, Ismail? From now on, this is Miveri. Come on, then, Miveri, let's see if you go as nicely as Zeba' At the touch of Miriam's heels the horse broke into a fast trot and they were soon heading away from the clinic, along the river's edge. As the sun rose, Miriam felt her doubts about the wisdom of making this journey into her past, without Iqbal's knowledge, fade away, vanishing like the frost. Within twenty minutes or so they left the road to follow a barely discernable track leading further into the mountain range. She relaxed, allowing herself to enjoy the sheer physical pleasure of the horse moving beneath her, the glorious morning, Ismail's company and her daughter's warm body snuggled against her own.

In the years since Miriam had last ridden, however, her body had forgotten and within a couple of hours her knees ached. From time to time she slipped first one foot, then the other, from the stirrup, straightening each knee in an attempt to ease the pain. She was glad when Ismail told her they would reach a *chaikhanna* after another half hour. When, after what seemed like hours rather than Ismail's estimated thirty minutes, she was finally able to dismount, her muscles screamed in protest. She hobbled into the low, dark building behind him. She must look like a ninety-year old. When her eyes were accustomed to the gloom she sank onto a mat, forcing her legs straight out in front of her. Ismail handed her his *patou* and, the woollen shawl covering her legs decently, she sighed in a mixture of agony and relief as Ruckshana pressed on them as she had seen the women do for each other since she was a baby. They were the only customers and Miriam wondered how the owner managed to make a living in such an out of the way place.

'He doesn't, really,' Ismail explained. 'He's a retired shepherd and runs his 'hotel' to keep himself busy. We may be his only customers today, though I know some of the herders call in for tea some days."

After breakfasting on fried eggs, *nan* and hot, sweet tea Miriam felt able to face the next stage of the journey. Often they rode companionably side-by-side without feeling the need to talk. When they did, she was careful to steer the conversation away from the past and anything connected with Jawad and her life in Zardgul. Ismail seemed content to follow her lead. He talked a little about Afghanistan's political situation, expressing his opinion that Taliban did not have the strength of numbers nor the military experience to take control of the country. As for the local politics Ismail told her the *shura* was keen to have a clinic in the area. 'I think there will be good co-operation from their side,' he said, 'and also they would be pleased to find an organisation to help fund a school.'

The landscape was changing now and they entered a rocky gorge, whose high cliffs towered above them on either side and in front of them. Ismail pulled up, pointing out a narrow path. 'Let me take Ruckshana for a while?' he suggested. Miriam gasped when she realised the route they were taking appeared to be almost vertical and allowed Ismail to lift Ruckshana, settling her in front of him before urging his horse on again. Hardly daring to breath, Miriam followed behind. The path was scarcely wide enough for a man to walk. Her view of the world narrowed to the space between her horse's ears and she was convinced each time one of Miveri's hooves slipped on loose stones they'd both go tumbling over the edge, but the only things to fall were small pebbles that rattled unnervingly into the chasm below. Not until she reached the top did she dare to look back, and down, catching her breath at the view of the flat plain so far below, the river from this height no more than a thin, silvery thread. The cloudless sky was huge above them, its blueness pierced by the jagged peaks of the Hindu Kush mountains.

As they continued the journey Miriam's delight at being once more on horseback lessened as the pain in her left knee increased. Occasionally she dismounted and walked for a short distance, trying to ease the stiffness. The last time she did this, however, Ismail spoke up. 'I know it's difficult Miriam-*jan*, ' he said, 'but if we're going to reach Zardgul before dark we have to move faster.' With a groan, Miriam swung herself back into the saddle, urging Miveri into a fast-paced, spine-jarring trot. Ruckshana, after being entertained by Ismail's stories about dragons had fallen asleep, safely encircled in the arms of her new *Caca*.

The sun was already dipping behind the tallest mountains as they approached the summit of what Ismail promised was the last pass. 'You'll be able to see Zardgul from the top,' he said. Miriam stopped, gripped by a sudden panic. She wished she were back at the teaching camp, finishing a shift in the clinic, that Ismail had never come to Charkoh. She looked at him.

'Ismail, I don't know how I'm going to cope with this. I don't think I can face meeting people, talking about… remembering…I shouldn't have come.'

'It won't be easy, Miriam-*jan* but you need to do this. Since meeting you in Charkoh, I've felt you are trying to shut out all your memories of Zardgul, of Jawad, of your life among us.' When Miriam didn't answer he continued. 'You haven't asked a single question about Jawad, about what happened. That's not normal – trying to bury it somewhere deep in your head won't work. It's always there, always hurting because you won't let yourself deal with it. Coming back to Zardgul will be painful, I know, but maybe it will help you somehow to…'

'Since when were you an expert in psychology, Ismail?' Miriam's voice was frosty.

'Oh, Jawad taught me quite a lot,' Ismail replied, adding with a shrug, 'but you don't want to talk about him. I'm sorry you don't want to come back to Zardgul, but right now you don't have a choice – unless you intend spending the night on the mountain.' He kicked his horse, 'Let's move. It'll soon be dark.' Miriam could feel her face flush with anger but, without making any further comment, urged her own horse on.

At the thought of stepping onto what would surely be an emotional roller coaster, she felt sick with dread. She was annoyed with herself for snapping at Ismail. In doing so she had inadvertently acknowledged he was right in his diagnosis of how she deliberately kept her memories buried. At the same time she was angry with him – what gave him the right to criticise the way she dealt with her loss? Had he contrived to bring her to Zardgul just to take some perverse delight in watching her misery? This last question brought her to her senses. It was inconceivable that Ismail would enjoy seeing her suffer. He had been a good friend to both Jawad and her – was, indeed, still her friend. Getting through the next few days was going to be difficult enough, without alienating the person who would be her greatest support.

Catching up with Ismail, she put out a hand to rest on his arm. 'I'm sorry. It's been a long day, I'm tired and,' she drew a deep breath, 'yes, I'm scared. But I shouldn't take it out on you. Still friends?'

'Always, Miriam-*jan*, always.'

The moon, almost full, had risen by the time they arrived at Ismail's house, situated half a mile before Zardgul village itself. Miriam slid to the ground, turning to greet the woman who stood in the doorway. Ismail's wife, Usma, had been her closest friend in Zardgul and seeing her now, arms open wide in welcome, made Miriam ignore the agonising pain in her knees as she rushed towards her. Wordlessly, the two women hugged tightly before moving together, arms linked, into the house. Calling to his sons Mustafa and Sultan to see to the horses Ismail followed the women, carrying Ruckshana in his arms.

Usma led the way from the ground floor, where the sheep and goats were penned in for the night, up a curved flight of steps into the guest room. With its whitewashed walls and bright, striped gillims on the floor it looked warm and inviting in the light from the pressure lamp. Miriam hobbled over to slide gratefully onto a *toshak*, pulling Usma down to sit beside her. As she studied her friend, she noted the lines etched across her forehead, the network of creases around her eyes although there was still no trace of grey in the hair that escaped from beneath her chaddar. When she smiled, however, Miriam couldn't help but notice she'd lost several teeth.

'Oh, Miriam, I can't believe you're here. I've missed you so much.' In reply, Miriam squeezed her hand, not yet trusting herself to speak without bursting into tears. Usma rushed on, 'Everyone's so excited. People haven't talked about anything else since they heard you were coming back. I expect half the village will be here tomorrow.'

A young girl, with a striking resemblance to Usma, entered the room carrying a tray. She greeted Miriam shyly before beginning to pour and distribute tea. 'Shahnaz?' The girl nodded. 'You weren't much older than Ruckshana is now when I last saw you,' Miriam said with a smile, indicating her daughter who, now awake, was gazing hopefully at the dish containing wrapped toffees. Mustafa and Sultan entered the room, along with a smaller boy who Ismail introduced as his youngest son, Habib. Miriam was sipping at her second glass of tea when without warning she surrendered to a jaw-breaking yawn. 'Sorry. Didn't mean to be so rude.'

Usma rose to her feet, 'You must be exhausted,' she said. 'I'll show you your room and you can have a rest until food is ready.' Assuring everyone she was too exhausted after the journey and had no need of food, just sleep, Miriam, taking Ruckshana's hand, followed Usma. When her friend opened a door to the left of the sitting room she closed her eyes.

'Our room,' she whispered.

'I thought you would like to be in your old room. If it's a problem we can change it.' Usma sounded anxious. Miriam shook her head, stepping into the room in which blankets had already been spread on two mattresses laid out side by side. There was little space for much else in the tiny, square room, which was exactly as she remembered, right down to the poster of a flower-strewn meadow in the Swiss Alps. The boys had brought her bags in, placing them on the recessed shelf behind a colourful, embroidered curtain. After checking there was nothing else she could do for her, Usma said goodnight, hugged her friend briefly and left the room, closing the door gently behind her.

Miriam stood for a few moments in the silence, as though listening. This had been their room – her and Jawad's, where they had spent the first few weeks in Zardgul before moving into their own home. Giving herself a shake she turned her attention to preparing Ruckshana for bed. No ghosts here – stupid of her to think there might be. Despite the long naps she had taken on the journey, her daughter was soon asleep and Miriam lay down next to her, stretching her sore muscles. She turned out the paraffin lamp Usma had left her and closed her eyes. Almost immediately she knew the welcome oblivion of sleep had fled. Despite her physical exhaustion, she was wide-awake.

She sat up, pulling the blanket around her shoulders. She thought about re-lighting the lamp but the moon shining in the one small, un-curtained window bathed the room in a gentle glow. Apart from her daughter's even breathing the only sounds were the occasional rustling of straw when a sheep stirred below. Memories came crowding in and for once Miriam made no attempt to drive them away. Here in this room she and Jawad had made love for the first time as a married couple.

FOURTEEN

Edinburgh to Zardgul 1986

Seatbelt unbuckled long before the plane taxied to a standstill at Kabul airport, Margaret urged her father to move into the queue in the aisle where she jiggled from foot to foot. What took them so long to open the doors?

Jawad had written to tell her he was driving from Mazar-i-Sharif, with his father, the day before. In her head danced a fuzzy, soft-focus picture of herself rushing towards Jawad's open arms. As soon as they disembarked, however, she realised how she'd confused her cultures. Had Jawad been arriving at Edinburgh airport they could indeed have flung themselves into each other's arms. At Kabul only men were hugging each other. Jawad caught Margaret's hand, briefly, in both of his, leaning forward to give her a daring peck on the cheek. In a gleaming white *salwar* suit that set off his dark skin, he took her breath away, as did the gleam in his dark eyes which told her he too was imagining a more physical reunion. She pulled herself together to introduce the two fathers.

Anwar looked resplendent in a karakul hat, a green striped *chapan*, worn cloak-like over his shoulders. He took her hand and kissed her forehead, welcoming her, as his daughter, to his family. 'I am very happy you proved me wrong, Margaret-*jan* and I look forward to knowing better the woman who has captured my son's heart.' Although he asked the travellers if they would like to rest in Kabul for a day, continuing the journey the following morning, Margaret sensed he was keen to set out immediately. Leaving now, they would be able to reach Mazar-i-Sharif before nightfall, though she wondered if her father was up to the journey after the flight. Jim waved away her concerns, climbing nimbly into the front passenger seat.

Margaret and Jawad sat in the back, their hands immediately seeking and finding each other's. As her body crackled and fizzed at his touch, she would not have been surprised to see sparks fly around the vehicle. With the two fathers getting to know each other in the front Margaret felt she and Jawad were in their own private world – a world from which she felt she'd been exiled for the past year.

'Look at this,' she said, handing Jawad a letter she took from her bag. 'It's been with me since the day it arrived.' She watched his lips curl into a smile as he read his father's reply to her request she and Jawad be allowed at last to marry.

Anwar's response had been brief. '*You had better come quickly,*' he wrote, '*before my son dies of a broken heart.*'

'I was so happy, I danced into work,' she said, smiling at the memory. 'And look,' she handed Jawad a 'Good Luck' card signed by dozens of her colleagues. 'I didn't realise I knew so many people. They took me out for lunch – for bacon rolls, because Janet thought bacon would be the thing I'd miss most after a few months here.'

'I hope not too much,' Jawad said. 'Pig meat is not possible. Though,' he mused, 'perhaps the Russians....'

'Don't worry. I won't miss it at all. Besides once I...' Margaret stopped, not wanting to tell him yet of the decision she'd made. She continued by talking instead of the generous gift of cash her colleagues had given her. 'It can go towards our work in Zardgul, although,' she paused, widening her eyes at him in mock anger, 'I did wonder if I'd have to use it to pay for excess baggage. All those books.' She shook her head, 'It doesn't do a girl's self-esteem much good when the first letter from her future husband is more about the books he needs than love.'

Laughter bubbled under his contrite words when he apologised for his lack of romance. 'But, you knew already how much I loved you, I think, but not which books I wanted.'

Jawad had spent time in Zardgul, talking to the villagers, assessing the needs in the area. 'What we can achieve is so little compared to what's needed – I even wondered at times if it was not so impossible it would be crazy even to think we can make a difference.' He paused, lost in thought, before continuing, 'It's like building a wall, so big it cannot be completed in our lifetime. But,' he squeezed her hand, 'if we can put one brick in that wall, at least we'll have done something worthwhile.' Watching Jawad's glowing face, listening to him talk about their future with the passion she remembered, Margaret began to feel the long, lonely months had been a dream; they'd never really been apart.

Soon the mountains, with their permanently snow-capped peaks, began to rise higher and higher above them, tiny villages clinging to the steep sides. 'My God, look at the height of those mountains,' Jim exclaimed. 'Make Munro bagging look like climbs for toddlers.' Miriam laughed at her father's excitement. Beside the river were orchards of mulberry trees, now laden with fruit, apricot and cherry trees. Anwar pulled up beside a trio of small boys, negotiating with them for a basket of mulberries. Margaret exclaimed in delight over the basket, fashioned from small branches and lined with leaves in which the berries, washed in the fast-flowing river, glistened. They sat under the trees to picnic on the berries, the first mulberries she'd tasted. 'Mmh, they're so sweet, lovely.' Jawad showed her how to pick out the best ones, his long fingers dancing over the surface of the berries, scooping up a handful at a time to throw into his mouth. She copied him, relishing the cool juiciness until she noticed her fingers were soon stained purple. 'Bit like brambles, dad,' she said, laughing, waving her hands at her father. 'Do you have mulberries in Mazar-i-Sharif?' she asked Jawad, 'because I think I'd like to eat them every day.' Jawad described the two huge mulberry trees in their compound, which produced more berries than she could possibly eat adding, though, their season was a short one.

It was early evening before Anwar pulled up outside the house in Mazar. He tooted the horn bringing Jawad's younger brother Daud to open the gate into the *auli*. His sixteen-year old sister Habiba and fourteen-year-old Farida stood waving beside their mother Zakia. She stepped forward to welcome them, as elegant and graceful as Margaret remembered, making her feel decidedly grubby and dishevelled after so many hours travelling. She was grateful when Zakia offered to take her and her father to their rooms to freshen up. After showing Jim his room, she led Margaret further along the corridor. On her first visit she had been given a room to herself – the one her father was now occupying – but this time she was sharing with Jawad's sisters. 'I hope you don't mind,' Zakia said, 'but with so many guests coming to stay for the wedding we're running out of space.' Margaret did mind, very much, but could hardly say she really wanted her own room so that her fiancé could sneak in during the night to make love to her. Perhaps when the girls were asleep she could visit Jawad's room. Almost as though she'd read her mind, Zakia told her Jawad would stay at his uncle's house until the wedding. Miriam was horrified to think Zakia had perhaps been aware she and Jawad slept together the year before. Feeling her face flush she knelt down and began opening her suitcases to hide her telltale blushes. Her future mother-in-law settled companionably on a *toshak*, chatting about wedding arrangements while Margaret unpacked.

'Your mother – you must be sad she is not here. She is too sick to travel?' Zakia asked causing Margaret to pause, considering her reply. How to explain her strained relationship with her mother to a woman for whom her children meant everything? Her mother, Muriel, had refused to consider a trip to Afghanistan, only daughter's wedding or not and Margaret was glad she hadn't come. Muriel would have spent her time imagining slights, been bristly and made life uncomfortable for her daughter, her husband and her hosts. She couldn't say such things to Zakia, though. Let her believe she's ill?

She shook her head. 'No, she's not sick but she doesn't travel well. The journey would have been difficult.' That was certainly the truth. She turned back to her open suitcase and continued to lift out books and yet more books, stacking them on the floor near the window.

Zakia, who had seemed to want to ask more about her mother, suddenly exclaimed, 'What about your wedding dress? Is it in the other case?'

Margaret froze. Wedding dress? Oh, shit! The only clothes she'd packed were the dress and *tunban* she'd bought on her first visit, the warm jumpers and thermal underwear Jawad had written she'd need in winter. She'd also brought an enormous green jacket, which would, reputedly, keep her warm even in Everest conditions, though now, wiping the sheen of sweat from her forehead, she couldn't imagine it ever being so cold – but no wedding dress. Zakia's expression, as she flew from the room, told her this was a major, major disaster.

After dinner Jawad led Margaret outside to sit on the veranda. She responded greedily to his kiss until from the open window of the dining room came the sound of throat clearing. They sprang apart. Jawad sighed, waving his arm in the direction of the house. 'I did not think about the fuss, the arrangements, the shopping. All I dreamed about is getting in the jeep and driving off to Zardgul with you. Although,' he teased her, 'it seems my future wife hadn't thought much about marrying me – not even a wedding gown, indeed.' He pulled her close again. 'We will soon be on our own – although I'm not sure if I can trust myself to behave until then, my beautiful Margaret. I wonder if you know how much I love you?'

'Do you think you could get used to calling me Miriam?'

'Sorry?'

'I'm changing my name. I'm going to be Miriam.'

'What do you mean?'

'I'm converting to Islam and, although I know I don't have to change my name I decided to choose something more Islamic.' When Jawad didn't respond, she rushed on, 'It's not something I'm doing on a whim. I've spent the last year studying…I thought you'd be pleased.'

'But I never asked you to become a Muslim.'

'I know. At first I was only reading about it because I knew so little and wanted to understand more and then, well, I suppose I began to think it was the path I should be on. Look, I find it difficult to talk about – personal faith has always seemed to me a very private thing. We Scots might argue about religion in the pub but we tend to shy away from the topic in our daily lives.'

'It's a very big step. As long as you have not felt under pressure – I mean, my father hasn't been writing to you about it has he? I'd hate to think you were doing it to please my parents.'

'No, Jawad, I told you – it's my choice.'

'Then I'm delighted.' He pulled her close. 'Did you make the *Shahadah* already?'

She shook her head. Although she knew there was no need for a ceremony, she'd wanted to make the declaration of her faith here in front of Jawad and his family. 'I hoped you would be a witness for me and, perhaps your father?'

Next morning, Margaret made the *Shahadah*, the first of Islam's Five Pillars. Standing before Jawad and Anwar she recited, '*Ash-hadu alla ilaaha illallah* – I bear witness and attest that there is no god worthy of worship but the One God Allah. *Wa ash-hadu anna*

Muhammad-ar-rasool ullaah – I bear witness and attest that Muhammad is the messenger of Allah.'

'*Alhumdalillah*,' Anwar smiled, 'May Allah bless you and shower His Mercy upon you.' He kissed her on the forehead and, although she had not made the decision for her father-in-law's sake, she was glad he was pleased. Wondering about her own father's reaction she looked to where, sitting next to Zakia, he was watching her. He looked pensive but smiled at her when she caught his eye.

'Not sure if 'congratulations' is the appropriate expression. You know I've never been a fan of any kind of organised religion myself, but if this is what you want and believe and it makes you happy, well, I'm happy too. You'll have to forgive me if I don't always remember to call you Miriam – after a lifetime of Margaret, it'll be hard to change.'

She nodded, giving him a quick hug, appreciating again her father's quiet acceptance of her actions. She hadn't discussed her intention to become a Muslim with her mother, knowing she could never make her understand. She wasn't sure she could fully explain her decision to anyone. Embracing everything important to Jawad, including his faith, was part of her commitment to him and wanting to be totally immersed in her life here. The Margaret who always felt she never fitted in anywhere in Scotland, was being replaced by Miriam, who was sure of her new identity and of her place here. She felt Jawad's eyes on her and looked across the room to where he sat. She blushed when he winked and she realised that rather than thinking about spiritual matters, his mind was focussed on more earthly pleasures.

Zakia and her daughters whisked Miriam off to the bazaar to choose material, not for a wedding dress – it was too late now for one to be made to order; it would have to be found, ready made – but for several suits. She stood, welcoming the sun on her back, feeling its scorching heat seep right through to her bones, melting her British chill, mesmerised as the shopkeeper unfurled bolt after bolt of cloth to fall in a rainbow of colour for her inspection. To each of Zakia's suggestions, Miriam agreed. She carried her parcels through the dusty streets to the tailor's shop as if in a dream.

Here, Zakia coaxed, bullied, threatened and, Miriam was certain, bribed the tailors to work round the clock to have everything ready in four days. In a shop window Farida spotted what she and her mother

declared was the perfect wedding dress – white satin topped with
layers and layers of netting. They urged Miriam to try it on. She
loathed every frill and froth of it but with the girls and Zakia in
raptures over how beautiful she looked she said nothing. Jawad would
think she was beautiful in a piece of sacking. She'd never in her life
had a positive thought about herself, but now believed herself beautiful
in the eyes of the man she loved. She hugged her happiness inside her
then, wanting to share it, grabbed her startled mother-in-law and
waltzed her around the tiny shop.

Shoes were impossible. Nowhere in the city could they find a pair of
broad-fitting size sixes. Zakia shook her head in disbelief when
Miriam admitted to having brought trainers and walking boots. 'Not
even one pair of sandals?'

'Rubber flip flops.'

'Bathroom shoes?' The horror in her mother-in-law's voice made
Miriam laugh out loud. Zakia stared at her, then she too laughed. 'Oh,
Margaret, sorry, Miriam, I can see why my son believes you are the
only woman to go with him to Zardgul. I can't think of a single
Afghan girl who would not be hysterical at the thought of not having
the right shoes for her wedding day.'

The evening before her wedding, Jawad's sisters Farida and Habiba
varnished Miriam's toenails an interesting shade of purple and applied
intricate patterns of henna to her hands. In the morning, they painted
her face as though they had shares in Max Factor before helping her
into her wedding gown and escorting her to the sofa on which she was
to sit while a seemingly endless procession of guests filed past,
offering congratulations and handing over gifts of money. To each she
murmured a smiling *tashakor*. Despite her mother-in-law's light-
hearted admonishment for not looking sad, as tradition demanded of
Afghan brides, she gave Jawad a huge grin when he joined her.

Her only moment of sadness came when she and her father spent a
few quiet moments together. She'd scarcely had a chance to talk to
him all day though she had been happy to see he appeared to be
enjoying himself enormously. From time to time she'd spotted him,
always in animated conversation, his arms gesticulating, with wedding
guests. He'd joined in the traditional dancing, swept up in the ring of
men, stamping and clapping as though he'd been doing it all his life.
When he came to say goodnight, though, she saw how tired he looked.

'Oh, dad...' Her voice faltered.

'Oh, dad, what?' He parried.

'I'm going to miss you. I...' She suddenly felt like crying.

He put a finger to his lips. 'Shh. No tears on your wedding. I'm sure it's written somewhere, it's not allowed.' He smiled at her. 'I'll miss you, too. So much, I'm going to have to come back to visit you – come and see this yellow flower place your Jawad's always talking about.'

'I'm going to hold you to that.'

He held out his arms, 'Come on, give your old dad a hug and let him get to his bed. Not been on a dance floor for years. Bit more energetic than a waltz.'

Before leaving for Hazara Jat and their new life in Zardgul the day after the wedding, Jawad wanted to meet with the mechanic for a final check of the vehicle as well as making countless other last minute arrangements. Almost as soon as the wedding feast was over, he excused himself, leaving Zakia wringing her hands in despair at her son's unorthodox behaviour. Miriam was determined to stay awake until he returned but, exhausted by the long day, she eventually fell asleep. She stirred once, vaguely aware of Jawad's body slipping under the cotton sheet next to her but hadn't awoken until he kissed her awake at three o'clock in the morning. 'It's time to go,' he whispered. 'Our life is about to begin.'

Although Miriam and her father had said goodbye the night before Jim rose, along with the rest of the household, to see them off. Miriam was tearful when she climbed into the jeep. The distance, which would soon separate them, suddenly seemed enormous. Looking back as they left the *auli* she thought again how her father was aging. Despite his talk about return visits, for the first time, she wondered when she would see him again.

Jawad reached over and took her hand, squeezing it gently. A sadness settled in the jeep. In a way it was a relief when they left the tarred road, Miriam clinging to the hand strap to stop herself from cracking her head on the roof. It was her first taste of country 'roads' and impossible to maintain the same level of emotional distress while being thrown around like a rag doll. In the grey light she studied Jawad's profile as he concentrated on avoiding the worst of the jarring boulders and potholes. They'd not made love since she arrived, not even on her wedding night, and now she was heading towards a remote village and a life amongst people she didn't know and whose language she didn't understand. Unbelievable. It was so ludicrous a situation she laughed, high spirits returning. Jawad took his eyes off the road to smile at her.

On her first visit, she'd scarcely been any distance from Mazar. Now, as it became lighter she watched, entranced, as the mountains ahead drew nearer. Standing out, bathed in an extraordinary clear light, they made the mountains of Glencoe look like small hills. Their blue black, jagged summits made her think of dragons' teeth. Small villages, huddles of half a dozen adobe houses, appeared occasionally, the same colour as the brown earth. Jawad talked about his last trip to Zardgul, his plans for their future.

'Oops, sorry.' In his enthusiasm he'd taken his eyes off the road and both he and Miriam bounced roof-ward as the vehicle hit a pothole. 'I'd like to see the school rebuilt in the area,' he continued. 'There used to be one – when the government wanted to make education compulsory – but the people thought they were trying to teach their children to be communists. They refused to send their sons. Some used to bribe the headmaster to mark them present on the register. Now they see education is a way forward.'

The first night of what, in theory, was her honeymoon, Miriam spent in a sleeping bag on the lower slopes of a mountain pass. A truck further up the pass had broken down. Nothing could move either up nor down until it was fixed in the morning. Jawad unpacked their sleeping bags, blankets and a box of foodstuffs. Snuggling close to him, Miriam thought how romantic it was to spend their first night together sleeping out in the open. Near by, truck drivers gathered in small groups and soon the mountainside was studded with flickering flames from tiny campfires made with what brushwood they could find supplemented, Jawad told her, by donkey stool and sheep droppings. When, picnic over, Jawad kissed her goodnight it was in such a chaste way Miriam understood making love under the stars while surrounded by truck drivers was not an option.

By the end of the second day's journey when they pulled up outside a 'hotel', Miriam ached in every bone and muscle. She hobbled after Jawad into the gloomy one, mud-walled room, the *gillims* covering the floor had faded to a dingy grey. Removing her shoes at the door Miriam tried to ignore the sticky things she could feel, but preferred not to investigate, under her bare feet. On the walls were posters, the largest of which clearly demonstrated whose war the Afghan people believed was being fought in their country. A map of Afghanistan, blood pouring from her many wounds, was clutched in the talons of a vicious looking American eagle while a snarling Russian bear clawed at it. Pictures of *mujahideen* martyrs who had died fighting the Soviet invaders were also tacked to the walls. Miriam shuddered at another poster showing a small boy, a cherubic expression on his chubby, baby face, dressed in a soldier's uniform, holding a Kalashnikov, while behind him were luridly painted scenes of bloody battle.

The dozen or so travellers already present looked up at their arrival. Self-consciously Miriam ducked her head making Jawad laugh. 'You'll get used to it,' he said. One of the men spoke to him and after a few minutes of questions and answers he turned to her saying, 'He was asking if you were Russian.' When she made an expression of surprise, he explained, 'Over the years of occupation some mixed marriages have been known. I have informed them of the history of our relationship, where you are from, how we met, and where we are going. Everyone can now concentrate on their own affairs, instead of ours.'

The kitchen boy brought *shurwa* and a few pieces of stringy goat meat. Miriam tore her bread into small pieces, pushing it into her soup, exactly as she had done as a child with a bowl of tomato soup. Instead of a spoon, though, here she used pieces of dry bread to scoop up the mixture. A small group gathered round a man who untied some cloth-wrapped, lumpy bundles. She nudged Jawad who glanced over at the group before turning his attention back to his food.

'Selling kalashnikovs,' he explained.

'So openly?' The man showed off his wares as though they were nothing more innocuous than brushes and brooms. His potential customers examined each weapon, squinting along the sights, hefting it, feeling its weight and balance. She'd assumed arms-dealing was conducted in secrecy, not in a roadside truck stop.

Jawad grunted. 'Major dealing happens behind closed doors. These were probably stolen in Kabul – or sold. Some of the Russian soldiers are selling their weapons to buy food.' He swallowed the last of his tea. 'Before we sleep do you need to go outside? I will be your *chowkidar*.'

She nodded. 'Where are we going to sleep?'

'Here.' Miriam looked round the room, where already most people had rolled themselves into their *patous* for sleep. Her dismay must have shown because Jawad continued, 'I did warn you life would not always be comfortable.'

Miriam was stung by the remark. Her concern was not for her comfort – she was tired enough to sleep on a rock – but once again love-making was clearly out of the question. When she whispered in his ear, she was amused to see him blush.

Late next morning they had a puncture. Climbing down from the jeep Miriam listened to the silence that descended when Jawad killed the engine. The only sound came from the teal-blue river rushing along beside the road, foaming white where it fought its way over and around gigantic rocks, which, who knew how many centuries before, had come crashing down the mountainside. On one side of the track the mountains rose sheer, from out of the river itself, while opposite, at the bottom of the sparsely grassed slopes huge boulders lay scattered around. So completely deserted was it, had it not been for the tyre tracks on the dusty road she could believe no one ever travelled this way. Reluctantly, she turned from the spectacular view to help change the tyre.

When they'd finished, Jawad leant towards her to remove an oil smut on her cheek. She tingled at the touch of his finger and they caught and held each other's gaze. Slowly he bent to kiss her. As their lips met a faint giggle came from above them. Looking up they spotted two small boys high on the mountain guarding a mixed flock of sheep and goats. 'My God,' Miriam exclaimed, 'is there nowhere in this country to be alone? I would've said we were the only humans here for miles.'

'Never mind, we'll soon be in our own home.' Jawad bent, kissing her swiftly on the lips, loud cheers resounding from above. 'Come on, we want to reach Zardgul before dark.'

At the top of the Zardgul pass Jawad stopped the jeep. Together they stood looking down on the village below. Miriam could see several small hamlets of flat-roofed houses, like miniature models from a toy box, clinging to the mountainside. Jawad explained there were several villages, some only three or four houses, in the immediate vicinity. The fields, small handkerchief sized patches, shone in the late afternoon sunlight jewel green and gold in sharp contrast to their grey, rocky backdrop. A narrow blue ribbon of river twisted along the valley floor, disappearing behind a copse of poplar trees.

He turned to her and she saw a hint of anxiety appear in his eyes as he scanned her face. 'I hope you will be happy here Miriam-*jan*. Life will be tough and I pray it will not make you be sad for what you have left behind.'

She smiled up at him. 'As long as we are together, I can put up with anything.'

FIFTEEN

Zardgul 1986-1987

By the time Jawad had negotiated the jeep down the twisty pass a crowd of people, adults and children, had appeared, the sound of their excited chatter heard before the jeep came to a halt. A tall, broad-shouldered man wearing a beige waistcoat over his light blue *kameez* detached himself from the group. A white circular cap pushed his crisp black hair off a high, tanned forehead. He moved towards them, his arms outstretched in a gesture of welcome. He and Jawad hugged, kissing each other on the cheeks. He turned towards Miriam and Jawad introduced her to Ismail. She replied with her stock of greetings phrases in Dari then they were swept off to Ismail's house where Miriam met his pregnant wife, Usma and at least a dozen more women and children all of whose names she forgot moments after being introduced.

She sipped tea feeling self-conscious under their gaze. Sometimes they spoke directly to her but she could only shake her head in apologetic incomprehension, looking over at Jawad, hoping for rescue but he and Ismail were deep in conversation. By the time Jawad moved to sit beside her, her jaws were aching from the strain of smiling and she was feeling self-conscious and foolish. 'I know it's not easy,' he said. 'Once you can talk to people it will be different. Ismail has invited us to stay with his family until our own home is ready.'

Later, in the evening Usma said something to Miriam, who looked to Jawad for a translation. 'She's asking if you want to go outside before going to bed.' Miriam rose, following the woman who'd picked up a plastic water pot from inside the doorway. Usma paused at the corner of the house before beckoning Miriam on but when she rounded the corner there was no sign of a latrine. Instead, in the light of the small paraffin lamp Usma held, Miriam saw from tell-tale evidence this was the designated toilet place. She smiled her thanks. Usma smiled back but showed no inclination to move away. '*Tashakor* – thank you,' Miriam murmured, smiling harder. Usma nodded, smiled, placed the lamp on the ground and squatted. Despite her acute embarrassment that she was expected to pee alongside someone else Miriam was impressed at how discreetly the other woman managed the performance. Not so much as a centimetre of bare skin was exposed.

Back in the house, Jawad was in the small guest room. He closed the door behind her, holding his arms out and as she slid into his embrace he murmured against her hair, 'Finally, after a lifetime, we are alone.'

'Are you sure there isn't a horde of kids outside that window?' she whispered, 'or a hundred more of Ismail's friends and relations waiting to be introduced?' He shook his head, slowly sliding her chaddar from her head, letting it drop to the floor. After having had her head covered in front of him for so long, his action made her suddenly shy, as though he had undressed her completely. He ran his fingers through her loosened hair. 'I feel like I'm in the middle of a Mills and Boon.'

'What is a Mills and Boon?' he asked, easing her down onto the mattress.

'Impossibly romantic novels.'

Only this is for real.

Miriam was the first to wake in the morning, the sun's rays creeping like warm fingers across the quilt. She stretched, then propping herself on one elbow gazed down at her sleeping partner. She was about to drop a kiss on his lips when a soft tap on the door made her jump. She nudged him awake. 'Someone's at the door,' she whispered. It was Usma telling them breakfast was ready.

Afterwards, Ismail escorted them down to the small cluster of houses that constituted the village of Zardgul to inspect what would be their new home. The house belonged to an old man whose wife died the year before. With no sons and unable to manage alone he'd moved in with his daughter's in-laws. Workmen had already started on repairs to the two-roomed house's flat roof. 'This will be the *mehmankhanna* – our room for guests,' said Jawad, 'and the other will be our room for sleeping, office, eating when no guests. We can build two more rooms for consultations and a storeroom.'

A doorway led to the bathroom, a tiny room with a recessed shelf and a hole in the outer wall to allow the water from bucket baths to escape. Miriam wandered round imagining how it would look. Colourful *gillims* on the floors and embroidered cushions would make it bright and cosy. The kitchen, however, defeated even her imaginative powers. Sandwiched between the two rooms, the doorway from the vestibule was so low she had to duck her head to enter. Other than a hole in the ceiling, intended to draw smoke from the cooking fire, there was no natural light, but most alarming was the 'cooker.' A mud platform, it was about two feet high, built out from two walls, with a hole at one end for firewood. Two more holes, one larger than the other, on top of the platform were for the cooking pots. On the other side of the room a bread oven, was sunk into the floor.

Miriam's heart sank as deep as the *tandoor* but she kept smiling. Jawad was enthusing about the speed the repairs were being done. Not likely to have much idea about kitchens and cooking. He caught her eye and shrugged. 'I've no idea how you cook on that thing either,' he said, 'but I'm sure together we'll manage to work it out.' She smiled at how easily he had read her mind, liking his use of 'we.'

Jawad went off each morning to work alongside the builders, leaving Miriam with Usma. She enjoyed learning the rhythms of Usma's life, which began, most days, with dawn prayers. She would next light the fire in the stove, take the huge kettle that had sat all night keeping warm at the bottom of the *tandoor* and put it on to boil for the morning tea. Several times a day she'd tramp the few hundred yards to the spring, fetching water for the house in an assortment of containers. In the small dam beside the spring, dishes and cooking pots were washed. In this same dam she washed clothes and wool from the sheep to be spun once cleaned and dried. Piles of rice or lentils had to be picked over for small stones and pieces of grit before being washed and put to soak.

She discovered how little smoke went out through the hole in Usma's kitchen roof. Mostly it billowed around the kitchen, making Miriam's eyes sting as though she'd rubbed them with chilli. Working in such primitive conditions, she'd never be as competent as Usma who could produce a variety of dishes, all ready at the same time, all still hot. Miriam still struggled to prevent the rice from burning onto the bottom of the pot whenever she turned away to slice onions for the salad and was even less successful in her attempts to bake *nan* in the *tandoor*. Usma, wearing a long leather gauntlet to protect her arm from the searing heat inside the oven reached inside, slapping the prepared dough onto the sides. When they were done she retrieved them with a metal rod. Miriam was relieved when Jawad told her a neighbour, Gul Chaman, was willing to supply them with fresh *nan* every day.

One task Miriam enjoyed was feeding the chickens after they'd been let out in the morning. Usma would stride down the slope below the house, calling to her hens who would hurry along behind her, clucking and squawking as though encouraging each other not to be left behind. It was when she stopped to scatter their food, the fun, for Miriam began: their arrival disturbed vast numbers of crickets which the hens decided would make the most delicious breakfast. Only there were so many crickets all leaping at great speed in every direction the poor hens would find themselves pecking at empty air. The first time she saw the hens' frantic darting here, there and everywhere, chasing the elusive morsels, Miriam laughed until she cried.

Visitors regularly climbed the mountain track to Usma's house to meet the foreigner, giving Miriam plenty of opportunities to practise her language skills. Although she didn't understand more than a tenth – if that – of what the women talked about she overcame her self-consciousness, learning to use body language, to mime what she was trying to say. When she succeeded in understanding something new or the women grasped what she was telling them they would beam at her so encouragingly she felt she was being awarded a gold star in primary school.

Sometimes, though, she was overwhelmed by everything happening in her life. Nothing was familiar – from drinking tea without milk to her own reactions and emotions. She longed for time by herself to think about all she was experiencing. Once or twice she set off alone up the mountain behind Ismail and Usma's house but within minutes a voice hailed her and a figure rushed breathlessly after her. Jawad explained that as she was still regarded as a guest people felt it was their duty to ensure she always had company. 'They can not understand why anyone would want to be alone,' he said. 'If you go off by yourself they are thinking you are sad. It is their duty to make you happy again. Besides, no one here is going 'for a walk' as you say it – if they are walking it is because they are going somewhere for their work – to fetch water, or take the animal to new grazing. You will have to be patient. In time I think they will stop treating you as a guest.'

Finally they were able to move into their house. Though she'd enjoyed staying with Usma and Ismail, it was wonderful to have their own place. There were times when Miriam felt guilty at how happy she was. It didn't seem right to be so enjoying life in a country in the midst war yet Zardgul seemed so distant from the conflict around Kabul and other parts of the country.

At the start of the winter news of fighting, only a few hours by foot from Zardgul brought home to Miriam that the war was not, after all, in some far distant country. A messenger brought a letter from a Party commander requesting medical help for injured *mujahideen*. Jawad prepared to leave almost at once.

'I wish you weren't going,' she said.

He stroked his hand over her rounded stomach, 'I promise I won't take any risks. You could go to Usma's if you're lonely. Ismail's coming with me so she'd probably be glad of the company.' The baby kicked and she shook her head. She wouldn't feel alone. But she was terrified for the five days he was away.

When he returned, she'd never seen him so angry. He hugged her tightly. 'It was so stupid. A stupid skirmish between two of the Parties – Sazman Nasr and Sepah. I cannot believe these people. They are too much idiotic and *maghrur*.'

'And what?' On rare occasions, when unduly excited about something, Jawad's usually perfect English would slip.

'They are arrogant.'

'Why were they fighting?'

'About who should control Hazara Jat when the Soviets have gone. Can you believe this? May Allah help us if these people are future leaders. The Soviets and government forces have killed almost twelve thousand civilians this year alone – never mind the number of children maimed or killed by mines disguised as toys.' He stopped for breath. 'Sorry, I did not mean to become an anti-war propaganda machine. It is making me so angry. These fools are falling out with each other like boys in the school yard.' He shook his head.

'Were people killed? Many injured?'

'One is unlikely to survive. He lost a lot of blood already, before we reached to him. His injuries were more serious than I could deal with. They were going to try to get him to Kabul or Pakistan.' He struck his open palm with his fist. 'By the time we left, they still could not decide which place they should take him.

'They gave us a room in someone's house. People brought their injured to us there. From both sides, wounds to be cleaned and dressed, some stitching, and everyone demanding painkillers. As far as I could tell neither one side gained anything for their trouble. On top of all that, some Commander told me that I should only be treating **his** *mujahideen.*' He sighed. 'I really struggled not to lose my temper with him. I am not sure if I succeeded. He went away looking not pleased with me.'

When she saw the first snow, Miriam's excitement amused Jawad. Big fat flakes swirled down all afternoon and by evening the ground was covered, the snow falling faster. She couldn't resist going outside to make footprints on the snowy carpet, sticking out her tongue to catch the flakes, teaching Jawad how to make snow angels. By mid-morning next day most of it had vanished. 'I promise you'll see plenty of snow,' Jawad assured her, 'more than you can imagine.' A few days later she awoke to a strange light in the room. When she looked out her eyes were assailed by a world of white; no horizon, no sky, nothing but blinding whiteness. This wasn't Christmas card stuff, Arctic weather more like. Jawad appeared with a couple of shovels, a 'told you so' expression on his face and, once she'd added several layers of sweaters, finally zipping herself into the Everest conditions-defying jacket, she followed him outside to start digging.

When they'd cleared a path from the house to the well, Jawad climbed up to shovel snow from the flat roof. Within days the temperature dropped well below freezing, forcing everyone to remain indoors, huddled round stoves. Preparing for the hundred metres dash to the latrine Miriam, swaddled in so many layers, felt like the Michelin man. Returning from fetching water from the well, having been outside for less than fifteen minutes, Jawad's moustache was frozen solid.

The house was overpoweringly hot and stuffy with the windows fastened tight, the stoves going full blast. Being pregnant hadn't helped. Sometimes, desperate to breathe some fresh air she would open the door, but the icy air was like a knife cutting inside her nostrils, the back of her throat. Within seconds the room was at fridge temperature, a happy medium never possible. The novelty of those first snowy weeks palled when Miriam understood how long an Afghan winter lasted. Other than Gul Chaman's husband who brought their bread, visitors were rare and she missed female companionship.

'Would you like to visit Usma and Ismail?' Jawad asked one day, adding as he patted her, by then rather obvious, bump, 'Do you think you'd be all right to walk up the hill?'

'Be ready in five minutes,' she grinned in delight. They stayed for almost a week. The house was overflowing as two of Ismail's brothers and their families had also come to visit Usma, Ismail, their two sons, and the beautiful charmer Shahnaz, who was the first baby Miriam helped deliver in Zardgul. At six months, the baby girl was healthy, bright-eyed and happy, with a radiant smile for everyone who entered her orbit. Her two older brothers adored her.

The house was overcrowded and overheated: the livestock, fed now on summer-harvested fodder, were confined inside too, the pungent heat from their bodies rising from their ground floor quarters to the families' living rooms above. A holiday atmosphere instantly cheered Miriam. Most evenings were given over to the children who took part in all kinds of games, some of their own invention, some organised by Ismail who, Miriam thought, was a wonderful master of ceremonies. The more she got to know the man, the more she liked and admired him. His nieces performed traditional dances – the younger ones without a trace of self-consciousness although the girls of around eleven and twelve years were inclined to be overcome all at once by attacks of shyness, sitting down abruptly, hiding their faces, giggling. The boys played *corjangi*, swiping at each other with cushions while blindfolded. They created strange beasts and monsters, disguising themselves in blankets and homemade masks to prance around the room terrifying the little ones – and one or two of the adult women, who refused to go outside unaccompanied for fear of what might be lurking in the dark. As the lamps burned lower, throwing huge shadows on the walls, the atmosphere was soon ripe for storytelling. Miriam loved listening to the stories of ghosts and mysterious, supernatural events, taking her turn by telling a few Scottish ghost tales herself.

During the day the adults had been left in peace by the children and spent many hours talking, interspersing their conversations with frequent card games. Miriam had learned enough of the basic rules to play the most popular game of *fiskut*, in which four people in two partnerships played, but now Ismail appointed himself her personal tutor, teaching her how to improve on her game by reading, and acting on, the signals partners made to each other. 'But that's cheating, isn't it?' she'd asked, laughing as Ismail slammed down a card, indicating he had no more of that particular suit in his hand. Once she overcame her innate horror of being considered a cheat at cards, she soon became a worthy partner.

'I've so enjoyed this week,' she said to Jawad as they prepared for bed on their last night before returning to their own home. 'It's been like a week-long ceilidh – even without a drop of whisky passing my lips.'

Farid's birth in the spring brought a happy ending to the long winter. And to think she once thought Edinburgh was cold.

'Miriam? Miriam, come, see what's arrived.' Wiping her eyes, Miriam emerged from the smoky kitchen where she'd been preparing the evening meal. 'Look,' Jawad waved a bundle of envelopes in the air, 'the postman's been. Or, to be more accurate, Hassan the shopkeeper at Sia Bomak brought them from Kabul and his son delivered them to me in school today.'

Miriam's heart leapt at the sight of the British stamps. Trying to remember when she'd last received post she reached out eagerly but Jawad held the envelopes above his head keeping them just out of her reach. 'Are you going to be a greedy child and devour them all in one gulp,' he teased, 'or are you going to take your time and savour them slowly?'

Last time letters arrived there had been two from her father and Miriam had torn them open, not bothering in her haste to check the dates. She read them in the wrong order and so fast that when she'd finished them she'd felt cheated, particularly as Jawad still had several envelopes to open.

'Okay,' she agreed. 'Dinner's nearly ready so I can wait until we've eaten. Listen out for Farid, in case he wakes.'

Humming off key, Miriam returned to the kitchen. Receiving letters meant such a lot now. She'd never been much of a letter writer before. Never needed to be, keeping in contact with her parents and friends in Dumfries by phone. Now, though, she set aside time each week to write to her father, and to Janet, detailed accounts of life in Zardgul. It was amazing so few letters disappeared in transit with the roundabout journeys they took to and from home. Jawad's family held letters until they heard of someone travelling to Hazara Jat who could be trusted as a courier. Sometimes they passed through several hands before reaching their destination. There were risks. If stopped and searched by either the Soviets or the *mujahideen* the person carrying letters from abroad, written in a foreign language, might be accused of spying. Over the winter, when the roads were virtually impassable no letters arrived.

As soon as she'd swallowed her last mouthful of food she held her hand out for her letters. While she ripped open the envelopes, sorting the three from her father into date order, Jawad cleared away the dinner things. Halfway through the first letter a squawk from the corner of the room alerted her Farid had awoken. 'I've got him,' said Jawad.

'He'll be hungry,' Miriam said, making faces at her son in his father's arms. 'Give him here.' She deftly undid a zip inset in her dress giving the baby easy access to her breast. Smiling down as he sucked voraciously she told him, 'I'm reading a letter your grandfather wrote before he knew you were born, when he was worrying about me having a baby so far from hospitals and doctors.' Apparently unimpressed by this information, Farid continued his meal with single-minded concentration and Miriam resumed her reading. The second letter offered congratulations on the birth of Farid, asking if it was possible for a photograph of his grandson to be sent. Six months earlier she and Jawad had taken a whole roll of film, sending it to his parents to have developed in the city. They would have sent copies to her father.

'Can you ask your father to make more copies to send to dad?' she asked Jawad, who nodded agreement though pointing out her father's last letter had been written two months ago so it was possible the pictures might have arrived by now. Though she still felt a stab of disappointment, it was no surprise to Miriam, her mother hadn't written. Her father always ended his letters saying she sent her love but she never put pen to paper herself.

That night in bed Jawad commented on how quiet she'd been during the evening. 'Have the letters made you homesick?'

She was silent for a few moments, considering his question. Then, with a shake of her head she replied, 'No, not homesick, but they've made me think how sad it is dad doesn't won't get to know his grandson as a baby.' She fell silent again trying to analyse how the letters had affected her. So hard to fathom it, harder to explain. She'd certainly felt a pang of longing – a longing for people to be able to share her experiences here. Finally, she said, 'I do love getting news of home but there's something disorientating about it. Sometimes I remember our arrival in Zardgul as if it was only yesterday. Reading about Janet's life – the parties, the work, I can't believe it's only eighteen months since I came here. Life in Scotland seems so distant it makes it feel I've been here for a long, long time. Almost as though my life there happened to someone I hardly know.'

'Oh, I don't know,' Jawad replied. 'I still remember the Margaret Adair who almost broke my nose in her eagerness to meet me at a party. You could've just come up and introduced yourself, you know.'

'You! You know perfectly well it was an accident. I was so desperate to escape, I hadn't even noticed you and…' She threw her pillow at Jawad, who retaliated by wrestling her onto her back before beginning to kiss her neck, starting just below her ear, slowly moving his mouth down her body. Afterwards, satiated and sleepy, Miriam murmured, 'I'm awfully glad I punched you on the nose,' before drifting off to sleep, her head cushioned on Jawad's shoulder.

A few hours later, anticipating Farid's demand for a feed, she awoke, lifting him before his first whimper developed into a hungry yell. She watched her nursing son as he waved one arm in the air as if keeping time to an invisible orchestra. She smiled. The confusion of her early weeks in Zardgul had by now acquired the hazy, disjointed quality of a dream half-remembered. So many new people had suddenly appeared in her life she'd taken to jotting down their names in a notebook – until Jawad commented, only half in jest, people were wondering if she were a *jaasus* – a spy. Sometimes she'd felt she was drowning in a sea of meetings; with the village elders with whom Jawad discussed his plans for a school and a clinic, with the commanders of the political parties who formed the local *shura* and with builders, poring over construction plans. They'd eaten in a different house every night for weeks because everyone wanted to invite the guests for a *mehmani*. Once, when Jawad said they'd been invited for dinner at Anwar and Fatima's home, she groaned. 'Can't we have one evening, just the two of us, in our own home?'

'Of course, we can. You are free to not accept any invitation. It is not *majbur* that we go.'

The following day when Jawad asked if she would go to Gul Bibi's house she agreed. The evening at home had re-charged her batteries. She could cope again with spending an evening not understanding half of what was said to her, not being able to ask the things she wanted to know about the women's lives here, being mindful of etiquette. About a week later, when they met near the well, Fatima returned her greeting but looked away and didn't linger to talk. Puzzled, Miriam mentioned the incident it to Jawad. 'She is hurt you refused her invitation.'

'But you said it was all right, we didn't have to go.'

'Mmh, it was my mistake. I should have known. And, of course, it made it worse when you accepted Gul Bibi's invitation. She feels she lost face.'

'What can I do? Shall we invite Fatima to dinner here?'

Jawad shook his head. 'Then she'll think her house isn't good enough for you, your house is better. You'll have to wait until she decides to forgive you.'

She suggested apologising to Fatima. Jawad advised against it. 'What can you say? That you were very tired? She'll think you are only too tired to come to her house. Feeling unwell – but recovered enough to eat with Gul Bibi?'

'Tell her…' Miriam's voice quavered with distress at her mistake and frustration at her inability to put matters right. 'Tell her I'm an ignorant foreigner who doesn't know any better.' She never refused another invitation, but it was many months before Fatima asked them again to a *mehmani* in her home.

As her command of the language grew, enabling her to communicate more easily and freely so did her confidence. It was Farid, even before he was born, who had done the most to give her the self-assurance she now had. Holding classes for the women had become much more relevant once she was able to speak from personal experience about pregnancy and childbirth, although she was still a long way – and hoped to remain so – from the experience of women like Chaman who had already given birth ten times, six children still living, and was expecting her eleventh any day now.

Realising Farid was asleep she settled him down and slid back under the warm blankets beside Jawad. In his sleep he sensed her, pulling her close, enfolding her in his arms. With a contented sigh she dropped off to sleep.

SIXTEEN

Zardgul 1995

A gentle tapping on the door roused Miriam. Disorientated, she sat upright. Where was Ruckshana? The tapping became more insistent and, recognising Usma's voice calling her name, she remembered where she was, telling Usma to come in.

'*Subakhair. Khau khub bud* – did you sleep well?' Miriam nodded. Considering how late it had been before she fell asleep she was surprisingly well rested. 'I brought you tea and egg for breakfast,' said Usma, setting a tray on the floor. Miriam squinted in the sunlight beaming in the window.

'You should've woken me earlier. It's so late.' she replied, peering at her watch. 'My God, Usma, it's almost eleven. And where's Ruckshana? She's not being a nuisance, I hope?

Usma smiled. 'Not at all. After breakfast she fed the chickens with me. She's a lovely little girl – a real chatterbox. Now she's 'helping' Ismail take the cow to graze. He'll be in soon to see what you want to do today. Eat up,' she added, indicating the fried egg. Miriam fell back against the pillows with a groan. 'What's wrong? Are you ill?'

'No, it's the thought of what's in front of me today. Oh, Usma, how am I going to get through it? It wouldn't be so bad if no one mentioned Jawad's death but the first thing they'll do is offer condolences. I don't think I can bear it.' Her friend crossed the room in two quick steps and enfolded her in her arms.

'You'll be all right. You're strong, Miriam-*jan*, stronger than you think. And you've got me and Ismail to support you.' She squeezed Miriam's shoulders. 'But you need to eat something.'

Miriam hugged her friend back, giving her a shaky smile. By the time she was up and dressed she could hear Ruckshana chattering to Ismail in the guest room. She couldn't face the egg, by now cold, but managed some dry bread, washed down with sweet tea before she joined them. She returned her daughter's kiss and enthusiastic hug, holding her on her lap while she launched into an account of her morning's activities. Miriam smiled at Ismail over the top of Ruckshana's head.

'So, what's the plan for today?' he asked when little girl paused for breath. 'People have been asking for you. I told them you were resting. Many women want to go with you to the graveyard.'

'No,' Her shrill voice made Ruckshana jump and stare at her with big eyes. 'Sorry, baby,' she murmured, her voice softening, comforting her daughter with a cuddle. She looked at Ismail, 'Not today. I need you to take me to the *qabrestan* on my own first.' Her voice faltered and she took a deep breath before continuing, 'and then to the school, to where it happened.' Ismail nodded. Usma offered to keep Ruckshana, to which Miriam readily agreed. Visiting the grave wouldn't be much fun for the little girl – she'd be happier staying with Usma. When Ismail said he'd get the horses ready, Ruckshana leapt to her feet and followed him.

'You've time for more tea,' Usma said, pouring two glasses. 'Now,' she demanded, sitting back against a cushion, 'tell me about Iqbal. Have you a photo of him? What kind of place is Sang-i-Sia? Why…'

Miriam laughed at the stream of questions. 'Sang-i-Sia's not a bad place – there's more water than here so people can grow fruit. I'm kept pretty busy in the clinic…'

Usma made a dismissive sound. 'Never mind Sang-i-Sia. I was only asking out of politeness. It's Iqbal I want to know about.'

'You'd like him. He's a nice man, kind. He works hard for his people and he's been good to Farid.' As she spoke, Miriam knew she was painting a dull, one-dimensional picture of her husband. She tried again. 'He adores Ruckshana. You should hear the two of them together. He can be fun and …'

'Is he anything like Jawad?'

She fell silent then, realising her silence gave the answer, shook her head. 'In the beginning I thought maybe he could be but…' She looked at Usma, reflecting on how close they had always been. That friendship deserved honesty. 'He's nothing like Jawad,' she burst out. 'Jawad and I were partners, sharing everything in our lives –friends, family, work, even the domestic stuff. I'm hardly included in Iqbal's life at all. D'you know,' she rushed on, hands gesticulating in time with her words, 'in the last year I've only been out of our compound twice. Once I went to pay my condolences to a friend whose husband died and once to a wedding. The clinic where I work is part of our home so I don't even need to go outside to work. I never go to visit friends – they come to see me at home.'

She stopped as a thought struck her. 'You know, I didn't even choose my friends. Some of the village women started visiting me in the afternoons. I do like them and enjoy their company but, apart from my neighbour, they're older than I am. Age has brought them the freedom to go out and about.'

'Why did you marry him? And so quickly?' Miriam heard a note of reproach in Usma's voice and sighed.

'I believed I was doing the right thing for all of us, especially Farid. I couldn't let him grow up far away from his father's family. I didn't know Iqbal would change. In Pakistan he wasn't always worrying about what people were saying. From the way he behaves it's as if everyone in Sang-i-Sia's watching everyone else, ready to criticise any infringement of any one of dozens of unwritten rules. And nothing should ever change.' She sighed again, her shoulders drooping.

'I don't mean Iqbal forbids me to go out but he gets in a state about what people will think and say if I do. It's easier not to bother.' Frustrated at her inability to explain what she meant, Miriam shook her head. 'If I had only lived in Sang-i-Sia I would probably have assumed it's how everyone lives in rural areas where most people are uneducated, illiterate – but it's different here. Although very few people are educated there's an openness here, a willingness to look forward, to accept change that Sang-i-Sia doesn't have.'

'Ismail has an idea that's partly because of where we are,' Usma said. 'Zardgul is in the very centre of Hazara Jat. Hazara people live in all the areas around us, but Sang-i-Sia sits on a boundary. Its neighbours on one side are Pushtoon so Hazaras close in on themselves to protect their way of life from being changed by their neighbours. He says he noticed it first in Jaghoray. He was surprised to find in an area where there is more education, and the people are wealthier, the women had less freedom than here. They are treated more like Pushtoon women – kept within their four walls. I've never been to Jaghoray or Sang-i-Sia so I haven't seen for myself.

Miriam considered Ismail's theory. 'Maybe he's right,' she said at last. 'When I came through Jaghoray I thought men kept their wives at home to show they were rich enough to not need their wives to work in the fields. Women in both Sang-i-Sia and Zardgul work on the land. The difference is if Ismail passes women working here, he says hello, might chat for a minute or two. In Sang-i-Sia Iqbal wouldn't speak and the women would pretend they didn't see him. I don't know how it will ever change.' She sighed again, staring into her tea. 'It's not that I spend my time regretting not going out – mostly I'm busy with work and the children and the house – it's more to do with feeling Iqbal doesn't see me as partner. He doesn't … Oh, I don't know how to explain it, Usma. Don't listen to me. I'm talking nonsense.'

'Maybe because in the beginning you'd decided he'd be like Jawad you didn't notice some things about him until it was too late.' When Miriam only shook her head, Usma continued, 'You can't change the way the village is – not on your own, anyway, but can you change things between you and Iqbal?'

'I really don't know. We need to talk, but he won't.'

'You know when something's wrong you have to try to change it. If it can't be changed, can't be put right, then you have to consider moving on.'

'That's a very British sort of way of looking at a problem.'

'It was you who taught me, Miriam. Years ago, in class.' She smiled gently. 'So what will you do?'

Miriam didn't know what to say. What would 'moving on' mean? She was relieved when Ismail called her name from the doorway. The horses were ready. She hurried outside to where Ruckshana, looking proud of herself, was standing holding Miveri's reins. Miriam kissed her goodbye, telling her to be a good girl for Usma, before swinging herself up in the saddle. She and Ismail headed towards the village.

How many times in the past had she walked or ridden this path between Usma's house and her own, never doubting her life in Zardgul would continue as happily as it had begun? The scenery was achingly familiar. Over there, on the right, in a small gully the deadly *Al Khatoon* was said to live. This supernatural being reputedly roamed the hills at night luring men with her unearthly beauty. The hapless men, unable to resist were then either struck dumb or blind or, in the worst-case scenario painted by the village women, they died. They told her the gorgeous creature with long dark hair to her feet could be mistaken for none other than *Al Khatoon*. Her feet, apparently, were back to front. Miriam had, at first, laughed at their stories until they told her the creature especially liked to catch people who professed to have no fear of her. She inclined her head slightly as though in greeting as they rode past the gully.

The wheat had been harvested, the tiny fields now bare. Two men were working at the threshing ground prepared, as always, in the centre of the village. Her first harvest in Zardgul, she'd watched fascinated as two cows yoked together plodded round and round the flat, hard-packed mud circle pulling the wooden thresher behind them. One of the men, holding an enormous riddle was throwing the grain up into the air, allowing the wind to separate the chaff, while a second raked the grain into a golden mountain. Several farmers shared the harvest ground. Men often worked half the night, in the light of the enormous, big-bellied harvest moon, which hovered above, seemingly within touching distance. She'd been amazed the first time she saw the harvest moon, calling Jawad to come and see. Together they'd stood, arms wrapped around each other, gazing upwards. Our moon.

Once, at midnight, in her first year she'd taken tea and scones to the men. They'd been surprised but had drunk the tea, commenting favourably on her scones, although as she was still battling to get to grips with her stove, they'd turned out more cookie than scone like. They listened to her explanation of how in Scotland women took food to the men in the fields at harvest-time. They'd laughed, telling her she should encourage their women folk to adopt the custom. It wasn't until she was back at home she realised she'd been talking about a time she'd never actually known. She considered going back to tell them these customs had long since died out in her own country but decided explanations would be too complicated. Jawad had been highly amused. She'd felt foolish.

Now, she looked beyond the men towards her old house. No one was sitting on the roof. It was too early in the day for anyone to have finished their work and be drinking tea, watching the life of the village around them. Gul Chaman had often used to join her, bringing a freshly baked, warm *nan* and news of the neighbours. Together, they'd watched children sneak into the rows of peas, filling their pockets with the emerald pods, before scampering off to devour them out of sight. Or, small bodies starved of vitamins when the previous year's harvest had been eaten, they'd creep along behind the house to a neighbour's field to pull young carrots, eating them, sweet and cool, the earth still clinging to them. Ismail asked if she wanted to visit the house but she shook her head. Not today, maybe another time.

Reaching the end of the village they turned right, riding in single file on the narrow path leading to the cemetery, situated outside the village. Miriam felt her heart begin to hammer painfully in her ribcage. Most of the graves had simple headstones, no more than pieces of flat rock stuck vertically in the ground. Many had slipped and lay slanting or even flat on the stony ground. At some of the graves, banners from strips of red, green and black cloth, the colours of the Afghan flag, fluttered from poles. Ismail led Miriam to one of those.

Jawad's grave had a cordon of white stones around it. She gave an involuntary gasp, never imagining this was how Jawad's resting place would look. Somehow she'd pictured it complete with a proper headstone as though he'd been buried in St Michael's kirkyard in Dumfries; somewhere green and neat and tidy, with flowers in urns. She dismounted, handing Ismail the reins, and approached the grave. She stared at the mound of earth and stones, at the faded flags fluttering in the soft breeze. Kneeling, she reached out a hand, resting it on the earth. Why hadn't she thought to bring some memento to leave? Instead of being swamped by feelings of grief, she felt nothing. Tears she'd been fighting back since she arrived in Zardgul now refused to flow.

She was conscious of Ismail standing close to her, watching her reactions. Was he judging her emotional response to report back to others? When he asked if he should leave her, she shook her head. 'I want to go to the school now, please,' she said, her voice clipped as she fought to control the sudden rage welling up inside her; anger Jawad had been taken from her, her son had lost his father, her life turned upside down and the happiness she had known swept away. Without speaking, leading the horses, they retraced their steps before turning off again in the direction of the school. When they were in sight of the simple mud-walled building Miriam stopped. How proud

Jawad had been of the school with its one big classroom and a second, smaller staff room and store. He'd worked hard alongside the masons, learning how to make mud bricks, arguing with the carpenter over the size of the windows, wanting them to be larger than the traditional small ones designed to keep out winter cold.

Miriam stopped walking and turned to Ismail. 'Tell me now,' she said, her voice quivering. She met his gaze as he looked at her as though trying to determine how much he should say. 'Everything,' she said more firmly.

Ismail cleared his throat. In a low voice he began, 'Jawad was here the day…' He swallowed hard. 'The day it happened he was working on the plans for the new classroom. I was to meet him later to decide how much wood we'd need. A man called Jan Ali – you didn't know him,' he said at her enquiring glance, 'He was in Sepah party. He came to warn Jawad. Armed men were on their way but Jawad refused to leave. Jan Ali came to find me, practically in tears. He'd pleaded with Jawad to run, but he'd just thanked him for the warning. Said he'd deal with it, talk to the men.'

'I don't understand. Most men around here carry guns. What was so dangerous about Sepah men coming to see Jawad?'

'You know they'd offered Jawad protection?'

'Protection! They wanted Jawad to belong to them, to treat only their people. He'd never agree to that. He always said he came here to work for everyone.'

Ismail nodded. 'The Sepah commander came several times to talk to him, trying to persuade him not to treat people from Sazman Nasr or Harakat. Jawad always refused. He tried to convince the commander – and anyone else who would listen – they had no business fighting each other, should be working together for the community – digging wells rather than trying to kill each other. Many people, including a lot of *mujahideen*, agreed with him. He could argue so powerfully, I think he might have persuaded Sepah if it hadn't been for Anwar…'

Miriam interrupted. 'Anwar? The mullah from Bomak?'

Ismail nodded. 'He hated Jawad.'

'Hated him? But why?'

'Jawad's popularity eclipsed his own. Actually, Anwar was never popular – powerful, but feared not respected – and certainly never loved the way Jawad was. Anwar couldn't stand to see how highly people regarded Jawad. He made a lot of money before your clinic opened, and he was angry people had stopped coming to him for treatment.'

'But he was ignorant about medical matters,' Miriam burst out. 'Of course people would come to the clinic.' She'd heard he prescribed a number of superstitious and dangerous treatments, on one occasion instructing a woman to feed her three-year old daughter spittle from a hen's beak to cure her chest infection. When he encouraged people to take *perhez* it was to the point of starvation. 'He was a great believer in beatings to force the *djinn* he maintained caused illness to leave a person's body. Remember the young woman Jawad had to treat? Her entire body black and blue? She had epilepsy.'

'How could I forget?' Ismail's voice was grim. 'But the problem wasn't only because people stopped going to Mullah Anwar for medical care. Even from his own village they were coming to consult Jawad about non-medical matters, asking his advice on problems from disputes between neighbours to arguments over land, even on questions about Islam. Anwar was furious. Surely you knew this?'

Miriam shook her head. 'I knew Jawad had a couple of meetings with him before I went away. I understood they had some disagreements, but wasn't aware of Anwar's jealousy – or hatred.'

She shivered, staring up at the sky where the mountain peaks jabbed into the vivid blue. 'I only met him once, when he came to the house. I think you were there, too. When I came into the room he acted like I wasn't there. Wouldn't touch the tea I brought, making a big thing about not taking any food or drink prepared by a non-Muslim. When Jawad explained I was a Muslim, Anwar grunted as though he didn't believe him. I left the room then.'

Ismail nodded, 'He'd come in a fury about Jawad's plan to encourage girls to attend the school. He tried to say Islam didn't allow it. A big mistake to start telling Jawad what Islam does and does not allow. His other point was Islam's insistence on modesty in girls and women. He said he'd heard Jawad examined women alone in the clinic. Nonsense, of course and Jawad didn't even bother to correct him. He did tell him it was wrong the modesty Islam decreed had been twisted to make women feel a dreadful sense of shame about their bodies. He said the prophet Muhammad, Peace be Upon Him, had never meant in his teachings for women to be denied medical treatment. And if women could only be seen by female doctors, where were they to come from if girls were not allowed to be educated?'

Miriam walked on, silently digesting what Ismail had been telling her. She'd believed Jawad shared everything with her, not only his ideas and dreams but also his problems. Now she was hearing about a major issue he'd not discussed with her and felt hurt by his silence. 'I wonder why Jawad didn't tell me any of this?'

'You were going to Scotland, upset about your father – he probably didn't want to burden you with more worries. Besides he thought it would be resolved.' She had been distraught at the thought of not seeing her father again and at having to leave Jawad – he would have wanted to spare her further anxieties.

'Go on,' she prompted Ismail. 'I still don't see how Anwar was involved in Jawad's death.'

'Anwar felt Jawad was turning people against him. He'd lost face and swore he'd drive Jawad out of Zardgul.'

There it was again, this thing about losing face. Iqbal's constant refrain. It seemed to permeate everything in this country. It went so deep, too deep for her to understand. Chaman's husband going through with a marriage he didn't even want, despite knowing it would cause misery to the person he loved. Could it really make a man hate another – enough to kill him?

'But Ismail, there's a huge difference between threatening to drive someone out of the area and actually having them killed.'

'I don't think it was what Anwar intended. He'd have been content to see Jawad forced to leave Zardgul. He went to Sepah. Reported that shortly after the commander had last warned him, Jawad had gone to Bomak to attend two injured Nasr *muj*. Anwar told the commander Jawad was laughing at him, saying Sepah couldn't stop him doing what he pleased.'

Miriam groaned. So then, Sepah's reputation was at risk. Ismail nodded at her unspoken understanding of the situation.

'So,' he continued, 'Sepah let it be known publicly unless Jawad agreed to come work only for them and their people they would kill him. Everyone knew he would refuse. We didn't know they were going to act so soon. We thought there was still a chance to find a way to …' He stopped, lifting his arms, palms out in a gesture of defeat.

Miriam asked, 'So what happened when Jan Ali found you?'

Ismail paused to tether the horses, letting them graze the sparse grass by the edge of the path. 'I knew as soon as I saw him, Jawad was in danger. Barely waited for him to tell me what was happening before starting out.' He shook his head, falling silent for so long Miriam had to prompt him to continue. 'I don't know what I thought I could do. Maybe intercept them before they reached the school – give Jawad time to escape? I ran down the mountain from there,' he said pointing to a path to the left of the one they had taken. 'It seemed I would never reach here. No matter how fast I ran I felt as if I was going uphill. My legs were lead.' He paused, wiping the sheen of sweat from his forehead, carried on, 'I saw them approach the school. Heard them call his name and, with what breath I had still in me I yelled out to Jawad to run.

'One of the men turned, pointing his Kalash at me.' He looked away from her, swallowing hard. 'I'm sorry Miriam-*jan*. I didn't dare move. I saw Jawad come outside. He looked up and waved at me. Greeted the men. So calm.' Ismail stopped, tears glistening in his eyes. Wordlessly, Miriam reached out, resting her hand on his arm. With a stab of guilt, she realised she'd been so wrapped up in her own loss she'd never considered others had also suffered from Jawad's death. In silence they moved closer to the building then Ismail, his voice unnaturally gruff said, 'They stood here. I couldn't hear what they said. I saw Jawad raise his arms, as though asking permission to speak. Of course,' he sighed, 'they knew very well if they listened to him they'd never be able to go through with what they had come to do...'

Miriam stopped, her eyes wide with horror. She clamped her hands over her mouth but they couldn't keep back the unearthly keening rising from deep in her body. She was staring at bullet holes around the door of the school. She took an unsteady step forward, then another until she was close enough to reach out a hand to touch the round indentations. Pressing her forehead against the splintered wood of the doorjamb she whispered, 'Jawad! Oh, Jawad!' then, shoulders heaving, she began to cry. When her legs would no longer support her she slid to the ground where she sat, arms clasped round her pulled up knees, rocking herself. Ismail's soft murmuring reached her ears but she waved him away, only vaguely aware of the sound of his footsteps receding as she surrendered to her grief.

When she closed her eyes she saw behind their lids Jawad standing in front of the doorway, smiling, waving to Ismail and greeting the men with guns as though they were welcome guests. She heard the shots – one, two, three – saw his broken body crumple in slow motion into a pool of blood. Had he known his life was about to end, or was he sure the men would listen to him? In the moments of his dying had he thought of her, of his son so far away? She tightened her arms around her knees, hugging them fiercely. The agony of accepting that she would never feel Jawad's touch again made her want to scream until her lungs burst.

SEVENTEEN

Zardgul 1995

Miriam had no idea how long she remained sitting on the hard ground, before she was conscious of Ismail's return. When she tried to stand, her joints locked. He put out a hand to help her, but she shook it off as though his touch was repellent, ignoring the hurt expression that flickered over his features.

'Miriam-*jan*, I know, I understand how this is for you. I…'

'Oh, yes, Mr Amateur Psychologist – it's good for me to go through this hell. Well, guess what, your therapy stinks. Like everything else in this bloody country. That man,' she pointed a shaky finger towards the bullet-holed doorframe, 'came here to help you. He hated war, was sickened by the way the Parties behaved. When you should have been united to ensure when peace came – God, he actually believed there would be peace one day – Hazaras would never again be so repressed. But no, you had to go on squabbling over who controlled this bit of territory or that.

'Even so, he never stopped believing your children deserved health care, an education, a chance in life and you,' she was on her feet now, her face inches from his, 'you killed him.' She raised her right arm and, before Ismail had time to react, her hand came down in a ringing slap across his cheek. 'Don't dare tell me you understand how I feel.' She raised her arm again but this time he was quicker and caught hold of both her wrists. Pulling against his grip, she shouted, 'Let go of me. At least before, I could remember Jawad as he was. Now, what I'll see is a blood-spattered broken body.' She stopped struggling as a fresh flow of tears began.

'It won't always be like this, Miriam-*jan*. This is the worst.' He released his hold on her wrists taking a step back With gentle fingers he tilted her chin up until she was looking at him. 'When Jawad died you buried your anger and grief. Instead of grieving, you shut him out of your life…'

'Rubbish,' Miriam snapped back, 'I didn't…'

Ismail continued as though she hadn't spoken, 'I think you were too afraid of the pain. When you were in Quetta I tried to imagine how it must be for you, far from family and friends, receiving the news of Jawad's death. Of course I can't experience your loss the way you do but I know you well, Miriam. An Afghan woman would've wept and screamed. She'd tear her clothes, her hair, let the world know she was mourning the man she loved. But you, you'd have kept it all inside, not wanting Farid to see his mother out of control.

'Keeping all that emotion deep inside where you couldn't feel it has become second nature to you. Today, for probably the first time since you heard Jawad was dead you've begun to let it out. In time you'll be able to remember Jawad as he was in life, the real Jawad.'

'Why do you keep on about **remembering** Jawad?' Miriam burst out, 'What's this thing you've got about the **real** Jawad? I don't want to hear any more, all right? I wish you'd just shut up and leave me alone.'

Ismail sighed. He looked down at the ground. 'What do you want to do? Go home?'

Miriam stared at the doorway. She had a desperate longing to hold her son, feel his skinny arms wrapped tightly round her neck, see her love reflected in his dark eyes, so like Jawad's. At the same time she felt thankful he was far away in Mazar, not standing here at her side looking at the place where his father had been murdered. Her mind jumped to a new thought and she swung round to Ismail. 'What happened to the men who did this – to Anwar and the man who pulled the trigger?'

'They fled immediately,' Ismail said. 'By the time the shots were fired,' he glanced towards the holes in the doorframe, 'people knew what was happening. The women – my God, Miriam, the women – they came from their houses, they left their work in the fields, they dropped whatever they were doing and ran to the school. If these men had still been around they'd have killed them. I never saw women so full of fury.

'The man who fired the shots – Hassan – came from a village three hours from here. When he reached home his mother had already heard. She refused to allow him into the house. Neighbouring women lifted stones to throw at him as if they were driving a dog away. He and the others fled to Kabul. We heard Hassan had been killed in a rocket attack but,' he shrugged, 'no one knows for sure.'

'And Anwar?'

'He stayed in Bomak. He…' Ismail interrupted himself to say, 'Look, Miriam-*jan*, it's getting late. Let's go home now. I'll tell you what happened to Anwar on the way.'

Miriam shook her head. 'No, I'm not ready to leave yet. Tell me about Anwar – then you can go. I – I need to say goodbye on my own.'

Ismail looked doubtful but continued, 'Anwar had no supporters. Even Sepah turned away from him. The commander sent a letter of apology to the people of Zardgul, saying he knew he was wrong to have Jawad killed. He was transferred to Bamiyan then to Kabul.

'We couldn't prove Anwar's part in Jawad's death. He denied he'd had anything to do with it. All he could think about was regaining what influence he once had. I think the man became *dawanna*.' Ismail tapped his forehead to indicate Anwar's mental state. He heard a new aid organisation had come to Bamiyan with funding for well-building projects. He went to persuade them to begin their project in his village. Fighting broke out between Nasr and Sepah and, according to the man who went with him, Anwar and he took shelter in a cave near the small Buddha. Anwar was terrified; convinced he was going to die. Even when things went quiet he refused to leave the cave. The man went on to the bazaar, promising to meet him on his return. Next day he found Anwar dead. He said it looked like he'd died of fright – his face was contorted and his body was crouched in a corner as if trying to get away from someone or something.'

'Good. I'm glad. He deserved a terrible death – alone and in terror,' she said coldly. 'If he wasn't already dead I'd kill him myself.' Softening her voice she added, 'Will you go now. I need time alone.' Ismail opened his mouth but Miriam shook her head at him. 'I know my way back.'

'I don't like to leave you…'

'I want to say goodbye.'

He nodded, turned away and mounted his horse. She watched him ride away then walked through the doorway into Jawad's school.

The classroom was empty except for the teacher's desk and chair, dusty and cobwebbed. The chair, Miriam noticed absently had a broken leg. Jawad had never used it anyway, preferring to sit with the pupils, cross-legged, on the *gillims* he'd begged from families. She imagined she heard a faint echo of boys chanting their lessons. She conjured up an image of Jawad teaching, enthusiastic, praising his pupils' efforts. For a long time she stood, lost in the past. How was she to say goodbye? With a forefinger she idly traced his name on the dust of the table.

All the time she was in Scotland, talking about him every day to Farid, to friends. Knowing he would be looking up at the same moon thinking about her. Impossible to believe she hadn't felt some connection break – no intuitive warning of danger, of his death.

She remembered the day the letter came. She'd known the moment she recognised her mother's handwriting on the envelope. In Jawad's arms, crying, 'It's cancer. She says they can't operate and the doctors can't say how long he's got. Now he'll never have a chance to meet Farid.' She gave a wry smile at the memory of her panicked departure from Zardgul, from Afghanistan. It had been a few months after the Soviets had finally left. Celebrations had been short-lived as in and around Kabul renewed fighting to oust President Najibullah began. Jawad, deciding Kabul was too risky had accompanied her and Farid to Pakistan. After a night in Quetta they journeyed on to Karachi – the bus took hours but she'd no visa, couldn't book a flight. She followed Jawad, numbly as he talked to officials, to the consulate, sorting out her papers. Then she was saying goodbye at Karachi airport, all the time wondering if she would reach home in time to see her father.

Although she'd found her father looking surprisingly well, it was a brief period of remission. At least he'd met his grandson, was well enough for a time to take him to feed the swans on the river, play on the swings in the park and scoff ice creams. So sad Farid would have no memory of the lovely times he'd shared with his grandfather. As she gazed unseeingly at the mud-plastered walls, blinking back tears, she heard a soft footfall. She stepped away from the table towards the door, calling out a greeting. It took her a moment to recognise the boy who hesitated in the doorway. 'Zahir? Gul Chaman's son?'

He nodded. 'My mother sent me. She invites you to take tea.'

'Please thank her, Zahir. Tell her I would love to come but not… not today. Perhaps tomorrow?' She saw the boy's expression change to one of confusion. Refusal was not a response he'd expected. He stood shuffling his feet in the dust, not sure what to say but clearly unwilling to leave without her. Relenting, she said, 'I don't want to trouble her to make tea.' Zahir gave her a relieved grin, while assuring her it would be no trouble at all. Miriam's eyes swept once more around the room, alighting on the name she'd scrawled in the dust. She moved as though to wipe it clean with her sleeve but changed her mind. She walked out of the school with Zahir who un-tethered her horse, leading it behind them.

Miriam ducked her head as she entered Gul Chaman's low doorway, kicking off her shoes. She sniffed at the warm aroma of baking bread. Her one-time neighbour, a tiny, woman, head always tilted to one side like an inquisitive sparrow, hurried from the kitchen to welcome her. '*Mudder-i-Farid* – Miriam-*jan* – a*fsos* – sorry, so very sorry.' At the sight of Gul Chaman's tears, Miriam felt her own eyes welling. She made no effort to wipe them away finding, for the first time, a comfort in these shared tears. Gul Chaman led her to sit, softly patting her back. Zahir, showing not the slightest trace of embarrassment at the sight of two grown women weeping together, brought in a tray loaded with tea things and busied himself setting out small dishes of nuts and dried fruits. He left the room, returning with something wrapped in a cloth. Gul Chaman spoke, 'Look Miriam-*jan*, specially for you – just baked.'

'Barley bread!' When Miriam spoke, the tears drying on her cheeks made her skin feel tight. She remembered the first time she'd eaten barley bread in Zardgul, how everyone had laughed at her when she'd remarked how delicious it was. Puzzled, she'd said, 'But it is. Why have I never had it before?' Jawad explained barley was considered a poor substitute for wheat and only eaten when the wheat flour was finished. Besides, he'd added, it made you fart, a major breach of manners. She looked at her friend now and with a surge of genuine delight, gave a gurgle of laughter. She leaned over and hugged her before helping herself to a chunk of bread. 'Mmh,' she murmured, her mouth full, 'as good as ever.' When she'd swallowed, she asked, 'How did you know where to find me?'

'Everyone knows where you went today. It's been a day of sad memories for all of Zardgul.'

Both were silent, each thinking their own thoughts. Finally Miriam said, 'An hour ago I thought nothing in this world would ever make me smile again – yet here I am laughing at the memory of eating barley bread. I don't understand myself. I don't know what or how I should feel.'

'You'll sort it out, Miriam-*jan*. Right now,' she said as Miriam's stomach gave a loud rumble, 'I suspect you're feeling hungry – and a bit windy. Come on, eat, then go home and sleep.' Smiling, Miriam reached for another piece of bread.

It was almost dark by the time she set out for Ismail and Usma's house. Knowing they would be worried she urged Miveri into a fast trot. Ruckshana leapt at her as soon as she came in the door, wrapping her arms around her mother's legs. Miriam scooped her up, saying, 'I'm sorry I was away so long. Did you miss me?' She squeezed her daughter tight, making her squirm. Usma and Ismail appeared together at the door of the guest room and Miriam felt a stab of guilt at their anxious expressions. Her palm tingled at the memory of striking Ismail and she flushed with shame at her behaviour. 'Sorry I'm late.' She explained about her visit to Gul Chaman and the barley bread before turning her attention back to Ruckshana.

She was glad of the little girl's chatter over dinner to prevent either Ismail or Usma asking her questions about how she felt, or about her future plans. She looked down at her daughter's upturned face. How much like Iqbal she looked. She hadn't given him a thought since talking to Usma this morning. After dinner Ruckshana went off with Shahnaz to hear a bedtime story, 'a real one from her mouth' as she put it. When Usma followed them out, heading to the kitchen to make tea, Miriam turned to Ismail and said quietly, 'I'm sorry about the things I said. I didn't mean you were in any way responsible for Jawad's death. And I apologise for slapping you.' She watched him raise his hand to rub at his cheek. 'I was…'

'It's been a difficult day. No need to apologise.' Ismail picked up a pack of cards, began to shuffle them.

'I think I'll say goodnight to Usma and go to bed.'

Ismail indicated the cards. 'Give me the chance to win some chickens.' Despite her protests that she was too tired to play he continued dealing the cards. 'Good,' he said, winking at her, 'gives me a better chance.' She understood he was trying to smooth away any discomfort she still felt about their earlier argument and picked up her hand of cards reluctantly. Usma brought in the tea and settled down to watch. Miriam found herself responding to Ismail's banter, to the amusement of his two sons, but it was not long before she threw down her cards in mock disgust. 'Should've gone to bed as planned,' she declared. 'I'll be bankrupt soon – how many chickens do I owe you?'

Usma said, 'I often think about the fun we had when you and Jawad came to stay in the winter. The games and the children dancing, the stories.' Despite her longing for bed Miriam sat on, reminiscing. Laughter was in Usma's voice when she asked, 'Remember the time you and Jawad fell out – when you came to stay here and left next morning owing Ismail hundreds of chickens.' Miriam stared at her in silence. 'Don't you remember?' Usma prompted.

'Jawad and I fell out? Never.' Miriam finally replied.

Now both Usma and Ismail grinned at her. Usma said, 'I'm not sure if I can remember what that particular fight was about – I think you were angry he'd arranged a meeting with the teachers and forgotten your birthday. You walked up here in the dark. You were so miserable I really was afraid you would pack your bags and leave as you threatened.' She shook her head at the memory. 'Ismail insisted you play cards – though goodness knows why, your mind was certainly not on the game.'

'Part of my strategy,' Ismail chuckled. 'I knew Miriam wouldn't leave Zardgul without clearing her debts and it would take her years. In fact,' he mused, 'I'm not sure you ever did.'

Listening to their teasing Miriam felt the first faint, stirrings of a long-buried memory – an image of herself in the kitchen, hot and flustered, sweat-soaked hair plastered to her forehead. It was to have been a special dinner – she'd worked so hard to make everything from the rice to the korma perfect. Jawad had rushed in, grabbed a piece of dry bread, kissed her and turned to leave, saying he was meeting with the teachers, would probably eat with them. Usma was wrong, though, about it being her birthday. She'd been going to tell him she was pregnant. Disappointment turned to fury. Jawad looked at her in astonishment when she'd screamed at him about always going out, never wanting to stay in with her, leaving her by herself. 'You know you're always welcome to come with me,' he'd said, furthering enraging her. She looked up at Usma and Ismail.

'Strange, I'd forgotten about it.'

'It wasn't the only time,' Ismail said. 'You wore a path between your house and ours. We both did – you coming up to see Usma, me going down to explain to Jawad what the problem was.' He laughed, 'Poor Jawad, he never understood why you were upset.'

'You're making it sound like we were always fighting,' Miriam tried to keep her voice light.

'Oh, Miriam, that's not what we're saying,' Usma replied. 'And Ismail's exaggerating. All couples have ups and downs. Look at us – we argue all the time – doesn't mean we're not happy together. Does it?' She nudged Ismail's bare foot with her own and Miriam thought her voice held a warning note as if to tell him to drop the subject.

Ismail, sweeping the cards together, said quietly, 'Miriam-*jan*, earlier today I said you needed to start remembering the real Jawad. He was a good man – it was clear to everyone you loved each other. But he was human. Sometimes he hurt you without meaning to; forgot you were thousands of miles from your own country and family, forgot you might sometimes feel lonely or unsure of yourself here.'

Miriam interrupted, 'I'm not listening to this.'

Ismail ignored her. 'You've made Jawad into a saint. In doing so you damage your relationship with Iqbal and, more importantly, with Farid.'

'Enough, now, Ismail,' Usma said quietly while Miriam, at the same time, shouted,

'How dare you say that?'

Ismail lifted the playing cards and slipped them back into their box before replying, 'Because I care about you. And about Farid. You hold Jawad up as this wonderful, perfect person, who dedicated his life to serve his people. Neither Iqbal nor Farid can ever achieve the standard you tell them Jawad set.

'Think what you're doing to your son, Miriam! He's going to feel a failure all his life because he knows he can never match up to how wonderful his father was. Let Jawad be human, with human flaws.'

Miriam stood up. 'I'm going to bed.' She swayed on her feet and Usma jumped up to steady her.

'No more, Ismail,' she said, 'she's exhausted. Come on,' she tugged Miriam's arm, 'let's get you to bed. I'll bring you some green tea.'

Ismail carried on, speaking quietly from where he still sat cross-legged on the *toshak*, his head tilted in Miriam's direction. She didn't want to hear any more but something compelled her to wait for his words. 'I've always thought of you as a very giving person. I was pleased when I heard you were continuing Jawad's work, even if it's in Sang-i-Sia and not here in Zardgul.' He paused, staring hard at her until her slight smile at his words of praise slipped. 'But, Miriam-*jan* I begin to see a selfishness in you. Jawad would be the first to ask why you give so much of yourself to others while neglecting the needs of those who are closest to you.

Miriam turned away, yanked open the door and rushed to her own room where she sank down on her *toshak*. Ruckshana stirred and she leant over, thinking she was about to wake, but her daughter remained fast asleep. She pulled the blanket more snugly up to her chin, smoothed the tangled curls off her forehead and kissed her. Her thoughts turned to Farid, wondering what he was doing, and so back to Ismail's words. Usma entered, bringing her tea. When her friend asked if she wanted to talk Miriam shook her head. 'No, I need to think.'

'You need to sleep,' Usma replied as she left the room. Miriam sipped her tea, brooding about Ismail's attack. When she put down her empty glass and turned out the lamp she lay staring into the darkness seeing Farid with his big, questioning eyes in the thin, solemn face. Was Ismail right? Was she really so blind to the needs of her family? Did Farid think he was a failure who'd never match up to his father's achievements? Was that why he worked so hard, spending so little time with his classmates out of school, desperate to achieve the highest marks? She'd often wondered, knowing Iqbal could sometimes appear aloof in his attitude towards Farid, if it was an attempt to gain his step-father's approval. Was she robbing her son of a childhood?

She shifted, trying for a more comfortable position – let her mind drift back to when Daud had come to tell her of Jawad's death.

***

She arrived in Quetta the day before the arranged date, checking in at Green's Hotel. The porter dropped her suitcases on the floor and rushed around opening curtains, flicking light switches several times to convince her they worked, showing her the location of everything in the room from the wardrobe to the television. He flicked through the channels but, failing to produce anything more exciting than a bearded man in a turban talking earnestly to the camera and several versions of snowy screen, he shrugged. 'English programme evening time,' he promised, grinning at Farid, 'cartoons.' She rummaged in her bag for some rupee notes and handed them to the young lad, thanking him for his help. When he left she hung the 'Do Not Disturb' notice on the handle and flung herself on the double bed.

Quetta was hot and their stopover in steamy, sticky Karachi had done nothing to acclimatize the travellers to the searing heat. Summer days in Zardgul were hot, yes, but with clear blue skies forming a high, overarching dome, breezes on which drifted the scent of clover and pink *shaftal*. Farid was cranky, wanting his toy tractor – the one at the bottom of a suitcase – refusing to play with anything else. With a sigh she rolled off the bed, turned the fan to its highest setting and set about unearthing the toy. 'Here you go,' she said, sitting on the floor beside him. 'Who're we going to see tomorrow?'

'Daddy.'

'Right! Only one more sleep.' Considering the possibility of delays on the road and Farid's disappointment if Jawad was late, she added, 'well maybe two. We'll be a proper family again.' Farid, making engine chugging sounds turned his attention to his tractor, pushing it across the floor. Miriam ruffled his hair, trying not to imagine her own disappointment if Jawad was late. She went off to shower. Later, unable to settle she and Farid went out, despite the heat, to wander round the bazaar.

Looking up at the craggy ring of copper coloured mountains shimmering in the heat Miriam couldn't imagine them covered in snow. The bazaar was colourful with mirror-work bags, bedcovers, shawls and brightly embroidered Balochi dresses, their deep front pockets glittering with sequins. Wall hangings, displayed in open doorways glinted in the sunlight. Usma would love those cushion covers. The shopkeeper, while insisting he was offering her a 'special discount', asked such an exorbitant price Miriam was about to walk away before remembering the importance of haggling when shopping in Pakistan. By the time she bargained the price down to a level acceptable to both parties she was exhausted, Farid was thoroughly fed up. The shopkeeper handed her the cushion covers in a paper bag, which in a previous existence, had been a newspaper. He called Farid to him and placed an embroidered Balochi cap on his head. 'Proper Baloch boy, now,' he said with a smile displaying brown teeth stained by *naswar*. Amused, Miriam watched her son admiring his reflection in the hand mirror the shopkeeper held up.

Back at the hotel they ate in the ground-floor restaurant. Miriam ordered the local speciality, *sajji*. She tore pieces off the leg of lamb for Farid who was busy colouring in a picture book. While she ate she watched the other, mostly male Pakistani, diners. A few foreigners, men and women who, she guessed, were here to work with Afghan refugees glanced frequently in her direction. In this city where the expatriates banded together they'd be wondering about her and Farid. She smiled to herself.

'Come on, Farid, eat up and let's get you to bed,' she said, rising from the table. Once he was asleep she watched him for a while, trying to guess how it would be when he met his daddy again. Would he be shy with him after such a long time apart? Although exhausted, she knew she'd never sleep and gave herself up to dreaming about their reunion. Although she did eventually drop off she was awake at first light, forcing herself to stay in bed for another hour before bounding up and heading for the shower. At this time in the morning the water was refreshingly cool and as she showered she sang, not caring how tuneless she sounded. She woke Farid who asked sleepily, 'Daddy here?'

'Not yet,' she replied, folding him in her arms, 'but he'll probably come today. Shall we have eggs and *paratha* for breakfast?' Later, Miriam re-packed the cases wondering what they could do to fill in the hours until Jawad arrived. Although he was unlikely to reach Quetta before mid-day, she was afraid to leave the room in case he did arrive early. She imagined him pulling up outside the hotel, taking the stairs two at a time. By late afternoon Farid was over-tired but refusing to nap until his daddy arrived. It had been stupid of her to tell him Jawad would be here today. Miriam was on her knees helping him to arrange his farm animals when the knock on the door came. Scattering cows and goats she leapt to her feet, crossing the room in three rapid strides. As her hand grasped the door handle she took a deep breath then flung open the door.

For a second she stared, stupid with incomprehension, at the figure in the doorway. Then she buckled at the knees and would have collapsed on the floor had Jawad's brother, Daud, not rushed forward to catch her. As he helped her to the nearest chair Farid, terrified, ran to her side. 'Is he my daddy?' he sobbed, pointing, 'Don't like him.'

Miriam lifted her son onto her lap, 'No, darling,' she said in a voice devoid of expression. 'Daddy's not coming now.' She looked at Daud, willing him to tell her that she'd misinterpreted his presence but his stricken face told her there was no hope. She wanted to scream but the shaking body of her son, pressed close to her own silenced her.

'I'm so sorry Miriam-*jan*. I… I don't… I…wish I did not have to bring you this news.'

She was finding it so difficult to breathe, could only whisper, 'When? What…?'

'Two months ago. He…'

Miriam, rocking Farid whose sobs had quietened, put a hand up to silence him. 'No, not now, not in front of the boy. He'll sleep soon. Perhaps you could ask room service to bring tea?' How could she even think of anything so banal when her husband had been dead for two months? She looked down at the top of Farid's head, laid her cheek on his soft hair. Only her son's need of her was keeping her breathing. When he was asleep she laid him on the bed and pointed to the door, indicating Daud should precede her into the corridor. He looked bewildered.

'Miriam-*jan*, this is not the place to talk about…'

'Nowhere in the world is a suitable place to hear about a husband's death,' she replied quietly, before bursting out, 'Two months ago! Why did no one write to tell me?'

'You know it is not our way to deliver bad news to people far away. It was agreed I would come…'

'What happened? Was he ill?'

Daud shook his head. 'He was killed by Sepah.'

Miriam shook her head in disbelief. This couldn't be real – but why else would Jawad's brother be standing here now? She opened her mouth but no sound came out. Her body began to tremble and she leant against the corridor wall for support. 'Let's go back inside, Miriam-*jan*,' Daud suggested, taking her arm. 'The boy's asleep.' Miriam allowed herself to be led into the room. Her eyes went immediately to the bed where Farid was sleeping, his face still streaked with dried tears.

'When are we leaving?' she asked.

'What do you mean?'

'When are we leaving for Zardgul?'

'It's not possible. You can't go to Zardgul. We still don't know exactly what happened – or why. The boy may be in danger. Perhaps they would try to kidnap him.'

Miriam sank onto the chair covering her face with her hands. She couldn't risk anything happening to Farid. Daud sat opposite her. She hated him for not being Jawad, for being alive. Why didn't he go?

He cleared his throat. 'You know in Afghanistan family is very important. My parents asked me to say they'll do anything they can for you and for Farid.' He fell silent for so long Miriam looked up at him. He swallowed hard before continuing, 'It is the duty of a brother to take care of his sister-in-law. Believe me Miriam-*jan* when I say taking care of you will not feel like a duty. I…well, if you agree…I am prepared – as is our custom – to marry you. If this is your wish.'

This really couldn't be happening. His expression told her he was serious. She threw back her head and laughed, feeling sanity slip away. Farid woke with a whimper. Immediately Miriam's moment of madness vanished as she hurried to comfort him. She glanced once over her shoulder at Daud, 'Please leave.'

***

Miriam sighed. She'd had to take care of Farid. She'd had to explain to him his daddy wasn't coming to meet them, they weren't going back to Zardgul just yet. She'd had to stay strong and calm for him, hiding her overwhelming grief, trying to reassure her anxious little boy she would always be there for him. As well, she'd had to decide, alone, what she was going to do to support herself and Farid, plan a way to return to Afghanistan, cope with daily life in a country she scarcely knew. When had she had the chance to grieve properly for the man who had been everything in the world to her?

EIGHTEEN

ZARDGUL 1995

Miriam was wide-awake now. She reached for the teapot and, finding it cold, decided to make some fresh. Wrapping her *chaddar* round her she went into the kitchen, which still retained some warmth from the evening's cooking. Poking the embers, she added a few small pieces of wood to bring the fire to life before putting the kettle on to boil.

She sat, her feet dangling inside the unlit but still warm *tandoor*. Good thing Ruckshana wasn't around to see her. Although it was a custom, almost universally adopted by women and children in kitchens, she'd forbidden her daughter to do it. Seen too many children seriously burned after falling in. She gave a shudder, pulling her feet up, turning her thoughts elsewhere.

Something fundamental had shifted in her life in the last couple of days. Outwardly, nothing had changed by coming to Zardgul. She'd go back to Charkoh the day after tomorrow. The teaching camp would be winding up, which meant an almost immediate return to Sang-i-Sia and Iqbal. What was different? Despite the misery she'd experienced here, today, over the last few weeks she'd known a sense of freedom, of being her own person, she never felt in Sang-i-Sia. Her life there seemed now to be increasingly claustrophobic, dark, like the slow extinguishing of a lamp.

'Oh, Jawad,' she murmured softly, 'I wish you'd tell me what to do, how to sort things out.'

Only the sound of steam hissing from the boiling kettle answered her. Was she really guilty of destroying her relationship with Iqbal and Farid by turning Jawad into some kind of super being? The idea filled her with shame. Of course Jawad wasn't perfect, they had argued –

occasionally. Times she'd been miserable because she felt Jawad didn't understand how difficult life sometimes was for her – far from home, from books, from cinemas, from people who knew her. Too proud to tell him she was struggling to deal with so much alien to her. Longing for a word of acknowledgement she was doing well, but too stubborn to ask for it. Memories of other incidents surfaced.

She'd been so jealous when Jawad, along with other men from the village, went swimming on a hot summer evening. The thought of feeling the cool water of the river flow over her was so inviting but, despite his usually progressive attitude towards equality of the sexes, Jawad had refused to let her join in. He'd forbidden her to suggest to the women they went swimming – or even paddling – on their own one evening. They'd had a huge row. Maybe Ismail's psychology wasn't as amateurish as she thought. She loved Jawad more than she'd ever loved anyone, but of course he'd had his share of human flaws. He'd be horrified if he knew she was telling his son he was perfection personified.

She stirred herself to make the tea, rummaging around in the gloom of the kitchen until she found where Usma had hidden the sweets from the children. She shook two or three onto a dish, replacing the packet behind the sack of flour and settled down again. Was it only this morning Usma asked her if she could put right the problems she and Iqbal were having? Change things or move on? Up until she went to Charkoh such an idea had never entered her head. Even at the teaching camp, although struck by how different her life was when he wasn't around, she'd not contemplated leaving him. The Iqbal of Sang-i-Sia was not the Iqbal she'd married in Pakistan but, although she didn't know what had changed him, she harboured a hope the old Iqbal would reappear in time. What if he was gone for good? She considered things continuing as they were now. It would become intolerable. Was it partly because she made him feel inferior to Jawad? When they first met she used to talk to him about their work in Zardgul. Since coming to Sang-i-Sia, though, she was careful not to mention him but perhaps she'd already planted the seeds, which had grown into feelings of inadequacy.

She'd experienced pangs of guilt since marrying Iqbal – guilty she was being unfaithful to Jawad by marrying again so soon after she'd learned he was dead, and there was always a niggling sense of guilt at using Iqbal, her means of getting back to Afghanistan and to Zardgul. Had she hoped back then there was a chance they might even live and work in Zardgul? Did Iqbal feel used? She remembered the day she first considered marrying him – the day Anna told her Iqbal was reluctant to return to Afghanistan to open a clinic in Sang-i-Sia. Knowing he would be there she accepted Anna's invitation to another seminar, making sure she appeared friendly and approachable when Iqbal joined them.

Anna – or someone – had told him about Jawad and when he expressed his sadness for her loss it had been surprisingly easy to talk to him about her husband's dreams. Iqbal was not only a sympathetic listener; he seemed to share those dreams and spoke with admiration about the work Jawad had begun. 'Hazara Jat needs more Jawads, hundreds of them throughout the region and,' he added with a smile, 'it needs more Miriams to work with the women.' It wasn't long before they were spending a lot of time together.

When she asked when he planned to return to Afghanistan, however, he shrugged. 'I'm not sure. I want to do some further training, specialising in tuberculosis. You must know already about the extent of the problem and difficulties in treating it in Hazara Jat.'

'Did you visit Sang-i-Sia recently?' she asked, knowing he'd not been back to Afghanistan in many years. She watched his face take on a closed expression. He shook his head but didn't speak for so long she thought he was not going to reply.

'I've never been back,' he said quietly. 'I left because of this,' he pointed to where his eyebrows should have been. 'I contracted leprosy when I was a small boy. When I was old enough I came to Pakistan because I heard it was possible to find treatment for the disease here.'

'Don't you miss your family? I'm sure they must want to see you.'

'Yes, of course I do. But…' He fell silent again until she prompted him to continue. 'But, it's difficult. There's so much stigma attached to leprosy,' his fingers smoothed a non-existent eyebrow, 'it made things difficult for my family, for me. Especially for me.' He stopped again, looking searchingly at her. 'I don't think you can really understand what it's like – coming from a country where there is no leprosy. You don't know what it is like to have people hate you because of your illness. People are afraid of you, afraid to touch you. They don't know where this disease has come from – don't understand about bacteria –

still believe it a curse from Allah. The person who has it is being punished for a sinful act. And they don't forget. If I go back I'll still be the Iqbal who has leprosy.'

'No, I'm sure that's not true,' Miriam said, 'Going back as a doctor will give you high status. I know how much doctors are needed, wanted. Jawad did some intensive paramedic training before going to Zardgul but he wasn't a qualified doctor. Even so, he was still given much respect.'

Iqbal shrugged, 'Maybe.' After a moment he said, 'Yes, of course, you're right. It's just …'

This time he didn't continue and Miriam, not sure if she should, asked, 'Is it why you've never married – the leprosy, I mean?' He nodded. She caught a glimpse of something in his eyes.

'I won't find a wife in my village now – I'm too old, even if anyone would agree to marry me. Coming home with a wife would do more to show people I'm as good as they are than any number of medical certificates. It's difficult to explain….' His voice trailed off into silence again.

Miriam said softly, 'I'm sure you can find a wife who will want to go to Sang-i-Sia with you.' She reached over, placing her hand on top of his for a brief second. She shuddered. How manipulative she could be.

But she had felt something for him – wouldn't have married him if she hadn't. He was a good man and a good father, devoted to Ruckshana who adored him. Leaving him would mean heartbreak for them and, although she realised a distance was between Iqbal and Farid, he provided the stability her son needed. Was it enough, though?

An image came into her head of herself and Iqbal walking along a dusty Karachi street. They were heading away from the hospital where he'd come to do a specialist course in tuberculosis. He was telling her about the morning's lecture, his face animated. He had a free afternoon and they were taking Farid to the beach, then to the funfair at Clifton. As they strolled towards the bus stop at the end of the street, Iqbal took her hand and squeezed it. Surprised, for such physical signs of affection between men and women in public were rare even in cosmopolitan Karachi, she'd looked up at the handsome face smiling down at her. She smiled back, returning the pressure on his hand. Yes, she was happy then – they both were. Could it be recovered?

Other images from the past few years came and went as she sipped her almost cold tea. Their wedding had been a low-key affair in Quetta. Not wanting Farid to be upset at her going away as soon as she was married they'd waited a few weeks before taking a delayed honeymoon. Anna had kept Farid while Miriam and Iqbal had gone up to the beautiful Swat valley for what had been a week filled with laughter and loving. The months in Karachi had been good, too. Iqbal had introduced her to some of the many Hazaras who lived there – a great number of whom seemed to be cousins. They'd enjoyed picnics at the beach, where they'd built giant sandcastles with Farid, swum in the warm waters of the Arabian Sea, hired a fishing boat to take them crabbing in the moonlight. She remembered his joy when Ruckshana was born. 'I never knew a baby could be so beautiful,' he'd said, his eyes full of wonder and love.

She saw a similar look of wonder in his eyes even now whenever they made love. The thought of his gentle loving made her ache with longing and she suddenly missed him terribly. If something is wrong, change it. Usma had quoted her own words back at her and she realised, before thinking about leaving Iqbal, she had to try first to make things right. If he loved her, they had a chance to sort out whatever had gone wrong. 'I've never told this man I love him,' she said aloud, 'not once. And I do.' It wasn't the same love she had for Jawad – something so special it could never happen again. But she'd experienced that – been luckier than millions of women who had never known such a love. Her memories of Jawad mustn't get in the way of her and Iqbal's chances of happiness.

Miriam left the kitchen and groped her way to the outside door, desperate to go to the loo. As she opened the door a blast of icy air made her shiver. A faint glow in the sky indicated, to her surprise it was almost dawn. She was glad to hurry back to her room and pull the blankets up round her. Putting things right between them, tackling whatever problems were making Iqbal so inflexible was going to be far from easy but she felt more positive about the future than she had in a long time.

In the morning Usma's knock on the door sounded peremptory. Blinking awake in bright sunlight Miriam found her cheeks wet with tears. As she lifted her hand to brush them away she paused, the memory of her dream nudging her subconscious. As usual, she'd been running after the man who looked like Jawad and, as always, he'd stopped and turned towards her, but this time he really was Jawad, not the faceless stranger. He'd been smiling, a hand held out to her. Recalling the dream, she experienced again, if only for a flash, an overwhelming happiness and, what she could only describe as the completeness, she'd felt in the dream. Jawad's smile absolved her from marrying Iqbal, reassured her she'd reached the right decision last night. How desperately she wanted to go back to sleep, re-capture the moment.

'Sorry to wake you, but you've half a dozen visitors waiting for you in the guest room – and more on the way. They're going to be very upset if you don't put in an appearance.'

'Oh, God I'm sorry Usma. I didn't sleep until almost morning.'

Usma looked concerned and her voice lost its asperity as she looked at her friend, 'Are you all right?'

Miriam, struggling to sit up, nodded. She flashed a radiant smile at Usma. 'Yes, I am. I did a lot of thinking last night – much of it thanks to you and Ismail. She fell silent for a moment before saying, 'I don't quite know how yet, but I do believe Iqbal and I can sort out our problems. When I get back to Sang-i-Sia I'm going to tell him I came here.' She drew a deep breath, 'Won't be easy, but we're going to have to learn to talk to each other in ways we never have, including being honest. I think I can make him understand why I came. Let him see it was a step towards letting go of the past – allowing us to make something of our future.'

She beamed up at Usma before throwing back the blanket ready to face the day. By then the half a dozen guests Usma had warned her were waiting had doubled. Gul Chaman was there, and Basma, Usra and Payish, three of the very first students who had attended her health classes; Fatima, who had given birth to *doganagi* – twins – the second summer Miriam spent in Zardgul, another Fatima famed for her sharp tongue but who, Miriam, knew had a soft streak a mile wide. For a while there was bedlam as the women hugged and kissed Miriam, laughter and tears mixing as they welcomed her back, offering condolences on the death of her husband, congratulations on her remarriage.

Usma provided endless pots of tea and the day began to feel like an Eid holiday. By the time the last guest said goodbye it was late afternoon. Miriam realised she'd not done anything about the report on the feasibility of opening a clinic in Zardgul. She wondered at Ismail's smug smile as he unlocked a storage trunk. From inside he produced a thick manila folder, which he handed to her. 'Ismail! You've already written a report. This is amazing,' she riffled through the pages, 'there's far more information here than I could have collected.' She looked up at him, 'You'd prepared this before you ever came to Charkoh. You could've given it to Jeanine.'

Ismail's smile broadened. He nodded. 'But then you might not have come to Zardgul.' She looked away and his smile faded. 'I'm sorry if you think I was being manipulative but – well, I'm not sorry I succeeded in getting you here. Are you? Do you regret it? I know I said some harsh things last night...?'

Miriam shook her head, meeting his troubled gaze. 'A sleepless night is a small price to pay for being able to see the way forward. No, I don't regret coming here. I'm only sorry it took so much deceit to bring it about. If Iqbal had...' She stopped. No point in going over old ground again. Before she could say more, Usma bustled in, her face flushed, her hands covered in flour.

'Ismail, come on – kitchen. You were the one who wanted a special meal for Miriam's last night. The kebabs won't cook themselves.' Ismail followed her out and Miriam went to pack ready for the morning's departure.

After an early breakfast the family walked outside with Miriam and Ruckshana. The saddled horses were waiting. Usma held out her arms to Miriam. Both women had tears in their eyes as they hugged, neither daring to think about when they might meet again. Ismail led the way, Ruckshana sitting in front of him, holding the reins and Miriam took one last swift glance back at her friend before following him. She would come back. She would bring Farid and, she hoped, Iqbal. 'Come on, Miveri,' she urged the horse into a canter, overtaking Ismail, 'let's show them what we can do.'

The journey was tiring but the nearer they came to Charkoh, the higher Miriam's spirits rose. She was looking forward to seeing Chaman again and Eva, even Jeanine. Chaman was the one she most wanted to talk to, the one who would understand. She spoke to

Ruckshana, who was now snuggled up in front of her. 'You'll see Feroza and Laila tonight. Won't that be good?' She felt Ruckshana's head bumping her chest as she nodded in agreement. 'And soon, we'll be going back home, to Daddy.'

'And Farid?'

'Yes, I hope so. Yes, I'm sure Farid will be home soon.'

They were almost at the clinic now and Miriam could see only one tent was still standing. Patients must be going home. Suddenly she let out a cry, 'Oh, God, no, please no!'

Ismail turned to her, his face showing alarm. 'What's wrong? What's happened?' Miriam reined in her horse. Her face white, she pointed towards the clinic.

'Iqbal's Toyota.'

'Well,' Ismail murmured dryly, 'you did say you were going to tell him you'd visited Zardgul.'

Miriam shot him a look of anguish.

'Daddy's come, daddy's come,' Ruckshana chanted, squirming so much in excitement, Miriam had to grab her daughter to prevent her toppling from her perch. As they rode forward again, slowed now to a walking pace Miriam saw Iqbal come out of the compound. Shading his eyes against the low sun he was looking in their direction. Ruckshana slapped at Miveri's neck.

'Go faster,' she commanded. 'Want my daddy.'

Miriam dug her heels into the horse's side, urging her into a fast trot. Might as well get it over with. No matter how slowly she covered the remaining few yards separating them, it would never be long enough to decide what she should say to her husband. When she pulled up, Ruckshana launched herself into her father's arms and Miriam sat for a moment watching her cover her father's face with kisses. How could she have considered separating those two? She dismounted and took a step towards her husband and daughter. Iqbal had not looked at her yet. She opened her mouth to speak just as Ismail rode up behind her. She saw Iqbal's eyes flicker over her before he strode past her to greet Ismail.

'Thank you for taking care of my wife and daughter. Will you come in, take tea before you leave?' His voice was quiet, polite but the tell tale tic was pulsing furiously.

Ismail declined the offer saying, 'Thank you, Dr Iqbal *khaan,* but I've some business in the village. I should reach there before dark.' He handed Miriam the folder of notes on Zardgul. 'I'll be there for a day or two if Dr Jeanine wishes to talk to me about anything.' He said goodbye to Ruckshana, shook hands with Iqbal then proffered his hand to Miriam. Aware of Iqbal's eyes on her she hesitated for a moment before taking it. She felt the warmth of his calloused hand send a message, 'Be strong. Fight for what you want.' As though he had spoken to her, she nodded once. He took her horse's reins and Miriam and Iqbal watched in silence as he rode away. Only Ruckshana, still in her father's arms, waved.

'Iqbal, I know how angry you must be. I'm…'

'No, you don't. You have no idea at all.' When he looked at her the hostility in his eyes was like a physical blow. She caught her breath, silenced. Iqbal put Ruckshana on the ground, hunkering down beside her. 'Feroza and Laila are inside waiting for you. D'you want to go and play?' He smiled after her as she ran to find her friends but by the time he straightened and was once more facing Miriam the smile had vanished. She looked away, desperately trying to think of words that might help.

Iqbal broke the silence, 'Jeanine tells me she wants to open a clinic in Zardgul. She sent you to make a report.' It was a statement but Miriam nodded as though he had asked a question, slightly raising the folder she held as if offering proof. Iqbal carried on, 'Until we leave I'll pretend to believe her story.' She winced. 'Jeanine was the first person to see me arriving so I was spared the indignity of finding out from anyone else my wife wasn't here. Everyone believes – or lets me think they do – I gave permission for you to go.' He marched towards the compound gate.

Miriam hurried after him. 'Iqbal, wait. Look, I'm sorry I…' He seemed not to have heard, was almost at the gate. 'Iqbal, please… We need to talk.'

He swung round. 'I'm in no mood for talking right now, Miriam. I'm not sure there's anything I want to hear from you. I don't know if I'd believe whatever you said.' He opened the gate.

'Is that why you came to Charkoh? Because you don't trust me?' she asked, appalled to hear the note of challenge in her voice. She heard the gate creak as he swung it to and fro and forced herself to meet his eyes. She noticed the tic had stopped and his eyes, instead of showing anger, were expressionless.

He spoke quietly, 'I came for two reasons. Firstly because your ex-father-in-law sent word that Farid was coming back …'

'Farid! Oh, that's…'

Ignoring her he continued, 'and I thought we could meet him together in Bamiyan. Secondly, since Taliban took Herat things are unsettled. I was concerned about my wife's safety. Though clearly, since she is a free and independent woman, answerable to no one, I needn't have worried.' He stood aside for her to enter the compound, closing the gate behind them.

She opened her mouth but before any words came out Ismail said, 'I'm going to see Jeanine now, to tell her we're leaving in the morning. You'll want to pack your things, I expect.' How the hell was she going to sort this out? Shit, shit, shit. She started up the stairs, hearing even before she was half way up, Chaman's voice and shrieks of laughter from Ruckshana, Feroza and Laila. Despite everything, she smiled at the sound. Moments later, with Chaman's arms around her though, she was nearer tears than laughter.

She stepped out of her friend's embrace, wiping her eyes with the back of her hand. 'When did he get here?'

'Yesterday. By chance Jeanine was leaving for her room and she saw him arriving. She talked to him before he came looking for you. Ali told me he's blaming Jeanine for sending you to Zardgul. Apparently he's been going on and on about how she doesn't understand our culture. How she should know by now you don't send women riding around the countryside with men who are not relatives – especially not with men as handsome as Ismail.'

'He called Ismail handsome?'

'No, I did.' Chaman grinned. 'He is, isn't he?'

Miriam groaned. 'You're not helping Chaman.' She sank down on a mattress, burying her face in her hands. 'He knows Jeanine's story isn't true. Knows why I went. At least he thinks he does. I'm not sure…' She twisted her fingers together, looking down at her clasped hands. Glancing up at Chaman she said, 'It's strange. I thought I knew why I was going to Zardgul but then things changed. I started to see my life differently – what happened to Jawad, how I dealt – or didn't deal – with his death, Iqbal and our marriage.' She sighed. 'I was going to tell him I went to Zardgul, to Jawad's grave. Try to explain why and…' she broke off with another sigh. 'I didn't have any illusions it would be easy but I thought – Oh, Chaman, he's not going to listen to anything I say – no apologies, no explanations will make any difference. He didn't want me to come here in the first place and going off to Zardgul just proves he can't trust me. It's going to be hell back at Sang-i-Sia. It'll take months of behaving as the perfect Afghan wife, grovelling, showing how sorry I am…' She buried her face in her hands.

'No, Miriam, that's not the way.' Chaman's voice was sharp and she pulled Miriam's hands away from her face, forcing her to look up. 'There's no such thing as a perfect wife, just as there are no perfect husbands. And Afghan wives don't grovel. Dogs grovel and they get kicked for it. When Ali was going through that business of taking a second wife I fought with everything I had in me. If I'd wept and wailed I'm sure today I'd be back in Pakistan in my parents' house, not here working alongside my husband – as his one and only wife.'

'It's different. You'd not done anything wrong.'

'Really?' There was a surprised note in Chaman's question. 'You really think you were wrong to go and see Jawad's grave?'

'No, but Iqbal does. He'll see it as one more example of how I've allowed Jawad to come between us. And it's true – I have.'

'If you want things to be right between you and Iqbal then you'll have to be strong. And remember if there had been no Jawad, Iqbal would never have met you. Fight for what you want.'

Hearing her friend deliver the same message she'd felt in Ismail's handshake Miriam gave Chaman a weak smile. 'I know you're right – just don't know how I'll manage it.'

'You will,' Chaman said, getting to her feet. 'Come on, it's time for dinner.'

'Oh, damn. I was going to take a bath. You go ahead. I'm not hungry anyway.'

'There's some water in the bathroom. You're not going to sit up here on your own – you have to face everyone, behave as usual. Now, go and wash your face.'

NINETEEN

Back to Sang-i-Sia 1995

Iqbal was already seated in the staff room, deep in conversation with Anwar. Miriam saw him glance up as she came into the room with Chaman and the girls. Ruckshana made a beeline for her daddy, who scooped her up and sat her on his lap. A chorus of salaams came from people around the room and Eva, with a huge smile, beckoned them over to places beside her. 'It's good to see you back. How was the trip?'

'Good, thanks.' Over the babble of voices Iqbal was straining to catch her every word. 'There's a good chance Hansease will open a clinic in Zardgul – certainly a need for it. I've given Jeanine a fairly detailed report, so let's hope she can find the funding.' Keeping resolutely away from personal aspects of her visit she spoke a little more about Zardgul before changing the subject by asking Eva how things had been at the camp. Listening to stories about the successes and failures of Eva and Chaman's work in the women's clinic Miriam relaxed a little. Absorbed in the conversation she scarcely noticed the *dustakhan* being cleared away and tea brought in until she heard someone call her name.

'Dr Miriam, shall we show them how to play?' Hussain grinned at her, a pack of cards in his hand. She froze.

'I… em, I don't think so. I'm really tired. I…' She didn't dare look in Iqbal's direction as she made her excuses. Bloody Hussain. Why did he have to open his mouth?

'Oh, come on. Dr Iqbal says you're leaving tomorrow. It's our last chance to show them.' At the same time as Hussain was making his plea, Miriam felt Chaman's finger jab her in the ribs, under her *chaddar*. Although her friend didn't speak, Miriam knew she was telling her, 'Start as you mean to go on. Be strong. Be yourself.'

She shuffled forward towards the group of card players, holding her hand out to take the cards from Hussain. 'All right, let's show them.' Aware of Iqbal watching her Miriam couldn't concentrate on playing and they lost the first couple of hands. The others laughed when Hussain threw her a despairing look. He so hated to lose. Miriam pulled herself together and began to play to win.

Anwar found another pack of cards and invited Iqbal to play. 'You and me against Moh'd Amir and – who'll partner Moh'd Amir? What about you Chaman?'

Chaman laughed, saying, 'I'm useless. You'll have to find someone else.' Anwar urged her to join in, promising he could teach her how to play.

Ali spoke up, 'If you can teach Chaman how to play *filscut* Moh'd Amir, I'll cook breakfast tomorrow.' Chaman joined the second group of players amid encouraging banter.

After twenty minutes Miriam looked round when she heard Ali say to Moh'd Amir, 'Looks like you'll be cooking breakfast after all tomorrow. She's hopeless at cards – but don't ever try to beat her at chess.' He grinned at Chaman who wished everyone goodnight and went out carrying a sleeping Raihanna, followed by Feroza and Laila. Tiredness soon caught up with Miriam. Every time she yawned her eyes watered so much she couldn't spot the cards in her hand. She longed to lie down where she was and sleep. Finally she gave up the struggle and rose to her feet. She went to take Ruckshana from Iqbal's arms where she was fast asleep but he indicated he would carry the little girl to the room.

They crossed the compound and climbed the stairs in silence. Miriam tapped on the door opening it enough to let her check Chaman was covered and warn her Iqbal was coming in. He laid Ruckshana down, said goodnight to Chaman and left the room. Miriam followed him out, closing the door behind her not knowing if she was hoping he would speak to her or not.

'We leave at six,' he said, not meeting her eyes. 'I've asked Moh'd Amir to prepare some food for the road and he'll bring tea for you and Ruckshana at half five.' He turned to go down the stairs, adding, '*Shubakhair* - goodnight.' She listened to his footsteps. They didn't slow down. He wasn't thinking about coming back to talk to her. She heard the outer door close and turned back into the room.

'Who won?' Chaman whispered.

'What?' Miriam wasn't sure what Chaman meant.

'The cards – who won?'

'Oh, we did.'

'Good. Well done.'

Miriam smiled in the dark. 'Thanks. Thanks for pushing me into it, though I'm not sure if it didn't hand Iqbal even more ammunition.'

'Well at least he saw that Afghan wives play cards, too.'

Miriam grunted. 'Not very well!'

Chaman was soon asleep but Miriam, too tired to think, too tired to sleep, lay awake for a long time. The brightest point in her life right now was the knowledge she'd soon have Farid back with her. He'd pick up on the tension between her and Iqbal – always did. She sighed.

When Moh'd Amir tapped on the door at five thirty Miriam was already awake. She called out her thanks, waiting for his footsteps to fade before opening the door to bring in the tray of tea. She went out to the latrine, shivering in the icy morning air. By the time she returned Chaman was awake. Ruckshana, still half asleep, sat holding a piece of bread in one hand, a hardboiled egg in the other. Miriam urged her to drink some tea.

'You all right?' Chaman asked, her voice still thick with sleep. Miriam paused. Her husband probably hated her, was certainly furious with her, she was setting out on a freezing cold morning on what would be a miserably silent journey to meet her son, whom she'd psychologically scarred for life. And she didn't know if her marriage could be saved.

'Fine. I'm fine.' She drank her tea then, mentally squaring her shoulders, replaced the glass on the tray. 'Let's go, Ruckshana.' She turned to hug Chaman, saying, 'Don't come outside. I'd rather say goodbye here.' She clung to her friend, tears blinding her, without the comfort of being able to say see you next year. She didn't know when, even if, they would meet again.

'I'll pray for you every day,' Chaman promised.

'I'm not sure Allah will listen,' Miriam replied sadly, 'I've not been paid him much attention lately.'

'Allah knows what's in your heart, even when you're not saying all the prayers.'

By the time Miriam and Ruckshana reached the compound the darkness was pierced by lanterns and torches held by the people who arrived to say goodbye. Eva came forward to hug her. 'Thanks for being such a great translator,' she said, 'I would've been lost without you. If Jeanine organises another teaching camp I'll come back – and insist you and Chaman translate for me again. Although I intend to learn some Dari before I return. Have a safe journey and good luck. The women of Sang-i-Sia are in good hands.'

Miriam felt Iqbal's impatience as the engine throbbed into life and hurried round to take her place in the Toyota. He had already wedged Ruckshana, still clutching her egg and piece of *nan,* into place in the back, surrounded by blankets and Miriam climbed in beside her. The moment she closed the door, Iqbal accelerated away.

Ruckshana soon fell asleep. Inside the jeep, the silence sounded louder than the engine. 'So,' Miriam asked with a determined cheerfulness, 'how's everyone in Sang-i-Sia? Your family? Your father – is he keeping well?'

'He's not good. My brother Hassan – the one in Iran – died suddenly. Father is taking it very badly.'

'Oh, Iqbal, I'm sorry.'

'Why? You never met Hassan, and I didn't like him.'

'You never told me you didn't like your brother. I know you didn't talk about him much but I didn't realise you...'

Iqbal cut her off mid-sentence, his voice clipped. 'You and I have got far more important things to discuss than my family tangles, though right now I really don't want to talk.'

'Fine. Don't talk. That's how you deal with most things, isn't it? I'm going to sleep. Let me know when – if – you ever feel like speaking again.' She didn't for a moment expect she'd be able to sleep but wriggled around until she found a more comfortable position, pillowed her head on a folded blanket and closed her eyes. She knew nothing more until Iqbal brought the Toyota to a stop and turned off the engine. She eased herself into an upright position, massaging her stiff neck. Ruckshana was just waking up, too, her eyes gummy with sleep. Seeing the sun so high, Miriam was astonished she'd slept for several hours.

'It's eleven o'clock,' Iqbal said. 'We've made good time but I need a break. There's tea in a thermos and some *nan* in that box by your feet.' She slid out of the jeep pulling the supplies box with her, glad to stretch her legs. Tea would be good, though she didn't feel like eating. Iqbal lifted Ruckshana down and spread a blanket on the ground. They were at the top of a steep pass and the rock-strewn road in front of them descended in a series of hairpin bends. Although the sun was bright in a cloudless sky the wind blowing at this height was chill, warning winter was on its way. From far below, the faint tinkling of goat-bells and the reedy notes of a shepherd's pipe drifted up to them. Ruckshana chattered to Iqbal, making him smile at some story about Feroza. Miriam sipped her tea and sighed. They could've been a happy family stopping for a picnic on their way to Bamiyan. If she'd come back from Zardgul a day earlier, or not gone at all… No, she'd been right to go. She didn't regret it. She sighed again when Iqbal stood up ready to continue. Carrying Ruckshana back to her seat in the jeep, he brushed by Miriam without saying a word.

From time to time Miriam tried to make Iqbal talk to her – shouting at her in anger would be preferable to this silence – but he would not be drawn. To her questions about when Farid would arrive in Bamiyan he only told her 'maybe yesterday, maybe today.'

They continued to make good time and when the first of the red sandstone cliffs, their faces pockmarked with caves, alerted Miriam to how close they were to Bamiyan it was still light. In the bazaar, Iqbal drew up outside the hotel. Miriam lifted Ruckshana out and with her daughter in her arms hurried up the stairs to find her son. The door to the first floor room stood ajar: she could hear voices but when she pushed the door wide and walked in a dozen *mujahideen* were tucking into kebabs and rice, their kalashnikovs stashed tepee fashion in the centre of the room. She knew Farid could not be there but continued to stand in the doorway staring round the room. At the sound of approaching footsteps she whirled round, but it was Sufi, the hotel owner.

'Welcome back,' he said. 'I'm sorry this room is full but I have another. It's smaller but for a family room it's good. Follow me.'

'Have you seen my son? Farid? Is he here yet?'

Sufi shook his head, clearly not understanding what she was talking about. He sorted through a bunch of keys until, satisfied he'd found the right one, unlocked the padlock on a door. She hesitated on the threshold, wrinkling her nose at the chill air and musty smell, before stepping into the room. She trembled from a combination of cold and searing disappointment. Iqbal came up the stairs carrying blankets and boxes, which he deposited on the floor.

'Farid's not here.'

Iqbal shrugged. 'There's still time for him to arrive today. If not then maybe tomorrow.'

'Maybe tomorrow?' Her voice was shrill. 'You said he'd arrive yesterday or today. Maybe he's in a different hotel?'

'Miriam, you know it's impossible to be certain how long a journey will take. Daud will bring him here as soon as they reach Bamiyan. Can we get this room sorted out?' He turned to Sufi hovering in the doorway. 'Bring us a *bukhari* – it's cold in here. And food. Miriam, Ruckshana, what do you want?' Ruckshana wanted kebabs, Miriam said she wasn't hungry. 'Three plates of kebabs – and get the *bukhari* sent as quick as you can.'

The kerosene stove was soon brought, its powerful smell disguised the mustiness, gave a promise of warmth. Miriam stirred herself to cover the thin none too clean *toshak* with blankets. Finding a bucket and water jug, she washed the dust from her own and Ruckshana's face and hands. When the food came she picked at it, fighting back tears. After the plates had been cleared away Iqbal suggested they go for a walk in the bazaar. Ruckshana was enthusiastic but Miriam shook her head.

'I'll stay here in case they come.' As soon as she said the words she knew she'd made a mistake. Iqbal's face closed up even more. Without another word he left the room with Ruckshana. Miriam almost ran after them, words of apology on her lips, but instead went to the window overlooking the dusty street. Her husband and daughter emerged below, Ruckshana firmly grasping Iqbal's forefinger in her tiny fist. Iqbal was leaning down, listening intently to whatever Ruckshana was saying. Miriam saw him suddenly throw his head back and the sound of his laughter, mingled with her daughter's giggles, drifted up to her. She felt hot tears sliding unchecked down her face.

It was dark when they returned, bringing a blast of chilly air in with them. Ruckshana's cheeks were pink from the cold and the excitement of her shopping spree. She showed Miriam all she'd wheedled out of her father: an embroidered waistcoat, some hair slides, an English alphabet book and a pair of pink plastic sandals. 'And *choclet* – one bag for me and one for Farid.'

'Right, young lady,' she said, 'let's get you ready for bed.'

'Not sleepy.'

'Yes you are,' Miriam replied in a voice allowing no further argument. 'Daddy can read you a story,' she added, softening her tone. Ruckshana was soon asleep, cradled in Iqbal's arms, still holding onto her plastic sandals. He laid her down, pulling the blanket up to her chin, before moving towards the door.

'Where are you going?'

'Out.' He opened the door.

'No, you're not,' Miriam hissed. 'We're going to talk. If you leave now I'll take it you have no intention of trying to make our marriage work.'

Iqbal stared at her, his hand still on the partly open door. The door creaked as he made a move. At the same moment came the sound of loud banging on the outside door. She heard a voice asking if Dr Iqbal was there. It must be Farid. She tore past Iqbal and down the stairs where she wrestled with the heavy bolt fastening the door.

Crying and laughing she called through the door, 'Farid, can you hear me?' Sufi came up behind her yelling at her not to open the door.

'At this time of night, it can only be *dozd*. They'll rob us.'

'No, it's Farid. It's my son. Oh, please Sufi, open the door.'

'It's all right,' Iqbal called from half way down the stairs, 'You can open up.'

Ignoring the two men standing on either side of Farid, Miriam pounced on her son, hugging him, covering his face with kisses until he pulled away, protesting, 'Mother, I'm not a baby.' But not before she felt his arms return her hug.

'Miriam-*jan* how are you?'

She looked over Farid's head at Jawad's brother, remembering the last time they met. She managed to smile at him, 'I'm well – happy now you've brought my boy back safely.'

'I'm sorry to arrive so late. We had one puncture after another.'

Sufi bolted the door again, shooing everyone back upstairs. 'Suppose you'll want tea now? I'm not cooking, you'll have to make do with what's left of the *yackhni*.' Iqbal led Daud and his driver into the big room, asking Sufi to take tea to Farid in the family room. Miriam turned the lamp up higher so she could look at her son. He's right. He's not a baby any more. The realisation gave her a fleeting stab of pain – in such a short time he'd be leaving his childhood behind. Ruckshana stirred in her sleep, waking fully the moment she heard her brother's voice.

'Farid!' she scrambled out of bed, rushing at him. Clumsily he hugged her, submitting to yet more kisses. 'Have you got me a present?' she demanded. 'I've got you one.' She burrowed under her blanket, pulling out the bag of toffees. 'Look, *choclet.*'

'I have got a present for you, but it's in my box. You'll have to wait until tomorrow.'

'What is it?'

'Wait 'til tomorrow.'

Miriam laughed at her daughter's pout. To distract her she said to Farid, 'So, how was Mazar-i-Sharif? Did you enjoy city life? We want to hear everything.'

Sufi brought in a tray of tea and food: Farid fell on it as though he'd not eaten for a week. He talked in between mouthfuls of bread and soup. 'We went to the *mazar* lots of times to feed the pigeons. Thousands of them – all white,' he told his sister.' Turning to Miriam he added, 'My grandparents are well. They have sent a letter for you. Uncle Daud has it. They want me to go back next year. Can I mother? If I go in the winter Uncle Daud will take me to the *buzkashi*. They only started playing before I left but I saw two games. Uncle Daud knows lots of the *chapandaz* – all the really best riders.' He paused for breath.

'Did your grandparents talk to you about your father?' The second the words were out Miriam wished she hadn't asked them. Too soon. Did she imagine the cloud passing briefly across her son's face? He nodded.

'Yes. They're still very sad. They gave me some photos of him to keep. They're in my box. Are we going home tomorrow?'

'I think so. You'd better get some sleep, you must be exhausted.' She unfolded more blankets, making up a bed, while he went to wash his hands. When he returned she knew how tired he was when he immediately lay down. Ruckshana snuggled in beside him. Miriam turned the lamp down, sitting beside her two children holding their hands until they fell asleep. She sat for a long time, listening to their even breathing, watching the lamp's shadow flicker and dance on the wall, waiting for Iqbal to return, wondering what she was going to say.

She glanced at her watch from time to time, fighting her own exhaustion. Daud and the driver must have finished eating by now. Surely they couldn't be still discussing punctures and politics? She was only aware that she had nodded off when her head falling forward snapped her awake. She rubbed at the back of her neck, yawning and disorientated. Iqbal's mattress remained empty. She rose and opened the door, listening. No sound of voices came from the other room and, taking the lamp, she tiptoed across the narrow corridor. Pressing her ear to the door she could hear only a symphony of snores. Quietly she opened it, peering into the darkness. In the faint lamplight she could make out the shapes of several sleeping bodies.

'Bastard,' she ground through clenched teeth before returning to her own room, resisting the urge, only because she didn't want to wake the sleeping children, to slam the door as hard as she could. There's your answer then – he doesn't think a discussion about our marriage is even worth staying awake for. She slid down between Ruckshana and Farid, pulling a blanket round her.

So now what? Back to Sang-i-Sia and a half-life of working, running a home for someone who doesn't mind an empty shell of a marriage? Go back to Scotland, leaving a big chunk of her heart behind? She shook her head to dislodge a picture of her mother's triumphant 'told you so' expression. That aside, could she go back to being a midwife, a cog in a hospital wheel? To Mazar-i-Sharif, then? With her experience it wouldn't be difficult to find work in the city amongst the many aid organisations. She'd be able to support herself and the children. How would Jawad's family feel about their one-time daughter-in-law turning up on the doorstep? She pictured Anwar's face – he would be as gallant as ever, welcoming her warmly but…he would, after a few days, gently let her know her place now was with her husband. Besides if they knew there were problems between her and Iqbal they would want to keep Farid and she'd have to fight for him.

Ruckshana stirred in her sleep, flinging out an arm. As Miriam absentmindedly stroked the back of her daughter's small, plump hand the image of her leaving the hotel with her father came back to her.

They loved each other so much, what would separating them do? Iqbal would never allow her to take Ruckshana away. She couldn't contemplate leaving without her. If only…she hadn't gone to Zardgul… had returned sooner… been there when Iqbal arrived… if he hadn't come to meet her…hadn't lost face in front of colleagues. 'I made my husband lose face,' she groaned, realising when both children stirred, she'd spoken aloud. Farid muttered something inaudible before sliding into sleep again.

It was so big, this thing about face – respect – reputation – honour. She wasn't even sure if it could be translated into English. Close approximations of the word, but not the whole sense of it. She thought about Ali being incapable of breaking off the engagement because he believed to do so would damage his 'reputation', thought about Mullah Anwar – prepared to have a man killed. She couldn't make the jump across the cultural divide to experience how it felt to lose face but understood she had to accept its importance and let Iqbal know she had done so. If he would listen to her. She buried her face in the blanket to muffle her sobs, thought of how much she wanted to feel Iqbal's arms around her, reassuring her they'd be all right. Her thoughts went round in circles until exhaustion overcame her and she slept.

The sound of Ruckshana and Farid's voices woke her. She raised her head from the pillow and with a groan let it fall back. 'Morning you two,' she managed. 'What are you up to?'

'Waiting for you to wake up,' said Ruckshana. 'We're hungry. Daddy's looking at the jeep.'

Miriam sat up noting, with the exception of her own, the bedding had been folded, bags packed. There was a tap at the door and Sufi carried in a tray stacked with plates of fried eggs. The boy followed him bringing bread and tea. Miriam was helping Ruckshana to an egg when Iqbal entered. She passed him a plate, poured tea and tore off a piece of *nan* for herself, dipping it in the sweetened tea. As soon as he'd eaten breakfast Iqbal rose to his feet.

'I'll take these to the jeep. When you're finished we'll be off.'

The journey would have been unbearable for Miriam, but now she had Farid back her heart felt less heavy. He entertained them, sometimes even making Iqbal smile, with stories about his time in Mazar. Like a sponge he'd soaked up every detail of all he saw and did and now brought it all to life for them as he described the busy bazaars displaying everything from plastic sandals to antique carpets, the ice cream parlours selling delicious pistachio and rosewater flavoured *sheeryakh*, kebab shops, the presence of the militia and the tanks rumbling through the streets in the dead of night. When he talked about the shrine, re-telling the legends Jawad had once told her, she thought what a fine gift of story telling he had inherited from his father. She smiled inwardly at the quick rush of pleasure this gave her.

Once, when both children had fallen asleep Iqbal glanced over at her. After a great deal of throat clearing he said, 'I know you wanted us to talk last night but...I...well, it was late and I couldn't leave Daud...' His voice trailed into silence. He glanced at her again before returning his attention to the road. She stared at his profile, willing him to say more, wondering at the note of appeal she thought she'd glimpsed in his eyes. She touched his arm, about to speak, when Ruckshana waking, demanded to be let out to pee. Miriam sighed as Iqbal braked, bringing the jeep to a stop and went to lift his daughter down.

The children stayed awake from then on, giving no opportunity for further personal discussion. Tonight. They had to start talking tonight. It was late afternoon when they arrived at Sang-i-Sia, still light enough for Miriam to note the changes since she left only four weeks ago. The harvest was in. The trees were almost bare, only a few brown leaves still clinging to their branches. She shuddered at the thought of the winter ahead, the thick snow isolating them, cutting them off from the rest of the world. She looked up to where the low, slanting sun spotlighted their house, turning the mud walls to a warm honey colour.

Below, outside Fatima's house she could see figures moving about and a bright splash of colour – orange and black. Her neighbour must be working on a *gillim*. The sound of the vehicle caused the figures to stop, look down the mountain and Miriam saw Fatima stand up, hand shading her eyes. Then she was waving and Miriam jumped out of the jeep to wave and climb up the path towards home.

TWENTY

Sang-i-Sia 1995

Within minutes Fatima's husband, Daud, with some of his older sons, was helping Iqbal carry the bags and boxes up to the house. Farid, carrying his own box, immediately disappeared into his room, Ruckshana shot off in search of her kitten and Miriam found herself standing alone in the living room.

Put the kettle on. Make tea. Organise unpacking. She crossed to the window, watching Iqbal bring the last bags. When he came in they must…She jumped, startled, when Fatima called her name.

'Tea's ready. Come down.' As Miriam turned from the window to her friend, Fatima, asked, 'What is it, Miriam-*jan*? Is something wrong?'

Miriam shook her head, made herself smile at Fatima. 'Been a long two days on the road.' She linked arms with Fatima, 'Let's go.'

Later, declaring Miriam too tired to cook after such a journey, her neighbour insisted the family eat with her and Daud. Her husband echoed the invitation, adding Malim Ashraf was expected from the village. Instead of a simple meal with Fatima, the evening was turning into a *mehmanni*. Daud's second wife, Shahnaz had to be invited so Iqbal and Daud could eat in her room with Malim Ashraf; the women occupying Fatima's room. Seeing Iqbal nod agreement, Miriam accepted reluctantly.

Though indeed too tired to cook, Miriam was also too preoccupied to make conversation. She asked for news of the village. Shahnaz shifted slightly in her place and Miriam detected a slight change in the atmosphere. She was astonished to catch the two women exchange a glance. Curiosity aroused, she started to ask what was going on but

Fatima began at once to rattle on with a story about a family dispute over the sinking of a well. Not knowing the people involved, Miriam's attention soon drifted. If they didn't go home soon it would be too late for her and Iqbal to talk. Probably what he was hoping when he accepted the invitation. She was relieved when Daud popped his head round the door to say Dr Iqbal was ready to leave.

Back in their own home, her exhaustion must have been apparent to Iqbal for he organised the mattresses and started preparing Ruckshana for bed. Miriam hugged Farid when he said goodnight. 'I'm glad you had a good time in Mazar,' she murmured, 'but I'm so happy to have you back home.' Hearing a giggle she turned to see something wriggling under her daughter's blanket. Iqbal extracted the kitten, assuring Ruckshana it would be perfectly happy in the kitchen. When he began to read the child a story, Miriam knew he was avoiding any talk with her. After a few minutes listening to the antics of Mullah Nasuridin, she removed the book from his hands.

'She's asleep, Iqbal. No more delaying tactics. You said we'd talk. I want to…'

'We're both far too tired, Miriam. Leave it tonight. In the morning, after we've slept.' He gave an exaggerated yawn.

'Nice to know you are so little concerned about our problems you're able to sleep.' Well done, girl, get straight up there on your high horse. Quickest way to make him clam up. She reached a hand out towards him. 'Sorry, didn't mean to snap. You're right, we're both exhausted but I need to explain about Zardgul. And I need to know why you've changed so much in the last year. I…'

Iqbal cut her off. 'What about my needs, Miriam?'

'What? What do you mean?'

'I'm hearing what you need. It seems to me it's all a bit one sided. Maybe I need…'He broke off, shaking his head as though he didn't know how to continue. 'Right now I know I don't need to hear anything about Zardgul.' He looked away from her.

She stared at his bowed head. A bit one sided? She heard Ismail's voice, telling her she'd become selfish. Was Iqbal saying the same?

'What do **you** want Iqbal?'

A long silence followed her question. Would he want her to give up her work in the clinic, devote herself to being a model wife and mother or pack her bags and go back to Scotland? At last he looked up, his face expressionless. 'I'd like to hear you laugh more often.'

'Laugh?' Taken aback by his answer she couldn't think what to say. Remembered Jeanine's comment in Charkoh, her laughter in the staff room after work.

Iqbal nodded. 'You used to laugh a lot. I'm not able to make you laugh any more.' He sounded sad, defeated.

'You changed,' Miriam said softly.

'Last night, in Bamiyan, when you questioned if I wanted our marriage to work, it was like you'd taken a knife and stabbed me.'

'And if Farid hadn't arrived just then, what were you going to do?'

He reached for her hand. 'I wanted to stay but I didn't know what to say. Still don't.'

Miriam squeezed his hand. If he wanted them to be together, they were over the first hurdle. Her sigh turned into a yawn. She tried to smother it. Had to tell him about what she'd learned in Zardgul.

Iqbal caught her yawn. He gave her a faint smile. 'Enough now. Let's sleep.'

'But I …Okay,' she agreed. 'Tomorrow. Promise we'll talk?'

Iqbal nodded. 'I'll ask Farid to see to Ruckshana in the morning – let you sleep.'

'Won't you be here? You're not opening the clinic tomorrow are you? I thought we would…'

'No,' he cut across her words, 'but I have some work to attend to in the morning.'

'I wish you wouldn't be so defensive when I ask anything about what you're doing,' Miriam said. 'It's not meant as an interrogation.'

After a pause, he gave a slight shrug. He muttered, 'I have to see my father about prayers for my brother.'

'Of course, yes. Shouldn't I come with you to offer my condolences?'

'You needn't go tomorrow. At the forty days prayer would be better. We'll have time to talk when I come back.'

Though nothing had been resolved, the huge issues not yet tackled, at least he was speaking to her again. It was a start.

Next morning Miriam woke late to a silent house. She lay still for a few moments, vaguely wondering where the children were. Turning her head she noticed someone – Farid or Iqbal – had placed a thermos and some *nan* wrapped in a cloth beside the bed. She sat up, stretching her arms high above her head, enjoying the feeling of having slept well. She poured her tea, sipping with appreciation. Before she'd drunk one glass she heard Fatima call her name and hurriedly stood up, folding the blankets. Trying to look as though she hadn't woken only minutes before, she returned Fatima's greeting, inviting her friend to come in. Returning from the kitchen after putting water on to boil for fresh tea Miriam suddenly asked, 'Do you want to go for a walk instead of sitting here?'

'Walk? Where?'

'I don't know – through the village, maybe. Or further up the mountain? Don't you ever feel like just walking – just getting out?'

'Why?' Fatima looked startled.

'Well, fresh air, exercise, see the view from another angle...' Miriam stopped, feeling foolish. She shrugged. 'Just an idea, forget it.' Over their tea Miriam told Fatima some of the funny incidents at the teaching camp. A loud rumble from her stomach reminded her she hadn't yet eaten anything and it was almost lunchtime.

'Come down and eat with me,' Fatima suggested. 'Farid and Ruckshana are down there, anyway. Ruckshana's making my girls jealous of the doll Farid brought her from Mazar.'

'Maybe I'll cook something here – if I can remember how after so long not doing any. I'm not sure if Iqbal will be back to eat or not.' She started putting their empty glasses on the tray along with the teapot. She rose to her feet, asking, 'Did you hear his brother died? The one who lived in Iran?'

'Yes, I know.'

Something in Fatima's tone made Miriam uneasy. She scrutinised her friend's face for a clue but couldn't read her expression. Fatima looked away first.

'What is it? What are you not telling me?' Fatima, plucking at the fringe on a cushion, seemed unable to meet her gaze.

Miriam sat down again. 'I sensed something last night when I asked what was happening in the village.'

Finally Fatima said, 'It's nothing, really. Just ...Well, Iqbal's brother's wife has come back to the village.' She shrugged as if to dismiss any import her words might have.

'So?'

'Did…did Iqbal tell you?'

'No. He only told me his brother died,' not adding that as, until late last night, her husband was scarcely speaking to her it was unlikely he'd bother to tell her anything.

'He's not mentioned his sister-in-law, Zohra?' When Miriam shook her head, Fatima gave a long sigh.

'Look, just tell me what all this is about, will you?'

'There's talk in the village – now she's back. People are saying, now she's free…' She swallowed, continuing in a rush, 'maybe Iqbal will marry her.'

Miriam gave a shout of laughter, breaking off suddenly when Fatima looked away. 'My God, you're serious, aren't you? You think Iqbal is going to marry his sister-in-law?'

'I'm not saying he is. Just warning you there's talk. I didn't want to say anything but I was worried you'd hear it from others.'

'But why would he want to marry her?'

'He loved her.'

'What?'

Fatima nodded. 'They loved each other from when they were small. Zohra was his friend; probably his only friend once people knew about his disease. I can remember seeing them together.' She smiled, 'Always talking to each other as if no one else existed in the world. People assumed when Zohra became a young woman, things would change. But they still saw each other, finding secret places where they could meet.' She laughed. 'They didn't know there aren't any secret places round here. Everyone knew. I was only small then, but I can remember hearing my sisters giggling about them. Zohra was teased a lot whenever she came to the well. Poor girl, she put up with a lot of tormenting but…well, she must have thought he was worth it.'

'What happened? How did this great love affair come to end?' Miriam was surprised at the bitter note in her voice. How could she be jealous – it was so long ago? Why hadn't Iqbal ever mentioned Zohra? She felt Fatima's eyes rest on her and met the woman's questioning gaze. 'What happened?' she repeated.

'They wanted to get married and go away to Pakistan. I didn't hear the details at the time – something to do with trying to find medicine for his leprosy. People thought he wanted to go somewhere no one would know about his disease.

'Anyway, they went together to Zohra's family. It was very unusual – not the way things are done here. Her parents agreed. They met with Iqbal's. That's where it all went wrong. It wasn't until I was older I learned what happened. All I knew was Zohra had become engaged and was married almost at once to Iqbal's brother Hassan. Afterwards, I heard it was Iqbal's father who opposed the marriage – to anyone – because he believed the disease would be passed on. Didn't want his grandchildren to get leprosy. But Zohra was a good catch. Her father owned a lot of land and old Sarwar was delighted at the chance to forge links with the family.'

'But, I don't understand. Why did Zohra agree to marry Hassan?'

Fatima shrugged. 'She had no choice. Sarwar told her father if she didn't accept he would go to the *shura*, make a report about her behaviour with Iqbal. You know, say they'd been having a sexual relationship. Even if it wasn't true,' she lifted a hand to forestall an outburst from Miriam, 'the talk would be enough to ruin the girl's reputation. As far as I know she and Iqbal never saw each other again. On the morning of the wedding he disappeared. His poor mother never recovered. She was a distant cousin of my mother and used to come to our house to cry on my mother's shoulder, saying she'd lost two sons the day Hassan was married. As you know, Hassan went to Iran after he married Zohra. And now she's back,' she ended thoughtfully.

Lost for words, Miriam stared at her friend. The story explained what had always puzzled her about Iqbal's coolness towards his father, the little amount of time he spent with his family. On a personal level, the fact Iqbal had never told her any of this was painful – as, stupidly, she thought, was the knowledge he had loved someone else. Had loved? It might even be expected that he should offer to take care of his brother's widow. She swallowed hard.

'How long has she been back? Has Iqbal seen her?'

Fatima's fingers were again entwined in the cushion fringe, smoothing and pulling at it. Miriam resisted her impulse to grab the cushion from her and hurl it across the room. Fatima nodded, once. 'He went to see her a week ago – before he went to Charkoh. We…I wondered if maybe you wouldn't come back. When you arrived yesterday I was very happy to see you. I thought then it was only talk. It didn't seem as if Iqbal had said anything to you – and surely he would, if he was planning on marrying Zohra I mean?'

Miriam felt dizzy. Everyone was talking about this, about her, about her husband taking a second wife. Unbelievable. She forced herself to take a couple of deep breaths, to be calm. It was ridiculous. Iqbal would never take a second wife. He'd been angry when he heard about Ali's engagement. While not openly disapproving of polygamy – after all Islam allowed it, therefore he wouldn't speak against it – he always said unless the man was certain he adhered one hundred per cent to the criteria he should not take a second wife. But in the light of Fatima's story, how well did she know her husband? She looked at her friend, hoping to see her grinning at the absurdity of the notion. There was sympathy in Fatima's eyes. Miriam wanted her to go away. She desperately needed time alone to think.

'I'm glad you told me. It would've been horrible to hear it from someone else. But I know there's nothing to worry about.'

Fatima rose to her feet. She put her arms out to Miriam, saying, 'It's only talk. People remember how much in love they were all those years ago and, well, you   know how everyone gossips here.'

Miriam returned her friend's hug but Fatima's last words did not comfort her as she walked with her to the gate. They sounded an echoing drumbeat in her head. Standing in the compound she stared up at the mountains wondering what Zohra looked like. She wandered back into the house and sat down, absently picking up the cushion whose fringe Fatima had all but pulled off. What would she say to him when he came back?

Maybe she should keep quiet about Fatima's news – at least until they'd dealt with their other problems? This Zohra creature needn't become an added complication. Did Iqbal still find her attractive? They'd be about the same age but Zohra – well – she'd look at least ten years older, wouldn't she? How many children had she had? Would Iqbal notice her wrinkles – or see the young girl he fell in love with? She gave herself a mental shake. Zohra wasn't the real issue – concentrate on the more important things – getting her husband to open up to her would be a good start.

At the sound of Iqbal's footsteps, Miriam sat up straighter. The door opened and she took a deep breath.

'So how's Zohra?'

Not the way she'd intended playing it. As an opening gambit, though, it certainly had impact. Colour drained from Iqbal's face, his jaw dropped, and for the first time in her life she understood the expression goggle-eyed.

'Wh…what did you…? I…I meant to…'

From where she was sitting on the *toshak*, the remains of the shredded cushion on her lap, Miriam tilted her face upwards to look him in the eye. 'Meant to what? Tell me about her?' He stared at her, nodded. 'When Iqbal? In time to invite me to the wedding?'

'Wedding? What're you talking about?'

'What the whole village is talking about – you marrying your childhood sweetheart.'

'Don't be ridiculous. Who's…?'

'Ridiculous? Yes, that's what I thought, at first. But the more I learned how little I knew of your past – your secret love, for example – the more I began to wonder if it was quite so ridiculous.' She watched the colour return to his cheeks, saw the tic start its staccato dance. What gave him the right to be angry?

'I'm not going to marry Zohra,' he said, his voice now flat, cold. 'I never …'

'Turn you down, did she?' Shit. This wasn't how it was supposed to go. So this thing twisting her insides, making her blood boil and rush into her head until she wanted to scream, wanted to lash out – this was jealousy. She took a deep breath, then another. She looked at him and knew he wouldn't marry Zohra.

'It was such a shock to hear about her… Iqbal, why did you keep it from me?'

He gave a shrug, raising his arms, palm outwards but before he could speak she rushed on, 'To know you chose not to share such an important part of your life with me …to find out from someone else, it was so hurtful.'

From where he was still standing in the middle of the room, Iqbal now moved slowly to sit down opposite Miriam. Leaning forward slightly he hissed, 'As hurtful as a wife abusing her husband's trust? Making him look a fool? As hurtful as that, Miriam?'

'That's dif…' seeing him move as if to stand and walk out, she stopped. This was her only chance to explain. She swallowed, dropping her eyes from his hard stare. 'I know you're angry with me for going to Zardgul, but I **had** to go.'

He snorted. 'As always, you had to show your devotion to your first husband – **your** past love. At least mine stayed in the past, didn't dominate our marriage.'

'But why didn't you tell me about her?'

'No point. By the time I met you I'd learned not to remember, not to be always thinking about what might have been. Besides, you were so caught up in your own loss...It would've looked like I was trying to compete.' He dragged his palms down over his face.

'Didn't you think I would hear about it eventually? Especially when she came back?'

'I was going to tell you when I came to Charkoh to meet you. You weren't there.'

Miriam groaned. 'Iqbal, please, let me try to explain why I went. Will you listen?' Finally, he nodded and she continued, 'I learned things about myself when I went to Zardgul – things I'm ashamed of. I realised how unfair I've been to you – and to Farid – by being so... so fixated, I suppose, on Jawad.

'You promised you'd take me to Zardgul. Perhaps you didn't understand how much it meant to me to see Jawad's grave. To be able to say goodbye.' Miriam's voice was shaky, and she fought to control it. 'It was the most important promise you ever made to me. I truly believe if you'd kept it we wouldn't be in this horrible situation now. I'm not only talking about saying goodbye to Jawad. I was able to lay ghost, something I should have done a long time ago.

'When I was in Zardgul I faced for the first time how much damage I've done. I hoped there was still a chance I could start to put things right between us. I admit I was wrong to go behind your back.' Her voice was steadier now and she added, 'but you have to take some responsibility for that.'

Iqbal's face tightened. He stood up and began pacing the floor. He turned at the door and moved towards her. Looking down at where she sat, he said, 'I did intend to keep my promise. At first, the reasons for not taking you were genuine but, as time went on, I couldn't bear the thought of it.'

'But why?' She already guessed what his answer would be, braced herself to hear it.

'What's been difficult to bear from when we met – knowing in your eyes I'll always be a lesser man than Jawad. I couldn't face going with you to Zardgul, being reminded every second of every day I wasn't as good as the man buried there.'

'Oh, Iqbal, I'm truly, truly sorry. I had no idea, until I was in Zardgul, what I'd been doing. I tried so hard to not keep talking about Jawad…'

'But that was part of the problem.' Iqbal sat down again. He glanced at her but looked away again, down at the rug. His voice was so low, Miriam had to strain to hear him. 'In the beginning, when we first got to know each other, you talked to me about Jawad. You told me about your life in Zardgul, the work you did, then – you stopped.' He was tracing the *fil-pau* pattern on the rug with a forefinger. She urged him to go on. 'Well…well, it was as though you'd decided to lock part of yourself away – a special part – because you didn't want to share it with me. Something you could only share with Farid.'

Miriam shook her head. 'I thought you didn't want to hear me speak of Jawad and our life together. I thought because…' her voice trailed away.

'Because what?'

'Whenever I mentioned Zardgul and how life was there, especially if it was about the greater freedom I enjoyed, it would make you angry. So as to not antagonise you I stopped talking about my past. Keeping silent about Jawad, not talking about friends I have there has been horrible. Iqbal, I never meant for you to feel you didn't match up.'

She looked over at him. He was nodding but, before he had a chance to speak she carried on, 'I'm apologising for my part in things going so wrong between us but I can't and won't take all the blame. Since we've been in Sang-i-Sia you've changed – you're nothing like the man I married. In Pakistan we did things together, now you come home to eat and sleep. Conversation has been reduced to talking about work and the children. Whenever I try to express any opinion you put me down. You're always making out I don't understand Afghan culture, implying I don't know how to behave. Recently, I've started to feel like a prisoner.' She drew another breath before adding quietly, 'It – I – can't go on like this.'

'This is Jeanine's doing.' Iqbal's tone was suddenly hostile.

'No, it's not. Oh, she may have brought things to a head by insisting I went to the teaching camp. While I was there my frustration about my life – our life – crystallised. The Iqbal I married, the Iqbal I lived with in Pakistan, wouldn't have stopped me giving English classes to twelve-year old boys. He used to walk down the street hand-in-hand with me – now he refuses even a walk on the mountain. The Iqbal I married wouldn't have tried to stop me going to the teaching camp – would've encouraged me. What changed you? It can't all be down to feeling inferior to a dead first husband.'

He was silent, shifting his position on the *toshak*, moving the cushion behind his back. She waited, half expecting him to get up and march out of the house. Instead he surprised her by asking, 'Do you think I feel free here?'

'What do you mean?'

'Oh, I don't know how …' The door burst open and Ruckshana, Farid at her heels, came racing in. She flung herself at her father who quickly changed his initial groan at the interruption to a mock bear growl as he opened his arms to his daughter. Miriam rose to her feet. 'I'll go and make some tea.' She crossed the room and pressed her hand onto his shoulder. 'Later, okay? We can't leave it here.'

She put water on. Waiting for it to boil, suddenly feeling half-sick with hunger, she chewed on some dry *nan*, while puzzling over Iqbal's last question. How could he not feel free here? She took the tray of tea through and returned to the kitchen to prepare the evening meal, listening to Ruckshana's giggles in the background. She could hear the murmur of Farid's voice – how he'd come out of his shell since his trip to his grandparents. Although she dreaded the thought of another separation, and the underlying fear they might not send him back, she'd have to let him go again next year. He seemed more eager to talk to Iqbal – she caught the word *buzkashi* from the other room. Maybe their relationship would have a chance to improve if she stopped reminding Farid about his wonderful father. She stopped. Was she so sure she and Iqbal were going to find a way out of this mess – still together?

She really hoped so.

TWENTY ONE

Sang-i-Sia October 1995

Later in the evening, while Miriam read to Ruckshana, Iqbal asked Farid to help shut the chickens in for the night. Ruckshana was asleep when Farid, a worried frown on his face, wished them goodnight.

Miriam poured tea, pushing the dish of sweets towards Iqbal. She turned down the lamp and moved closer to where he sat, his eyes fixed on the shadows flickering on the walls. She heard him draw a deep breath, knew he was wondering what to say.

Finally she broke the silence. 'Iqbal, I have one question.'

'Go on.'

'Do you want us to stay together?' He swivelled to look directly at her. Would he read in her eyes a sudden need for reassurance?

'Yes. Yes, Miriam, I do.'

'So, then surely we can sort things?'

He dropped his eyes, adding, 'I don't know if it's possible.'

Miriam stared at Iqbal. Oh, God – he'd decided to marry Zohra after all. It would be too humiliating to share her husband. She'd have to leave. She realised he was still speaking.

'I know things have to change if I'm to keep you. I don't think I can do it.'

'But, why, Iqbal, why can't you change. If I can, then…Or do you think I can't make the effort to leave Jawad in the past? It's …'

He held a hand up to stop her. 'I'm not talking about Jawad. This is about me. You talk about freedom like you're the only one denied it. Do you think I liked being sucked back into village ways, its rules and customs? Sucked into a family that only wants me now I'm a big doctor, an important man whose status reflects on them. I hoped I could come back and continue to be my own person – the person I became in Pakistan – but I was wrong.'

After a long silence, Miriam said, 'You'll have to explain what you mean. Help me understand.'

He sighed. 'Problem is I don't know how. While I was in Pakistan part of me wanted to come back to my *watan*. I don't think there is an Afghan – Hazara or Tajik or Pushtoon – anywhere in the world who doesn't feel the pull of his homeland. It's in our blood. Maybe returning to a city like Kabul would be different. Amongst so many strangers you can be anonymous, not have the weight of your past pulling you down. Since coming back I'm drowning in customs, though I have no respect for them – where reputation, the good of the family name, counts for more than anyone's personal happiness.'

'Is this to do with Zohra? With how your father stopped you two getting married?'

'No – well, yes and no. It goes back before that, even. Do you remember I told you about what happened at Band-i-Amir?'

Oh, not again – surely a ducking in icy water so many years ago couldn't still be a major trauma?

'Go on,' she prompted when he remained silent.

'Well, I thought my father must've hated me. Zohra tried to convince me he did it out of love for me. She might have persuaded me – only she didn't know the whole story. I've never told anyone.' He closed his eyes and buried his face in his hands. At last he turned to face Miriam.

'At Band-i-Amir I saw a man murder his daughter. Then, he and his son dropped her body into the water. Like me, she had leprosy. I grew up believing my father wanted me dead – convinced if he'd found me when I ran away from him he'd kill me.' The lack of emotion in his voice made what he was saying all the more chilling and Miriam stifled a gasp of horror.

He continued, in the same deadpan tone, 'As I got older, of course, I became less afraid of a stone smashing down on my head – my father would never have done such a thing. It was an extreme action, done in desperation. My father may have been foolish to believe the waters of Band-i-Amir would cure me but, unlike the man who killed his daughter, he didn't expect it to be instant. Maybe the girl's father couldn't bear the stigma of leprosy attached to his family. Perhaps he thought it a kindness to his daughter, ending what would be a miserable life. In those days they still used to force people out of their village, to wander from place to place begging for food. Maybe a quick death would be preferable?

'Those nightmares, when I wake in the night – I see the girl's body, with blood streaming from it, floating in the water. Strange, in reality I never saw her body – didn't even see her face. Yet I could swear I'd recognise her if she walked into the room now. Sometimes, years ago, in my dreams I saw a boy sitting beside a rock, a shadow behind him holding a big stone above his head. I knew I was the boy.' His eyes had a glazed look, as if he was re-living, not re-telling an event from his past. He seemed scarcely aware of Miriam reaching for his hand.

He said, 'Then Zohra came into my life. For a while I knew what it was to be happy. I should've known it wouldn't last. Maybe I'm destined to lose....' He sighed but didn't finish the sentence. After a minute or two of silence, broken only by their daughter's gentle breathing, he said, his voice more animated, 'Zohra liked me. That was... astonishing to me. 'You can't imagine how it felt, to be liked. My heart was hers from the first day she spoke to me.'

Miriam felt again the stab of jealousy. Iqbal stopped talking, looking quizzically at Miriam. 'Why are you looking at me like that?' he asked.

'Just wondering...if... does she...Zohra... still own your heart – part of it?' Hoped the light was too dim for him to see the hot flush rising in her cheeks. Ridiculous. Made her feel she was fifteen. She could feel his eyes searching her face

'No,' he squeezed her hand, a tiny smile twitching his lips. 'You have it all.'

She wasn't sure where Iqbal's story was going. 'I understand now why your relationship with your father is so distant. Go on.'

He shrugged. 'You've heard the story – Zohra married my brother. My mother tried to convince my father to let us marry. She was always on my side. It was she who persuaded him to let me stay on in school, but in this matter she couldn't change his mind. I had to go away. Couldn't bear to stay and see Zohra marry Hassan. I didn't tell anyone and in all the activity on the wedding day I simply left the house and started walking along the road away from the village.

My only regret,' his voice dropped, 'is not saying goodbye to my mother.'

'Is that when you came to Pakistan? How did you manage? Did you have money?'

'A few afghanis – enough to buy bread once a day. I walked. I scrounged lifts on trucks, sitting on top of their loads. It took four, five days. Most of the time I was numb with misery. Other times consumed by hatred for my father.

'From the border I was lucky to find someone going to Quetta. It was dark and I remember seeing lights in the distance – it looked like a great sea of light. I was terrified. I'd no idea what could produce so much light. When the driver dropped me off he told me to go to Mariabad, the Hazara area. I slept in the mosque the first night and in the morning when the mullah saw me he knew at once I had leprosy. He told me about the clinic.

'I remember thinking Zohra had been right – there was medicine available for leprosy. I've never known such a mixture of happiness and misery. If my disease could be cured then I could have married Zohra…You know the rest. I was admitted to the clinic. They gave me a job helping the cook but when the clinic in-charge realised I was educated they sent me for paramedic training in Karachi. Good days. I liked Karachi. I loved my work and would have been content to stay there. Later, when Dr Kramer came she arranged for me to go to medical school. I don't know how she managed it because they don't usually allow refugees.'

Miriam interrupted with a laugh, 'Anna was pretty good at getting what she wanted, one way or another.'

'True. She wanted me to go back to Afghanistan. You say in English she used the carrot and the stick. No agreement to go back, no medical training. I knew I was a fraud. I didn't want to come back.' He sighed. 'That's not true. There were times when I was so homesick for the mountains, the clear air, flowers in spring and, I suppose the feeling it was where I belonged, I felt my heart would break. I'd stay in my room listening to Daud Sarkhush singing in Hazaragi, songs about our homeland, tears pouring down my face. It was hard not to think of Zohra at those times. Then I'd remember how life would be back here.'

He fell silent as though trying to put his thoughts in order. 'Oh, Miriam,' he gave a quiet laugh, 'I'm rambling. Talking too much rubbish. I can't see what use it is to remember such things. How does it help us now?'

She squeezed his hand, leaning towards him. 'We'll only know if you carry on. Perhaps if you'd told...' she stopped. 'Please keep talking.'

After a few moments he continued, 'I'd think about coming home then... You know how it's said here a woman is nothing without a husband in Afghanistan? Well, a man is nothing without children. And who would marry Iqbal, the leper boy?

'Oh, there might've been people willing to marry their daughter to Iqbal the doctor – despite the fact I would be regarded as old – but they would be uneducated girls. I once tried to explain this to Dr Kramer but she didn't understand. She laughed, said I'd be fine once the clinic was established. I kept postponing the date for returning – finding more courses useful for my future work. Then I met you.'

'Are you saying I pushed you into coming back?'

It seemed to Miriam he considered her question for a long time before replying, 'In Quetta, listening to you talk about the work you – and Jawad – were doing in Zardgul, your enthusiasm for each tiny success, made me think again. If you had not agreed to marry me, though, I would never have come back. You made me believe returning home wouldn't be as bad as I feared.'

She gazed past him at the lamp, biting her lip, twisting the fingers of her free hand in the end of her *chaddar*.

'Is that why you wanted to marry me? Because you thought a foreign wife would make it easier to come back?'

'No!' At his angry shout Ruckshana stirred, crying out in her sleep. Miriam hurried across the room to pat the child's back, soothing her back to sleep. Iqbal stood up, saying he would make more tea. She could hear his angry clattering of glasses in the kitchen. Damn. Would he clam up again? Her question had slipped out. It wasn't even what she'd meant. Wanted to know he didn't blame her for his decision to come back. Iqbal's return stopped her tangled thoughts. He set the tray down between them.

'Miriam, I can't deny there's status in having a foreign wife.' He shook his head. 'Unfortunately we Afghans have such low self-esteem we are always deeply impressed by anyone who has one. My God, what a wonderful man this must be if a foreigner wanted to marry him.' He gave a contemptuous shrug. 'So you may not believe me when I say I wanted to marry you because… well, because… I…I loved you.' His voice dropped to a whisper, 'And I hoped one day you would love me.'

'You didn't think I loved you? But you still wanted to marry me?'

'I knew you wanted to come back to Afghanistan more than you wanted anything else in your life. I hoped bringing you here might make you happy enough to...love me.' He shook his head. 'Instead, trying to make your dream come true seems to have driven us apart.' He made a helpless gesture with his hands.

'Oh, Iqbal,' Miriam said softly. 'I don't know what to say. What a mess. I feel so guilty.'

'No need.' He smiled at her, stretching a hand to wipe away her tears. 'I knew coming back wouldn't be easy but I thought maybe people were ready to change their old ideas.'

He shrugged. 'I was wrong. There are still people who won't shake my hand because they fear they might catch a disease cured years ago. Still men who insist on marrying off their daughters before they start menstruating – passing the burden of honour to another man so they don't have to worry about it. When I tried to talk to them about waiting until their girls were older, they accused me of being un-Islamic, bringing foreign notions into the village.'

'But Iqbal, these things take time to change. You can't expect people to accept new ideas overnight.'

'I know.' He sounded exasperated, scrubbing hard at his face. 'Oh, I knew I couldn't explain properly. It's not…there's other stuff…the hypocrisy. People greet Malim Ashraf with respect because he's the headmaster, then take their children out of school because they don't see the point of education. The watchfulness – knowing everyone is watching everything you do, ready to criticise. That's why I asked you to see patients here rather than work with me in the clinic – they had plenty to talk about when we came here without giving them more.'

'But would it really matter? It's not so different from small towns and villages anywhere. In Scotland people are always watching what others are up to. They'll always find someone and something to talk about.'

'I knew you wouldn't understand. I'm not talking about natural curiosity and harmless gossip. What a poor world it would be if weren't interested in our neighbours. No, this is to do with reputation – losing face…'

'Ah,' Miriam broke in. 'I'm beginning to grasp its importance – maybe not understand it, but at least have an idea of its relevance to life here. Chaman talked about it – and Ismail told me about the Mullah who believed Jawad had made him lose face. Partly what got him killed.'

Iqbal nodded. 'Can you see now why I seem to have changed? To keep face, to be accepted by this community – my own people – I have to live by their rules. Otherwise I'd never be able to do my work. What would be the point of a doctor with no patients?'

Miriam shook her head. 'You're not doing your job properly if you don't start to make changes.' Her voice dropped to little more than a whisper, 'I can understand what you're saying but, I can't accept it.' When he didn't reply she went on, 'I've admitted how wrong I was to cling to my past with Jawad. Admitting it is one thing, being able to change how I think and behave will be hard, won't happen all at once. But, Iqbal, I believe our marriage is worth saving so I'll try my damnedest. But I can't do it on my own – I want the old Iqbal back.'

When Iqbal spoke again there was a catch in his voice she'd never heard before. 'I… I don't know if I can find him again.'

'Why not?'

'I've realised trying to pull against the culture doesn't work – and it makes me feel weak and spineless – not easy to live with, Miriam. 'D'you know the only time I've refused to bow to custom and tradition was when the news came Hassan had died. It is my duty to comfort my father in his loss. Instead I walked away, offering to send him a sedative.' He gave a mirthless chuckle. 'I made a stand and felt like a piece of shit afterwards. What difference would it have made if I'd stayed with the old man for an hour or two, offering the customary words when someone is grieving?'

'At least you weren't prepared to be a hypocrite. It's a start.'

Iqbal threw himself back against the cushion behind him. He stared into space, lost in his thoughts.

'So what are we going to do?' she asked. 'You want me to stay. I want to stay. Now we've actually looked the problem in the face, we know what we've got to confront. Are we going to find a way to live here, fight together against what's been pulling us apart?'

'I'll try, Miriam, though I don't honestly know if I have the strength to do it.'

'At least tonight we've made a start. I think,' she added with a grin, 'you've talked more to me tonight than you have in months. We have to keep talking to find our way forward.'

He pulled her towards him, holding her close. 'I'm exhausted, Miriam. Can't we go to bed now?'

'I didn't mean tonight, you idiot,' she punched his shoulder, smiling up at him. 'Unless you've any more secrets you should tell me about before Fatima does.'

'Ah, I suspected she was the source. No, you know all my secrets now.'

TWENTY-TWO

Sang-i-Sia October 1995

Next morning, a few patients were waiting to see Miriam. None had anything seriously wrong, had come more to say hello than consult on medical matters. She was touched by their welcome and the small gifts – a still-warm *nan*, a couple of eggs, a small dish of cream – brought a lump to her throat.

Everyone asked about her time in Charkoh. They were also, she knew, dying of curiosity about what was going on between Dr Iqbal and Zohra but too polite to ask outright. She ignored their oblique hints. When she said goodbye to the last patient she headed for the kitchen, thinking maybe she would invite some of the women round one afternoon. Maybe even for dinner one evening. Give the village something to talk about – a *mehmanni* only for women – no husbands allowed.

She wondered if Iqbal had many patients. Last night, she'd fallen asleep with his arms around her but had woken several times, disturbed by his restless tossing and turning. This morning, when he brought her tea, the dark shadows under his eyes meant he could not deny he had slept badly. She sighed. How long would it be before she could mention Jawad without making it sound like he had been Mr Perfect – or without seeing Iqbal wince at the mention of his ghostly rival's name. How would he react when she told him she wanted to take Farid to visit Zardgul his father's grave? Would he ever find it easier to open up about his feelings?

She shrugged – she wasn't so easy herself with emotional outpourings. They were actually quite alike in many ways – more than a touch of the dour Calvinist in Iqbal.

Once the new clinic was built she would have her own consulting room there. How fantastic it would feel leaving home every morning to walk down the path beside Iqbal, both of them going to work. Not until the end of next spring, though, a long time to wait for change to take place.

She decided she would take up Iqbal's offer to have a girl in to help with the housework. It would give her some free time. She could go out for a walk, drag Fatima up the mountain to look at the view. She'd love it once she got her up there. Let people talk about the doctor's crazy foreign wife – he'd get used to it. She'd start her English classes again – though maybe she'd arrange for the boys to come to the clinic, then Iqbal wouldn't worry about them being alone in the house with her. Or they could come to the house when he was there.

She gave a luxurious yawn. She was glad there hadn't been too many patients. A pile of clothes was waiting to be washed, but she could enjoy a nap first. She let her eyes close and was still fast asleep when Iqbal, calling her name, woke her. 'I must've been asleep for a couple of hours,' she said, groggily peering at her watch.

'You needed it,' Iqbal replied, his voice muffled as he yawned in sympathy. He poured tea for her, placing a saucer of dried mulberries beside it.

'I've not even cleaned the rice for dinner,' she said, chewing on a couple of mulberries. 'This is one of the few times I miss Scotland. Wouldn't it be great to get a takeaway? Course you can in the city. I remember takeaway kebab shops in Mazar.'

He smiled, but she could see it was half-hearted. Now what was bothering him? 'Come on, Iqbal, I can see there's something you don't know how to say. Don't tell me Zohra's changed her mind and said yes?' She laughed up at him to show she was joking but he didn't smile back at her. 'Sorry, was that in bad taste?'

'Just not very funny. I told you I didn't ask Zohra to marry me, nor will I. Though it did cross my mind it might be a possibility.' Miriam's mouth opened. He added hastily, 'Only for a second, though. I mean, when I first heard she was coming back.'

'Is that why you went to see her?'

'I went to offer my condolences on the death of her husband. And I admit I was curious. I wanted to see if …well, if there was anything left of …how we used to feel.'

'And?' She wasn't sure if she liked this much openness in Iqbal. She certainly didn't like the nasty sensation in her stomach when she thought of him and Zohra together.

'It was strange. Awkward at first. We were polite and impersonal. Other people were around, and it wasn't until I was leaving we had a few minutes to speak alone. She asked about you – if you were happy in Afghanistan, and said she hoped to meet you soon. I think you'll like each other.' Miriam raised her eyebrows but said nothing. 'What we once shared is long gone, a distant memory. She's a nice woman – good and kind.'

'So what's on your mind if it isn't Zohra? I know there's something. Sit down and say it.'

He sat on the space she patted beside her, taking one of her hands in his. 'I didn't sleep last night. Everything we talked about repeated itself over and over. I know it's been difficult for you here. I hadn't realised how difficult. In some ways,' he squeezed her hand, 'you've played the part of an Afghan wife too well. Maybe you should've spoken up sooner so I could understand better.' When she opened her mouth to protest, he squeezed her hand again, saying, 'I'm not blaming you. It's my fault. I should never have allowed myself to be so engulfed by the old ways. But I did. I can't undo that. So I spent last night wondering how to reconcile my need to be accepted by the community, my need to be respected with your – our – need to have the freedom to work towards changing things.

'I thought about Farid and Ruckshana. I don't want them to grow up believing it's all right for a girl not to be educated or …Oh, I don't want them to absorb old and dangerous belief systems not even rooted in Islam. Regardless of what we teach them at home, community pressure will be too great for them to resist. I've thought so hard all morning about how things will be if we start going against custom.' He took a deep breath, expelling the air slowly. 'Miriam, I can't. I'm not able to shake off the ropes forcing me into being what they want me to be.'

'So what are you suggesting?' Miriam asked.

'Leaving Afghanistan.'

'What?'

'It's too late to fight for change. Maybe our children's generation will be the ones to do that – I can't.'

'But we can't leave. The new clinic, our work. This is your home – you told me last night how homesick you used to be. How can you think of leaving?'

'Is saving our marriage not reason enough? I know you, Miriam. You'll start pushing at the boundaries too quickly, I'll try to slow you down and we'll be back to where we were two days ago.'

She remembered her plans of earlier in the afternoon. Yes, she was full of schemes to push the boundaries to their limits. Would almost certainly be at perpetual war with the men of the village and her husband. But leave Afghanistan? What about her promise Farid grow up here, part of his father's land and culture, always a part of his father's family? This was her country, too. She said so.

Iqbal shook his head, 'No Miriam. It's not. Your adopted country, maybe. And yes, I know all the arguments you'll make about Farid. I'm not suggesting we never set foot on Afghan soil again – that, I couldn't bear. Farid can still visit his grandparents. He'll still have an Afghan stepfather – hopefully a better one than he has now.'

'So you've got it all worked out.' She pulled her hand free from his. 'The Afghan patriarch decides what's best for his family without any need for consultation. Would you care to tell me where you plan to take us? Or should I just wait and see? For God's sake, Iqbal, what was last night all about? I thought we were going to try to work through problems together.'

'I am consulting you.'

'No, you've told me what you've decided we're going to do.'

He stood and began pacing the room. She watched him turn at the door, come back towards her, turn away again. Finally he came back to her side and sat down, rubbing his eyes with the heels of his hands. When he dropped his hands, she could see his eyes were red-rimmed whether from lack of sleep or held-back tears she wasn't sure.

He said quietly, 'Maybe I could have found a better way of saying it. I'm not telling you we're leaving Afghanistan. I'm saying we should consider it as a possible solution. I'm afraid if we stay here in Sang-i-Sia I'll lose you. One day you'll say you've had enough because I've not turned back into the Iqbal you married. I know as long as we are here, I never will. I'll always feel weak and spineless because I'm too worried about losing my reputation, being out of step. Maybe I'm a coward, but that's how it is.'

She didn't pull away when he took her hand. He kissed the back of it, turned it over and kissed the palm.

'You're not a coward, Iqbal. What a strange, mixed up pair we are. The foreigner wants to stay in Afghanistan, the Afghan wants to leave his homeland – not because of drought or famine or war but...'

'Because he loves his funny foreign wife, sees this as a way of keeping them together.'

She nodded slowly. 'Where were you thinking we'd go?'

'Well, I suppose Scotland is out of the question?'

'Unless you want to drive a taxi or clean hotel bedrooms.'

'No, I'd rather stick to what I know – something in the medical line. Pakistan? Not too far away. We have enough connections between us to find work – maybe Jeanine will have something? Good schools for the children in Karachi.'

'But what about the work here? We can't leave the people in Sang-i-Sia without a doctor.'

'I'm not suggesting we pack up and go tomorrow, or even next week. We'd have to give notice to Hansease, wait until they find a replacement. It'll take months. Will you at least think about it?'

'Yes, all right, yes, I will. But we also need to keep discussing it, together. Together, Iqbal – no more unilateral decisions, okay?'

'Okay.'

She put their glasses on the tray beside the empty mulberry dish. 'It's time the children were back from Fatima's – want to come down with me to collect them? We could even go for a walk before coming back.' She smiled impishly at him. Months, he said, before a replacement could be appointed. They'd be here for the winter and into spring. Gave her some time to start helping Iqbal to become the man she married. Plenty of time. No need to think just yet.

***

Karachi, October 1996

Miriam stood on the balcony of their tenth-floor flat looking down on the heaving rush hour traffic on Shahrah-i-Liaquat. The temperature was in the high eighties and the faint breeze that blew in off the Arabian Sea had little coolness to it. Iqbal had suggested, after work, they take the children to Clifton for an ice cream and a walk along the seafront, where the breezes were fresher. She watched for his Suzuki van to pull into the compound. From inside the flat she could hear four-month old Daud gurgle as Ruckshana tickled him.

For a moment she thought about how cool it would be in Sang-i-Sia right now, before resolutely turning her thoughts elsewhere. For the last month she and Iqbal had listened with increasing horror to the litany of atrocities perpetrated by Taliban since they captured Kabul. Thank God, Jawad's family had already left Mazar for Pakistan. Although until now the city remained free, who knew when it too would fall?

She saw Iqbal's vehicle arrive and went into the living room to tell the children it was time to go. She picked up Daud, hugging him to her and hurried out to the lift.

Lightning Source UK Ltd.
Milton Keynes UK
17 November 2009

146363UK00002B/89/P